THE BEST SHORT STORIES
OF 1932

THE BEST
SHORT STORIES
OF 1932

and

THE YEARBOOK
OF THE
AMERICAN SHORT STORY

Edited by
EDWARD J. O'BRIEN

88

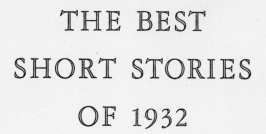

Short Story Index

Dodd, Mead and Company

NEW YORK · MCMXXXII

PRINTED IN THE UNITED STATES OF AMERICA

TO
JOSÉ GARCIA VILLA

31535

BY WAY OF ACKNOWLEDGMENT
AND REQUEST

Grateful acknowledgment for permission to include the stories and other material in this volume is made to the following authors, publishers, and editors:

To the Editors of *The Atlantic Monthly, Harper's Magazine, The Midland, Scrip, Story, Clay, Pagany, The New Yorker, Scribner's Magazine, New Copy, The Frontier, The American Mercury, The Saturday Evening Post,* and *The Boston Evening Transcript;* to Garrett and Massie, Inc., Farrar and Rinehart, Inc., The Columbia University Press, and The New Review Editions; and to Mr. Bill Adams, Mr. Alvah C. Bessie, Mr. Clifford Bragdon, Mr. Louis Brennan, Miss Wanda Burnett, Mr. Whit Burnett, Mr. Erskine Caldwell, Mr. Morley Callaghan, Mrs. Helena Lefroy Caperton, Mr. John Cournos, Mr. David Cornel De Jong, Mrs. G. E. Diefenthaler, Mr. William Faulkner, Mr. Manuel Komroff, Miss Meridel Lesueur, Mr. Scammon Lockwood, Mr. William March, Mr. George Milburn, Mr. Ira V. Morris, Mr. Peter Neagoe, Mr. Dudley Schnabel, Mr. Laurence Stallings, Mr. Bernhard Johann Tüting, Mr. José Garcia Villa, and Rev. Leo L. Ward, C.S.C.

I shall be grateful to my readers for corrections, and particularly for suggestions leading to the wider usefulness of these annual volumes. In particular, I shall welcome the receipt from authors, editors and publishers of stories printed during the period between May, 1932, and April, 1933, inclusive, which have qualities of distinction and yet are not printed in periodicals which are brought regularly to my attention.

Communications may be addressed to me at 118 Banbury Road, Oxford, England.

E. J. O.

INTRODUCTION

INTRODUCTION

I AM prompted by the remarks of an English novelist to look backward over the field of my work for the American short story during the past eighteen years and to cast up a balance of failure and achievement since 1914. My study of the short story, as it happened, began with the outbreak of the war. Chance could not have provided me with a more significant date. In 1914 everything went into liquidation. I came to my work at the end of an historic period. In 1914 no American writer had thought of stock-taking. The writers of this time were incredibly complacent. They were satisfied that they were writing the best short stories in the world, that they lived in God's own country, and that no one could teach them anything. They were well-paid and they knew that nothing succeeds like success. To my mind at that time their complacence seemed to have little justification. It seemed to me, however, that a purpose would be served if I were to isolate and call attention to the best that was being written. It might be possible to level up the mass. I had even a mad hope that I might help to give a genius a chance. As literature is an act of hope as well as an act of faith, this probably did no one any special harm.

Mr. H. E. Bates, the English novelist to whom I have just referred, has been reading a volume which I published recently in which I reprinted the best American stories which I have found since 1914. My selection was not drawn from stories published after 1930. The stories were arranged chronologically and dated. It is as clear to Mr. Bates as it is to me that the years from 1915 to 1922 were a lean time. These were the years of greatest complacence. They were the most triumphant years of the machine. The machine and the story-writer were both over-producing cheap standardized goods. It was a boom period. Like the hero of Scott Fitzgerald's story, the American writers of those days, all but one or two, lost everything they wanted in the boom. They still make money.

INTRODUCTION

From 1922 to 1930 was the shaping period. The standardized stories still appeared. There was unlimited inflation. The popular story became more and more gaseous. A critic had to look more and more closely to find what he was seeking. But it was there, and it had never been there before, at least since Stephen Crane died and was buried and forgotten. I sought hard for whatever was stirring on the face of these very muddy waters, and I found Sherwood Anderson. A little later I found Ernest Hemingway. These were two homeless artists who loved their own people. Their own people did not seem to care much for them. Little by little they won a foothold and found an audience in American youth, the youth which was growing up gropingly and seeking gropingly for self-expression.

This youth was homeless and looking for something in which it could take root. It found something in Anderson and Hemingway. These two men released American youth and helped it to find itself. Their reward is a generation of young writers of which America will some day be as proud as it should be now. The proof of my statement is in the stories which I shall print this year. "The Best Short Stories of 1932" is for the most part a book of youth, of youth which knows where it is going and what it is going to do. I started my work eighteen years ago as an act of faith. It was regarded as a mad act of faith, but it was the substance of things hoped for, and what I then hoped for has largely come to pass. 1930 inaugurated the period of artistic maturity in the American short story.

The new mature generation is not yet accepted by editors. The editorial moles are still grubbing blindly in the old furrows. *Scribner's Magazine* is a distinguished exception. Fortunately this does not deter the creative artist who is serious. He founds his own magazines. *Story*, which is published for its own sake, is now the most distinguished short story magazine in the world. I am compelled by my own sense of critical integrity to reprint seven stories from its pages this year. *Clay*, which has been founded by José Garcia Villa during the past year, bids fair to rival *Story* successfully. Several other magazines of the sort have either appeared or are announced. Now that the boom has collapsed, the machine can be mastered. It is the young writers whose task it will be to point out the way.

INTRODUCTION

II

To repeat what I have said in these pages in previous years, for the benefit of the reader as yet unacquainted with my standards and principles of selection, I shall point out that I have set myself the task of disengaging the essential human qualities in our contemporary fiction, which, when chronicled conscientiously by our literary artists, may fairly be called a criticism of life. I am not at all interested in formulæ, and organized criticism at its best would be nothing more than dead criticism, as all dogmatic interpretation of life is always dead. What has interested me, to the exclusion of other things, is the fresh, living current which flows through the best American work, and the psychological and imaginative quality which American writers have conferred upon it.

No substance is of importance in fiction unless it is organic substance, that is to say, substance in which the pulse of life is beating. Inorganic fiction has been our curse in the past, and bids fair to remain so, unless we exercise much greater artistic discrimination than we display at present.

The present record covers the period from May 1, 1931, to April 30, 1932, inclusive. During this period I have sought to select from the magazine stories published by American authors those which have rendered life imaginatively in organic substance and artistic form. Substance is something achieved by the artist in every act of creation, rather than something already present, and accordingly a fact or group of facts in a story only attains substantial embodiment when the artist's power of compelling imaginative persuasion transforms them into a living truth. The first test of a short story, therefore, in any qualitative analysis, is to report upon how vitally compelling the writer makes his selected facts or incidents. This may conveniently be called the test of substance.

But a second test is necessary if the story is to take rank above other stories. The true artist will seek to shape this living substance into the most beautiful and satisfying form by skilful selection and arrangement of his materials, and by the most direct and appealing presentation of it in portrayal and characterization.

The short stories which I have examined in this study, as in previous years, have fallen naturally into four groups. The first

INTRODUCTION

consists of those stories which fail, in my opinion, to survive either the test of substance or the test of form. These stories are not listed in the yearbook.

The second group consists of those stories which may fairly claim that they survive either the test of substance or the test of form. Each of these stories may claim to possess either distinction of technique alone, or more frequently, I am glad to say, a persuasive sense of life in them to which the reader responds with some part of his own experience. Stories included in this group are indicated in the yearbook index by a single arterisk prefixed to the title.

The third group, which is composed of stories of still greater distinction, includes such narratives as may lay convincing claim to a second reading, because each of them has survived both tests, the test of substance and the test of form. Stories included in this group are indicated in the yearbook index by two asterisks prefixed to the title.

Finally, I have recorded the names of a small group of stories which possess, I believe, the even finer distinction of uniting genuine substance and artistic form in a closely woven pattern with such sincerity that these stories may fairly claim a position in American literature. If all these stories by American authors were republished, they would not occupy more space than a few novels of average length. My selection of them does not imply the critical belief that they are great stories. A year which produced one great story would be an exceptional one. It is simply to be taken as meaning that I have found the equivalent of a few volumes worthy of republication among all the stories published during the period under consideration. These stories are indicated in the yearbook by three asterisks prefixed to the title, and are listed in the special "Roll of Honor." In compiling these lists, I have permitted no personal preference or prejudice to influence my judgment consciously. Several stories which I dislike personally are to be found on the "Roll of Honor." The general and particular results of my study will be found explained and carefully detailed in the supplementary part of this volume.

Edward J. O'Brien.

Oxford,
June 9, 1932.

CONTENTS

THE BEST SHORT STORIES
OF 1932

THE FOREIGNER [1]

By BILL ADAMS

(From *The Atlantic Monthly*)

I 'M a "Limey." I served my four-year apprenticeship in a lime-juice ship. That's another way of saying a British ship, sir. Under the law every man in a British ship had to be served a half gill of lime juice a day as a preventive of scurvy. I'm talking of sailing ships, of course. That's why I say "had." There are no sailing ships left now.

Thanks for the drink, sir. . . . Oh, very well. I'll spin you a yarn if you say so, sir. I'll tell you about the bloody foreigner.

Steam was fast crowding sail from the oceans when I went to sea, and sailing-ship owners were being forced to economize in every possible way. A sailor's work was very hard, because, from economy, ships invariably went to sea with barely men enough to handle them. That wouldn't have mattered so much if the food had been good, but the food was never enough and what there was was vile. Most white men wouldn't go to sea under such conditions; we Limeys called none but British and Americans "white men."

With the exception of Frenchmen, our crews were made up of men from every seagoing nation. You seldom saw a Frog in any but a Frog ship. Men from the Northern nations were most numerous, though there were plenty of others. More than once in my apprentice days I went to sea with no two men of the same nationality in the forecastle. Jabber, jabber, jabber, in all manner of languages. It made a fellow savage to hear it in a ship that flew the old Red Duster at her peak. You'd see some young apprentice walk up behind a foreigner and kick him. "English aboard of an English ship!" he'd say. If the jabberer was a big six-foot Scandinavian, or one of those chunky, broad-chested Russian Finns, the young lad would maybe just shake a fist in the fellow's

3

face and say, "That talk doesn't go in this packet! Cut it out!"

And one needed to be a bit careful with the Dagos, too. The South Europeans and South Americans were apt to be handy with a knife. But the foreign sailors were commonly a very peaceful lot—stolid or cowed. If they were not being kicked and cursed by hard-case mates at sea, they were being preyed upon by the crimps and the sailors' boarding-house masters ashore. Enough to break any man's spirit, such a life was. A patient lot of poor sea slaves they were.

We young apprentices were a proud lot. "One Froggy Frenchman, a Dane, a Portugee—one jolly Britisher can lick 'em all three." That was our credo. Our history books had omitted to mention that even Lord Nelson's ships were manned largely by foreigners. Well, I'm older now, and I learned something from the bloody foreigner.

II

I was just turned twenty-two when, having finished my apprenticeship, I took the exam and passed for my second mate's ticket. The luck was with me, for on the very next day I chanced on a ship that wanted a second mate and on a skipper who had no objection to a young chap just out of his time.

The mate was on the quarter-deck when I came from interviewing the skipper in his cabin. He was pacing to and fro, his pipe in his lips and his hands in his pockets, and he looked as though he owned the earth. A man of around thirty-five or so, he stood better than six feet and was broad in proportion. "Who in hell are you?" he asked when he saw me.

"I'm the second mate, sir," said I, and his scowl changed to a comradely grin.

"You've struck a good ship and a damned fine skipper," said the mate.

I was relieved to hear that, for I'd thought the skipper rather stony and had been half afraid that I'd shipped with a hard man to get along with.

The mate told me all about it while we sat on the hatch together, and the more he told me the better I liked it. The skipper's name was Mostyn. His father had commanded one of the grand tea clippers in the days before steam came to spoil the sea for sailors—

days when our ships were manned by crews in which a foreigner
was very rarely seen.

"Mostyn's chock-full of the good old tradition. He hates bloody
foreigners like the Devil himself," said the mate.

"He don't hate 'em any more than I do, sir," said I.

"You and me both," he replied. "And that's what I meant
when I told you he was a damned fine skipper. There'll be no
foreigners in this packet. He's signed an all-white crew."

"Glory be!" said I, and added, "Who's the kid?" A little slip
of a lad had just come from the deck house amidships.

The skipper's fifteen-year-old son was coming in the ship as an
apprentice—her only apprentice. "He's been a bit delicate," the
mate told me. "The skipper's been pretty much worried about
him, but now the doctors have told him that the sea'll probably
be the making of the boy."

"Fresh from home and mother, and delicate at that!" said I.
"I suppose we'll have to favor the little lubber, sir, eh?"

"His mother's been dead quite a while," replied the mate.
"The skipper's had some old woman taking care of him. And as
for favoring him—not on your life! The skipper wants us to
treat him just as we'd treat any apprentice. He'll sweep decks,
chip rust, scrape cable, and start at the bottom same as you and
I had to."

The ship was going to sea next morning, and the crew came
aboard soon after dark. They'd all been drinking a bit, of course.
When we went to the forecastle to look them over we found that
there was one man short. "He's probably drunk, sir," said the
mate, reporting to the skipper. "He'll show up before very long."

But when the tug came to take us out next morning the missing
man had not joined. "We'll have to take a pierhead jump, eh,
sir?" asked the mate.

"See that you get a white man," tersely ordered the skipper.

When the ship came to the last lock, just before entering the
river, there was the usual crowd of idlers on the pierhead. "Now
then," called the mate, "who wants to make a voyage in a good
ship?"

None of the idlers made any answer, but in a minute we saw a
lean, shabby little fellow pushing his way toward the ship.

"Where the devil do you come from?" asked the mate when the

little fellow jumped from the pierhead to the deck. "You look like a bloody foreigner to me."

Making no answer, the little fellow grinned placatingly up at the mate.

The skipper was furious, for, with the tide at the flood and the wind fair, he couldn't lose time hanging round to wait for a white man. "Very well, mister," said he, "put him to all the common deck work. I'll have no foreigner doing any sailor work in my ship." So while the rest of the hands went about setting sail the foreigner was put to sweeping the decks down.

Pretty soon the skipper looked down from the poop and saw his kid and the foreigner sweeping the decks side by side. He immediately called the mate. "I'll not have that boy working with a foreigner, mister. Find him something else to do," said he. So the mate told the kid to lend a hand setting sail, and the foreigner was left to sweep by himself.

It wasn't long before the hands were growling because they had to do the foreigner's share of the work as well as their own. He caught on at once, laid down his broom, and started forward to help them. "You, damn you! Get hold of that broom!" bellowed the mate.

You can know how popular the foreigner was by the way he was treated when the hands went below for breakfast. It was mighty little breakfast for him! Just the few scraps of fat and gristle that they left him. When the meal was done they ordered him to take the empty mess kid back to the cook, and by way of putting him in his place one of them booted him. He took it all without a murmur of remonstrance—meek as he was shabby.

A dog's life the little foreigner led from the first. When he wasn't sweeping the decks he was chipping rust from the bulwarks, or wiping off the paint work, or polishing the brass, or down on his knees scouring the planks with a holystone. As for sailor work, he wasn't allowed so much as to coil up a rope. When he was off duty the hands made him wait on them. Instead of the forecastle's being scrubbed out on Saturday morning, as was customary, they made him scrub it every day. They made him wash their clothes when Sunday came round. They made him dubbin their sea boots and oil their oilskins. Nothing more than a poor common servant he was; and in the minds of every one, from

skipper to skipper's son, being just a poor common servant was all
that he was fit for. "The meek shall inherit the earth," grinned
the mate. "I'll be damned if they'll inherit the sea!"

III

Thanks to the foreigner's presence in the ship, young Mostyn
had a good time from the first. There was no sweeping, no chipping rust, no polishing or scouring for him. Instead of having to
wait a year before being allowed to do any sailor work, he was
set to helping the hands right away. For all that he looked a bit
sickly, he was full of devilment, and the hands very naturally
made a pet of him and went out of their way to teach him to
splice, knot, hand canvas, and so forth. It was easy to see how
pleased the skipper was. While he hadn't intended to have the
lad shown any favors, circumstances had played into his hands.
You'd hardly blame a parent, I suppose.

You can't blame the kid for taking his cue from the mates and
the men, either. And of course he knew how his old man felt
about it. He was forever ragging the foreigner. He'd grimace at
him. He'd mock his broken English. If the fellow had a shirt
hung out to dry, he'd tie it into knots and break the buttons. If
he was at work a little way up the rigging and the foreigner happened to be at work right below, he'd manage to spill tar down
the foreigner's neck.

Maybe the fact of his being a bit sickly made the boy more of
a tease than he'd have been otherwise. He was a regular young
devil at finding ways to torment the little foreigner, and of course
no one interfered. It was a big joke with the hands. They were
always watching to see what he'd think of next, and sometimes
they'd make suggestions. They never had to suggest anything
twice. And the queer thing was that the foreigner never became
the least bit mad. He'd look at young Mostyn and he'd grin, and
his eyes would shine as though he actually enjoyed it all. It
wasn't long till the hands were setting him down as half-witted
even for a foreigner.

As was often the case, there was one man in the crew who stood
out above his fellows. He was a first-rate sailor, and of magnificent physique. He could box, wrestle, run, and jump better than

any man in the forecastle—agile as a monkey when he was in the rigging, light-footed as a cat when he was on deck. It was with him that the skipper's son usually worked as helper. In the dogwatch, when the day's work was done, the sailor would call the kid out to the deck and give him a boxing lesson, or, having set the boy to wrestle with some light member of the crew, would teach him the different holds.

One day a week or two after we sailed, the wind died and the sea fell flat. In the dogwatch that evening the big sailor climbed up to the topsail yard. He had stripped himself naked, and for a moment he stood on the slender yardarm sixty feet above the sea with the setting sun shining on his bare hide. All hands gathered at the rail to watch his dive. Down he went, and down, and out of sight in the sunset-shadowed water. The ripples died. The sea was still. Long seconds passed.

Craning their heads over the side, the hands peered down to the sea. Perhaps the dive had been too high. Perhaps, though we were too far north for many sharks to be about, a shark had got him.

"By God," said the mate at my side, "that fellow's gone!" And then, when all hands were giving the big man up, there was a shout from the sea at the other side of the ship. He'd dived clear under her, and had come up on her opposite side.

"I'll teach ye to swim one o' these days, sonny," called the big sailor to young Mostyn, who was looking down at him from the rail. And down he went again, out of sight, under her keel, and up at the opposite side. A whale of a man, he was; and it was always he who was hardest on the little foreigner. Over the rail he climbed now, and saw the foreigner staring at him. "Ye bloody furriner, go git me clothes!" he ordered. And the foreigner fetched his clothes and held them while the big sailor took them one by one. "Now, damn ye, put on me boots!" he ordered. While he sat on the hatch the foreigner put on his bluchers, and laced them.

"An' now ye can go to the devil!" said the big man, and pushed his foot against the little fellow's chest and sent him sprawling. The deck rang with laughter.

What with shark, barracouta, squid, and so forth, it was against orders for men to go swimming from a ship at sea. When the hands gathered on the quarter-deck at eight bells the skipper looked down on them. "There'll be no more going over the side. D'ye hear me? No more swimming under any circumstances!" said he.

"Aye, aye, sir," responded the big man, and, as the hands turned to go forward, he grasped the little foreigner by the neck. "D' ye hear that, ye bloody furriner?" he demanded. "Let me catch ye takin' a swim, an' just look out for yerself!" A big joke, the hands thought that. Even the skipper had to smile.

A few days later the ship was rambling along with the northeast trade in her canvas. Dusk fell, and, their forms dim in the starlight, the hands sat yarning on the hatch. Beside the rail, alone as always, stood the foreigner. All day he'd been down in the dark, smelly chain locker, chipping rust from the cables, while the others worked in the bright sun and balmy breeze. The mate and I had forgotten him, and he hadn't been called up till after supper was done. None of the hands had given him a thought. They'd eaten all the supper hash and had drunk all the skilly by the time he came to the forecastle, so that there was nothing for him but hard-tack and cold water. His hands and his face, his dungaree shirt and pants, were grimy with rust stain. If it hadn't been for young Mostyn he'd have had clean things to change into. Young Mostyn had taken his spare shirt and pants from the line where he had left them to dry and had daubed them with fresh tar. The kid was in the half deck now, in the snug little quarters that he had all to himself.

Suddenly there was a flapping on the deck halfway between the hatch and where the foreigner stood. A flying fish had come over the rail. The one to get it would have a fine breakfast next morning. All hands started up, but the big man was in the lead and the others sat down again.

"Hand it over, damn ye!" ordered the big man, for the foreigner had come first to the fish.

Without a word, the foreigner turned away and stepped to the half-deck door. "Here ees nice feesh for leeder poy," said he, and handed the fish to young Mostyn, who took it without so much as a word of thanks.

"Playin' up to the kid, eh? A lot o' good that'll do ye!" sneered the big sailor. And it did the foreigner no good, for thenceforth the big man was harder on him than before and young Mostyn ragged him no less. But there was never a murmur of complaint from him. Meek as a lamb among wolves he was.

IV

That was the way of things all the way down the Atlantic. Always dirty, always denied his full share of the grub, the little foreigner grew leaner and shabbier as the weeks passed.

We were a few hundred miles north of the corner when, going forward one evening, I heard a lot of laughter in the forecastle. The door was open. The big sailor was seated on his sea chest, pointing at the little foreigner, who stood before him. "Ye blitherin' fool," said he, "ye can't go round Stiff without oilskins and sea boots. Ye got to go aft an' git 'em from th' Old Man."

All down the Atlantic we'd had no weather bad enough to necessitate the wearing of oilskins or sea boots. I'd never realized that the foreigner lacked them. Now I remembered that all he carried when he jumped from the pierhead had been a small canvas bundle.

The big man winked up at me. "Take a squint at the bloody furriner's dunnage, will ye, sir?" said he.

They had fetched out the foreigner's bundle. It lay open on the table, its contents in full view. An extra dungaree shirt, an extra pair of dungaree pants, both of them ragged and tar-stained, a couple of pairs of old socks—and the picture of a kid of about the age of young Mostyn.

The foreigner picked up the picture and held it out to me. "Mine leeder poy, sir," said he, and you should have seen how his eyes shone! I felt sorry for the poor little swab, for I understood now why it was that he had always been so patient with young Mostyn. But I said, "You can't go round the Horn without oilskins and sea boots. You'll have to get some from the skipper."

He shook his head. "I safes mine moneys for mine leeder poy, sir," he said.

I didn't ask about it then, but later I found out that his wife was dead and his kid was being taken care of by some woman to whom he sent all his pay.

I've seen some hard cases among crews, but not till that voyage had I seen a man hard enough to face Cape Stiff without oilskins or sea boots. And it was June, the black heart of the Horn winter!

We were two weeks beating round the Horn, two weeks of screaming gale and mountain seas. Hail bouncing from mast and spar and deck house; snow flying; spray, bitter cold, slapping over the rails unceasingly; always the deck deep in wintry white water.

"There's no law to make a man buy oilskins and sea boots if he don't want to," said the mate. As for the skipper, he never so much as saw the foreigner, I think. Certainly he took no notice at all of him.

Down there off Stiff the foreigner was allowed to go aloft, to take his share of the sailor work. There was not a better man aboard. He was often first man into the gale-battered rigging, often the last man down. Always he was wet to the bone. Saltwater boils came at his wrists, his knees, his ankles. Yet, while the white men damned old Stiff and cursed the raging seas, no murmur came from his blue lips.

After twenty-four hours off Stiff, young Mostyn began to look a bit white about the gills. Though the hands tried to keep an eye on him, he was knocked down and washed round the decks a time or two that first day. He started to cough. "Fetch him to the cabin, mister," ordered the skipper when the mate told him that. It was blowing like the devil just then, and all hands were on the way aloft to furl a topsail—all but the foreigner, that is. A "grayback" came roaring aboard and bowled the foreigner over before he could get into the shrouds. He was washed across the deck and back before he could regain his feet.

At the moment that the mate came from the half deck with his hand on young Mostyn's arm, one of the hands shouted something from aloft. The foreigner had found his feet and was close to the half deck. The mate ordered him to take the kid to the cabin, and hurried aloft to see what was wrong with the topsail.

You should have seen the skipper's face when the little foreigner came to the cabin door! He was carrying the kid tucked under one arm, and hanging to the life line with his other hand. The kid was dry, but the foreigner was soaked, of course. The skipper looked at him as one might look at a leper. The thought that that skinny little ragged foreign chap could face the Horn without oilskins or sea boots while his own son couldn't face it with the very best possible outfit was too much for him. He shoved the lad through the door and banged it in the foreigner's face. And d'you suppose the little foreigner cared? Why, by the shine of his eyes you'd have supposed that the skipper had given him a hot shot of the best Jamaica!

V

At the end of two weeks we headed her nor'ard, and away she went with a souther in her canvas, every one merry. The hands let up some on ragging the foreigner now. Even the big man quit badgering him quite so much. He'd earned his mite of respect. The mate and I would have set him to work with the others had we dared, but we knew that the skipper would not have allowed it.

When the souther died we picked up a fine westerly, and out of the cabin came young Mostyn. His cough was gone, and he was going back to the half deck. The hands gave a cheer when they saw him, and it was easy to see how pleased the skipper was at that.

If the hands quit ragging the foreigner, young Mostyn didn't. Maybe it was the spleen that you'll often find in those who are sickly. He tormented the little fellow even more than before.

On a Sunday when we were just at the edge of the tropics the westerly left us and we lay becalmed for a day. The mate and I were walking the quarter-deck together when the big sailor turned from looking over the flat sea and ran to the galley. "Shark-oh, doctor!" said he to the cook. "Gimme a hunk o' pork fat, will ye?" From the galley he went to the carpenter's shop for the shark hook.

It was a small shark, not over seven or eight feet long, but it took four men to haul it aboard.

"Keep clear there, boy!" called the skipper to his son, who was interestedly watching the hauling aboard of the first shark he'd seen.

"Aye, get away! Stand back, lad! He'll be takin' a leg off ye!" said the big sailor.

When the shark lay flapping on the deck the big man fetched an eight-foot wooden capstan bar from the rack and rammed it down the brute's throat. "Bite on that, ye devil!" said he. They drove sheath knives into its brain, cut off its tail and fins, and, last, severed its head.

"Look at that, will ye, sonny?" said the big man, as the jaws of the severed head still gnashed on the bar. "If ever ye fall over the side, look out as it ain't in the tropics, for no one's goin' to go in after ye."

Just as they were about to throw the shark back to the sea the little foreigner came up. "Vait," said he. "Vait yoost a leeder."

"What's he doing that for?" asked young Mostyn as the foreigner cut off a slice of the warm flesh.

"Think o' eatin' shark, son! Them bloody furriners is no diff'-rent from dogs," said the big man.

Young Mostyn looked disgustedly at the foreigner. "You dirty beast," said he.

That night we picked up the southeast trades and footed it nor'ard again. When we were a degree or so south of the line the wind left us and we lay becalmed once more, idle canvas hanging flat from idle spars. Blue cloudless sky above, unshadowed blue sea beneath and all about the ship. For a couple of days she lay so, and then the black doldrum squalls appeared. One after another, blowing up now from one quarter and now from another, they passed over us, each bringing its brief breeze and torrent of rain.

With the exception of the big man and the foreigner, the hands were down in the sail locker that morning. The foreigner was scouring rust spots from the bulwarks. In the rigging a little way above him the big sailor was at work, with young Mostyn to help him.

In mid-forenoon a squall heavier than any we'd had yet came over the water. I could see the whitecaps at its forefoot and the solid wall of the rain while it was still far off. It was almost on us when the big man glanced up. He dropped to the deck, and, looking back up at young Mostyn, called, "Ye'd best be comin' down, son, till yon squall's blown over."

Young Mostyn looked down. The foreigner looked up. Their glances met. "Why don't you stay in your own ships?" sneeringly asked young Mostyn. The big man laughed, and next instant the squall struck the ship and over she went till her lee rail lay level with the seething sea.

A scream rang high above the noise of wind and seething sea and hissing rain. A yell rose from the big sailor, and, hearing him, the hands came rushing from the sail locker. I flung a life-buoy to the sea. The skipper sprang from the chart room to the poop deck.

"Who is it overboard?" the skipper asked me when in a few moments the boat was away.

"Your son, sir," I replied.

Torrents of rain lashed down. Wind boomed. Searching for the hidden boat, Captain Mostyn from his poop gazed white-faced into the gloom.

The big sailor's voice came from the quarter-deck. "Where's yon bloody furriner? W'y wasn't 'e 'elpin' to get the boat away?"

In vain I looked up and down the deck for the foreigner. "He's somewhere shuddering below," I thought.

The rain thinned. While Captain Mostyn stood too horrified to move, I strode to the chart room and fetched the telescope.

The squall passed on; the sun shone bright upon the stilled blue sea. Beyond the distant boat I saw young Mostyn clinging to the buoy. "What luck!" I thought, supposing that, since he could not have swum to it, I must have thrown the buoy right to him. Next moment, close to the buoy, I saw a man swimming—and then, with the swimmer between it and the buoy, I saw a sharp triangular fin!

The fin vanished. The shark had dived! And instantly the swimmer vanished too. And then in another moment I saw him again, and between his lips was something that flashed in the sun. "By God, he knifed the shark!" I cried.

And now, on the other side of the buoy, I saw another fin, and at once saw the swimmer making fast toward it. That fin dived too, and the swimmer also dived again.

The boat was nigh the buoy now. Faintly there came to me the distant uproar of the mate's and rowers' voices.

"He got that shark too, sir," I said to Captain Mostyn, for now I saw them hauling both swimmer and skipper's son into the boat. "Your son's safe, sir," said I.

Captain Mostyn took the telescope from me, looked through it, and murmured, "Thank God!"

VI

They lifted the foreigner first from the boat, and very gently they passed him up over the ship's high side. And I saw that the bottom of the boat was red.

The little foreigner's face was deathly white, but his eyes were unafraid and shining. We bore him into the cabin and laid him there, on the deck; and, as the bottom of the boat had been, the deck grew red.

At sunset that evening we stopped the ship once more. The trade wind thrummed softly in the rigging and the sea was brightly blue when four sailors entered the cabin and came forth again bearing a stretcher.

Upon the silent quarter-deck young Mostyn stood beside his father.

"We therefore commit this body to the deep," read Captain Mostyn, and there his voice faltered. All hands gazed at him, all save his son, who gazed at the old Red Duster covering the canvas-sewn form that lay so still upon the stretcher.

"We therefore commit—this body—to the deep," read Captain Mostyn again, and stopped for a space ere he went on with the words of the burial service for such as die at sea.

"According," continued Captain Mostyn, "according to the mighty working—whereby He—He is able—*to subdue all things unto Himself.*"

And then Captain Mostyn turned away and took his son's arm, and without a gesture, without another word, went falteringly through the cabin door and shut it after him; so that it was the mate who must raise a hand, must make to the stretcher bearers that final gesture at which we of the sea commit to the sea our dead.

HORIZON [1]

By ALVAH C. BESSIE

(From *The Criterion*)

AFTER the ninth day at sea he found himself able to write
again. Before that, any efforts he made had foundered even
before their inception, through disinclination, ennui or sheer dis-
ability. Standing at the rail he tried to image himself writing
again and he laughed—there could be no more absurd incongruity
than the contrasted images of the sea, and a man writing at a
desk. So for eight days he stood at the rail or wandered up and
down the deck, or paced the bridge of the ship. Here he was most
at home, and he buttoned the old army overcoat about his neck
and stood with what he enjoyed thinking were steel-cold eyes,
gazing over the sea at the circular horizon. Day after day the
horizon presented an unbroken line, dim and vaguely beckoning.
His eyes were strained to such a pitch that he continually saw
puffs of smoke or the funnels of non-existent vessels, and he called
the mate's attention to them. Then they both looked through
binoculars: "I can't see it," the mate would say. "I must have
been mistaken," he replied. But when an occasional ship did
come in sight, he felt his heart pounding proudly and joyfully in
his breast, and he paced the deck more vigorously than before.
A symbol, his unheard voice would say to him—here we are,
hundreds upon hundreds of miles from any land—two isolated
human beings touch hands for a brief moment, and are gone. He
could hear the thin buzzing of the apparatus in the wireless shack,
and when he saw the operator later in the day, in the saloon, he'd
say: "What ship was that we spoke this morning, Sparks?" And
Sparks said, "Southern Cross—bound for Baltimore." But most
of the time no ships were visible, and he had to content himself
with watching the terns floating on curved and rigid wings behind
the ship, waiting patiently for the cook to throw the garbage over-

[1] Copyright, 1932, by Alvah C. Bessie.

16

board. Occasionally, he could see them turn their sharp heads with a quick movement, and at those times he felt peculiarly close to them in spirit, and could almost hear the conversation in which they were undoubtedly engaged: "You watch the port side," said one tern, "and I'll watch the starboard," and they hung absurdly suspended over the ship, rolling in the air on rigid wings, just as the vessel rolled upon the sea.

He picked up his pen and wrote: "The thing that hurt him most was the fact that at the first few dinners aboard, no one spoke to him. He sat at the captain's table with the captain and the other officers, and was constantly amazed at the silence that prevailed. Of course, he was used to the stories of the taciturn men who sail the seas in ships, so it was with real astonishment that he encountered a legend that for once seemed true. They all ate with their eyes on their plates, and hurried to stow the food away inside; so that when he felt an extreme necessity for butter, it was all that he could do to summon courage enough to say in a weak voice, 'Pardon me, may I trouble you for the butter?'"

He paused and dipped his pen, then held it in his mouth. Strange, he thought, how strange that was the first day out—I must be developing an inferiority complex, to have been so abashed by the presence of these men. They had all looked up at him when he spoke and they all looked so far away and alien that he'd felt the hot blood course up his neck and cursed himself for a fool for having spoken. One of them had reached him the butter, then they all looked down again into their plates and resumed eating.

These men do things, he had thought—here are men, silent and mature, men who are as stable and well-orientated as the tested compass in the binnacle. They knew what was what—they knew their business and they knew their lives. They had every single moment of their lives on tap—mapped and charted, ready to consult. Give them a crisis and they were on deck, steady-handed, cool-eyed, tight-mouthed and, above all, in action. While I, he had thought, am a spineless jelly-fish. I am a creature of moods and dreams and passions, of impulses and tics. Here are men who are solid and substantial—their feet are planted on the deck, and their eyes too are on the horizon—but not for the same romantic reason as my own, and not with the same focus.

And so he had attempted to cultivate the officers, probe gently into their quietude, and see what pearl of wisdom he might fish out of the depths. Of course, he would reason, they are human beings—their occupation is responsible for their silence—four hours on watch and eight hours off give little time for the amenities of polite society—there is little to say and no time in which to say it. A man who paces the bridge on a rainy night for four hours, back and forth in the same tracks, his eyes on the invisible horizon, his ears utterly open and alert, becomes something more and less than human—becomes a machine—a receptive organ of the finest sensitivity, and the darkness of the night and the low soughing of the wind across the sea and the incessant dash of the water along the side, all combine to make him turn inward upon himself, and whatever thoughts he may have remain inarticulate and sealed away.

So he stood up on the bridge at night and waited for the mate to speak to him. The first night as he came up the stairs, the young third mate barred his way. "Is it all right," he'd say, "to come up on the bridge? I can't sleep." The third mate turned away and mumbled, "Have to ask the captain, he's in the pilot-house." He felt his way across the bridge to where he knew the pilot-house door stood open. He walked in, straining his eyes to see, and could see nothing but the face of the helmsman, wanly lit by the light from the binnacle in front of him, and hear nothing but the creaking of the wheel as he turned it to and fro, and the ticking of a clock. "Captain?" he said, in a surprisingly loud voice. "Yes," a voice said, almost at his elbow, and with the snap and precision of a shot. "Is it all right to come up on the bridge? I can't sleep." "What seems to be the trouble—" He wondered what the captain looked like—he had not seen him yet. "—seasick?" "Not yet," he'd say, "but I—oh, just the strangeness of it all, the vibration and the noise." "First trip to sea?" "Yes, sir." "Well," the voice replied, "you sure picked a good time o' year. December and February are the worst months on the North Atlantic." "Yes?" he said alertly, and was silent, and stood rigidly looking out of the window of the pilot-house, afraid to say another word. Not that there was anything to be seen; for after his eyes had become accustomed to the darkness, he was only rewarded with a view of a dark, starless sky and a darker sea, and two pale wakes where the prow of the freighter pried the sea apart and sped it backwards. Little lines and spots of phosphoresence swelled and glowed amid the wakes, and glowed and disappeared.

He gave up writing for the day and lay back on his bed and stared at the ceiling of the cabin. He was sole passenger on a freighter, and although he hated to admit it, he was lonesome. Lonesome? ridiculous, he thought—now I know why men go to sea. It is impossible to be lonely on the sea—the sea is your friend and companion and it whispers in the hollow of your ear. Standing on the bridge at night in utter darkness and detachment, he had failed to note the loneliness he'd felt at night, in the woods, even with a cheerful fire and the homely sound of frogs croaking down by the shore. Here, as he stood with the salt spray whipping across his cheek and mouth and stinging his eyes, with nothing to connect him to the earth or the presence of man but the lonely topmast light and the realization that after all, although there was a man nearby, he might just as well be dead, here he could not be lonely or unhappy, but there was nevertheless a sense of isolation all about—it was so keen and persuasive that he buttoned his coat closer about him and turned his mental eyes within and shut his physical eyes to the night and the topmast light and the fireflies that played among the waves.

The roar of water was in his ears, and the myriad uncatalogued and unidentified sounds that mingled with that roar. Somewhere a bolt was banging against the hull; Clank, it said and was silent for a long time, and then it said clank again when he least expected it. There was an endless high note from amidships—the engines, he thought, and counted the minutes till inside the wheelhouse the brass clock said, Ting-ting. One o'clock, he thought, and then the helmsman pulled the cord of the ship's bell that hung in front of the wheelhouse, and that bell said, Tang-tang. There was an interval which the wind's moan and the water's rush and the vibration of the engines filled, and from the prow came the echo of the bell pulled by the lookout on the forecastle-head. Far away, it said Tang-tang and paused, and a voice far away said: "All lights burning brightly, sir." He could barely hear it above the medley of other sounds. "All-*right*," the mate inside the wheelroom said.

So after he had gained the master's sanction to visit the bridge whenever the mood seized him, he spent more time up there and finally got on speaking terms with the young third officer, Pearson. Pearson was a tall, red-faced young fellow, with a reticent, almost surly air. As he paced the deck the first few times the passenger Perry was there, he scrupulously avoided looking at him. He'd pass in back of Perry, as he leaned against the rail, and turning, look right through him and walk back. This annoyed Perry, so he said, "Fine weather," and the third said, "Yeh," and went back in the wheelhouse and disappeared. But after the first few visits, Perry discovered that Pearson was more than willing to talk—in fact, he did most of the talking, and when he felt that he was running down, Perry would prod him with a leading question and Pearson sailed away again upon another tack. He usually talked about women, and his red face grew much redder as he spoke. "I knew a girl on Telegraph Hill," he said. "God, she was a hot baby—funny thing," he said, "she used to play around a lot with me, then one time a girl got ahold of her and, by God, if she didn't go and live with her. I've never understood that," Pearson said, "but I dunno—I've sort of got to expecting anything of women." Then he looked puzzled and scratched his head and shook it a few times and resumed his feline pacing back and forth.

Then a curious thing happened—for it shook Perry even more than it did Pearson, and he was jarred enough: they were talking about books, and Perry said, "I've had a little experience with publishing—I once had a book printed—it was illustrated by Rokàl." "You don't mean that book called *The Piper*," Pearson gasped, "why, you didn't—" "Yes, that's it; my God, don't tell me that you bought a copy of that thing," Perry said, and Pearson, "Why, Jesus Christ—now isn't that funny—you didn't—you didn't *write* that book? Well, I'm damned!" "Don't tell me you bought a—did you like it?" Perry said. "Well, now if that isn't the best ever," Pearson said. "You bet I bought a copy—in San Francisco—ye-es, I liked it," he said, "but—say, I've got it in my room—will you autograph it for me?" he cried, his face as red as a beet. "Delighted," Perry said, leaning back upon the sliding door and looking worldly. He suddenly wished that he were ten years older. After that Pearson and Perry thought a little more of each other.

II

When they were presumably two days from shore, Perry sat down again and took his pen: "In analysing the strange behaviour of Pearson," he wrote, "I shall only attempt to write as a scientist now—there will be time enough when I've got to Vienna, far from the sea, to sit down and try to acquire a perspective which will permit of a more imaginative treatment of both Pearson and the sea in general. All the seamen on this boat—Pearson corrected me when I said boat—'Ship,' he said, and looked at me, 'ship.' Then I said ship. 'And also—' Pearson said, 'chart, chart, not map,' and to tantalize him I said map and boat.—however, all the seamen on this—ship, agree that Conrad was a lousy writer. To put it more precisely, what they mean, I gather, is that as far as they're concerned, as a writer of the sea he fails to touch accurately and illuminatingly upon the very things with which these men are most concerned and should understand. Now whether Conrad found it necessary to alter the facts of sea-life in order to satisfy the sort of audience he catered for, or whether he was just so poor an artist that his creative mind did not select the right details and when it did, perverted them beyond their importance, I know not, but clinging to the latter supposition, I also feel that a large part of his lack of success was due to the fact that he had the wrong perspective, or worse, no perspective at all . . . being at all times too close to the thing he was attempting to express. Thus, in the case of Pearson—" Here Perry paused and laid his pen down and closed his ink-bottle. I'll wait till I get to Vienna, he thought, and went up on the bridge.

It was a cold clear day, the sun was low in the south and gave no heat and the ship was rolling, pitching and labouring heavily. Great waves shot up from her bows suddenly, geyserlike, and exhausted their energy in furiously hissing sprays. The fume from the wavetops snapped viciously across the decks and drenched the tarpaulins stretched across the hatches. Perry delighted to stand for a half hour at a time and watch the shipped water wash to and fro across the steel deck, and note the multifarious courses it pursued. The great rocking waves sprang and leaped and sank and died away, then leaped the rail and landed bodily on the forward deck with a dull boom that shook the ship from end to end. She shuddered to the surface, dripping from every pore and shaking side to side, her nose pointing twenty degrees above the taut horizon. As the great palls of spray rose from the ocean and drifted across the ship, the sun caught them and flashed momentary rainbows through the mist, that died as soon as born. Alongside, where there was a continual slaver of froth and spray, the rainbow rode triumphantly along, plunging and dipping like a painted veil. Perry conjured the poor dejected shade of Conrad and challenged it to write a single line that could express, however poorly, the beauty that surrounded him on every hand. Conceive of it, he thought, thousands of miles of living, leaping waters, girdling the globe from continent to continent—no mere mud-puddle this, but a titanic force, majestic even in repose, terrific and fearful when whipped up by a gale, a force greater than all the other forces put together—an overwhelming hive of energy, unbounded and unharnessed. Even though he felt like Napoleon whenever he stood on the bridge—even though he could not help feeling that somehow he was in control of the great ship that bore him over the sea, it was impossible for him, try as he would, to feel anything but humble in the presence of the only real god whose sanctum he had ever dared invade. "I feel humble," he said aloud into the wind, and the wind tore the very words out of his mouth and flung them down his throat.

III

After his sudden burst of confidence, which lasted a week and even permitted him to invite Perry to his room, Pearson had withdrawn into his shell, and his red face expressed the complete inanition that had masked it heretofore. It came on slowly enough —he spoke less and less day by day, until within another week he answered once again with grunts and nods and avoided looking at Perry when he passed. There was no explanation. I know what it is, Perry thought, he is afraid of me; afraid of me. His inherently modest mind fought against the idea, but he finally had to admit that the impending silence dated from the revelation of the printed book, and that it was the shock of knowing a flesh and blood author that had sealed the springs of Pearson's confidence. Surely that day they had been at their flood—he'd taken Perry to his cabin and shown him the copy of *The Piper*, which Perry signed, "With gratitude and much astonishment, L. Perry." and when Pearson was at his best, Perry had said, "I've always wanted to ask, but was rather timid—we read so much about the fascination of the sea, and how it holds men to it—I personally can't see it—it looks the same to me every day, sometimes a little rougher—but what is this miraculous lure of the . . ." "Bull," Pearson said, then, "aw, I don't know. I guess there is something though (the second mate had said he thought so too, only he'd been a little more particular—with his southern accent, Caverly had said, 'Waal, ah don' know—ah guess it's mo' the sea than the life at sea, fo' that ain't so pleasant') . . . well, y'know," said Pearson, "I lived ashore for six months this year, down in the Village, with a nice apartment and a sweet girl to love, but I just didn't feel right somehow—then I got a job and believe me, boy, when we got standing out to sea and I smelt that breeze— boy! you know (he took up a pencil), when you get up late at night and go to the galley to get your coffee, and then go up on the bridge and pace back and forth, and every half-hour the clock goes like this (he rapped on the desk), taptap-taptap, and fo'ard another bell goes, taptap-taptap, and the lookout on the foc'sle head says, 'All lights burning bright, sir,' and you say, 'All-*right*,' —boy! that's it," he said, "I guess that's it."

But day by day Pearson said less and less and Perry felt embarrassed in his presence—he got to coming up on Pearson's watch and only staying long enough to look at the pilot's chart and see how far they'd gone since noon the day before. Then he stood in the pilot-house while Pearson paced and carefully avoided seeing him, and finally he said, "Making good time to-day." "Uh huh," the third replied, and went into the chart-room. Perry wanted to be able to say, "Look here, old man, how have I offended you, what's the matter?" but somehow he couldn't do it. He knew he hadn't offended him and was completely baffled. He did manage one night at mess to say, "You've crawled back into your shell again, I see," and Pearson grinned and passed the butter to him. He determined to make Pearson talk, so he didn't go up on Pearson's watch again and he didn't talk to Pearson at the table; and Pearson didn't talk to him at all.

I give it up, he thought, on deck one night, the last night before the freighter docked at Havre. I'll send him a letter from Vienna, and ask for a response. To hell with him, he thought, and remembered how the day he'd come aboard he'd seen Pearson looking at him and talking him over with another mate, with a sly grin on his face. He remembered that he'd hated him that day, so he picked the thread up where it had been broken, and hated him again, and stood on the deck in the clear winter night with the stars wheeling back and forth and round and round overhead, and Orion lying on his side far to the south and the Big Dipper almost on its back. Somehow the stars seemed very far away and utterly impersonal and cold, at sea; they did not comfort him as they had so many nights in the summer, as he lay alone in his blanket in a hay-field, winking merrily and keeping him company. Now they wheeled and soared like terns, miles above, majestic and ironical and cold . . .

He looked out to sea—the fabric of waves tossed and soared and swayed away and sank, and the cold salt spray flashed back and forth across the deck and swished against the ports and dripped warm phosphorescent lights off the bulkheads. The miracle, he thought, of passing ships at sea . . . one star in Orion went out beneath a bank of low clouds at the dark horizon, and the whole night was tremulous with the high, thin howl of the wind through the cables, and the high voice of the engines, and the sibilant hushing of the sea against the steel plates . . .

LOVE'S SO MANY THINGS [1]

By CLIFFORD BRAGDON

(From *The Midland*)

THE first four hours out of Cleveland were not bad. The bus was hot as the devil, but almost empty, and I had the whole back seat alone where I could make myself comfortable stretched out. But when we hit Youngstown, it was all over. Everybody in eastern Ohio got on there—fat women with bundles, slick boys with panama hats and several suitcases, girls in couples, and a sailor. I had to sit up to make room for a fellow and his wife.

The man looked as if he thought he were pretty hard—tight blue suit and long hair plastered back and parted in the middle— like a million others; all they seem to care about is how smooth their hair is. When he smoked, he pulled his lips tight and made the smoke spurt out of the corner of his mouth, first up and then down. They all do that, millions of them. They want you to think they are pretty hard. This one's eyes were little and grey. His wife was pretty, poor kid, though sort of pale and thin, it seemed to me.

Anyway, every chair was taken, and the heat was terrific. I began to wonder whether it was worth the twelve or fifteen I would save on it. If it had not been for the sailor and a couple of girls, I don't know how we could have stood it. As it was, every one was glad to have them along. They sang songs and giggled and carried on almost all night. Sitting right in back of them, I got the benefit of the really good part, the hot give and take, so to speak. For instance, the sailor asked the thinnest one where they were going, and she said, "No place, friend. We're just traveling for our health." Then the other one began singing.

"I wonder how the old folks are to-night.
Do they miss the little girl who ran away?"

25

It was like that almost till morning. Sometimes one would sing, sometimes both—harmony—and it really wasn't bad, except once in a while. Then the sailor would groan, and they would laugh it off and get talking.

The fellow next to me—the fellow with the wife—was all ears. Every time one of them would make a wisecrack, he would hawhaw and stamp his feet. His wife would look up at him now and then and smile as if she thought it was pretty good too, and blink her eyes. But as a matter of fact, I don't think she was even listening, because the minute she got on the bus she just curled up in a corner, coughed a few times—she had a pretty bad cough —and closed her eyes. Her husband didn't seem to mind, though. He ate three or four plums and took in the entertainment. He was sitting so that his wife could rest her head on his lap and he had to lean over on me to hear everything the sailor and the girls said.

As soon as he finished the plums, he got friendly. First he winked at me after he had nearly fallen over from laughing once, and then he leaned even closer than he was already, nudging me.

"They're rich, ain't they?" he whispered. His voice didn't sound at all the way he looked.

"Yeah," I said. "Your wife mind if I smoke?"

"No. Where you from?" he said, "Youngstown?"

I told him, no, I was from Cleveland, and he mentioned how bad the Indians were doing. Just then his wife sat up and coughed. She asked him for a cigarette, but he shook his head. Then he kissed her.

When she was curled up again, he turned to me. "It must be swell being a sailor," he said. "Lots of fun, them fellows."

"Yeah," I said, "but they don't get on land only once in so often."

"That's right," he answered, nudging me again, "but when they do, oh, boy—uh?"

I moved over a little. "It's pretty good, I guess."

"You bet," he said. "You know I used to be pretty quick on the pickup myself. I used to have a pretty good line—and they fell for it, too, if I do say it."

Neither of us spoke for a while then. We were scrouging around trying to get a little less cramped and hot than we were, or else listening to the clowns in front of us. Everybody else was doing the same thing or just sitting still with their heads back and their mouths open—especially the fat women. All the women on this bus were fat—except the little girl on the back seat—and they appeared not to mind the heat as much as the thin men. They sat as if they had been dumped down and a few yards of crumpled stuff thrown around them.

My new friend seemed to be turning something over in his mind, and so I had a chance to take a peek at his wife. I couldn't see her very well unless we were passing under a light. It gave a funny effect then, as if she were alive for a second and then dead, about to wake up and then just dropped asleep again. I was getting so I could hardly keep my eyes off her.

When we were pulling out of Pittsburgh where some one got off, leaving us three the back seat to ourselves, he started in again. "Where you bound for, Bud?" he asked me.

I told him New York and asked him where he was going.

"Harrisburg. I got an aunt," he said. "Well, we're getting off the bus at Harrisburg, that is, but we're going up to the Pocono Mountains. We been over two thousand miles on the roads in the last five days. We been out to Denver."

"Is that so?" I said. "Nice out there, they tell me."

He laughed a little. "Well," he said, "yeah, it's a nice enough place, but no work."

I asked him what he'd been doing out there then, thinking he might be one of these auto-hoboes. Neither he nor his wife looked like money at all—even cheap money. He didn't answer my question, so I said, "What did you do, drive out and then take the busses back?"

"No," he answered, "we took the busses both ways. Was you ever in Harrisburg?"

"No," I said.

It was getting late, and the entertainment was off for a while because one of the girls, the less fat one, had paired off with the sailor. The other pretended she didn't care and sang by herself for a minute but not long. She tried to get hold of a red-headed fellow across the aisle, but there was nothing doing, so she flopped around and pretended to go to sleep. I was ready for sleep myself, but didn't like to sleep sitting up, and besides, I kept glancing over at the girl curled up in the corner. I lit another cigarette and asked the girl's husband what he was going to do in Pocono.

"I don't know," he said.

"A little vacation, maybe?"

"No, I'll get work up there if I can," he said. "One reason for going up there is maybe my uncle can get me some work. I got a trade—glass worker, but I don't care much what I do." He settled himself a little. "It don't make any difference," he went on. "There are some good farms up there—Dutch. Maybe I'd make a good farmer. Yeah, a swell farmer—not. But it's O.K. with me." He stepped carefully on the cigarette I had just tossed on the floor, and smiled.

"Well, but what's the idea going up into the hills though?" I asked him. It was about two in the morning. The time and the heat both must have made me feeble-minded. Anyway he didn't answer my question, because his wife woke up just then and put her fingers through his hair as if she liked the stuff. She was just a kid. He must have been about thirty-one or -two; hard to tell exactly. But she didn't look more than twenty at the most.

Well, for a while then he didn't even know I was alive. A big change came over him. He took out his handkerchief and fanned her like they do a fighter. It seemed funny to see this tiny little kid sitting in a corner of the back seat on a bus, all slumped down like a fighter just saved by the bell, and being fanned like one, too. It made me feel sore at something because I wanted to do something for her. Of course there wasn't anything I could do— I just felt like it ought to have been somebody else fanning her and kissing her. Not that there was anything wrong with this fellow exactly; she ought to have been married to somebody else, that's all. The poor kid must have been boiling hot—though it had cooled off a little by this time—because there were little beads of sweat all over her forehead, and she coughed so much I finally had the sense to quit smoking.

Her husband fanned her like that until she smiled at him and closed her eyes. Then she curled up again, and her husband made her as comfortable as he could. At about the same time the sailor and the girl split up. The girl came back and sat with her friend. At first the fat one pretended she was still asleep,

but she soon got over that, and the two of them started in singing
again. It was late, and some man up front didn't like it.

"Aw, pipe down, lady," he hollered, "and go to sleep."

The girls came right back at him. "If you don't like it, why
don't you get out?" one of them said.

This got a good laugh; we were in the mountains without a
house in sight. Just the same the girls quit singing.

"If he was back here, I'd slap his mouth," the fat one said.

The sailor turned around. "Well," he said, "your friend here
bit mine."

"Oh, hush up, you big liar," answered the girl he had been
sitting with. Then they all three laughed and started another
conversation.

The fellow sitting with me laughed so hard at what the sailor
said, I thought he would roll off onto the floor.

"That was a fast one," he said, rubbing his nose. "Like I said
to a girl friend once." He reached in his pocket as if he wanted
a cigarette, but changed his mind. He slid down in his seat so
that he was talking up sideways at my chin. "This girl was in
swimming, see?" he went on, grinning all over, "so I come up
behind her under water and pinched her on the—well, you get
me, haw, haw, haw—just kidding, see, but she made out she didn't
notice it, and she says to her friend who was standing there with
her, she says, 'Oh, wasn't that a big wave, Betty—or Beth, or
whatever her name was.' I heard her and came right back, 'Yeah,
that was swell,' I says. Swell, see, me pinching her," and he
laughed hard and nudged me for the hundredth time. He was
looking the way people usually do when they tell a joke—like a
kid watching some one else eating a piece of candy. I thought it
was a pretty bum joke, but we got talking along those lines for a
while. He told a few pretty fair ones about his adventures—just
the usual stuff, and then I asked him again how he happened to
be going up to the mountains with the hill-billies. I preferred
hearing about that though I guess it was really his wife I was
interested in.

Every now and then I would look over at her, but she made
me feel so foolish, I kept trying to listen to her dumb husband
instead. She made me feel like I wanted to hold her like a little
kid and give her a drink of water—in little sips. She would sip,

I thought, and then look up and catch her breath and smile with her eyes. It made me feel foolish, thinking like that.

Well, her husband said something after a minute, answering me, I guess, but I missed it. Then I heard him say,

"I said she's pretty, ain't she?"

Of course I felt like even a bigger yap then than before; he couldn't have helped noticing me staring at her, not even him. But he didn't seem sore. I said, "Yes, but she don't look very well."

"No," he said, "she's got a cold."

He turned so that he could look at her, and patted her arm. "She's only twenty-two," he went on. "We been married five years, would you believe it? She was seventeen then."

"Is that a fact?" I answered, not knowing what else to say.

"Yeah. She's Irish. Look at that nose and you can tell she's a little mick all right. She's only been in this country five and a half years. She come over six months before I married her."

He just seemed to be talking for talking's sake. I guess he didn't want to fall asleep, either. But I wanted him to keep on about her, so I said, "What's her name? Colleen?"

"No," he said, "Mary. She's not really Irish I guess though. She says she's Manx from the Isle of Man. Sounds like a cat, don't it? There's a cat named Manx, ain't there? Anyway I tell her she ain't got it right. She's a minx, not a Manx, I tell her."

He stopped suddenly and looked at me as if he was afraid I might think he was a sap, and yet as if he wanted me to laugh at the same time. One dirty, stubby hand was still on her arm, stroking it. It was dark, and he didn't know I could see that. But I could. Her arm was so white. It was impossible now to keep from looking at her; I was beginning to think she was the prettiest girl I had ever seen.

Pretty soon her husband started talking again. "She was working at my aunt's house when I was there for a while. They lived in Brooklyn then. That's how I come to meet her. Ever been in Brooklyn?"

"Love at first sight, uh?" I said.

He chuckled. "Hell, no," he said. "She wouldn't have a thing to do with me at first. I was carrying on around there with some other girls at the time. But, you know, I cut all that out. It's funny, ain't it, how you'll do that."

All I wanted to do was to keep on asking him questions. "How did you finally bring her around then?" I asked him.

"Oh, she come around all right in the end," he whispered, winking at me. "You can't keep the girls away from a good-looking fellow, uh?" His little grey eyes opened wide, and he nudged me. "Ain't that right?" he added, laughing when I looked at him. "Of course I was just kidding, Bud," he said. "I guess I ain't no John Barrymore, all right."

He sounded so serious I had to laugh. "Sure, I knew that," I said.

I didn't mean it the way it sounded, but I was just as glad to let it go. I was so sick of his nudging me I could have hit him anyway. Besides, as I said, looking at his wife made me sore at things in general, and I guess I was taking it out on him. He wasn't really such a bad guy.

But he got over it all right, and pretty soon he laughed. "We was married in Brooklyn. She's a Catholic," he said.

"But how did it all happen?" I broke in on him, wanting to hear all I could. It seemed as if I had to.

"Well, I'll tell you how it was, Bud," he answered, sitting up again and crossing his legs, but keeping one hand on his wife's arm, "we got to keep awake, huh? But there ain't much to tell. There wasn't anything romantic about it or anything. I'd just been kidding around with her for a while—you know how it is—taking her to a show now and then without meaning much. She never let on one way or the other till the very end—but—but she said then she'd been crazy about me. Anyway I didn't hardly believe it myself for a long while. She was just a kid, see?"

"Oh, yeah, I see," I said.

He went right on. "She would be around the house cooking and dusting and so on and I'd just sneak up behind her and kiss her on the neck—that's about all. She was too tired for much gallavanting around most of the time usually."

I didn't like him telling me all this, and yet I kept egging him on. "Didn't she mind you kissing her like that?" I asked.

"Oh, no," he answered. "She wouldn't stand for a lot of fooling, but I wasn't never rough with her. I—I—she seemed to take it all right. Anyway we didn't court long. In fact it was just a month before I popped the question like they say. It come on me like a bolt of lightning, but Mary said afterward the only thing that surprised her was—and worried her too, she said—was why I didn't get on to myself earlier."

"Yeah, go on," I said.

"Well, one night she was out in the kitchen and I was sort of helping around when my aunt come in. 'Mary,' she says, 'Mrs. Link's out here with her baby. Come on out and take care of him while me and her go to the show, will you?' she says.

"So Mary and I went out and played with this kid for about half an hour. It was a cute kid—falling around. And then all of a sudden I felt something sort of come over me. It was the funniest feeling I ever had—like—like I wanted to pick her up and . . . Oh, well, anyway I stood up, see?—we were sitting on the floor—and Mary looked up at me as if she was surprised— the little bum. She wasn't no more surprised—but believe me I was. I was so surprised I was afraid if I opened my mouth I'd holler and act crazy. But then the first thing I knew I heard myself talking—like I was way away.

" 'Well, Kid,' I says, 'I guess you better set the date.' Right like that. 'Make it whenever you like,' I says, 'but the sooner the better.' That was all there was to it. I didn't mean to say it that way, believe me, but that's the way it was. Funny, how things happen so different from what you'd have said they would when you were thinking about it, ain't it? That was May, and we was married the following September. Mary carried roses."

I didn't say anything. I just took a quick look at his wife. Apparently the poor kid was sound asleep.

We were coming into a small town at the moment and stopped to gas up. Everybody that was awake piled out for a cup of coffee. I drank two. I was trying to think straight, but I guess I was too sleepy. The fellow and his wife both stayed in the bus.

When it came time to climb in again, I noticed it had gotten quite chilly while we were talking, so when I'd picked my way back to my seat, I told the fellow I was going to try to get a little sleep on the floor and his wife could stretch out and make herself comfortable. She was sitting up then and heard me.

Neither one of them said anything, but the girl did stretch out, and he sat crunched up in one corner. I was hoping the girl would smile or something, but she didn't.

Pretty soon everybody else piled in and we started out again. The sailor and the two girls were just as full of pep as ever and began kidding around out loud. One of them said something funny, and my talkative friend let out another one of his horse laughs. I was feeling foolish still, so I took off my coat and put it over the girl's feet; she was coughing a little. Her husband already had his over her shoulders. He had the window open and I was glad it was warm on the floor. I asked him why he didn't put the window down, but he pointed to his wife, and shook his head. He was laughing so hard at the wisecrack from the seat in front he couldn't speak, but when he got through, he leaned over—I was stretched out on the floor in front of him then.

"Say, Bud, listen," he whispered, "did you ever hear the one about the Irishman and the girl in Hoboken?"

Well, I couldn't see him, but I knew just what he looked like. Something jumped up inside me, and I said, "No, damn it, and I don't want to, either."

He didn't say anything, but I could hear him sit back and move around trying to get comfortable. I was feeling so bad I could have killed him. Pretty soon I heard a kiss and some whispering, but from where I was, I couldn't tell whether it was in front or in back of me. That was all I knew for about three hours.

It was light when I woke up. I sat up on the floor and looked around. The girl was lying stretched out, fast asleep with her head in her husband's lap. When he saw me sit up, he winked at me, and grinned. I almost felt sorry for him—he looked so cold. I said, "How is she?"

He looked down at her and put his hand on her forehead. "Her cold's pretty bad," he whispered.

They got out at Harrisburg.

POISONER IN MOTLEY [1]

By LOUIS BRENNAN

(From *Scrip*)

THE horizon had been retreating before him all day. But now it had stopped and he knew that over the flatness of the prairie it was creeping around him. There was no longer any sun; his only direction was the washed-out track of a road that had the sole quality of a narrow twisting length. A storm had beaten the epidermis from it, leaving a raw surface, hole-marked, uncrossed as yet by any travel, crawling its feeble course away from itself. The boy dragged after it; its fortunes were his fortunes, and he hoped that it had a belly as lean as his and a destination for the night. So far it had not been a valuable companion; it had found neither hospitality for him, nor for itself that end of wandering toward which all roads, like sea-bound eels, tend and aspire. If meals have a name and appointed time for the hungry, his last one had been a breakfast from two frightened old ladies who gave him a glass of milk and two apples because their cat had rubbed him kindly on the leg. It had been easy to laugh at them then, and apologize with a bow. He had been just starting his second day. Behind him there, very far behind, because he intended never to turn back, was an office. His clerkship in it had vanished, as his stool might have vanished in smoke had it been burned; it had left him nothing.

The road seemed to be the only thing on the whole plain that could have seen or heard of man; but the storm had destroyed all evidence of any such a creature. The boy felt some relief in wording his feeling conversationally. Without speaking he addressed a remark to the road:

"I'll never reach twenty-six . . . or even the next town, if you don't make up your mind to go somewhere."

To him the road's knowledge of his hunger was as complete as

34

his own. His association with it seemed in its intimacy to have been long enough for confessions of secret sins. Yet, still and inscrutable, it attended him in callous silence. Though all the gravel and stones were gross to the feel of his thin shoes, the boy took careful steps in his seeming plodding along to save his stomach the painful jerk of a slip or stumble. Inside him the hollow that the day had left was spreading, widening, deepening; harsh movements caused it to re-echo with shrill small pains that were long in quieting.

It was so dark now that he thought that, standing on tiptoe, he could have touched the sky. Straight ahead, he did not know whether he could see a foot or a mile. A swirling mist was dissolving into the dark, then steaming off again in faint grey uncertain lines, following a breeze or vanishing completely in a gust. Things of material and substance, occasional trees, the ground itself, were robbed of their shape and existence to the eye; they might have drifted themselves in a mist. The road was only a scratching under his feet, and jouncing of his leg.

After a while the darkness began to thin out, to clear. Still nothing was visible, but the murky, muddy composition of mist and darkness seemed to settle, and growing less dense, to be of great depth and extension as though it might cover the whole world.

He was alone in this world. The thought seeped in. Like a man waking from stolid sleep, he shook off the painful mood of hunger, breathing it out in the same respiration in which he inhaled his feeling of loneliness. Remote, untouchable, unrestrained by the presence of any eyes or living brain to think or judge, he burst out of the everyday bounds of his mind into a sense of his freedom and supremacy in this world. Towns and the iron walls of neighbors' minds had dropped into the tenacious fingers of That Which Is Past. The fields and the road and the air were his. Whatever walked here, whoever peopled it, he was Adam of; stripped of the imperfection of being Robert Carl, he was a man to whom God had given a planet. He would have spoken as a peer to kings, presidents, to Michael, to the devil. He was belabored by no question of right and wrong. Wrong was no wall equatoring his mind to the fields that he might walk and the fruits that he might eat, or dare not. Yet feeling himself capable of anything he did nothing; freedom to wish his mind to any pole, freedom to act, immune to accusing eyes, meant freedom not to go or do. Shivering, he trod the prairie road and was unconscious that he moved. The feeling was so incoherent, so formless and so risen without effort, so unsatisfiable that it satisfied itself, lasting longer in its emotional instability than the pleasure of sweets or music or cool water to the senses.

Having burned its tender fuel, the elation collapsed. Bolder the hurt of hunger advanced up his side and down his legs to meet the jumping ache there. He found that hunger is not a pain that stops in its own province like a bruise that cries out only where the wound is. By patient advance it besieges the whole body, being careful never to throb so unbearably that it makes itself insensate. The boy found that he could hinder the advance by folding his arms under his stomach, where the unevenness of his gait became magnified to a shock. Bent over so, he walked along watching each foot push itself behind and reappear suddenly again to catch up to the other in a kind of stupid race.

Even if he had been upright he would not have seen the mote of light much sooner. At first he half-expected it to disappear like a fuelless spark. He played with its image in his eyes, closing them against it, then opening them to bear on where it ought to be; it flickered to his blinking and was found in his eyelid. He blew his breath in its direction, and then striking a finger like a match, lit it again. Out of nothing it gained strength; he warmed his hands at it. With a flourish like a magician he made it appear out of his sleeve. He counted it the only star out that night.

The road shunted off here from a direct line to the light. Distrustful that it would ever get there the boy abandoned it and went stumbling across the field, holding to the light as though it were a line by which he was pulling himself along. By long searching of the immediate background of the light he uncovered the outline of a cottage overtopped by a tree, now with a lucid gash in its side. The road reached it before his uncertain painful feet. Cutting across in front of him it continued off to his right.

The cottage sat back from the road on a slight rise. He walked up to it between two rows of awkward young trees, more ungainly still with their half invisibility. A coat of new white paint cut it sharply out of the darkness, its single gable a high triangle jutting up into the thick enclosing gloom. Over the porch that was half the face of the cottage sparse new vines were trained in a lattice-work. In a window overlooking this the light from the inside was strained through half-open white curtains. Where this slightly illuminated dashes of the paint, the house looked as moist and fresh as at a weighty touch of dew.

No dog warned him off, no cat discovered him as he poked his way around the side to find the back door, slipping at almost every step on the grass, heavy from the rain. But he was careful on the small porch to look for pans or boxes which if he kicked might be alarums to the inmates calling him out a marauder. He dared do nothing that would cause him to be driven back to that road with its wandering stupidity and callousness. This was a course of action he had planned, coming across the field when the dwelling was a fort to be taken tactically. That thought had passed like a mood, but the plan having graved its outlines on his immediate mind, guided him along it when the last arduous jolting rod or so toward his goal made his stomach his mind, and the unbearable hunger pains his thought.

He knocked twice; before the door called out his presence the second time, it had swung back sharply into a light that pounced blindingly on his head. He forgot what he had wanted to say, that he meant to say it ingratiatingly. He nodded toward the figure in the door, pointing his words toward it, and his stomach spoke:

"I'm hungry."

Without further revelation of himself, without invitation, as naturally as into the invited home of a friend, he crossed the border of the doorway into the house. For a second he stood unaware of himself; then having turned about toward the door he saw standing with the door-knob still in her hand, regarding him with the startled emotions not yet risen to her face, a small slim young woman, a full apron covering her from bodice to hem. She was pretty and unexpected; her dark hair, though full-blown around her head, was in a trained array. In the frame of it her face slanted a little from cheek to chin that was softly rounded underneath. Her cheeks, faintly alive, were smooth and cared for.

"I'm hungry." This one information was the only bid he made for her attention: he was hungry and she could feed him. With sudden remembrance he took off his hat. "I haven't eaten since yesterday." He nodded, almost bowed to her, puzzled a little that she had said nothing, with the half-formed notion perhaps that she might respond to the speech of gesture. Having finished this he sat down on a chair in his damp, untidy clothes, holding his beaten hat in both tired hands.

The woman stepped out of her pose toward him, and since she had not relinquished the knob, the door opened on the black outside.

"But you can't . . ."

"I know. I'll be all right if you give me something hot. I'm cold inside and wet out. I'm very hungry. The last house is a long way from here, and I'm walking. I hope you're kinder than the others on this road, because I haven't any money . . . out of work."

This skeleton of monologue he offered to her bewildered look as it changed in slow transition from fright to an enforced accept-ance of him and whatever he threatened.

"Yes, yes, I can give you some biscuits and coffee. Of course, I'll feed you. It's too bad my neighbors aren't more hospitable. How far did you say the last house was the way you came?"

Her first words were a little tangled in her voice, but as these straightened out, her low tones began to flow with a determined force which was now evident in her action as she began to move about the kitchen. She did not speak further or appear to expect any conversation. In a kind of doze in which only those things that were looked at steadily appeared through, he sat and waited. About her as she worked the details of the kitchen seemed to fall in: the new kitchen cabinet, its metal shining, its glass windows unobscured even by recent dust, its china and dinner-ware ar-ranged on white paper napkins; the stove gleamed with such a polished face that it reflected steadily the neat blue flame on the oil wicks. The powerful illumination of a gasoline lamp showed the ceiling and walls, sending back as white and clean a light as they received. This much gave him an impression of tidiness and cleanliness, but there was another impression that he could give no name to; it was in the color and hang of the curtains; in the arrangement of the furniture; in the vased flowers and the white table cloth. And it was very strong to him even in his insensitive coma.

Her swift movements produced some half-worn biscuits, butter, and a dish of jam. This food she set down for him on the side of the table opposite to where he was, so that the wall was at his back, and the table between him and the corner of the room where she was working. Over his head was a shelf with pots of trailing plants; he had to duck his head as he sat down, and brush away the pendent tendrils. Across the room, he saw, as he reached for the butter, the door to another room; it was closed. These chunks of information remained undigested in his mind while with bungling quickness his hands tried to keep pace with his long unused jaws. The first bites, swallowed down almost without the benefit of teeth, hurt like small sharp stones. But in the sweet taste of the food, the zest of biting and chewing, the pain was forgotten. Even the woman was, as she worked, until the smell of frying ham and eggs drew his attention to them and her. As she brought the plate of round brown-edged eggs and thick slices of ham to his table, she spoke to him.

"Something warm for you."

She covered his figure apparent above the table with her eyes. "It must have been a long time since you've been to . . . I mean seen a town. There aren't many out here, you know. That storm has almost ruined your clothes." She paused. "You must have been out of work a long time."

She tried to make her voice sound compassionate, but in it was a note of the fascination, a desperate interest that made her say more than she meant. She started at his regard: her eyes took on a queer fleet darkening; turning away to hide it, she went on rapid little feet out of the room, closing the door so that he did not see what she did thereafter.

He put no interpretation on the fact immediately, but as his attention began to be less on the meal, he thought that she might have been worried about something—a tardy husband, perhaps. Of a certainty there was no husband in the house. His thought paused; a faint grinding, muffled only partly by the closed door interested his ear. It was repeated, he thought, with more impatience. Then, as he looked at the door opposite, the sound broke out unmuffled into snatches of grinding whirr that soon were almost an uninterrupted revolution of small sound. Though it was not loud, he half rose, puzzled, from his chair. The door was tugged slightly open, and through the aperture at the bottom a long striped cat squeezed his head and skinny ribs. The boy stared, and the cat, coming to a sudden halt, backed on his haunches and accepted the challenge. His eyes were suddenly chilled to slant green pieces of stillness, his ears went stiff in hostility. These seemed to be on the top instead of at the sides of his head, surmounting a face which was not round and suavely catlike, but triangular and hungry-looking. He would have been vicious and menacing were it not for his size and the patchwork coat he wore. Its Joseph's coat design gave him the air of a poisoner in motley.

For a second the boy was on the defensive. The small malevolence of the cat made him laugh queerly. His whole mood would have fitted well an answering growl at the animal. The moment of normal balanced emotion that food and rest and warmth had brought him was gone again. In the place of the former pain deep but clear was now an atmosphere of unsteadiness that made unreal sounds and sights real, and real ones grotesque. He still tried gazes with the cat.

As he looked now, he was aware that the bottom of the door had widened its angle with the threshold. His glance fled upward along the widened opening. There was only time enough to show the woman in the door; her whole attitude was poised on a second of sudden numbing revelation. The key to that revelation was not in the cat, nor on the boy's person. Her eyes were above his head and they were focused inexorably; then like a hope gone from the heart, she vanished and left the flat door where she had been.

The boy came to his feet as though the rapidity of her going had left a current that sucked him in, and as he was drawn up, the last inch of him straightened into a blow against the forgotten flower shelf. As solid and instant as was the pain that the blow left, it left another impression in his head, the thud of a heavy body grudgingly moved by the shock. When the lessening of the first pain gave sight back to his eyes, they awoke on the brown fat bulk of that thud, most of which was lying in shadow. He

reached for it; it fitted his curved hand smoothly; it was something to soothe the touch of his trembling from the warning just
rung in his head. And when he brought it out into the light, a
polished black flash slid along it and dripped from its end.

He held it in his hands, under his eyes. Where he had been
a moment ago, as solidified, as unshakable in himself, in his one-
ness as this gun, he was now an excitement, an evanescence of
alien desires. The room fell away and in with the coolness came
a million rebellions. Any one of these could have overcome his
gravity of habit and carried him across to the door.

The gun, which he had not thought of as a thing to make war,
to force and threaten, was exuding its audacity into his arm. He
paused before the door, touched it, and stood in its place in the
doorway.

The whole room pointed her out to him in the far corner of
it as a long corridor points down to the door at its end. She was
crouched in a great chair, bigger than she, and a deal table had
been pulled over in front of her. Beaten and disarmed she lay
here, flung into this last retreat by a fear that had got into the
muscles of her small body by seizing her mind. In her face a
strange sentence wrote itself; it was as though the natural order
was reversed and the image that had been first on her eye, the
image of her fear, had by reflection taken form and was now a
man in the doorway with her gun in his hand. With a low sound
that was less a cry than the uncontrolled escape of long sup-
pressed breath, her small head fell into the huddle of her figure,
and she was still.

For the boy she had dropped out of the world of moving beings
into the world of stones and walls and of the beings in the room
that now relapsed into their endurance of time. She had entered
the soul of the chair. The cool night air came in, and the gusts
of the great rebellions swept him and were gone. He grew. The
room was his now; it was his universe, empty of a rival to judge,
or condemn, or despise, or see him in whatever he did. His first
steps were giant steps; they cost him all the resolution thought
takes to become action when the mere contemplation of it seems
to require all the verve of mind and effort of body. But the near-
ness, the touchability, the helpless bulk of the things in his world
tempted him to action; on the road his world had been barren:

now it was full, blindingly full. His first steps released him to effortless motion.

He moved about touching all the things in the room with eyes newiy come to feel possession. The vase, and pictures, books, the ivory elephant, candlesticks, the chairs, the feather duster, shone like the gold of the forty thieves because he had laid on them the fingers of his possession. But the final treasure that was to be his, more intimately his than the mere having to touch, was kept from his sight in its sanctuary. With a weapon guarding his supremacy he hunted it. He peered, and crept, and prowled, and the gun that had drooped at the end of his arm was rigid and alert in the hand before him. Money, the purse that it was in, had a place somewhere in this room, and the room was his. That which was valuable in his world, that which had a place in it, no one had to tell him, for he knew. The purse had a place.

High up on a shelf he saw it, brown, looking like the books it was hidden among. There remained but the taking: steps across the room and reaching it from its high repose. He groped for a stool to elevate himself; then as he straightened up, a man was before him. Full statured, gun rigid in hand, he saw in the metallic turn of a second this other god in his world. His fingers, taught by instinct alone, tightened in their slow deadly squeeze to unleash his lightning and his thunder.

The man's face looked evil. Between the black thick cap of hair and the rough mask of beard, his eyes were two intense, unholy desires. In the movement of a chin thrusting itself bold in challenge, the two lips touched each other in lines of scarlet. His clothes had been beaten and torn, this man's, exposing, despite their lean damp clinging, a body bigger than the boy thought his own. The very wrinkles of the sagging coat had life and threat. Their slackness over a body contracted in arrested motion promised action hanging on the twitch of a thought; and in his still pose they made him an image of menace and fevered life. The accumulation of all this was in the boy's heart as he looked, a burdened impression, so full that anything added to it must break it open, burst it like too full fruit, and let the pulp run out. Then he who knew nothing of men handling guns, a book clerk, saw that the gun was in the man's left hand, its thin mouth pressed against the hard lips of his own. He laughed, without moving a muscle of his face, without a surge of his belly, he laughed, and in the metallic flash of a second the man in the mirror was dead. Of flesh, of soul, of terribleness the looking-glass was robbed, and like an impostor who, discovered in his borrowed identity seems to have the opposite of those features he pretended, it was a clown in a bad man's clothes. The boy laughed and looked, and the laugh was like water breaking through a winter's ice.

"Me! Jesse James, Deadwood Dick! The circus ought to give you a job, old boy! Better stick to stage-coaches and leave ransacking houses to second-story men. Welcome, Mr. Carl, to the hall of the Robber Barons! Me! John of the Roads. Dr. Jekyll's Mr. Hyde! I never knew you had it in you!"

He looked a moment at the woman in the chair, her white face pitifully sunk against the hard arm of the chair.

"Me, the monster king of the plains, and my name hushes little children!" And he went out into the kitchen for some water.

"No, madam, I had no gun in my hand . . . Of course, I didn't know you had one, where you kept it. I'm very, very sorry. You see, it was impossible for me to know how like a tramp I looked. . . . I came to say 'Thank you.' Of course, I went for water immediately. . . . Your phone is out of order. I tried to call a doctor. . . . No, madam, I'll go right away. How far to town? . . . Will you please accept my apologies? If I'd known you were so frightened, I'd not have stopped to trouble you. . . . Certainly. . . . Yes, I know the way to the road; goes west, doesn't it? Thank you."

He went out into the unfamiliar darkness, and left her holding a trembling light to show him the way. He was scarce off the small porch when it was gone, followed by the click of a latch. Feeling his way along to the road he groped into a wet pole, and, shying away, tripped over a loose wire. He felt it with his fingers. Two strands of wire, telephone wire, broken some place, he thought by the feel of slackness.

"Thief . . . I couldn't be one! I never was. But . . . almost."

The thought and he and the road went toward town together.

SAND [1]

By WANDA BURNETT

(From *Story*)

SOMETIMES the wagon jolted into a hole and a cloud of dust rolled away to the side of the road and settled like a smother over the small blue berries of the scrubby spruce. But mostly the road was smooth and ran ahead and behind the wagon—a string, long and thin, stretching across the desert. Only the sagebrush, the road, and the dusty blueberried spruce for miles and the sun pricking the sand. Now and then the dust, caught by a slight breeze, twirled like a funnel into the sky and was gone. Ghosts. Desert ghosts. Dancing.

I felt all scooped out and empty looking down at the desert and the purple mounds that ran like the rhythm of a song along the desert's edge. I remember. I was five then and I sat in the back of the covered-in wagon with my brother. I had on black stockings and the dust kept turning them grey. I brushed and brushed, but it did no good. Once the wagon stopped and my mother came around the back and winked at me. I told her no, but she said I'd better anyway. So I went with her. I gathered a few of the wrinkled berries and some sagebrush. When we came back my dad was standing in front of the wagon, one hand shading his eyes and the other pointing ahead. "Look," he said, "there's our road, way down there ta hell'n gone!" I didn't know where we were going. No one had told me. I had forgotten to ask.

Then we got back into the wagon and the horses went plop-plopping along the road again. Then it must have been noon because my mother opened a package and gave me a cheese sandwich and a tomato. I ate the tomato because I was thirsty and I poked a hole through the sandwich and wore it for a ring till my mother saw me, then I nibbled the crust and dropped the sandwich into the dust.

.   .   .   .

The house, standing there on the edge of the road, was gaunt and scarred and two hollow-eyed windows stared out from beneath the rusty tin roof. Steps, worn and rough, slobbered down over the lip of the open doorway. It stood there with its hands on its hips and its head cocked to one side, a fat old woman of a house. Toothless. Dirty. Old and complaining. And when the wind sweeping down the gulch whistled around the house it moaned and swayed back and forth, and on bad nights it cried. There were no coverings on the floors and a long plank table ran the full length of the dining room. The whole house smelled of sour bread dough and the kitchen shelves were lined with cans of tomatoes, opened and spoiling. I went snooping around. Some one told me it was a boarding house and that all the men from the mines would eat at our house now. I guessed that was all right. My mother was a pretty good cook, anyway.

There was an awful racket going on in the kitchen. My mother was sweeping out cans and rubbish, brushing off shelves, shaking stoves, opening cupboards, and talking fast about filthy Japs and pigs and all. Her hat still bobbed up and down on the top of her head and a streak of soot ran from under her nose like a big flowing moustache.

My dad and another man brought in the two trunks, funny fat trunks with wall-paper linings. They set them in a small room just off the dining room, and that night when we slept there, we had to put pans and big, square bread drippers all over the beds and floor to catch the rain that poured down through the leaky tin roof. Once, when the house no longer cried and the rain had finally stopped, I saw something run along the floor. It came close to my bed and drank from the black pan of water and its eyes were little lights there in the dark room. My mother set up a candle, but the water dripping from the ceiling kept putting it out. But I guess it was a rat all right, because the next morning my dad went down into the town—there were only two stores there—and bought three big traps and I helped him carry them home.

.   .   .   .

Elva was the tall one with the sad blue eyes and her hair was a cloud of fluff above her broad face. But she wasn't much good in the kitchen, my mother said. She was slow and she kept getting in the way. But I liked her. She used to chew my gum for me—the hard spruce gum that we gathered from the pine trees. Then my mother found out and I had to chew my own gum. I remember once Elva peeled a whole water-bucket of potatoes and the potatoes were like a handful of marbles there in the bottom of the bucket and the peelings over an inch thick. My mother was mad about it, too. So Elva and I went for a walk. We walked up past the mines, through the little grove of pines, and out to the very edge of the hill. And down below we could see the desert sleeping there in the sun and the paths wandering lost-like through the sand. But when I looked, my face got stiff and my ears grew tight and I felt all choked up inside. Elva was a statue staring down—all quiet and smooth. Then she slipped away, down the hill toward the desert. She kept sinking deeper and deeper into the sand and when I caught up with her she was making a funny little crackled sound way down in her throat. I thought she was laughing, but I guess she wasn't because when I laughed she just dug her fingers into the sand and told me not to. We went back to the house then, but that night she went for a walk alone and I didn't see her any more.

My mother liked Bertha best. She was big and brown and healthy. Big Brown Bertha, the men called her. She moved like a house afire. She could swing an ax like a man and lift a hundred pound bag of sugar with no effort at all. Once she came right through the kitchen swinging the ax back and forth in front of her and yelling—"Out of my way, out of my way, I'm mad!" Straight for the wood pile she went. She chopped her anger into little pieces and the chips flew away. Bertha—and her wood-chopping-madness.

I remember the first time my dad rang the big triangle dinner bell. He kept looking at his watch and asking my mother if it wasn't time yet and I kept telling him that I was sure it was time. I wanted to see what would happen. So he finally went out on the front porch and gave the big triangle half a dozen good smacks with an iron bar. It was like stirring up an ant hill. The men came swarming down the hill. One man fell face down in the dirt. No one bothered. They ran up the front steps and into the dining room. And when three of them jumped over the railing and fell on the porch I yelled to my dad to hit 'em—hit 'em hard, but he just stood there with the iron rod in his hand and didn't move. I peeked in through the window. The men were running around the table and bellowing, *"White bread!"* *"My God, it's white bread!"* They filled their pockets and the fronts of their bibbed overalls. They ate till their eyes bulged. They were heavy dirty men. Wild animals from the mountains. Sometimes, when my mother looked tired, I hated them and I hid the iron rod so my dad couldn't ring the dinner bell. I thought it opened the door of the mines, too.

There was a long man there in the dining room. Long and sort of tied in the middle—a jellybean man, bulging at both ends. He stood off in a corner alone. He didn't yell about the white bread either. And when the men sat down to eat they edged him off the end of the long bench. He just sat on the floor looking around dazed and empty and once, before my mother noticed him and made him sit by the kitchen where she could serve him, he hopped under the table and began picking up the bread crumbs like a bird and the men whistled and threw handfuls of crumbs to him and caged him in with their knees. I always whispered when he was around because I thought he was deaf and dumb.

. . . .

Sometimes I went with my dad to buy cigars, but mostly we just went there to talk. It was a good excuse though, the cigars. The old storekeeper had a fuzzy short beard. He was always waiting for the weather to warm up a bit so he could shave. When he talked he rubbed his hands and peered over the rims of his glasses and his voice was thin and crackled. An old granny voice. Once, when I went there alone, he invited me into his parlor. You just stepped down one step from the store and through an old worn curtain and there you were. He always kept the blinds down halfway, he said, because the dust didn't show up so much then. I guess he didn't have a wife. But he had a phonograph that blossomed from its small wooden box in the corner like a huge purple morning glory and in another corner of the room a glass cabinet squatted on its short curved legs. There were a few samples of ore scattered around on the shelves of the cabinet and way back on the bottom shelf, slumped over and dirty, there was a doll with a waxy pale face and hair that fell in yellow-brown strings over its eyes. He didn't like me to look at the doll. He got nervous when I went near the cabinet and made me sit in the little brown rocking-chair close by the phonograph. I thought it was fine listening to the record played over and over again and I rocked back and forth waiting for the words, "Oh, you great big beautiful doll, I'd like to squeeze you, but I'm afraid you'll break." I rocked closer to the cabinet. Then some one rapped on the counter and the old man slipped through the curtain, up the step, and back into the store. I went home. I told my mother about the doll and the phonograph. . . . After that my brother went for the cigars.

. . . .

Big Mrs. Rawls was coming down to make jelly-roll for the men. We took the kitchen door off so she could come in. She lived up the hill from our place in a tent. I guess it was easier, that way, without doors. She waddled over to a chair and oozed down over the sides and kept fanning herself and "whewing."

It should have been a good jelly-roll. She used almost a half a sack of flour and all the bottled jelly in the house. She rolled the dough out in big white slabs and smeared them thick with jelly, then she rolled them from one end like a carpet. But the jelly kept running out of the ends and the sides so she fastened them together with toothpicks. I followed her around with a spoon and ate all the jelly that wouldn't stay in the roll. My mother kept ahing and ohing and saying what beautiful jelly-rolls they were and Mrs. Rawls just swelled all up with pride when she slipped them into the oven. "Don't jump!" she said, "or you'll spoil the whole shootin' match." So I held my breath and tip-toed over to the corner and sat high up on a stool. She plumped herself down in a chair and all the dishes on the shelves clattered. She made jelly-roll for every one when she was a girl, she said. She'd even won prizes at fairs with them. And roly-poly pudding! Well, that was something, too. She bet the men would like that.

I didn't say anything, but I could see the smoke curling out from the sides of the oven door. My mother sniffed the air a couple of times. Mrs. Rawls went on gabbing. Not noticing. Finally she went over and opened the oven. She pulled out one pan. Then she pulled out another pan. "Only the jelly burning on the edge," she said. She tried to slip them back in a hurry, but I ran over with my spoon and looked into the pans sitting on the open oven door. It was a tired jelly-roll all flat and panting. Little rivers of jelly ran around in the gluey mass of dough and the picket fence of toothpick standing tall and thin in the middle guarded a small breathing bubble pushed up by the stream. It was like the grave on the hill back of the house.

Then I don't know. I guess every one went kind of crazy. My mother and Bertha made Mrs. Rawls sit down in the middle of the floor and they circled the pans, steaming and hot, around her. And one empty pan, a round one with handles on both sides, they put on her head and called her Roly-Poly, the Queen of the Jelly-Rolls. They danced round and round, in between the pans and out again. I thought my mother would be mad about not having any dessert for the men and all, but she just laughed and danced around the pans. I laughed too, then. I laughed all inside till I got a pain and had to roll all over the kitchen floor.

Bertha said to wait a minute. She ran out and brought in the screen door from the back porch and they caged Mrs. Rawls in the corner. The top part of the door had little black bars running up and down and in one place the screen was broken and loose. Her hair fell sloppily down her face and she clumped back and forth and tried to roar. Once she reached her big paw through the cage and cuffed Bertha on the head. I ran back and forth with pans of jelly-roll. My mother said she roared because she was hungry, so we stuffed the roll through the bars and the jelly ran in tears through our fingers and down our arms. Once I threw a piece through the bars and into the cage. It landed in her hair and the jelly ran down her big face and into her eyes and when it dried there it looked like drops of blood.

The men came stomping into the dining room for lunch. My mother said, Oh, Lord, and the screen door fell to the floor and Mrs. Rawls waddled away. Her eyes were glassy and she kept swallowing the air in big gulps. I sat on the steps and watched her going home, up the hill, slowly, and little Mr. Rawls running along beside her like a nervous whisper.

The wagon came in with the supplies that afternoon and I went out to see them unloaded. The canned goods were all battered up and tomato juice was oozing out of the cans. Sometimes they left the meat and butter down on the spur for days before they brought it out to the camp and the meat would be spoiled and the butter rancid. And once they were unloading a barrel of water from the wagon. It slipped and the water ran down the thirsty road and was gone. We didn't have any water then for two days. I remember, my dad had to hire a wagon and make the thirty mile trip to the next town. It was always the water. This time the water had been put in gasoline barrels and was so strong that it couldn't even be used for dish water. I didn't mind though. I liked the smell. When my mother wasn't looking I smeared some of the grease from the fat black barrel on my dress for perfume. It smelled of the city where we used to live.

My mother talked a lot about going home that day, and about what we could do when we got back. But that night Bertha made taffy, stretching the hot candy till it shone like fine silk threads. Some of the men came over, too, and we cleared out the dining room and danced. It was fine then. Every one forgot about the water. There was plenty of beer anyway. Some one brought an old concertina and before the night was over a violin showed up and wheezed along beside the concertina.

And I sat high on the table and watched . . .

I guess he'd been knocking a long time out there on the front porch. He didn't generally walk right in like that. He looked tired and small and scared. He'd been running, too. "Give old man Rawls a drink!" some one said. But when he got the drink he just kept picking it up and setting it down again, all lost. And finally they pulled him into the square of dancers and he danced round and round.

There was a terrible racket then. Every one clapped and stomped louder than ever. And when Mr. Rawls yelled, "Cupped! God damn it! Cupped, I say!" every one thought he was drunk and they clapped him on the back and danced faster and faster. My mother gave him another glass of beer and my dad told him to dive right in, but he wouldn't take it. He said, she's being cupped again, my wife, and sort of whimpered. Then he ran out of the door and into the dark.

My mother said, Oh, Lord, and ran after him. And I ran after her. Straight up the hill we went. It was black. I kept stumbling. Then we were there, in front of the tent. The shadows from the candle inside the tent made the figures moving around look old and bent in the middle and I was afraid to go in. I sat outside in the dark listening to the moaning inside. Once a coyote howled far up in the hills and I wished I'd gone in then. I looked in under the tent. A mountain covered with a white sheet moved up and down on a long bed. Hands came out from the sheet and clawed the air—big hands—Mrs. Rawls' hands. And a doctor walked back and forth with bottles and spoons. Pretty soon my mother came out and we went home. She didn't say much. I asked her what about Mrs. Rawls and she said, what did I mean tagging along when I was supposed to be in bed? So I didn't say any more.

The next morning a wagon came slowly down the mountain, past the boarding house, and on through the town. It was all covered in and solemn. I waved to Mr. Rawls, but he just walked on with his head down—following back of the wagon.

I don't know. I guess it must have been the jelly-roll that did it. My mother and Bertha were putting the screen door back on its hinges and wiping the bars with a big cloth and crying a little. I heard my mother tell Bertha that it was from excitement and overeating that Mrs. Rawls had died. And her heart. I went away then. I went out and gathered pine cones and I wondered about Mrs. Rawls, and why Mr. Rawls walked back of the wagon with his head bent down. I thought of the awfully big hole they'd have to dig for Mrs. Rawls. They couldn't dig it in the sand. The sand would crawl back in and there wouldn't be room for her.

He never came back, though—Mr. Rawls. The people waited and waited for him. Some one said he had gone all the way to California—walking right on through the Nevada desert. Following the sun. No one knew. The tent stayed on the hill for days and days and the wind rushing through the open flaps of the doorway pulled and tore at the canvas. Then one morning I ran up the hill, and the tent was gone and only the big square, vacant and smooth, was left. I never went back any more.

.   .   .   .

It was no use, my mother said, she wouldn't stay another day. Saloons, and everything springing up right next door and all. Drunken men lolling on our front porch. And our bedroom window looking into a saloon. Hammering. Hammering. All day long. And cussing, and spitting and chewing. I thought it was pretty bad, too, and I went out and kicked the toes out of my shoes. I kicked the blocks of wood that had been cut from the planks. I kicked them right at the men. I found a big box of nails and lugged them away. I hid them in the cellar. I thought saloons must be pretty bad.

I kind of hated to see my mother go, but I helped her pack and I sat on the top of the trunks so she could fasten the locks. I didn't know what I'd do when she left. Just go on shelling pinenuts, I guess, and maybe walk up the hill and look down into the desert. And maybe go down and see the old man and listen to the phonograph. But I wished Elva would come back. Bertha was no good. She wouldn't walk. I watched my mother take the heavy sack of pinenuts down from the shelf and tie a knot in the top.

I went out and picked an armful of the wild goldenrod that smiled around the dismal grey sheds in the back yard and thought of the time Bertha had drenched the feathery blossoms with a pan of steaming water. The blossoms had turned brown and slumped to the earth like a heavy sigh. I hated Bertha then. I hated her now when I thought of it. When I go home, I thought, I'll take some of the roots buried in the sandy soil and plant them in our town—I'll take the desert, and its warm yellow smell back home.

I ran around the house and out to the front with the flowers and my mother boosted me up into the back of the wagon. There were a lot of people there and they stood in a fringe around the wagon. Some of the women dabbed at the corners of their eyes with their white aprons. And Sam gave my mother a box of candy tied with a bright red ribbon. He didn't look like a jelly-bean any more and I noticed his hands, bony, loose, and worried, hanging from his wrists.

Then, somehow, I had the big doll in my arms and its eyes opened and shut and its hair still hung in long yellow-brown strings. Its face was dusty and smudged with tears and I held it tight in my arms.

.   .   .   .

The wagon moved slowly down the hill and into the desert. The wind had blown the sand into crinkled waves along the sides of the road, and on the hill, just before we dipped into the desert,

I noticed the little blue berries of the spruce were withered old faces hanging dead on the branches. The dust still rolled from under the wagon in clouds and settled over the bushes and the long thin tongue of a road slipped from under the wagon, down the hill.

Then we were there—there in front of the depot and I had a big lump in my throat and I couldn't cry. The depot was all hollowed out inside and dark and dirty. My dad bought me an all-day sucker, an orange one, and a little glass pitcher that sparkled like the sand in the sun away back there in the desert. When I looked at the pitcher, the lump in my throat got bigger and bigger and I felt all pulled out from the middle again. I ran away, then. I ran up back of the depot. The roofs of the houses on the hillside were flat black hands stretched out in the sun.

It was no use. I wouldn't say good-bye to them, to my mother and father and brother, down there waiting for the train. I'd stay on the hill of sand back of the depot. I took off my shoes and stockings and dug my toes deep into the sun-warmed sand.

I filled the pitcher and the sand poured out, trickling through my fingers, and fell in a spatter of diamonds down the front of my dress. I filled it again and again. The sand was like a river flowing on and on down to the depot and over the tracks. And I waded knee-deep in the river.

The train. Howling. I'd wash it off the tracks. I'd bury it deep in the river. I filled the pitcher again.

Faster! Faster! More sand poured from the pitcher and danced down the hill. The moaning whistle grew louder. The train hissed and screamed and coughed white clouds into the sky. They floated up over the depot roof and I watched them go to nothing.

Then my mother, puffing and panting, whisked me out of the river and down the hill. The pitcher slipped from my fingers and the sand trickled away, a patch of tiny broken smiles scattered in the sun.

SHERREL [1]

By WHIT BURNETT

(From *Story* and *Clay*)

I DO not know whether I can do this thing or not. Maybe it is just a thought, maybe I just think it is necessary to do it. I mean about the name. I have thought about it a lot though and it keeps urging at me. It is not easy to understand. But I must try to understand and explain it.

You see, I actually did have a brother. People sometimes asked me, Are you the only boy in the family? and I've said, Yes. This wasn't a lie wholly. I was the first born in my family. But there were others, two others. One died in long clothes. We have his picture at home. The other was named Sherrel.

It is easy to remember him. My mother had us photographed together, for instance. And one especial print was transferred onto little smooth discs the size of a saucer. The discs fit into small twisted wire easels and my brother and I used so sit on the easel like that on my mother's bureau in the bedroom.

He was, as I said, younger than I. This is important. The neighbours used to say, It's the difference in their ages. They tried to explain in that way why I was so mean. And you can see the difference clearly enough on the picture discs. We both stood by the photographer's chair, a plush chair. But I was up to the top of it. My brother's hand rested on the arm. It looks pretty small to me now because I'm twice as old as I was then. We both wore black velvet tam-o'-shanters and dark red velvet coats and pants. My mouth was a little open, too, looking at the photographer. I did not touch my brother. He had one hand, which was very small, on the chair, and the other one had hold of me. His hair was lighter than mine and softer and his eyes wider and bluer. He had a small mouth like a flower and it was smiling. He was a beautiful child. This was the brother I killed.

I am not telling you about a melodrama. I won't be arrested and hanged. I did not kill him yesterday. It was a long time ago, in fact, and I do not remember it all the time, only sometimes when something suggests the way I was then or when some one asks, Have you any other brothers? And I say, No. And here too in this other town at this school except for a girl I know I am quite alone in certain ways and in the winter as now I have seen any number of things to remind me. There is, for example, an epidemic of smallpox here and instead of smooth fast automobile hearses they still have funeral carriages that drag along slowly through the streets. Only once have I ridden in such a carriage. And that was then.

There are some things difficult to remember out of childhood. I do not remember when my brother was born. There was not so much difference then. Only four years before, I had been born. But I remember clearly when I was nine. My brother then was five. And we were two in the family. But I was the first.

Do you know how this is? Nine and five? Well, nine is somebody. Five is still curls. At nine I have seen something of the world. What have you seen at five? Go on, you can't come with us! Go on back to the house! We're going down to the store. You'll get run over. Go on, you can't play with us. You ain't big enough. Go on, grow up some before you come tagging around after us. Who asked you along? Beat it! I know how that is. I said all that, more brutally even. He didn't say anything. He didn't cry or whine or crab. I probably would have. He stopped following simply and stood there. And then we ran off. He stood alone. Sometimes I found him other places alone, sitting still in a corner thinking quietly about something. I am always a little puzzled now I am older. I have talked it over with others. He would have been important. . . . But at nine one is a weed, growing wild. Five is still in the hothouse.

We lived near the sandhills. It wasn't until several years later that I really got into the hills exploring them with a cousin of my own age. Sherrel never did get there. And there was a great liking in both of us for the hills, his maybe different from mine.

I often found him sitting dreaming, looking at them. But one day late in the Spring the hills in a way came down to our house. A cloudburst drenched them, rolling down soft sand, cutting great ditches in the road in front of our place. We weren't long in discovering that, I'll tell you. When Sherrel wandered out of the kitchen the ditch was full of us kids. It was a peach of a ditch as high as our heads, gnawed with caves and dangers.

I started the discoveries. There's some hole, I yelled. And down I had gone, doing what the others wanted to do, the first to absorb their wishes. Then they followed, yelling too. Sherrel, I suppose, could hear my voice coming up out of the ground. He came over to the ditch and looked down, standing alone above us. Go on back, I shouted, you'll fall in. He moved away. I paid no more attention then to him and the rest of us ran racing, hiding, searching, together in the wash.

And then, separated from the others for a moment or so, I noticed something odd about my hands. Hey, kids, I cried, lookee! Look at my hands! They looked. They stood back in wonderment. They looked at their own hands. No, they couldn't, they said. It was something funny. Look what Martin can do! Lookee, he can peel off his hands! It was true, something had happened to my hands. I took hold and pulled off long shreds of skin. I amazed them all. They stood astounded.

Let me see, said somebody. It was Sherrel.

Say, I yelled, didn't I say not to come down here? You ain't big enough to be in this here ditch. Let me see your hands, he said. The kids were all looking at me. I'll let you see, all right! I said. He stood his ground and didn't go. That makes me mad, I felt. No, I said. I took him by the shoulder and talked straight in his face, hard. How many times do I have to tell you to get out of this ditch! He turned around and walked up the gorge to a shallower spot and climbed slowly out.

A day or so later Sherrel stayed in bed. There's something the matter with him, my mother said. She didn't know what. Then he took a high fever, they said, and was delirious. I thought it was strange about delirious. Sherrel's eyes were shut and he looked as if he was sleeping but he was talking without any sense. We'll have to have a doctor, my mother said. And that afternoon the doctor came to our house, wiping his feet at the door and

entering with a serious look. Let's see the other young fellow, he
said. Anything wrong with him? He had a little sore throat,
my mother said, but he's all right. He looked down my throat.
Look at my hands, I said, ain't they funny?

What I thought, he said.

The same afternoon a man from down town came and nailed
up a yellow flag. It was a cloth sign saying, black on orange,
Scarlet Fever. I couldn't go out of the yard. That's sure tough,
the kids said, peering through the pickets. I even had to keep
back from the fence, too. It was catching.

I sat on the steps fronting north from our bare two room brick
house and looked at the hills. I had had the Scarlet Fever and
hadn't even known it. Why, my mother said, he was playing
around all the time. Why, he was out there playing in the ditch
with all those children. That's bad, said the doctor. But my
brother was worse. He had it good.

I remember the windows in the front room were darkened and
my mother never went to bed. She never took her clothes off.
And my father didn't go to work. My aunt came to the fence
with a bag of oranges and bananas. How is he? she asked. If
he isn't any better Dr. Anderson says he'd better have a consultation, said my mother. How is Dr. Anderson? asked my aunt.
He is the best doctor in town, my mother said.

I sat in the sun all tired now and weak. But I wasn't sick. I
was big and nine.

I remember the consultation. There were four doctors in the
kitchen standing around and talking low and sitting down and
getting up. I could see in from outside. My mother was nervous
and walking around and my father, who was a big heavy man,
stood around too and sat down and then got up. They were waiting for something definite they spoke of that I could not understand. It was the Crisis. I asked what it was, and my mother
had said, Sherrel will get better then. I didn't know what a Crisis
would be like and I opened the door slowly and got into the house
quietly, past the doctors.

My father and mother were in the front room by the bed where
Sherrel lay. He was still and wasn't talking deliriously. And
then my mother, who was standing by him with my father waiting, suddenly cried terribly for a minute or so, and then she took

hold of my father and pulled him down by the bed to the floor. I didn't know what was happening. I was frightened, too. Pray, she sobbed. Pray, if you never prayed before. Oh, God, she began . . . and she was crying more and more. My father was kneeling heavily and strangely in a big dark bulk. He put his arm round my mother. There, there, he said. I never saw them like that before. My father is English, my mother is German. I did not think about that though then. I thought, I am scared; this is all different, and dark. I stood in the doorway, too frightened to move.

Come in, Martin, my mother suddenly cried out to me. Come in to your brother. Come here with us. I came over, and there we were all kneeling down together.

Do you want your brother to die? she asked. No, I said. I was frightened at her, at the strange heavy silence on my father, at my brother even. Go and look at him, she told me.

I got up and looked at my brother's white face. It was like a face of ivory with pale lips. I looked hard. He was different too. What do I do? I thought. I am rough, not like that. My mother is looking at me terribly. Kiss him. I bent over and touched his face. His lips opened with a quiet breath, like a little flower bursting on my cheek.

The Crisis came and passed. It came while we were in the room there. My mother could not wait. She went to the bed, trying to wake my brother. Look, Sherrel, she whispered, we are going to get you the nice pearl-handled pocketknife to-morrow. You won't have to wait till Christmas. To-morrow. You just get well, now. Sherrel! Do you hear me, Sherrel?

Or, he can have mine, I thought.

But he didn't hear us. He didn't hear anybody. Then my mother went to sleep suddenly, it seemed, and drooped down by the bed and they put her in the other room on a couch.

I stood in the dark by a curtain when the doctors came in. Too bad, said Dr. Anderson. He leaned over my brother. Remarkable head, said one of the others. Isn't it! spoke up another one. Artist's head, said the one with the beard. Yes . . . Then the doctors walked out together into the room where my mother was and in a little while they all left the house.

A few days later there were the strange preparations for the funeral. I don't want to dwell on the funeral. That is not the point. But we rode in a carriage shut in by ourselves, still quarantined, the others following slowly behind us. I remember we passed the Watsons' place. They were standing at the gate, the family, staring stupidly at the procession as the horse carriages jogged down the hilly street rolling off to the cemetery.

This is all strange, I thought, riding along past the Watsons' house in a carriage like this. My mother and my father and myself. I was taken up with the thought and looked back out of the carriage window now and then at the carriages behind me. My mother pulled me back to sit up straight. My mother's face was drawn and tired and she was crying. My father's eyes had tears in them too. I could not cry. I thought, I ought to cry. How can I cry? I am not hurt in any place where I can feel. I squeezed into the corner of the carriage opposite them, pressing up against one hand hard to make it hurt. It turned numb and pained, but not in a crying way. You cry easy differently, I thought. Onions, for instance, make you cry. Would it have been a trick, I thought, or right and honest if I had put an onion in my handkerchief, no one seeing me, and then smelt it now and then in the curtained shadows of the carriage? I would have cried then. I wanted to cry. But all I could think was, Sherrel was a queer kid. Were we brothers sure enough? Am I anybody's brother? Why don't I cry? . . .

You see, he would sit in a corner quiet and frailly beautiful. I was nine and active. It's the difference in their ages. Maybe so. There were the Elwell brothers, now. They were twins. They had a carpenter's shop. It was a peach of a shop down in the cellar and they worked together great, making book-ends and rabbit hutches and things like that.

I gave him that sickness. I knew that. That killed him. That is why my brother is dead. But I am trying to remember, to clear things up. I am trying to remember if I thought that then. I remember I thought, It's funny just he got it. Why not Leona Eads, Ed or Billy Simons? They touched my hands. I wondered if I hadn't forced my sickness on my brother out of hatred for him, out of my own peculiar older-brother hatred. Did I slap him, maybe strike him in the face with my peeling hand? Perhaps I did. I wondered over this for many weeks now and then.

I'm not even sure now. I might have. It's funny how mean, you see, a person can be. I've thought of that. I've got a girl. I've talked things over with her, not everything, but generally you know. She doesn't like meanness either. I remember when I was about twelve, my sister was just coming along then. She was about two and I had to tend her occasionally. I didn't like it. Once my mother said to me, Do you want your little sister to die too? Well, no, I said. She might even have said, Do you want to kill your little sister too? Maybe this was it, because I asked myself that a lot later, trying to be better. I said, Do you want to kill your sister too? No, I said.

I didn't either. But I remembered what I'd said when she was born. I said, There's enough in this family already. But I didn't want to kill her. Still I had killed my brother. I had killed Sherrel. Not only by giving him sickness. But by meanness.

This is how I figure it now. I killed my brother by meanness. And it is too bad. I wouldn't do it now. I am not that way. I could have got him a job here in this other town where I am now after he got out of school. I'll be out of school here pretty soon. I'm eighteen next week. Then I'll go on a paper where I've got a stand-in. I'd have said, Now you keep on at school and read a lot of good things, good books, you know, poetry and good things and learning how to write. You've got good stuff in you, I can tell. You're going to be an artist. So am I. We'll be two artists, brothers, maybe different, but we can help each other. You've got a poetic style, and I've got a stronger style. I see things more as they are. I'm a little tougher. I can digest more. But that's all right. When I get going, I'll help you. You've got fine things in you. I'll help you bring them out.

That's the kind of person he would have been. He would have been an artist. There's nothing any bigger than that. Nothing finer. It's the best, in a holy way. It has to be in you first. It hides sometimes and doesn't get a chance to come out where people are.

I've talked that over with people, with that girl I spoke of. I want to be an artist. A writer. I can see back from where I am, though. I've been pretty mean, pretty contemptible. It's funny to look back like that and see yourself in old pictures and things. It's hard to think you had the same name, even.

And that's what I'm puzzling over now. There's nothing wrong with my name, actually. Mark. Mark Stowe. It was first Martin. It was even Martin Tilton Stowe. I didn't like it. All that, I mean. I cut it down to Mark Stowe. It made me feel surer, quicker, stronger.

But even that doesn't quite go. It doesn't all fit. I'm not all blunt, like that. Mark. Mark Stowe. I've got other things. I've written poems, even, and I wouldn't kiss a girl hard. I know how my brother was. He would have been like that too, only a lot more.

And, you know, about the name . . . My folks are getting along now. Sisters don't count, the way I mean, that is. I'm the only boy in the family. And I've been thinking, what if I should write a poem, a long, good one—here I am, alive and everything—and sign it not Mark Stowe but well, Sherrel Stowe? Do you see what I mean? And then by and by there would be another poem, and after awhile I would just go ahead and use it right along. Can you understand that? How I would be more him too, then—Sherrel?

WARM RIVER [1]

By ERSKINE CALDWELL

(From *Pagany*)

THE driver stopped at the suspended footbridge and pointed out to me the house across the river. I paid him the quarter fare for the ride from the station two miles away and stepped from the car. After he had gone I was alone with the chill night and the star-pointed lights twinkling in the valley and the broad green river flowing warm below me. All around me the mountains rose like black clouds in the night, and only by looking straight heavenward could I see anything of the dim afterglow of sunset.

The footbridge swayed with the rhythm of my stride and the momentum of its swing soon overcame my pace. Only by walking faster and faster could I cling to the pendulum as it swung in its wide arc over the river. When at last I could see the other side, where the mountain came down abruptly and slid under the warm water, I gripped my handbag tighter and ran with all my might.

Even then, even after my feet had crunched upon the gravel path, I was afraid. I knew that by day I might walk the bridge without fear; but at night, in a strange country, with mountains towering all around me and a broad green river flowing warm beneath me, I could not keep my hands from trembling and my heart from pounding against my chest.

I found the house easily, and laughed at myself for running from the river. The house was the first one to come upon after leaving the footbridge, and even if I had missed it, Gretchen would have called me. She was there on the steps of the porch waiting for me. When I heard her voice calling my name, I was ashamed of myself for being frightened by the mountains and by the river flowing below.

She ran down the gravel path to meet me.

"Did the footbridge scare you, Richard?" she asked, holding my arm with both of her hands and guiding me up the path to the house.

"I think it did, Gretchen," I said, "but I hope I outran it."

"Every one tries to do that at first, but after going over it once it's like walking a tight-rope. I used to walk tight-ropes when I was small; didn't you, Richard? We had one stretched across the floor of our barn to practice on."

"I did, too, but it's been so long ago I've forgotten how to do it now."

We reached the steps and went up to the porch. Gretchen took me to the door. Some one inside the house was bringing a lamp into the hall, and with the coming of the light I saw Gretchen's two sisters standing in the doorway.

"This is my little sister, Anne," Gretchen said. "And this is Mary."

We went on into the hall. Gretchen's father was standing by a table holding the lamp a little to one side so he could see my face. I had not met him before.

"This is my father," Gretchen said. "He was afraid you wouldn't be able to find our house in the dark."

I shook hands with him, and told him how easily I had found the place.

"I wanted to light a lantern and come down to the bridge and meet you, but Gretchen said you would get here without any trouble. Did you get lost?"

"The hack driver pointed out the house to me from the other side of the river, and I never once took my eyes from the light. If I had lost sight of the light I'd probably be stumbling around somewhere in the dark getting ready to fall into the river."

He laughed at me for being afraid of the river.

"You wouldn't have minded it. The river is warm. Even in winter, when there is ice and snow everywhere else, the river is as warm as a comfortable room. All of us here love the water down there."

"No, you wouldn't have fallen in, Richard," Gretchen said, laying her hand on mine. "I saw you the moment you got out of the hack, and if you had gone a step in the wrong direction I was ready to run after you."

I wanted to thank her for saying that, but already she was going up the stairs to the floor above, and calling me. I went behind her, lifting my handbag in front of me. There was a lamp sitting on a table at the end of the upper hall, and she picked it up and went ahead into one of the rooms.

"There is fresh water in the pitcher, Richard. If there is anything else you want, please tell me. I tried not to overlook anything."

"Don't worry, Gretchen," I told her. "I couldn't ask for anything more. It's enough just to be here with you, anyway. I want nothing else."

She looked at me quickly, and then lowered her eyes to the floor. We stood silently for several minutes, while neither of us could think of anything to say. I wanted to tell her how glad I was to be with her, even if it was only for one night, but I knew I could say that to her later. She knew why I had come.

"I'll leave the lamp for you, Richard, and I'll wait for you downstairs on the porch. Come as soon as you are ready."

She had left before I could offer to carry the light to the stairs for her to see the way down.

I went back and bathed my face and hands, scrubbing the train-dust with brush and soap. There was a row of embroidered towels on the rack, and I took one of them and dried my face and hands. After that I combed my hair, and found a fresh handkerchief in the handbag. Then I opened the door and went downstairs to find Gretchen.

Her father was on the porch with her. When I walked through the door, he got up and gave me a chair between them. Gretchen pulled her chair closer to mine, touching my arm with her fingers.

"Is this the first time you've been up here in the mountains, Richard?" her father asked me, turning his chair towards me.

"I've never been within a hundred miles of here before. It's a different country up here, but I suppose you would think the same about the coast, wouldn't you?"

"Oh, but Father used to live in Norfolk," Gretchen said. "Didn't you, Father?"

"I lived there for nearly three years."

"Father is a master mechanic," she whispered to me. "He works in the railroad shops."

"Yes," he said, "I've lived in many places, but here is where I want to stay."

My first thought was to ask him why he preferred the mountains to other sections, but suddenly I was aware that both he and Gretchen were strangely silent. Between them, I sat wondering about it.

After a while he spoke again, not to me and not to Gretchen, but as if he were speaking to some one else on the porch, some one whom I had failed to see. The warmth of the river covered us like a blanket in the chill night.

Gretchen moved her chair a few inches closer to mine, her motions gentle and without sound.

"After Gretchen and the other two girls lost their mother," he said, almost inaudibly, bending forward and gazing out across the broad green river, "I came back here to live. I couldn't stay in Norfolk, and I couldn't live in Baltimore. This was the only place on earth I could find peace. Gretchen remembers her mother, but neither of you can understand how it is with me. Her mother and I were born in these mountains, and we lived here together almost twenty years. Then after she left us, I moved away, believing that I could forget. But I was wrong. A man can't forget the mother of his children, even though he knows he will never see her again."

Gretchen leaned closer to me, and I could not keep my eyes from her darkly framed profile beside me. The river below us made no sound, but the warmth of its vapor would not let me forget that it was still there.

Her father had bent forward in his chair until his arms were resting on his knees, and he seemed to be trying to see some one on the other side of the river, high on the mountain above it. His eyes strained, and the shaft of light that came through the open doorway fell upon them and glistened there. Tears fell from his face like fragments of stars, burning into his hands until they were out of sight.

Presently, still in silence, he got up and moved through the open door. His huge shadow fell upon Gretchen and me as he stood there momentarily before going inside. I turned and looked at him, but even though he was passing from sight I could not keep my gaze upon him.

Gretchen leaned closer against me, touching my shoulder with her cheeks as if she was trying to wipe something from them. Her father's footsteps grew fainter, and at last we could not hear him again.

Somewhere below us, along the bank of the river, a train crashed down the valley, creaking and screaming through the night. Occasionally its lights flashed through the darkness, dancing on the broad green river, as its echo rumbled against the high walls of the mountains.

Gretchen clasped her hands tightly over my hand, trembling to her finger-tips.

"Richard, why did you come to see me?"

Her voice was mingled with the screaming echo of the train that now seemed far off.

I had expected to find her looking into my face, but when I turned towards her I saw that she was gazing down into the waters of the warm river. She knew why I had come, but she did not want me to tell her that.

I did not know why I had come, now. I had liked Gretchen, and I wanted her. But I could not tell her that I loved her, after hearing her father speak of love. I was sorry I had come, now after hearing him speak as he did. I knew she would gladly give herself to me, because she knew I was coming for that only, and because she loved me; but I had nothing to give her in return. She was beautiful, and I had desired her. That was before. Now I knew I could never again think of her in the way I had come prepared.

"Why did you come, Richard?"

My eyes closed, and what I saw was the star-pointed lights twinkling in the valley and the breath of the warm river flowing below and the caress of her fingers as she touched my arm.

"Richard, please tell me why you came."

"I don't know why I came, Gretchen."

"If you only loved me as I love you, Richard, you would know why."

Her fingers trembled over my hand. I knew she loved me. There had been no doubt from the first.

"Perhaps I should not have come," I said. "I made a mistake, Gretchen. I should have stayed away."

"But you will be here only for to-night, Richard. You are leaving early in the morning. You aren't sorry that you came just for this short time, are you?"

"I'm not sorry that I am here, Gretchen, but I should not have come. I didn't know what I was doing."

"But you do love me just a little, don't you, Richard? You couldn't love me nearly as much as I love you, but can't you tell me that you love me a little bit? I'll feel much happier after you've gone."

"I don't know," I said.

With her hands in mine I held her tightly. Suddenly I felt something come over me, a thing that stabbed my body with its quickness. It was as if the words her father had said were becoming clear to me. I had not known before that there was such a love. I had believed that men never loved women in the same way that a woman loved a man, but now I knew there could be no difference.

We sat silently, holding each other's hands for a long time. It was long past midnight, but time did not matter.

Gretchen clung softly to me, looking up into my face and laying her cheek against my shoulder. She was as much mine as a woman ever belonged to a man, but I knew I could never take advantage of her love, and go away knowing that I had not loved her as she loved me. I had not believed that when I came. I had traveled all that distance to hold her in my arms for an hour, and then to forget her, perhaps forever.

When it was time for us to go into the house, I got up and put my arms around her. She trembled when I touched her, but she held me as tightly as I held her.

"Richard, kiss me before you go," she said.

She ran to the door, holding it open for me. She picked up the lamp from the table and went ahead up the stairs to the floor above.

At my door she waited until I could light her lamp, and then she handed me mine.

"Good night, Gretchen," I said.

"Good night, Richard," she said.

I turned the wick of her lamp down to keep it from smoking, and then she went towards her room.

"I'll call you in the morning in time for you to catch your train, Richard."

"Don't let me over-sleep, because it leaves at seven-thirty."

"I'll wake you in time, Richard."

The door closed after her, and I walked across the hall to my room. I shut the door and began slowly to undress. After I had blown out the light and got in bed, I lay tensely awake. I knew I would never be able to sleep that night, so I tried to make the time pass more quickly by smoking one cigarette lighted from another. The house was quiet, except for muffled movements in Gretchen's room.

I could not tell how long I had lain there, stiff and awake upon the bed, but suddenly I had jumped to the floor. I opened the door and ran across the hall. Gretchen's door was closed, and I turned the knob noiselessly. A slender shaft of light broke through the opening I had made. It was not necessary to open it wider, because I saw Gretchen only a few feet away.

She had not heard me, and she did not know that I was there. Her lamp was burning brightly.

I had not expected to find her awake, and I had not thought I would find her where she was. She knelt on the floor beside her bed, her head bowed over her arms and her body shaken with sobs.

I stood at the door, not wanting to close it and go back to my room, and afraid to stay there and look at her.

Gretchen's hair was lying over her shoulders, tied somewhere with a pale blue ribbon. Her nightgown was white, hemmed with a delicate lace, and around her neck the collar of lace was thrown open.

I knew how beautiful she was when I saw her then, even though I had always thought she was lovely.

She had not heard me open the door, and she still did not know I was there. She knelt beside the bed, her hands clenched before her, crying.

When I first opened her door, I did not know what I was about to do, but now that I had seen her in her room, kneeling in prayer beside her bed, unaware that I was looking upon her and hearing her words and sobs, I was sure that I could never care for any one else as I did for her. I had not known until then, but in the revelation of a few seconds I knew that I did love her. I had come to her home prepared to take all I could from her, giving her nothing of any worth in return. But as I stood in the door I realized that I was just beginning to know my own self.

I closed the door softly and went back to my own room. There I found a chair and placed it beside the window to wait for the coming of day. At the window I sat and looked down into the bottom of the valley where the warm river lay. As my eyes grew more accustomed to the darkness I felt as if I were coming closer and closer to it, so close that I might have reached out and touched the warm water with my hands.

When the sun rose, I got up and dressed. Later, I heard Gretchen leave her room and go downstairs. I knew she was hurrying to prepare breakfast for me before I left to get on the train. I waited a while, and in a few minutes I heard her coming back up the stairs. She knocked softly on my door, calling my name several times.

I jerked open the door and faced her. She was so surprised at seeing me there, when she had expected to find me still asleep, that she could not say anything.

"Gretchen," I said, grasping her hands, "don't hurry to get me off—I'm not going back this morning."

"But, Richard—last night you said—"

"I did say last night I was going back early this morning, Gretchen, but I didn't know what I was talking about. I'm not going back now until you will go with me. But first of all I want you to show me how to get down to the river. I want to go down there and put my hands in the water."

THE RED HAT [1]

By MORLEY CALLAGHAN

(From *The New Yorker*)

IT was the kind of hat Frances had wanted for months, a plain little red felt hat with the narrow brim tacked back, which would look so smart and simple and expensive. There was really very little to it, it was so plain, but it was the kind of hat that would have made her feel confident of a sleek appearance. She stood on the pavement, her face pressed close against the shop window, a slender, tall, and good-looking girl wearing a reddish woollen dress clinging tightly to her body. On the way home from work, the last three evenings, she had stopped to look at the hat. And when she had got home she had told Mrs. Foley, who lived in the next apartment, how much the little hat appealed to her. In the window were many smart hats, all very expensive. There was only one red felt hat, on a mannequin head with a silver face and very red lips.

Though Frances stood by the window a long time she had no intention of buying the hat, because her husband was out of work and they couldn't afford it; she was waiting for him to get a decent job so she could buy clothes for herself. Not that she looked shabby, but the fall weather was a little cold, a sharp wind sometimes blowing gustily up the avenue, and in the twilight, on the way home from work with the wind blowing, she knew she ought to be wearing a light coat. In the early afternoon when the sun was shining brightly she looked neat and warm in her woollen dress.

Though she ought to have been on her way home Frances couldn't help standing there, thinking she might look beautiful in this hat, if she went out with Eric, her husband, for the evening. Since he had been so moody and discontented recently she now thought with pleasure of pleasing him by wearing something that would give her a new kind of elegance, of making him feel cheerful and proud of her and glad, after all, that they were married.

But the hat cost fifteen dollars. She had eighteen dollars in her purse, her salary for the week. It was ridiculous for her to be there looking at the hat, which was obviously too expensive for her, so she smiled and walked away, putting both hands in the small pockets of her dress. She walked slowly, glancing at two women who were standing at the other end of the big window. One of the two women, the younger one, wearing a velvet coat trimmed with squirrel, said to the other: "Let's go in and try some of them on."

Hesitating and half turning, Frances thought it would be quite harmless and amusing if she went into the shop and tried on the red hat, just to see if it looked as good on her as it did on the mannequin head. It never occurred to her to buy the hat.

In the shop she walked on soft, thick, gray carpet to the chair by the window, where she sat alone for a few moments, waiting for one of the saleswomen to come to her. At one of the mirrors an elderly lady with bleached hair was fussing with many hats and talking jerkily to a deferential and patient saleswoman. Frances, looking at the big dominant woman with the bleached hair and the expensive clothes, felt embarrassed, because she thought it ought to be apparent to every one in the shop, by the expression on her face, that she had no intention of taking a hat.

A deep-bosomed saleswoman, splendidly corseted, and wearing black silk, smiled at Frances, appraising her carefully. Frances was the kind of customer who might look good in any one of the hats. At the same time, while looking at her, the saleswoman wondered why she wasn't wearing a coat, or at least carrying one, for the evenings were often chilly.

"I wanted to try on the little hat, the red one in the window," Frances said.

The saleswoman had decided by this time that Frances intended only to amuse herself by trying on hats, so when she took the hat from the window and handed it to Frances she merely smiled politely and watched her adjusting it on her head. Frances tried the hat and patted a strand of fair hair till it curled by the side of the brim. And then, because she was delighted to see that it

was as attractive on her as it had been on the mannequin head
with the silver face, she smiled happily, noticing in the mirror that
her face was the shape of the mannequin face, a little long and
narrow, the nose fine and firm, and she took out her lipstick and
marked her lips heavily. Looking in the glass again she felt
elated and seemed to enjoy a kind of freedom. She felt elegant
and a little haughty. Then she saw in the mirror the image of
the deep-bosomed and polite saleslady.

"It is nice, isn't it?" Frances said, wishing suddenly that she
hadn't come into the store.

"It is wonderfully becoming to you, especially to you."

And Frances said suddenly: "I suppose I could change it, if
my husband didn't like it?"

"Of course."

"Then I'll take it."

Even while paying for the hat and assuring herself that it would
be amusing to take it home for the evening, she had a feeling that
she ought to have known when she first came into the store that
she intended to take the hat home. The saleswoman was smiling
warmly. Frances, no longer embarrassed, thought with pleasure
of going out with Eric and wearing the hat, without detaching the
price tag. In the morning she could return it.

But as she walked out of the store there was a hope way down
within her that Eric would find her so charming in the red hat
he would insist she keep it. She wanted him to be freshly aware
of her, to like the hat, to discover its restrained elegance. And
when they went out together for the evening they would both
share the feeling she had had when first she had looked in the
shop window. Frances, carrying the box, hurried, eager to get
home. The sharp wind had gone down. When there was no
wind on these fall evenings it was not cold and she would not
have to wear a coat with her woollen dress. It was just about
dark now and all the lights were lit in the streets.

The stairs in the apartment house were long, and on other evenings very tiring, but to-night she seemed to be breathing lightly
as she opened the door. Her husband, Eric, was sitting by the
table lamp, reading the paper. A black-haired man with a well-
shaped nose, he seemed utterly without energy, slumped down in
the chair. A slight odor of whiskey came from him. For four

months he had been out of work and some of the spirit had gone out of him, as if he felt that he could never again have independence, and most of the afternoon he had been standing in the streets by the theatres, talking with actors who were out of work.

"Hello, Eric boy," she said, kissing him on the head. He hardly looked up.

" 'Lo, Frances," he said.

"Let's go out and eat to-night," she said.

"What with?"

"Two bucks, big boy, a couple of dollar dinners."

So far he had hardly looked at her. She went into the bedroom and took the hat out of the box, adjusting it on her head at the right angle, powdering her nose and smiling cheerfully. Jauntily she walked into the living-room, swinging her hips a little and trying not to smile too openly.

"Take a look at the hat, Eric. How would you like to step out with me?"

Smiling faintly, he said: "You look snappy, but you can't afford a hat."

"Never mind that. How do you like it?"

"What's the use if you can't keep it?"

"But hasn't it got class? Did you ever see anything look so good on me?"

"Was it bargain day somewhere?"

"Bargain day! I got it at one of the best shops in town. Fifteen bucks."

"You'd bother looking at fifteen-dollar hats with me out of work," he said angrily, getting up and glaring at her morosely.

"I would."

"Sure. It's your money. You do what you want."

Frances felt hurt, as if for months there had been a steady pressure on her, and she said stubbornly: "I paid for it. Of course, I can take it back if you insist."

"If I insist," he said, getting up slowly and sneering at her as though he had been hating her for months. "If I insist. And you know how I feel about the whole business."

Frances felt hurt and yet strong from indignation, so she shrugged her shoulders. "I wanted to wear it to-night," she said.

His face was white, his eyes almost closed. Suddenly he

grabbed hold of her by the wrist, twisting it till she sank down on one knee. "You'll get rid of that hat quickly, or I'll break every bone in your body; then I'll clear out of here for good."

"Don't, Eric, please don't."

"You've been keeping me, haven't you?"

"Don't hurt me, Eric."

"Get your fifteen-dollar hat out of my sight quick. Get rid of it, or I'll get out of here for good."

"I will, Eric."

As he let go her wrist he snatched the hat from her head, pulling it, twisting it in his hands, then throwing it on the floor. He kicked it far across the room. "Get it out of here quick, or we're through," he said.

All the indignation had gone out of Frances. She was afraid of him; afraid, too, that he would suddenly rush out of the room and never come back, for she knew he had thought of doing it before. Picking up the hat she caressed the soft felt with her fingers, though she could hardly see it with her eyes filled with tears. The felt was creased, the price tag had been torn off, leaving a tiny tear at the back.

Eric, who kept on wetting his lips, was sitting there, watching her.

The hat was torn and she could not take it back. Hurriedly she put it in the box, wrapping the tissue paper around it, and then she went along the hall to Mrs. Foley's apartment.

Mrs. Foley, a smiling, fat woman with a round, cheerful face, opened the door. She saw Frances was agitated and felt sorry for her. "Frances, dear, what's the matter with you?"

"You remember the hat I was telling you about? Here it is. It doesn't look good on me. I was disappointed and pulled it off my head and there's a tiny tear in it. Maybe you'd want it."

Mrs. Foley thought at once that Frances had been quarrelling with her husband. Mrs. Foley held up the hat and looked at it shrewdly. Then she went back into her bedroom and tried it on. The felt was good, and though it had been creased, it was quite smooth now. "Of course, I never pay more than five dollars for a hat," she said. The little felt hat did not look good on her round head and face. She was sure that Frances was trying to sell the hat cheaply just to irritate her husband.

"I hate to offer you five dollars for it, Frances, but . . ."

"All right. Give me five dollars."

As Mrs. Foley took the five dollars from her purse Frances said suddenly: "Listen, dear, if I want it back next week you sell it to me for five, will you?"

"Sure I will, kid."

Frances hurried back to her own apartment. Though she knew Eric could not have gone out while she was standing in the hall, she kept saying to herself: "Please, Heaven, please don't let me do anything to make him leave me while he's feeling this way."

Eric, with his arms folded across his chest, was looking out the window.

Frances put the five dollars Mrs. Foley had given her, and the three dollars left over from her salary, on the small table by Eric's chair. "I sold it to Mrs. Foley," she said.

"Thanks," he said, without looking at her.

"Eric, I'm absolutely satisfied," she said, softly and sincerely.

"All right, I'm sorry," he said briefly.

"I mean I don't know what makes you think I'm not satisfied— that's all," she said.

Sitting beside him she put her elbow on her knee and thought of the felt hat on Mrs. Foley's head: it did not look good on her; her face was not at all the shape of the long silver face of the mannequin head. And as Frances thought of the way the hat had looked on the mannequin head in the window she hoped vaguely that something would turn up so she could get it back from Mrs. Foley by the end of the week. And just thinking of it, sitting there, she felt an eagerness and a faint elation; it was a plain little red hat, the kind of hat she had wanted for months, elegant and expensive, a plain felt hat, but so very distinctive.

THE HONEST WINE MERCHANT [1]

By HELENA LEFROY CAPERTON

(From *John o' London's Weekly*)

A DISTINGUISHED Virginian, dying, left a fund for the restoration of the family burying ground, where in the shadow of their living kinsmen his race slept its last, long sleep. Soon came landscape gardeners, who cleared away the clinging honeysuckle from about the crape myrtle and magnolia, revealing quiet, grey stones, over long-forgotten resting places. In so far as possible, all was to be left as originally designed by an early Cavalier ancestor, though centuries had caused box and yew to meet overhead with the sweet gloom of a cloister.

The work was well on its way when the architect directing the restoration came to the mistress of the place. "We cannot continue as planned, for in the centre of the plot we have struck an unmarked grave. I would suggest that we move it on one side under the west wall." The mistress drew herself up to a yet more slender height. "What? Disturb the guest? Oh, no! That is quite impossible! We have a stranger within our gates. Do not touch the resting place."

The chords of memory vibrated within me on hearing this, and I called to mind the story of the Honest Wine Merchant, and wondered.

In those days of too soft living before the Civil War, when our grandfathers wore stocks, ruffles, and very tight trousers; when, in fact, young men looked as if they might have stepped out from daguerreotypes, there lived in our town an Honest Wine Merchant, a German of the gentle, Goethe, Heine type, beloved and trusted by all. God rest his soul! He made of his trade a poem to uplift the hearts of men. Nothing but good he wrought, and well it is that he has passed beyond the knowledge of our reign of bloodshed, blindness, and death, which to-day supplants that which was once a beneficent vocation.

This Honest Wine Merchant was a great friend of all the young bloods around him, and whenever a sailing vessel, freighted with a precious cargo, came to rest in the James River, the Honest Wine Merchant would send his Negro body-servant with invitations to join him in his office above the wine cellars to sample the vintage. Such a vessel had just weighed anchor. Twice round Cape Horn she had carried her priceless cargo. This time it was a "pipe" of Burgundy. Now, "pipe" is somewhat misleading. It is in reality a huge cask, or tun, such as rests in the Schloss at Heidelberg. The body-servant bore the invitation, and, as usual, the young gallants came to the little office above the cellars to quaff the nectar that had been twice around Cape Horn.

"A rare wine indeed!" So spoke the Young Doctor. "I drink to the very good health of our host." He held the goblet aloft that the sun might strike through the wine, which glowed with the colour of an Irish setter's eyes. Drinking deeply, and in silence, as behoves those with real appreciation, the Young Doctor set down his glass and, raising his ruffled hand, removed from his moustache something which clung there. Manœuvring with his fine linen handkerchief, he discovered, to his great disturbance, a long, a very long, golden hair. Hastily he set down his glass, and in so doing beheld the Young Colonel regarding, with eyes of horror, something which lay in the fold of his fine linen handkerchief.

A wordless signal brought them together. Turning their backs upon the assembled company, they laid two golden hairs side by side upon the Young Doctor's plum-coloured sleeve. Now, neither of these young men would deny that golden hair is pleasant company upon a sleeve, but not when so mysteriously come by.

Both agreed that, painful as the task would be, they must tell the Honest Wine Merchant. So, lingering after the other guests had departed, they showed him the two golden hairs, borne from the golden wine. To say that the good man was horrified is to say nothing. He was distracted. He was aghast. In his sacred calling he knew nothing short of perfection. Most prayerfully he entreated the Young Doctor and the Young Colonel to accompany him at once, in order to examine the pipe of Burgundy. Together with the Negro body-servant, the three descended into the crypt-like cellars. Lanterns and torches threw bat shadows upon its Gothic arches. All about stood precious vintages, and, lofty among the other wines, the pipe of Burgundy but lately laid down after two voyages around Cape Horn.

Removing their coats and turning back their ruffles, the Young Doctor and the Young Colonel set to work to help the Honest Wine Merchant decant the wine. They removed the bung from near the base of the pipe and the wine pulsed out, crooning a slow melody of its own, catching the rays of lanterns and torches, as though broken rubies melted and flowed forth. All night they worked, in secret, for this strange thing must not be known outside those grey and flickering walls, lest dishonour come to a good man and a noble trade.

Towards dawn the gushing decreased to a slow, voluptuous murmur. Sighing, the wine at last brought forth that which made the three white men and the Negro recoil beneath the leaping torchlight. Gleaming golden, yet red as blood with wine, there coiled out slowly, lovingly, as a tired woman lets down her hair, a rope of golden tresses. With every leap of the wine an added glittering strand lay upon the stone floor of the cellar. Hypnotized, they gazed, while the Negro, crazed with terror, cowered against a pillar and hid his eyes. In vain his master commanded him to take a hatchet, mount the ladder, and knock out the top of the cask. At last, threats being of no avail, the Young Colonel seized an axe, and, standing upon the topmost rung of the ladder, brought down a crashing blow. Having made an opening, he reached for a torch. Thrusting it into the aperture, he seemed suddenly frozen as he stood.

"God's blood! What is it, man?" whispered the Young Doctor.

The man on the ladder beckoned, as one in a dream, and gave place so that the other could look into the cask. Nimbly, the Young Doctor mounted, and he too seemed turned to stone, while the Negro moaned and rolled the whites of his eyes and called upon his Maker. The Young Doctor gave place and motioned for the Honest Wine Merchant to ascend. He also gazed down in horror and amazement, for upon the floor of the cask there lay, naked and perfect, the body of a woman.

Flung down in a dreamless sleep, she lay sumptuously carved in ivory, and warmly stained with wine, deeply red her mouth and palms, and her small ears the colour of a pigeon's foot. About and around, making a pillow for her head, the golden hair sprang and surged, for the pipe of Burgundy had been sealed a century before; and for a century the wine had caressed and preserved her in a glorious mausoleum.

How came she there? That will never be known. No evidence of any violence did they find upon her splendid body, which the Young Doctor pronounced to be that of a very young girl. As the men gazed upon her, they could only surmise, each according to his inclination. Some act of love and violence, provoked by the sight of her lovely form as she had trod the wine press alone, had ended by her being thrust out of sight, the cask filled and sealed, and she forgotten, one hundred years ago, according to the date burnt into the lid.

But what of the Honest Wine Merchant? Had this awful discovery been laid bare, his gracious work would have been defamed and he, himself, disgraced. Therefore, at dawning, a covered wagon left the town. It was drawn by two spirited, astonished horses, upon whom never before had such indignity been put. Nay, more, the Young Colonel, their master, who spoke to them usually as a lover to his mistress, shouted and laid whip across their satin backs. And so, carrying a strange burden, they drew rein at last beside an old graveyard.

And there were three things the Young Doctor and the Young Colonel shrank from, and yearned towards, and did so until the end of their days. Those three things were: very golden hair, old ivory, and the smell of Burgundy.

Under the crape myrtle and magnolia, beside those who sleep the years away, marked with distinguished name and pious verse, lies the stranger within our gates. The young summer moon waxes and wanes. The mocking-bird casually breaks a heart with memory. The syringa scatters pure blossoms upon this unmarked grave. They do not wonder. Perhaps it is as well that we should also forget.

THE STORY OF THE STRANGER [1]

By JOHN COURNOS

(From *John o' London's Weekly*)

"I HAD been living in Russia for some years—mostly in St. Petersburg and Moscow, and when I had mastered the outlandish tongue sufficiently, it occurred to me that I'd like to see more of the country, particularly the small provincial towns and villages, and the people Tolstoy and Chekhov wrote so much about. I followed Chekhov's advice of travelling in third-class carriages, for that's where one's likely to get to know the simple people of a country. As you know, first-class passengers are generally too haughty to enter into conversation with a stranger, and there's nothing to be learned by travelling in first-class carriages in this country or any other.

"It was while on the way from Moscow to Nijni-Novgorod that a prosperous peasant got into my compartment. He was well about forty, tall and healthy, with a long dark beard, and he was well dressed in peasant fashion. Russians do not stand on ceremony. We plunged at once into conversation, and it wasn't long before he called me 'Brother'!

"When lunch time came he opened a parcel and, spreading its contents on a newspaper, begged me to join him in a repast. Being an Englishman and a stranger, I politely refused, but on his repeated insistence I yielded, rather gladly I must admit, for I was getting hungry, and the things spread out before me looked appetizing. 'There's plenty for us both,' he said. 'I always take enough for two, so that if I meet a stranger on the way he can share with me. It is not good to live alone and to eat alone. I've done a good piece of business in lumber hereabouts, and am on my way home to wife and little ones, and I've brought a little present for each!' He pointed to a large clean sack he had fetched into the compartment with him . . . 'And what brings you this way, brother?'

"I had already explained to him that I was an Englishman, and, in answer to his questions, told him a great deal about my country which astonished him, sometimes pleasantly, more often unpleasantly. 'That's not good, brother,' he would say, as when for example I told him about the huge factories and the immense slums and all that sort of thing. 'People are not meant to live like that. God has meant people to live by their hands, by the sweat of their brows, as the Book says. It's the work of Antichrist! . . . And are the people happy?' he asked. 'I don't think they're either happy or unhappy,' I said. 'They work hard and some of them have their small pleasures. As for happiness, that's a different thing!' 'So that's it!' he went on saying, scratching his head as Russians do when they're perplexed. 'Happiness lies in faith. Do your people have faith?' 'They have many beautiful churches,' I said, 'and men go to them, but mostly out of habit, I should say.' 'So that's it,' he went on saying, 'so that's it!' 'And do you have pilgrims as we do who forsake home and family and all they possess and wander to holy places for Christ's sake?' 'No. We had them about five hundred years ago,' said I, and I told him all about Canterbury, and about the wonderful cathedral there, and how the feet of pilgrims had worn away the paving-stones of the place. 'They must have been happy men,' he said, 'though even among us there are unbelievers who say that such men are out of their wits! Well, maybe they are, but I see it's not they who fleece the poor brother, but the clever ones! But what good is their cleverness, I ask myself, if it stands in the way of their entering the kingdom of God? The only judgment is the Last Judgment. Isn't that so, brother? The miserable sinners will be put into one place, where they can fleece one another to their hearts' content, eh?' 'That will provide an excellent test for their cleverness,' said I, laughing. 'So it will,' he agreed, and also laughed. 'But they will have Satan to deal with, and they will be hard put to fleece *him!* That will be a just punishment. Ha ha ha!' It was then he offered me lunch, and sprang the question at me. 'And what brings you this way, brother?'

"I said, 'I like what I've seen of your people, and I am taking this journey to see how the simple folk live.'

" 'That's fine! What do you say, brother, to getting off with me? It's the next stop. We're a large family—there are seven of us—but there's always room for a stranger. You can stop as long as you like, and I promise you won't go cold or hungry!'

"I was, of course, overjoyed at the opportunity to see peasant life at first-hand, and only too readily agreed. He was hugely delighted, and said: 'We stop at Podevka. There a team will be waiting to take us to Yarkoe, my village, a matter of ten versts or so.'

"Well, at last we got out, and, true to his word, a handsome troika awaited us. I shall never forget that wonderful sleigh ride. The fields were deep with snow drifts, and we passed through forests of pines and firs adorned with snow and ice shining like crystal in the sun. The air was sharp with frost, and crisp. You can have no idea of the exhilaration of a Russian troika going at full speed. An incomprehensible gaiety gets into your blood, and the crack of the whip in the crisp air and the jingle of the bells are a part of that enchantment.

"We passed a smallish town on the way. Here was a white many-domed church, its tiny golden minarets glinting in the sun; a little farther on, a little roadside chapel all lighted up with candles. . . . In some places these roadside chapels are almost as frequent as gasolene stations here. . . . We scarcely emerged from the town than on the very outskirts we passed between rows of thatched-roofed cottages, and just beyond them on the very edge of this semi-civilized oasis there stood side by side two largish buildings with barred windows. The first was pointed out to me as the county jail; the second, said my host, served as the 'House for Cracked Wits.'

" 'Ah, even here—' I murmured.

" 'Yes,' my host agreed, 'even here. But,' he added, significantly, 'there are always more out than in. And that is as true of the jail, brother. We are miserable sinners, a dark people . . . !'

"We went another five versts or so before the troika slowed down. We turned into a road running between two rows of gigantic firs: straight ahead of us was a hospitable-looking, rambling, well-cared-for, thatched-roofed house, and on both sides were huddled the barns and the threshing-floors and high piles of fire-logs. It was altogether a prosperous-looking place. We drove into the yard and stopped before the door of the house.

"All at once, the place became animated. The driver jumped from his seat, and opened the sleigh-door for us. A young man, one of the farm hands, came sauntering from the barn and greeted his master. The door of the house opened, and a comely, buxom woman of about thirty-five, with a red shawl around her head, appeared, followed by three or four children of various ages between six and twelve.

" 'Well, Marusya, how have things been going?' my host asked.

" 'Not so bad,' replied his wife. 'Only poor Vaska hasn't been himself. He's got the fever or something. He's been crying all day!'

" 'So. . . . I've brought a guest, Marusya!'—She and the children have been studying me with some curiosity. 'He comes from a far country—he's an Englishman—and he's come to see how we Russians live. Give him the large room with the soft bed, that he may see that we are hospitable, God-fearing people. . . . *Bozhe moi*—My God!' he said, turning to me, 'and I don't even know your name!'

" 'Richard Henryovitch, I suppose you'd call me.' The Russians, as you doubtless know, use the patronymic.

" 'And I am Anton Antonovitch,' he said. 'This is my wife, Marusya—and this is my eldest boy, Vladya—and this Artemy— and this is Marta—and this Nactasya. Vaska—he's the baby— is in bed. You can hear him crying. . . . Have you given him anything?' he asked his wife.

" 'Yes, I've soaked some herbs in hot water, and I've given it to him to drink, but he won't stop crying. I've sent for the doctor.'

" 'We're forgetting our guest, Marusya. Get a samovar ready, and a snack to eat.'

"And soon such a hospitable table was spread before me. . . . Well, I won't go into that. . . . The interesting thing I started telling you about happened in the evening. . . .

"It was the eve of some saint's day and there were the blazing logs and lots of candles. And Marusya had prepared quite a feast. It was a place of good cheer. Only that child went on crying. . . . The district doctor—an oldish man who had learned all he knew forty years before and hadn't looked at a medical book or journal since—had been there in the afternoon and given him quinine and a sedative, but both had worked off, and just as we sat down to enjoy our dinner the little fellow started bawling harder than ever. . . . Now Anton Antonovitch, now Marusya, left the table to minister to his wants—without much success. Vaska went on crying. We were all beginning to feel uncomfortable.

"We already had had some *zakuski*—the Russian *hors-d'œuvre*—and a drop of vodka—and were starting on *stchi*—a kind of cabbage soup—when there was a loud knock on the door. Anton Antonovitch went to open it. A stranger appeared in the doorway. He was tall, and as yet only the folds of his monk's cassock falling to the ground were visible in the shadow. But we heard his voice, a deep, melodious bass:—

" 'Do let me in—*radi Khrista*—for Christ's sake!'

" 'Enter, father. Food and shelter await thee.'

"The stranger, emerging from the darkness, paused on the threshold, surveying the faces of the household. It was the strangest face I'd ever seen, and as near like a holy man's as I ever expect to see in this life. He was about forty, he had a handsome long face and a magnificent flowing beard. His pointed hood fell to his shoulders, and newly-fallen snow, turned to ice and sparkling like diamonds, clung about his flowing hair, giving the impression of a halo. And ice crystals formed on his tufted eyebrows. The strangest thing of all were his eyes. They were genial and kind, yet burned like two glowing coals with a kind of inner ecstasy.

"Inevitably—as it were, helpless before the stranger—Anton Antonovitch made way for him and bade him sit down in the vacant chair at one end of the long table. Anton Antonovitch had previously told me that this vacant chair was always there for the chance wanderer.

"The remarkable stranger was about to sit down when it became apparent that he was listening to the crying of the child.

" 'Is the laddie ill?' he asked. 'He is crying as if he were ill.' How did he know it was a boy, I asked myself.

" 'Yes,' said my host. 'Poor Vaska has been crying all day

long. The doctor's been here and quieted him down for a bit. And now he's crying again.'

" 'The doctor is for the unbeliever,' said the stranger, with a contemptuous shrug. 'But the Orthodox should heal with faith and the laying on of hands. . . . Let me see the little one,' he added in a commanding voice. 'Is he in there?' he asked, pointing to the closed door whence the cries came.

"While we all watched with bated breaths, Anton Antonovitch —as it were, submitting—went before the stranger, opening the door for him and standing aside to let him pass. The room into which the door opened was dark. 'Would you like a candle?' the host asked. 'No,' replied the other. 'Haven't you heard it said, "I am the Light . . ." and again, "The light shineth in the darkness, but the darkness comprehendeth it not . . ." ?'

" 'A healer,' whispered Marusya to me. 'May God grant that he puts Vaska right!'

"We were all, including the children, awed by the stranger's presence, and waited for what would happen. No one dared follow him into the dark room. We heard murmurs as of a holy chant or a prayer. . . . Barely a minute elapsed when the shrill cries of Vaska suddenly ceased. The stranger, smiling benignly, re-emerged quietly, closing the door behind him.

" 'A miracle!' we all thought to ourselves.

" 'He's asleep,' said the stranger. 'Let him sleep. . . . And you, good woman, don't worry about the little fellow,' he said, turning to Marusya, who had a worried look on her face. 'Your little son is quite all right now, the pain and fever have left him. They shall not come back again . . . I promise you. . . . Blessed be He in whose Name we exorcise the griefs and aches of the living and help come to pass the Kingdom of Heaven on earth! . . . And now let us break bread and drink wine—for there is wisdom in bread and wine not understood by unbelievers. But we Orthodox men shall live in Jesus Christ and He in us through atonement and sacrifice. Amen!'

" 'Amen!' repeated after him Anton Antonovitch, his wife, and the eldest of the children.

"And the stranger drank a small glass of wine. . . . Then he broke some bread and dipped his spoon into the *stchi*.

"For a while we ate in silence. I was intensely fascinated, as you may suppose; feeling rather uncomfortable too—rather out of place, I should say. The stranger glanced at me once or twice —not exactly unkindly, but with curiosity—as if he detected the fact that I didn't belong there, in spite of my disguise in the shape of a Russian embroidered shirt buttoned askew across the chest. . . .

" 'Who's this?' He suddenly turned to the host, indicating me.

" 'He's a stranger, father, and he's come a long way, across land and water, to see how we Orthodox men live.'

" 'Well, he's come to the right place,' said the stranger, dryly. 'The world is full of unbelievers, and Christ with bleeding feet is walking across the travailing Russian earth. . . . The young man will learn a great deal here.'

" 'I trust so, father,' said I, scarcely knowing what else to say.

"He suddenly laughed—for the first time, and his strange eyes lighted up as at some recollection. 'I've lived as a novice in a lonely monastery in the far North—Archangel-way. And there is a marvellous old picture there painted by some ancient monk whose name has been forgotten. The picture is called "The Last Judgment." Upon a golden throne in golden sunlit clouds the Russian Christ sits surrounded by winged angels. And below Him on the earth are those on whom He sits in judgment divided in two camps. . . . A marvellous picture. . . . On one side are the saints and the good men judged worthy of the Kingdom of God, on the other are the sinners condemned to eternal perdition. . . . All the saints and good men are Orthodox Russians. . . . All the sinners are foreigners . . . Englishmen, I think. Ha ha ha!' He laughed immoderately. I laughed too, even though the joke was at my expense. Still, I was pleased. Our saint was human. . . . His humour was 'That touch of nature' that Shake-speare speaks of. It restored my confidence in myself, I was beginning to feel more at home.

" 'They say that in your land,' the stranger said, 'men no longer walk on bare feet and that men are beginning to ride in carriages that go by themselves without horses; and that there are even men who are learning to fly in the air in iron machines built to look like great birds; and that you have boxes in which you shut a man's voice, so that when the man's not there you can hear him sing or speak as if he were there! Is that the truth?'

" 'Yes, father, that's the truth!'

" 'That's bad! Bad! It's Antichrist at work!' he said, with a fierce gusto. 'Black magic. Yes, black magic. Men are turning to Antichrist. . . . Let me tell you what I saw at the Fair at Nijni-Novgorod. . . . I saw a magician standing up on a box. . . . He was a German, I think, or a Swede, though he jabbered our tongue almost as well as an Orthodox Russian. There was a big crowd round him and he was showing them tricks—such tricks! Black magic, I call it. . . . He called upon men in the crowd to give him their watches. A dozen or so were handed up to him. And what do you think he did? He put all these watches in one little heap on a stone block and, with a hammer, smashed them all into bits right before their eyes. Then he put the kerchief on the block, untied it, and called upon all who gave their watches to come and claim their property. And just imagine it—there were all the watches just as before—the works going and keeping time up to the minute. . . .

" 'There was a priest there in the crowd, a tall meagre fellow as thin as a tallow-candle and the light of God in his eyes, and he in a fury about it all. He started to exhort the crowd about black magic, and called the man a blasphemer, and challenged him to show that he wasn't a servant of Antichrist. The magician laughed, and said if the priest could show any better tricks than he, why didn't he show them? 'Yes,' shouted the crowd. 'Show us a better trick, if you can!' The priest, a fine honest fellow, took him up. He called for the watches, and the same fools came forward to give them up. The priest piled them up all in one heap as the other chap had done, and took the same hammer and with a single blow smashed them into smithereens. Then, with the bits before him, he began to talk to the crowd in this wise:—

" 'What do you folks want watches for? To keep time, you will say. What's the good of keeping time? What's a minute, an hour, a day, or even a year in eternity? You have daylight—the sun—to tell you when it's time to labour; you have night, darkness, the stars and the moon, to tell you that it's time to sup, to pray, and to go to bed. Time was given man to prepare for death —for eternal life. Time was given you that ye might bethink yourselves and repent ere it is too late. What are you doing to

prepare for the life to come? When God's hammer has descended
on your heads, and ye are as these smashed watches, ye—' 'What
about our watches?' some one shouted at the priest. 'What about
them?' the priest asked. 'When are we going to have them
back?' 'Here they are! Come and take them!' 'But they are
all in bits!' Came up one hefty fellow, threatening. 'So they
are! So they are!' answered the priest. 'Why don't you get this
clever fellow to put them together for you?' 'Yes, yes,' shouted
some one. 'He's put them together before. See if he can do it
now?'

"Well, there was a great hullabaloo, let me tell you, before the
thing was over, and the priest nearly lost his life. . . . The police
got there in time to save him. . . . As for the magician, he got
some rough handling, too, for not being able to do again what he
seemed to be able to do so easily before. . . .

" 'Who was right in this affair?' Anton Antonovitch, very much
perplexed, ventured to ask his visitor.

" 'The priest, of course!' said the stranger, with no indecision
in his voice. 'The man of God spoke for God. The little watch
ticks off the minutes, but God ticks off the millenniums. Isn't
that so?' The minutes of a man's life tick off as the sands ebb
in the sand-glass. . . .'

" 'There's something in what you say, father!'

" 'As for that, look at the children! And didn't the Lord bid
us to become as little children? Do little children ever think of
time? They don't bother about anything. . . . I cherish the
little ones as the source and goal of human being. . . .' And as
if to demonstrate his faith in this, he began after dinner to enter-
tain the children by telling the most marvellous tales, and he
knew how to tell them, too. . . . The most illiterate peasants
often have a natural eloquence rare in more civilized society. . . .
The children were in the seventh heaven and clung round
him. . . .

"He was in the midst of a particularly fascinating tale, to which
the elders as well as the children intently listened, when there
came a violent knock on the door, impetuously repeated.

"Anton Antonovitch went to the door and, opening it, peered
out. We heard voices out of the darkness. One voice said:—

" 'We are from Brodnoe—from the Insane Asylum. An inmate

has escaped this afternoon. And as it's a cold night, we thought he might be asking for shelter hereabouts. Has any one passed this way? . . .'

" 'No one but a holy stranger . . .' answered Anton Antonovitch.

" 'In a monk's clothes?' asked the second voice.

" 'Yes. . . .'

"Suddenly, two pairs of eyes, in heads leaning forward, peered in. . . .

"Before we knew what had happened two big men ran in and pounced on the stranger. . . . There was a brief scuffle. . . . He was terribly strong. . . . So were they. . . . Presently, his arms tied, they led him out to the waiting sleigh. We were all very much frightened. It was as if we had seen a ghost. . . .

"That wasn't the end of our excitement—for, suddenly, Marusya rose from her chair and, snatching a candle, rushed to the bedroom where Vaska lay in his crib. . . . We all followed, sure that the stranger had strangled him. . . . 'Poor Vaska! My poor Vaska!' cried Marusya. Holding a candle in one hand, she bent over the crib. We all looked. There was Vaska asleep with the most beatific smile on his face. On Marusya shaking him, he opened his eyes and surveyed us with a grave calm. . . . He was a handsome youngster of three. . . . He asked in a sleepy, lisping voice:—

" 'Mamma, was there any one here? . . . Such good hands touched me. . . . Who chased him away? . . .'

" 'I leave it to you—was the man mad? Or was it we who had gone out of our wits?'

" 'He must have escaped from the House of Cracked Wits I pointed out to you!' said Anton Antonovitch, and crossed himself.

SO TALL THE CORN [1]

By DAVID CORNEL DE JONG

(From *Scribner's Magazine*)

THE day was hushing to evening quiet, a quiet wherein all voices haloed themselves in melancholy, and late wagons over the hill sounded tragic. Not that all the light was waning, or that bats already fluttered. After supper Culver had saddled Cyrus, the white horse, but when he had gone in to wash his hands and face he had changed his mind abruptly. Now Cyrus was in the pasture again, and Molly, who had prepared herself for a long evening of whinnying at the gate, rubbed her chin contentedly over the white horse's rump and flicked her ears. Cyrus looked very white and slender in the soft light, with pines and lighter sycamores behind him. Now the sun reclined to the horizon, but birds still sang, though somewhat plaintively.

Culver sang a little. He idled for a short while over the whip. Then there were crows, two old and two young, above the neighbor's corn; raucous, because they were aware of him; impartial, though Culver seldom handled a gun; wary, even though it was not he, but his brother, who was really a crack shot. Likewise, it was his brother who could actually get voluble over the damage crows do to the farmer. But the crows, too, were gone with their strident alarms, while his sister banged the car door shut, and disappeared down the driveway. Now he was alone, with mother evident in the rattling from the kitchen. He was alone, with Cyrus still whiter against the trees and Molly silent with him.

Father had left again, immediately after supper, to look at the corn. This evening he would stand in the living room, three feet from the table, and say, "Look, mother, and you, Culver. See. Right here to this third button from the top, that's as high as the blades reach now. Oh, they're coming fine. Even the smallest ain't so small." Perhaps he would vary it just a little, one button

up, another stalk surpassing yesterday's in rarity and luxurious-
ness, and then mother would say, "Harry, I do need wood for the
stove to-morrow, and could you fix those shelves? I really don't
see how I can carry on another day, and that with all you able-
bodied men around." Here, too, there was possibility for varia-
tion, but not much. Then father would be silent, and mother
would show no evidence of appreciation for tall corn, and would
only huddle a little more over her sewing. Then father would
say, "All right," and demand the newspaper at once.

And all the time father spoke about the corn the night would
be glossily black behind the panes and the owl in the spruces
would be hooting, and no one but Culver seemed to wonder about
the darkness in the cornfield. He did not like it. He did not like
this at all. Why should he be aware of the darkness all the time,
while his father wanted them all to ask about the corn, and his
mother was unconcerned? Then he would sit down and read
about an aged woman killed by a non-stop driver, about yesterday's boatrace, about a cure for ringworm, until he felt composed
again to do other things. Why should he bother? Clif and
Louise, excited with father, asked questions, exclaimed, measured
and remembered last year's corn. And all that time he would
wonder about the darkness and the owl's hooting.

There was nothing to do now. Water gurgled in the kitchen
and kettles clattered, people sang and shouted from passing cars,
and the cows grazed and grazed, hungry after milking. He whistled for the dog, but the cat came, rubbed a purring head against
his knees and stared at the orchard, where gophers were. "Nice
kitty," he said. "Nice, nice, nice," until the cat crawled through
the fence and looked back once with large, incomprehensible eyes.
He rose.

He would walk to the corn and see its tallness. There were
buds on the catalpas, and by the fences the raspberries grew
plumper. "I could sing, I could sing, I could sing," he sang, but
stopped when he saw the chickens in the parsley bed. He swore
and threw sticks, and they cackled off, blatantly frightened. He
whistled then, and listened to the voices of the Nelson boys, who
shouted about cows behind the catalpas. Each young bull on his
chain lifted velvet eyes, and they passed long, blue tongues up
their noses and waited. Each one he tapped fondly rude on the

head. The last, October, passed a hot, rough tongue all along his arm and jerked at his chain to follow him. Vesper sparrows sang, and he whistled again, noting the light through the tree rows and swift flies.

Culver was tall, and sun-red. The sun played along the hairs on his arms, and the five bulls stood still and stared at him. With Clif and Louise gone, the evening would be long and still, and he could sit alone in the grass till the very last light was darkened from the west. The Durban train came then, grinding tiredly behind its engine, then Nelsons' lights would gleam from their front room and Clara at the piano would start "In the Gloaming," her voice too fast for the groping on the piano, and he would rise because there would be very little else to do. So the evening would come and go. Then the prospects for the morning would loom so meagre, so monotonously meagre, that he would read a book to make the most of the day that was left. Culver was the silent one of the family, the stubborn one, his mother had told her sister; the bright one, his father had said to the insurance agent; a peach, Louise would say a hundred times because he did not bother her; and Clif would go morning after morning to look at the skunk traps, thinking, "What's a guy like that much good for on a farm anyway?" Of course Clif would think that, levelling a gun at a woodchuck, while he, Culver, walked away because he did not want to see the animal rise and tumble, no matter how much of the lettuce had been destroyed. And he would walk in the rain and get thoroughly wet. That bothered all of them. In fact, it hurt them. He laughed derisively, at the thought of Clif.

He walked on. The cows lifted slow heads and marvelled at him with wide eyes, spinning long strings of saliva. Their moist lips moved and moved, and the evening had come like dusk to their eyes. He could not bear to look at those eyes long in such a light. From beyond some border which never could be passed, they stared. They were always on thresholds of things solemn, nearly terrific and full of melancholy. "Peace, peace, peace, terrific peace," he muttered. Too much to bear and to whistle, "I love you so much, I can't conceal it," and all that, so he was silent and walked past them till he could hear their lips no longer.

Past the oats was the corn. Then he recalled that his father would be there. The corn, his father's corn, his father always in the corn, with blades reaching nearly to his shoulders. "Just look, mother, look, Culver." No, he decided he would walk around and avoid his father. Could one worship corn and lie in it, worshipping, till night was over one, and then rise full of ecstasy? "What drivel, what soft stuff," he growled, and kicked the dead mullein stalks of last year.

"Culver! Culver!" his mother called from the windmill. He turned around and waited, but she looked the other way, and he did not consider the matter important enough to let her know where he was. She wanted one of her endless pails of water pumped, and no doubt she had seen Cyrus without a saddle in the pasture. "Culver! Culver!" she ended waningly, and he went on, and saw that the flowerbuds of the catalpas would soon burst, and that the raspberries ripened along the fence. Then everything was silent and came to a pause. Everything paused. He ceased his walking. Even sound hovered for a while, spent, holding its breath, as it were, before sudden outcries.

Then sound came, with the laughter of a woman beyond the corn. There were three peals of laughter and then a wind ruffled the corn, and all the blue-green sheen shuddered and wavered and flagged until the wind was past, and hollowing the oats. He walked between the rows of corn near the catalpa row. The corn tips fingered his ankles, his legs, his thighs and even his hips. Small animals scampered from the catalpas and birds twittered, already on the wing when he saw them. Bull Selkirk had said, past his three huge, yellow teeth, "Hell, guy, no fellow can withstand a healthy woman, I don't care how old he is." That past those yellow teeth from which the pipe drizzled had had little of truth then or significance, but he remembered it, because the laughter came again, low, healthy, past the corn.

He had reached the end of the corn where the catalpas merged with tangles of sumachs and cottonwoods. He stood still, his lips curved, his mouth open. Then he stepped back among the sumachs. Sounds of voices came, and laughter. His father was there with Nan Nelson, leaning over the fence, where the creek slowed through a shallow. She laughed again, and his father's voice muttered. He stood taut, without emotion and without thought. "So tall the corn, mother, so tall, Culver. So." That brought thought, but wildly and without aim. What right had he to look at this? He grew violently angry. He stripped the large catalpa leaves from a branch and dropped them on his feet.

His father was climbing over the fence, and Nan laughed, pulling at his legs and shouting, "Now watch, watch out, you'll tear; watch." Then he brushed himself and she brushed him and then came laughter again. A bluejay scolded from the cottonwoods. "Shut, you," he hissed, and watched as the two walked arm in arm along the creek to a clump of elms. There they sat down on the bank of the creek, muttering and laughing. He still tore the catalpa leaves and stared open-mouthed, the sun glistening his teeth.

Suddenly, he crouched and ran toward the house, and when he knew the hill slope hid him he straightened and ran on. Thoughts would not come connectedly and with order. Nan Nelson past tall corn, look mother. Look, Culver, nearly to my shoulder. Nan Nelson, who had left her husband and had come home again to reign over the Nelson brood, with Mrs. Nelson browned with cancer. Tall, tall corn, so tall. Nan full of laughing, full of bold blue eyes and loud words, with a cast-off man somewhere. But tall grows the corn, tall, right to your shoulder, Culver. That was the tall corn he liked, he boasted over. And Louise, so tall and so tall it was last year, remember, father, and Clif cleaning his gun, and mother insistent over nails and boards, and I don't know how I can go on another day without them. All you able-bodied men. All you.

Then he suddenly slackened his pace. How could he face her and tell her? "All you able-bodied men," he shouted at the bulls, "get you to the corn. Get you to the corn." The bulls jerked at their chains and stumbled back on frantic legs. He tapped the head of the last one, who lowered his head to charge him, impotently wild on his short chain. "You able-bodied man," he shouted to him, and the bull circled violently around the stake and snorted. He laughed again and walked on. His palate felt hot and dry, and his throat was parched.

Then he saw his mother by the house, spreading the milk cloths on the grass. He hesitated and looked at her. Then he brushed his hair impatiently and very slowly he walked toward her. But his voice would not come, so he stooped to the cat and said, "Get them, get them, kitty," pointing toward the orchard. The cat sat and stared and swung her tail twice. "Nice kitty," he said. "Nice."

His mother had heard him and waited. When he straightened himself she said, "I need another pail of water, Culver. My back is too sore to pump more."

"Later," he said. "I'll get it later."

"No, now. You can get it now."

He grew impatient at the petulance in her voice. "No, later. Come along now and let's look at the corn. Come."

She shook her head, "Now?"

"Yes, now. Look at the sun; it's almost gone. Come, you want to see the corn."

She looked at the sun. The sunlight glinted in the broken blue of her eyes and when she shook her shoulders it moved orange gleams over her dress. "Why, I can see that some other time."

"Oh, you can come now." He hesitated. Why should she come, why? But then he grew afraid of himself. "Why must you always have excuses?"

"Always, always?" she scolded. "But my legs are too sore to walk that far. You know that, don't you? You know that I can hardly carry on through the day. You can't compare me to yourself. I've gone through too much for that."

"But come now, mother."

"All right."

She came along, holding on to his arm. She was going to stand in the corn, broken and pathetic compared with Nan, Nan red and loud with laughter. He hated the contrast, he who would not see a woodchuck killed, but she must see him, she should. "Is the corn tall?" she asked.

"Yes."

"It is such a nice evening, but this is really too far. There is so much to do in the house yet."

"Look, haven't the calves grown? Don't they look great?"

"Yes. That'll mean a lot of work canning all that meat. There is always work."

They walked on, past the calves. Their shadows grew very faint and long, and when he looked toward the west he saw that the sun was nearly gone. He must not think. When he thought, he would not go on, and he must. She should see Nan, Nan, the tall corn that came to his shoulder.

"But it is awful far," she complained.

"We can walk slower, if you wish."

"No. Any walking makes me tired."

"We are nearly there. Look, the catalpas are going to bloom."

"I must fix a rent in your father's jacket to-night. That can't wait."

"Do you see the corn, mother? Look."

"Yes, it does look nice, doesn't it?"

He stood still and listened. There was only the ruffling of the corn, and to the left sparrow calls. Corn leaves flagged against the evening red and voices came and shouted up and waned again. They stood still. There was no laughter. She slid her finger up and down a corn blade and lifted her eyes impatiently to a peremptory horn which sounded from the road. "What's that good for?" she grumbled. He stood very still and hesitated. The corn blade sound in cumulation was like the rushing away of many frightened people. The ground was soft and reeked earthy when he dug into it with the toe of his shoe.

"But, come along. There, past the catalpas, there it is highest. Come." He had driven the words out as if they had no particular goal, or no hearer. They were like the corn rustle, fugitive to unnamed places, fleeing from the impossible. He did not want her to come. But he took her arm and said again, "Come and see."

"But this is the corn. I see it."

"Yes, but come."

She came unwillingly and muttered. They skirted the corn rows and walked beneath the fringe of catalpas in benediction over them. Come, son, lead her on, lead her on, your mother to your father. He struck at low-hanging leaves. Come, come to tall corn and laughter. He repeated the thought insistently. Everything was too lucid; everything was bathed in a hideous clarity with spectators watching and pointing. A nude light, he thought. A nude clarity and corn blades, the spectators, rustled and entered to something. They reached the end of the catalpas. "Really, Culver, I must get back."

There was the sound of voices now, but so soft they belonged to anything, to the whole muted evening. "Look," he said.

"Look at the corn."

Then there came laughter. He stepped between his mother and the laughter. He pounded his fist impatiently on his left hand. "Look, isn't it tall?"

She stood still again and fingered the corn. The green slid through her yellow hand and whined a fine sound. He also took a blade and slid it through his fingers. It fluted thinly against Nan's laughter. "It is nice corn," she said.

"Mother, you and father, and we all do have a decent time. We do, don't we?"

She looked suddenly away and then up in his eyes. "Why, yes. Why, how funny you speak. What makes you say such things?"

"Nothing. Nothing, just this evening. See. The quiet and all that." He waved his arm over the corn and to the budding catalpas. "Look how it's getting dark by the woods." And again when Nan's laughter came, "Look at the light."

She looked. "We are contented. We all are. I and your father and you too, of course. But, Culver, I must go back. And I am tired."

"Yes, you must go back."

"It's getting damp. That won't do my legs any good."

"No."

They turned and walked away toward the house. Five cow-birds tumbled into the catalpas from a vague south and fluted short notes before they stirred. They whirled away again into the rustle of the corn, sagged in simultaneous flight, rose to a height, shouted and scampered back over their heads. The light passed away from places beneath trees and silhouetted Nelson's cows against orange, tall and mysterious. "This is such a walk. Where is your father?"

"I don't know."

"I must fix his jacket. I really can't lose so much time. And don't forget that pail of water, Culver." She leaned heavily upon his arm and held him back. The young bulls came forward to look at them. She looked at the house and said, "Anybody might get in the house with us all back there."

"Nobody will."

"No? You don't know. I can't just go off like that."

"No, you shouldn't. You are right."

"Why do you say that? You know I can't. Your father . . ."

He interrupted. "Why don't you stop complaining now? Why do you always go on like that, why always the same? What does it matter to you what father does? You always drone on about the same things." He shook her arm from his.

She stood still, rather helpless, her mouth open and her arms loose along her hips. Her lips moved impotently toward speech, but no words came. Then he was sorry. But he turned his eyes away and looked at Cyrus and Molly, quiet together by the fence. She still moved her lips and stood straight. "Why," she said. "Why?"

"I'm sorry. I'm so sorry." He scuffled his feet violently on the grass. "Really."

"Why, Culver, you should go out more. You should, like Clif and Louise. Aren't you young? Why, you think of the strangest things, the strangest things." She shook her head, kindly, defeated, wondering.

They walked again, aloofly near each other, and silent. The cat slid through the orchard and hens fretted on the roost. The house waited blandly white between the spruces, as if it were aware of their quarrel and tried to forget it before they noticed that it too was disturbed. "Listen, the owl starts already." The owl whined a twisting, wavering shriek which trembled off in thin shivers and merged with cricket sounds. The chimney smoked tiredly. Along the barn a faint echo repeated their footsteps on the stamped ground. "Listen to that owl."

They stood still and looked at the spruces where the owl sounded. Their faces were lifted and their eyes sought the blackness in the green, but saw nothing. She walked on ahead of him. "Here is the pail. Get water first now, will you? Don't wait, please."

He took the pail and walked to the pump. She slammed the screen-door and was lost in the blackness of the house. Darkness came rapidly and stirred up from everywhere. He pumped with fast, truculent motions, and listened to the water's plump burling into the pail. As he moved the pump handle up and down he repeated an inflectionless monody, "So tall, so tall, so tall," till the pail was full. Then he pressed his forehead against the cold steel of the windmill and waited thoughtlessly, letting all sound come to his ears, hundreds of strands of sound, which he tried to unravel separately. There was nothing to do, nothing to be said, nothing to feel. There could be no misery and pain. This all meant nothing. He had looked at something, at healthy laughter, red, strong flesh, tall corn, and it could mean nothing. There were no changes, only knowledge, which pained, but could not be remedied. He stooped and took the pail and carried it to the house. "Here's your water, mother." That is what life would do. An endless carrying of water, and the rest would go on with laughter, growth of corn and whispers. "The water, mother," he shouted.

She came to the door. "There, there on the porch. I want it there."

He put the water on the porch and waited. "That's all," she said. "Not that I myself haven't plenty to do. More than plenty." She moved into the house again. When he watched her motions, he turned his head. They seemed so impotently tired and useless, as if they only existed for themselves, tauntingly aloof and unnecessary. What should she know? Why? She would stir the fire again and stoop over her needle, more awkwardly desirous to go on, to brunt awful obstacles which always waited. He walked to the front and stopped. The Durban train came and belched sound and creaked discords against the deep silence. Voices stirred. Then the light came from Nelsons' windows and the piano thumped. He listened. The piano tugged at the stillness and tumbled dull blocks of sound upon a floor of long, wide silence. Then Clara sang with a raw, girl's voice, gracelessly. He rose.

He would meet his father and say, "How was the corn? How tall?" And he would talk about the laughter by the fence and Nan's concern over his clothes and then about her laughter again. He would stand casually beside him, and say all that with a level voice, as if the matter were of no personal concern. He walked toward the back of the house.

Then he heard his father's footsteps on the hard clay by the barn. His mother stirred inside in the midst of busy sounds. He stopped, and bent over the poppies, black-red in the darkness. There was no scent and no movement. Only the footsteps came louder, then brushed through the pigweed and camomile, then paced softly on the grass. He straightened himself.

"Hullo, Culver. Looking for something?"

"No." He twisted his fingers deeply into his pockets. "No, just enjoying the night."

"It is a nice night. Wonderful."

"Yes." Then he turned his face and peered at the whiteness past the fence that was Cyrus.

"The corn is coming fine. Everything is coming fine."

"Yes." He saw the whiteness of Cyrus, moveless. "Yes, I must take a look at the corn to-morrow."

"Do, sure. Are you coming in?"

"No." He turned his back and leaned his arm on the gate. "I'll be in later."

The footsteps crunched off over the gravel, the door slammed and the kitchen floor creaked no longer. The piano thumped through katydid shouting, and Clara recapitulated noisily everything that was the Nelsons. Now he would stand by the table, three feet away, the eyes blinking beneath the unaccustomed light, measuring, urging, and she would stoop over the jacket rent and remember the kindling wood that had to be cut, and the clothes pole.

The whiteness of Cyrus moved. He drummed his hands palms down, fingers spread, on the top bar of the gate. "So much for that," he said. The horse moved on.

HANSEL [1]

By ANDRA DIEFENTHALER

(From *New Copy, 1932*)

THE farm house was dark within. Blackness slid in deep
hush across the winding valley. A wooded mountain suddenly hid the face of the setting sun. For Hermie, the half-wit,
oncoming night possessed soothing like the soft stroke of gentle
fingers—his grandmother's fingers. Quiet came into him as he
sat at the foot of her bed where he stole at evening along with
dusk. Presently grandmother's voice would add to the soothing.
Soothing would somehow weave itself in with the telling of her
tale. Grandmother was good. She alone understood his thick
talk and many tears. And now it was too dark in the room to see
her. It brought her nearer. He felt her dearness up there at the
edge of the quilt where her old hands lay still. They had ceased
caressing his cheeks.

"She walks now in the barn to see if I do everything right,"
Hermie said. "Soon she comes with the lamp. Then we have no
more nice here." It was his father's wife he spoke of.

"Yah, Hermie, you got right," the old woman answered. "Always with a lamp she comes. What could cure her from lamps, I
don't know. For the light she don't care so much; for the fire
she does. Everything with fire she must settle. Well, we don't
think on that now. To-night I tell you over again about the
broom-maker's childrums, Hansel and Gretel."

The half-wit interrupted, "Before the hex is here with the
lamp?"

"Yah, but we talk about the one in the story who is pushed in
her own fire—the oven—you know."

"I know, Grossmutter. She wants to fix the children—the boy
Hansel and the girl." Hermie laughed. He laughed often. His

imbecility was pain to the old woman.

"When I was the last time to Weimar I hear Humperdinck's music for the Hansel and Gretel opera. Never I forget it—so beautiful! I wish if you could hear it like that, Hermie. In America we live so far from the city, and anahow, we have no money now. In Europe we love music, and so much we have it, but in this house is only fighting. Right away she comes with the lamp—that Lydia."

The old woman began the German version of the nursery legend, Babes in the Wood, and told it with much feeling. She concluded, "and so—they pushed the hex in her own fire—the big oven, and shut the door quick. Dose childrums had each one, a pretty good head. What you tink on it, Hermie?"

The half-wit had no words for his delight. He grunted and rubbed his feet on the floor.

Lydia Frobish came into the kitchen and closed the door. She was a big, gaunt woman; vital and quick-moving. Time and fret had not altogether marred her handsome face. She lighted a lamp and carried it into a bedroom that was a box adjoining the kitchen. "So you stay like always in the dark and wait for me to bring the lamp? When you get enough from foolish stories?" she asked.

The half-wit shuffled out. Lydia followed. She lighted another lamp and placed it on the kitchen table. Then she laid more wood in the stove.

"Always with fire she works. In the lamp, in the stove is all right but not when it don't stay there," the old woman mumbled, for it was her habit to mumble. Lydia never paid heed to that.

Out in the yard the half-wit sat with a rough-haired, tawny dog. "In her own fire, in her own fire," he kept repeating to the friendly little animal.

The next morning at the breakfast table Lydia said to the half-wit, "You lazy, good-for-what? To eat, yes, and to sleep! Look how you can't get enough! Five or the six times I have to call you from the bed. You go now cut potatoes for planting—two eyes every piece. You cut right, hear? From one eye maybe they don't grow, and they *have* to grow, how you eat them. After, come back and carry water for the wash. I want you should rub your own clothes—Grossmutter's in with. First, bring dry wood. Wet makes me mad. You know that. Better you build the fire yourself for hot water, then for sure you do it right. Come now, wake up your feet once, stoffle."

"Ain't he the one to look in the air?" she turned to her husband and said.

John Frobish, a slight, blond man with faded blue eyes and small voice, pleaded for his unfortunate son. "Yah, Lydia, he does look in the air but you have to know he can't help it. To me it is awful how he was born so dumb. Why you don't give him enough to eat? Before he is through, you chase him up from the breakfast. Hard he works—too hard, how he is growing. You should think from that. He ain't a man yet for awhile."

" 'Hard he works,' you say? What you call this playing all the time jack-the-beanstalk from Grossmutter's stories? How many times I see him throw some beans from the window? And when I can't find the ax, I look where the beans wait to grow, and there it is. Some night for sure the stalk gets high and the ax is all ready to chop the giant down. And when he leads one from the cows up to Kruger's to be bred, he asks anybody on the road for three beans. Maybe mine, they ain't the right kind. Always with Grossmutter's stories his head is full. Better you stop talking about that dummy and think on a new barn. You should build one. Nothing is togeder. Not bins, not stalls, not mows. Soon the roof she slides off when we get heavy snow or a good wind."

"Yah! but the money! Where that comes from?"

Lydia lifted her shoulders for answer.

"Hermie! Hermie!"

"I come, Grossmutter," the uncouth boy called as he hurried through the kitchen into the box that was a room.

"They make me sick," Lydia said. "That old woman always calling, and knocking with her stick. The dumb-head runs every time to see what she wants. When *I* want something, he growls and pulls his feet."

John Frobish got up from the table. What was the good of words? He took his case of tools and went on his way to work. He was one of three carpenters building a new house for Doctor Ulric.

Sometime before midnight, impact of the thorny, black stick

sounded again through the rooms of the house. The old woman shrieked, "Hermie! Herm-ie!"

"Yah, Grossmutter, I come!" the half-wit in sleep and haste stumbled down stairs from the attic.

"Look! Fire! Hermie! the barn!"

"No one is to call, Grossmutter. Papa is by Strubble's store playing pinochle. She, Lydia hex, is not in her bed."

"Gott in himmel! Look at it burn! Nothing will be left!" The old woman screamed and rocked back and forth in the billows of her feather-bed yellow with wear and heavy with the odors of her aged, neglected body.

"With fire she would scare me to death, that Lydia. She *wants* I should die. The horses! Hermie, run. Loose them up. With fire they go crazy, the same like me. That Lydia, where she is?"

The half-wit ran out of the house toward the flames that rode up and down against the black of night. He saw the horses and cattle safe within the pasture fence below the barn. In shadow, Lydia walked with a lamp.

During the long, humid summer the old woman thumped more and more with her thorny, black stick, wanting the boy.

"I can't stand it to hear her call all the time, 'My poor Hermie. My poor John!'" Lydia said to the carpenter when he returned one night from Doctor Ulric's new house.

"Have more patience," he replied. "Old people could be a little bother. We come old ourselves some day. Please, I ask you don't be mean to my old woman—fast she is going now. And Hermie, you let him alone too."

The little meek man may as well have held his tongue, for the next day Lydia called the boy into the kitchen and said, "First you have to know that I want you to stop pulling the pigs' tails. Pretty near the whole day you make them squeal. You hitch up and draw turnips to the cellar, now. After, you paint the henhouse with whitewash, outside and inside the same. To-night you have to help cut kraut. We don't lose time with Grossmutter's stories, hear that, dumbhead?"

The old woman shouted from the box that was a room, "You should feel something for that boy. Why you don't ask him decent to work? Poor Hermie without his right mother—without his right brains! My John is blind when you he takes to marry. He gets him a bellyful of pretty face, all right. I hear how you said you would take the first man who comes along. That poor devil was my John. You take him for spites because Chris Hemp fools around with another girl. What you care if John is older as you are, fifteen years?"

"Fifteen! Why not make it a hundred? That would be more like it."

"I should send for the justice of the peace to stop you from fighting with me. Anyway, I should call him about the fire that burns the barn for insurance money. Before I die, for sure I go out from my head living with you."

"Already you are crazy. When I didn't know it, how I could stand you, pig?"

Supper over, John Frobish heard the old woman repeat hysterically all that had happened during the day. Distracted, he put his hands to his head and exclaimed, "Mix-up—nothing but mix-up in this house." As he did not know what to do, he made no effort to prevent the impingement that would inevitably continue.

November brought blasts of cold. Two men who had repaired a bridge blew upon their hands to warm them. They passed the Frobish house and one called to the other, "Smoke! Out of the window! From the chimney it should come!"

Entering the house they could hear the old woman scream, "Hermie! Herm-ie! Come, boy, come now. I must go like the barn when you wait too long. Lieber Gott! Lieber Gott!"

Fire crept along the bottom of her bed. She sank back into her dingy pillows and gasped.

Lydia came from the woodshed carrying a broom. When the blaze was beaten down, one of the bridge-menders said, "A lamp on the floor to burn the covers—how you make that out?"

"She could upset it. Or Hermie, the dumbhead," Lydia said.

Later the half-wit came into the smoke-blackened room. "Grossmutter," he sobbed. "Grossmutter, you are dead. But what I don't know is, how you could get the lamp when your legs they are paralyzed? Wait, I get you what warm. You are cold."

The bewildered boy slipped into the kitchen and returned with

Lydia's thick, red shawl. He spread it carefully over the still and bony body. In the morning he saw it hanging in its accustomed place on a nail behind the door.

The half-wit mourned and moved about more dumbly than ever. He clung to his father for the affection that was so deeply his need. He often refused food and absented himself from the house to escape wielding of the black, thorny stick. He had struggled for possession of it but Lydia was strongest. When he returned at night from aimless wandering to see his father, black brooding was still upon him. "Lieber grossmutter! Lieber grossmutter!" he wailed until it was more than John Frobish could bear. He wrung his hands and paced the kitchen. Why must the wretched boy bring that all before him again, the terrible fact of the old woman's death in a burning bed? Why did he hold the rough-haired, tawny dog and say, "In her own fire! In her own fire!" He silenced the sick-minded fellow with soft words, wanting to escape both him and Lydia, since his courage was so frail a thing.

"Hermie, come, stop the crying. Why you don't play your stories? Lydia lets you have the beans and the ax and what you need."

"Yah, papa, but a oven I want."

"John, we had enough with the old woman's play-business when she was alive. Now you want to keep the dumbhead going with it some more."

"Well, so he is still, that's all."

"He's better off if he was where she is."

"Lydia, you have to look out you don't go too far. When the pot comes too full it boils over. You should not let Hermie hear you talk like that. Only it make things worser as they are."

Hermie was quieted by his father's sympathy, and shuffled off to bed with the rough-haired, tawny dog at his heels.

Winter was well on its way. Bitter cold stung the big ears of the half-wit as he made his way among new sheds that sheltered the animals. The sheds stood sharply black in the twilight. Hermie listened for Lydia feeding the stock. Cattle crunched at corn-stalks. They had been fed and milked. Pigs grunted, satisfied on their straw—the old hog and her litter. Now to pull their tails. He did it heartily and smiled with pleasure. Lydia would be bound to hear that much squealing in the house. But she was not in the house. She lay beside the tall and wide cone-like straw stack in the cow-yard. Her moaning drew the half-wit as words could not. Curiosity urged him closer. Mutely he stood before her.

"Fool," she cried. "Go get somebody. I am bad hurt. The old ram knocks me down and hooks me with his horns. I can't move, and nearly I am stiff with cold. Run for a light, and tell your father to come if he is in the house."

The boy sped. Cunning and madness seized his brain. He returned almost at once with a lamp. His hands and chin trembled while he drew off the chimney and put the wick to straw, up and down and across the stack. Fire took hold of the dry wisps and spread, driven by wind. It ran in hissing, frantic flames. Smoke poured in wide and rolling mass from the bottom of the stack.

"Stop, stop, you devil's boy! From smoke I choke and soon from fire I burn. Come here on this side and pull me away."

The half-wit grinned. Then he shouted, "See, I bring you Grossmutter's lamp."

In a moment he was gone. He ran laughing his idiot's laugh along the river-bank with the tawny dog at his heels.

"In her own fire—the hex is in her own fire," he called to the faithful little animal, "me, I'm Hansel now."

SMOKE [1]

By WILLIAM FAULKNER

(From *Harper's Magazine*)

ANSELM HOLLAND came to Jefferson many years ago. Where from, no one knew. But he was young then and a man of parts, or of presence at least, because within three years he had married the only daughter of a man who owned two thousand acres of some of the best land in the county, and he went to live in his father-in-law's house, where two years later his wife bore him twin sons, and where a few years later still the father-in-law died and left Holland in full possession of the property, which was now in his wife's name. But even before that event, we in Jefferson had already listened to him talking a trifle more than loudly of "my land, my crops"; and those of us whose fathers and grandfathers had been bred here looked upon him a little coldly and a little askance for a ruthless man and (from tales told about him by both white and negro tenants and by others with whom he had dealings) for a violent one. But out of consideration for his wife and respect for his father-in-law, we treated him with courtesy if not with regard. So when his wife, too, died while the twin sons were still children, we believed that he was responsible, that her life had been worn out by the crass violence of an underbred outlander. And when his sons reached maturity and first one and then the other left home for good and all, we were not surprised. And when one day six months ago he was found dead, his foot fast in the stirrup of the saddled horse which he rode, and his body pretty badly broken where the horse had apparently dragged him through a rail fence (there still showed at the time on the horse's back and flanks the marks of the blows which he had dealt it in one of his fits of rage), there was none of us who was sorry, because a short time before that he had committed what to men of our town and time and thinking was the unpardonable outrage. On the day he died it was learned that he had been digging up the graves in the family cemetery where his wife's people rested, among them the grave in which his wife had lain for thirty years. So the crazed, hate-ridden old man was buried among the graves which he had attempted to violate, and in the proper time his will was offered for probate. And we learned the substance of the will without surprise. We were not surprised to learn that even from beyond the grave he had struck one final blow at those alone whom he could now injure or outrage: his remaining flesh and blood.

At the time of their father's death the twin sons were forty. The younger one, Anselm, Junior, was said to have been the mother's favorite—perhaps because he was the one who was most like his father. Anyway, from the time of her death, while the boys were still children almost, we would hear of trouble between Old Anse and Young Anse, with Virginius, the other twin, acting as mediator and being cursed for his pains by both father and brother; he was that sort, Virginius was. And Young Anse was his sort too; in his late teens he ran away from home and was gone ten years. When he returned he and his brother were of age, and Anselm made formal demand upon his father that the land which we now learned was held by Old Anse only in trust, be divided and he—Young Anse—be given his share. Old Anse refused violently. Doubtless the request had been as violently made, because the two of them, Old Anse and Young Anse, were so much alike. And we heard that, strange to say, Virginius had taken his father's side. We heard that, that is. Because the land remained intact, and we heard how, in the midst of a scene of unparalleled violence even for them—a scene of such violence that the negro servants all fled the house and scattered for the night— Young Anse departed, taking with him the team of mules which he did own; and from that day until his father's death, even after Virginius also had been forced to leave home, Anselm never spoke to his father and brother again. He did not leave the county this time, however. He just moved back into the hills ("where he can watch what the old man and Virginius are doing," some of us said and all of us thought); and for the next fifteen years he lived alone in a dirt-floored, two-room cabin, like a hermit, doing his own cooking, coming into town behind his two mules not four

times a year. Some time earlier he had been arrested and tried
for making whiskey. He made no defense, refusing to plead
either way, was fined both on the charge and for contempt of
court, and flew into a rage exactly like his father when his brother
Virginius offered to pay the fine. He tried to assault Virginius
in the courtroom and went to the penitentiary at his own demand
and was pardoned eight months later for good behavior and returned to his cabin—a dark, silent, aquiline-faced man whom both
neighbors and strangers let severely alone.

The other twin, Virginius, stayed on, farming the land which
his father had never done justice to even while he was alive.
(They said of Old Anse, "wherever he came from and whatever he
was bred to be, it was not a farmer." And so we said among ourselves, taking it to be true, "That's the trouble between him and
Young Anse: watching his father mistreat the land which his
mother aimed for him and Virginius to have.") But Virginius
stayed on. It could not have been much fun for him, and we said
later that Virginius should have known that such an arrangement
could not last. And then later than that we said, "Maybe he did
know." Because that was Virginius. You didn't know what he
was thinking at the time, any time. Old Anse and Young Anse
were like water. Dark water, maybe; but men could see what
they were about. But no man ever knew what Virginius was
thinking or doing until afterward. We didn't even know what
happened that time when Virginius, who had stuck it out alone
for ten years while Young Anse was away, was driven away at
last; he didn't tell it, not even to Granby Dodge, probably. But
we knew Old Anse and we knew Virginius, and we could imagine
it, about like this:

We watched Old Anse smoldering for about a year after Young
Anse took his mules and went back into the hills. Then one day
he broke out; maybe like this, "You think that, now your brother
is gone, you can just hang around and get it all, don't you?"

"I don't want it all," Virginius said. "I just want my share."

"Ah," Old Anse said. "You'd like to have it parceled out right
now too, would you? Claim like him it should have been divided
up when you and him came of age."

"I'd rather take a little of it and farm it right than to see it all
in the shape it's in now," Virginius said, still just, still mild—no

man in the county ever saw Virginius lose his temper or even get ruffled, not even when Anselm tried to fight him in the courtroom about that fine.

"You would, would you?" Old Anse said. "And me that's kept it working at all, paying the taxes on it, while you and your brother have been putting money by every year, tax-free."

"You know Anse never saved a nickel in his life," Virginius said. "Say what you want to about him, but don't accuse him of being forehanded."

"Yes, by heaven! He was man enough to come out and claim what he thought was his and get out when he never got it. But you. You'll just hang around, waiting for me to go, with that damned meal mouth of yours. Pay me the taxes on your half back to the day your mother died, and take it."

"No," Virginius said. "I won't do it."

"No," Old Anse said. "No. Oh, no. Why spend your money for half of it when you can set down and get all of it some day without putting out a cent." Then we imagined Old Anse (we thought of them as sitting down until now, talking like two civilized men) rising, with his shaggy head and his heavy eyebrows. "Get out of my house!" he said. But Virginius didn't move, didn't get up, watching his father. Old Anse came toward him, his hand raised. "Get. Get out of my house. By heaven, I'll . . ."

Virginius went, then. He didn't hurry, didn't run. He packed up his belongings (he would have more than Anse; quite a few little things) and went four or five miles away to live with a cousin, the son of a remote kinsman of his mother. The cousin lived alone, on a good farm too, though now eaten up with mortgages, since the cousin was no farmer either, being half a stock-trader and half a lay preacher—a small, sandy, nondescript man whom you would not remember a minute after you looked at his face and then away—and probably no better at either of these than at farming. Without haste Virginius left, with none of his brother's foolish and violent finality; for which, strange to say, we thought none the less of Young Anse for showing, possessing. In fact, we always looked at Virginius a little askance too; he was a little too much master of himself. For it is human nature to trust quickest those who cannot depend on themselves. We called

Virginius a deep one; we were not surprised when we learned
how he had used his savings to disencumber the cousin's farm.
And neither were we surprised when a year later we learned how
Old Anse had refused to pay the taxes on his land and how, two
days before the place would have gone delinquent, the sheriff received anonymously in the mail cash to the exact penny of the
Holland assessment. "Trust Virginius," we said, since we believed we knew that the money needed no name to it. The sheriff
had notified Old Anse.

"Put it up for sale and be damned," Old Anse said. "If they
think that all they have to do is set there waiting, the whole brood
and biling of them . . ."

The sheriff sent Young Anse word. "It's not my land," Young
Anse sent back.

The sheriff notified Virginius. Virginius came to town and
looked at the tax books himself. "I got all I can carry myself,
now," he said. "Of course, if he lets it go, I hope I can get it.
But I don't know. A good farm like that won't last long or go
cheap." And that was all. No anger, no astonishment, no regret.
But he was a deep one; we were not surprised when we learned
how the sheriff had received that package of money, with the
unsigned note: *Tax money for Anselm Holland farm. Send receipt to Anselm Holland, Senior*. "Trust Virginius," we said. We
thought about Virginius quite a lot during the next year, out there
in a strange house, farming strange land, watching the farm and
the house where he was born and that was rightfully his going to
ruin. For the old man was letting it go completely now: year by
year the good broad fields were going back to jungle and gully,
though still each January the sheriff received that anonymous
money in the mail and sent the receipt to Old Anse, because the
old man had stopped coming to town altogether now, and the
very house was falling down about his head, and nobody save
Virginius ever stopped there. Five or six times a year he would
ride up to the front porch, and the old man would come out and
bellow at him in savage and violent vituperation, Virginius taking
it quietly, talking to the few remaining negroes once he had seen
with his own eyes that his father was all right, then riding away
again. But nobody else ever stopped there, though now and then
from a distance some one would see the old man going about the

mournful and shaggy fields on the old white horse which was to kill him.

Then last summer we learned that he was digging up the graves in the cedar grove where five generations of his wife's people rested. A negro reported it, and the county health officer went out there and found the white horse tied in the grove, and the old man himself came out of the grove with a shotgun. The health officer returned, and two days later a deputy went out there and found the old man lying beside the horse, his foot fast in the stirrup, and on the horse's rump the savage marks of the stick— not a switch: a stick—where it had been struck again and again and again.

So they buried him, among the graves which he had violated. Virginius and the cousin came to the funeral. They were the funeral, in fact. For Anse, Junior, didn't come. Nor did he come near the place later, though Virginius stayed long enough to lock the house and pay the negroes off. But he too went back to the cousin's, and in due time Old Anse's will was offered for probate to Judge Dukinfield. The substance of the will was no secret; we all learned of it. Regular it was, and we were surprised neither at its regularity nor at its substance nor its wording: . . . *with the exception of these two bequests, I give and bequeath . . . my property to my elder son Virginius, provided it be proved to the satisfaction of the . . . Chancellor that it was the said Virginius who has been paying the taxes on my land, the . . . Chancellor to be the sole and unchallenged judge of the proof.*

The two other bequests were:

To my younger son Anselm I give . . . two full sets of mule harness, with the condition that this . . . harness be used by . . . Anselm to make one visit to my grave. Otherwise this . . . harness to become and remain part . . . of my property as described above.

To my cousin-in-law Granby Dodge I give . . . one dollar in cash, to be used by him for the purchase of a hymn book or hymn books, as a token of my gratitude for his having fed and lodged my son Virginius since . . . Virginius quitted my roof.

That was the will. And we watched and listened to hear or see what Young Anse would say or do. And we heard and saw nothing. And we watched to see what Virginius would do. And he did nothing. Or we didn't know what he was doing, what he was thinking. But that was Virginius. Because it was all finished then, anyway. All he had to do was to wait until Judge Dukinfield validated the will, then Virginius could give Anse his half—if he intended to do this. We were divided there. "He and Anse never had any trouble," some said. "Virginius never had any trouble with anybody," others said. "If you go by that token, he will have to divide that farm with the whole county." But it was Virginius that tried to pay Anse's fine that time," the first ones said. "And it was Virginius that sided with his father when Young Anse wanted to divide the land, too," the second ones said.

So we waited and we watched. We were watching Judge Dukinfield now; it was suddenly as if the whole thing had sifted into his hands; as though he sat godlike above the vindictive and jeering laughter of that old man who even underground would not die, and above these two irreconcilable brothers who for fifteen years had been the same as dead to each other. But we thought that in his last coup, Old Anse had overreached himself; that in choosing Judge Dukinfield, the old man's own fury had checkmated him; because in Judge Dukinfield we believed that Old Anse had chosen the one man among us with sufficient probity and honor and good sense—that sort of probity and honor which has never had time to become confused and self-doubting with too much learning in the law. The very fact that the validating of what was a simple enough document appeared to be taking him an overlong time, was to us but fresh proof that Judge Dukinfield was the one man among us who believed that justice is fifty per cent legal knowledge and fifty per cent unhaste and confidence in himself and in God.

So as the expiration of the legal period drew near, we watched Judge Dukinfield as he went daily between his home and his office in the courthouse yard. Deliberate and unhurried he moved—a widower of sixty and more, portly, white-headed, with an erect and dignified carriage which the negroes called "rear-backted." He had been appointed Chancellor seventeen years ago; he possessed little knowledge of the law and a great deal of hard common sense; and for thirteen years now no man had opposed him for re-election, and even those who would be most enraged by his air of bland and affable condescension voted for him on occasion with a kind of childlike confidence and trust. So we watched him without impatience, knowing that what he finally did would be right, not because he did it, but because he would not permit himself or any one else to do anything until it was right. So each morning we would see him cross the square at exactly ten minutes past eight o'clock and go on to the courthouse, where the negro janitor had preceded him by exactly ten minutes, with the clock-like precision with which the block signal presages the arrival of the train, to open the office for the day. The Judge would enter the office, and the negro would take his position in a wire-mended splint chair in the flagged passage which separated the office from the courthouse proper, where he would sit all day long and doze, as he had done for seventeen years. Then at five in the afternoon the negro would wake and enter the office and perhaps wake the Judge too, who had lived long enough to have learned that the onus of any business is usually in the hasty minds of those theoreticians who have no business of their own; and then we would watch them cross the square again in single file and go on up the street toward home, the two of them, eyes front and about fifteen feet apart, walking so erect that the two frock coats made by the same tailor and to the Judge's measure fell from the two pairs of shoulders in single boardlike planes, without intimation of waist or of hips.

Then one afternoon, a little after five o'clock, men began to run suddenly across the square, toward the courthouse. Other men saw them and ran too, their feet heavy on the paving, among the wagons and the cars, their voices tense, urgent, "What? What is it?" "Judge Dukinfield," the word went; and they ran on and entered the flagged passage between the courthouse and the office, where the old negro in his cast-off frock coat stood beating his hands on the air. They passed him and ran into the office. Behind the table the Judge sat, leaning a little back in his chair, quite comfortable. His eyes were open, and he had been shot neatly once through the bridge of the nose, so that he appeared to have three eyes in a row. It was a bullet, yet no man about the square that day, or the old negro who had sat all day long in the chair in the passage, had heard any sound.

It took Gavin Stevens a long time, that day—he and the little brass box. Because the Grand Jury could not tell at first what he was getting at—if any man in that room that day, the jury, the two brothers, the cousin, the old negro, could tell. So at last the Foreman asked him point blank:

"Is it your contention, Gavin, that there is a connection between Mr. Holland's will and Judge Dukinfield's murder?"

"Yes," the county attorney said. "And I'm going to contend more than that."

They watched him: the jury, the two brothers. The old negro and the cousin alone were not looking at him. In the last week the negro had apparently aged fifty years. He had assumed public office concurrently with the Judge; indeed, because of that fact, since he had served the Judge's family for longer than some of us could remember. He was older than the Judge, though until that afternoon a week ago he had looked forty years younger—a wizened figure, shapeless in the voluminous frock coat, who reached the office ten minutes ahead of the Judge and opened it and swept it and dusted the table without disturbing an object upon it, all with a skillful slovenliness that was fruit of seventeen years of practice, and then repaired to the wire-bound chair in the passage to sleep. He seemed to sleep, that is. (The only other way to reach the office was by means of the narrow private stair which led down from the courtroom, used only by the presiding judge during court term, who even then had to cross the passage and pass within eight feet of the negro's chair unless he followed the passage to where it made an L beneath the single window in the office, and climbed through that window.) For no man or woman had ever passed that chair without seeing the wrinkled eyelids of its occupant open instantaneously upon the brown, irisless eyes of extreme age. Now and then we would stop and talk to him, to hear his voice roll in rich mispronunciation of the orotund and meaningless legal phraseology which he had picked up unawares, as he might have disease germs, and which he reproduced with an ex-cathedra profundity that caused more than one of us to listen to the Judge himself with affectionate amusement. But for all that he was old; he forgot our names at times and confused us with one another; and, confusing our faces and our generations too, he waked sometimes from his light slumber to challenge callers who were not there, who had been dead for many years. But no one had ever been known to pass him unawares.

But the others in the room watched Stevens—the jury about the table, the two brothers sitting at opposite ends of the bench, with their dark, identical, aquiline faces, their arms folded in identical attitudes. "Are you contending that Judge Dukinfield's slayer is in this room?" the Foreman asked.

The county attorney looked at them, at the faces watching him. "I'm going to contend more than that," he said.

"Contend?" Anselm, the younger twin, said. He sat alone at his end of the bench, with the whole span of bench between him and the brother to whom he had not spoken in fifteen years, watching Stevens with a hard, furious, unwinking glare.

"Yes," Stevens said. He stood at the end of the table. He began to speak, looking at no one in particular, speaking in an easy, anecdotal tone, telling what we already knew, referring now and then to the other twin, Virginius, for corroboration. He told about Young Anse and his father. His tone was fair, pleasant. He seemed to be making a case for the living, telling about how Young Anse left home in anger, in natural anger at the manner in which his father was treating that land which had been his mother's and half of which was at the time rightfully his. His tone was quite just, specious, frank; if anything, a little partial to Anselm, Junior. That was it. Because of that seeming partiality, that seeming glozing, there began to emerge a picture of Young Anse that was damning him to something which we did not then know; damned him because of that very desire for justice and affection for his dead mother, warped by the violence which he had inherited from the very man who had wronged him. And the two brothers sitting there, with that space of friction-smooth plank between them, the younger watching Stevens with that leashed, violent glare, the elder as intently, but with a face unfathomable. Stevens now told how Young Anse left in anger, and how a year later Virginius, the quieter one, the calmer one, who had tried more than once to keep peace between them, was driven away in turn. And again he drew a specious, frank picture: of the brothers separated, not by the living father, but by what each had inherited from him; and drawn together, bred together, by that land which was not only rightfully theirs, but in which their mother's bones lay.

"So there they were, watching from a distance that good land going to ruin, the house in which they were born and their mother was born falling to pieces because of a crazed old man who attempted at the last, when he had driven them away and couldn't do anything else to them, to deprive them of it for good and all by letting it be sold for nonpayment of taxes. But somebody foiled him there, some one with foresight enough and self-control enough to keep his own counsel about what wasn't anybody else's business anyway so long as the taxes were paid. So then all they had to do was to wait until the old man died. He was old anyway and, even if he had been young, the waiting would not have been very hard for a self-controlled man, even if he did not know the contents of the old man's will. Though that waiting wouldn't have been so easy for a quick, violent man, especially if the violent man happened to know or suspect the substance of the will and was satisfied and, further, knew himself to have been irrevocably wronged; to have had citizenship and good name robbed through the agency of a man who had already despoiled him and had driven him out of the best years of his life among men, to live like a hermit in a hill cabin. A man like that would have neither the time nor the inclination to bother much with either waiting for something or not waiting for it."

They stared at him, the two brothers. They might have been carved in stone, save for Anselm's eyes. Stevens talked quietly, not looking at any one in particular. He had been county attorney for almost as long as Judge Dukinfield had been chancellor. He was a Harvard graduate: a loose-jointed man with a mop of untidy iron-gray hair, who could discuss Einstein with college professors and who spent whole afternoons among the squatting men against the walls of country stores, talking to them in their idiom. He called these his vacations.

"Then in time the father died, as any man who possessed self-control and foresight would have known. And his will was submitted for probate; and even folks way back in the hills heard what was in it, heard how at last that mistreated land would belong to its rightful owner. Or owners, since Anse Holland knows as well as we do that Virge would no more take more than his rightful half, will or no will, now than he would have when his father gave him the chance. Anse knows that because he knows that he would do the same thing—give Virge his half—if he were Virge. Because they were both born to Anselm Holland, but they were born to Cornelia Mardis too. But even if Anse didn't know, believe, that, he would know that the land which had been his mother's and in which her bones now lie would now be treated right. So maybe that night when he heard that his father was dead, maybe for the first time since Anse was a child, since before his mother died maybe and she would come upstairs at night and look into the room where he was asleep and go away; maybe for the first time since then, Anse slept. Because it was all vindicated then, you see: the outrage, the injustice, the lost good name, and the penitentiary stain—all gone now like a dream. To be forgotten now, because it was all right. By that time, you see, he had got used to being a hermit, to being alone; he could not have changed after that long. He was happier where he was, alone back there. And now to know that it was all past like a bad dream, and that the land, his mother's land, her heritage and her mausoleum, was now in the hands of the one man whom he could and would trust, even though they did not speak to each other. Don't you see?"

We watched him as we sat about the table which had not been disturbed since the day Judge Dukinfield died, upon which lay still the objects which had been, next to the pistol muzzle, his last sight on earth, and with which we were all familiar for years— the papers, the foul inkwell, the stubby pen to which the Judge clung, the small brass box which had been his superfluous paper weight. At their opposite ends of the wooden bench, the twin brothers watched Stevens, motionless, intent.

"No, we don't see," the Foreman said. "What are you getting at? What is the connection between all this and Judge Dukinfield's murder?"

"Here it is," Stevens said. "Judge Dukinfield was validating that will when he was killed. It was a queer will; but we all expected that of Mr. Holland. But it was all regular, the beneficiaries are all satisfied; we all know that half of that land is Anse's the minute he wants it. So the will is all right. Its probation should have been just a formality. Yet Judge Dukinfield had had it in abeyance for over two weeks when he died. And so that man who thought that all he had to do was to wait—"

"What man?" the Foreman said.

"Wait," Stevens said. "All that man had to do was to wait. But it wasn't the waiting that worried him, who had already waited fifteen years. That wasn't it. It was something else, which he learned (or remembered) when it was too late, which he should not have forgotten; because he is a shrewd man, a man of self-control and foresight; self-control enough to wait fifteen years for his chance, and foresight enough to have prepared for all the incalculables except one: his own memory. And when it was too late, he remembered that there was another man who would also know what he had forgotten about. And that other man who would know it was Judge Dukinfield. And that thing which he would also know was that that horse could not have killed Mr. Holland."

When his voice ceased there was no sound in the room. The jury sat quietly about the table, looking at Stevens. Anselm turned his leashed, furious face and looked once at his brother, then he looked at Stevens again, leaning a little forward now. Virginius had not moved; there was no change in his grave, intent expression. Between him and the wall the cousin sat. His hands lay on his lap and his head was bowed a little, as though he were in church. We knew of him only that he was some kind of an itinerant preacher, and that now and then he gathered up strings of scrubby horses and mules and took them somewhere and swapped or sold them. Because he was a man of infrequent speech who in his dealings with men betrayed such an excruciating shyness and lack of confidence that we pitied him, with that kind of pitying disgust you feel for a crippled worm, dreading even to put him to the agony of saying "yes" or "no" to a question. But we heard how on Sundays, in the pulpits of country churches, he became a different man, changed; his voice then timbrous and moving and assured out of all proportion to his nature and his size.

"Now, imagine the waiting," Stevens said, "with that man knowing what was going to happen before it had happened, knowing at last that the reason why nothing was happening, why that will had apparently gone into Judge Dukinfield's office and then dropped out of the world, out of the knowledge of man, was because he had forgotten something which he should not have forgotten. And that was that Judge Dukinfield also knew that Mr. Holland was not the man who beat that horse. He knew that Judge Dukinfield knew that the man who struck that horse with that stick so as to leave marks on its back was the man who killed Mr. Holland first and then hooked his foot in that stirrup and struck that horse with a stick to make it bolt. But the horse didn't bolt. The man knew beforehand that it would not; he had known for years that it would not, but he had forgotten that. Because while it was still a colt it had been beaten so severely once that ever since, even at the sight of a switch in the rider's hand, it would lie down on the ground, as Mr. Holland knew, and as all who were close to Mr. Holland's family knew. So it just lay down on top of Mr. Holland's body. But that was all right too, at first; that was just as well. That's what that man thought for the next week or so, lying in his bed at night and waiting, who had already waited fifteen years. Because even then, when it was too late and he realized that he had made a mistake, he had not even then remembered all that he should never have forgotten. Then he remembered that too, when it was too late, after the body had been found and the marks of the stick on the horse seen and remarked and it was too late to remove them. They were probably gone from the horse by then, anyway. But there was only one tool he could use to remove them from men's minds. Imagine him then, his terror, his outrage, his feeling of having been tricked by something beyond retaliation: that furious desire to turn time back for just one minute, to undo or to complete when it is too late. Because the last thing which he remembered when it was too late was that Mr. Holland had bought that horse from Judge Dukinfield, the man who was sitting here at this table, passing on the validity of a will giving away two thousand acres of some of the best land in the county. And he waited, since he had but one tool that would remove those stick marks, and nothing happened. And nothing happened, and he knew why. And he waited as long as he dared, until he believed that there was more at stake than a few roods and squares of earth. So what else could he do but what he did?"

His voice had hardly ceased before Anselm was speaking. His voice was harsh, abrupt. "You're wrong," he said.

As one, we looked at him where he sat forward on the bench, in his muddy boots and his worn overalls, glaring at Stevens; even Virginius turned and looked at him for an instant. The cousin and the old negro alone had not moved. They did not seem to be listening. "Where am I wrong?" Stevens said.

But Anselm did not answer. He glared at Stevens. "Will Virginius get the place in spite of . . . of . . ."

"In spite of what?" Stevens said.

"Whether he . . . that . . ."

"You mean your father? Whether he died or was murdered?"

"Yes," Anselm said.

"Yes. You and Virge get the land whether the will stands up or not, provided, of course, that Virge divides with you if it does. But the man that killed your father wasn't certain of that and he didn't dare to ask. Because he didn't want that. He wanted Virge to have it all. That's why he wants that will to stand."

"You're wrong," Anselm said, in that harsh, sudden tone. "I killed him. But it wasn't because of that damned farm. Now bring on your sheriff."

And now it was Stevens who, gazing steadily at Anselm's furious face, said quietly: "And I say that you are wrong, Anse."

For some time after that we who watched and listened dwelt in anti-climax, in a dreamlike state in which we seemed to know beforehand what was going to happen, aware at the same time that it didn't matter because we should soon wake. It was as though we were outside of time, watching events from outside; still outside of and beyond time since that first instant when we looked again at Anselm as though we had never seen him before. There was a sound, a slow, sighing sound, not loud; maybe of relief—something. Perhaps we were all thinking how Anse's nightmare must be really over at last; it was as though we too had rushed suddenly back to where he lay as a child in his bed, and the mother who they said was partial to him, whose heritage had been lost to him, and even the very resting place of her tragic and long quiet dust outraged, coming in to look at him for a moment before going away again. Far back down time that was, straight though it be. And straight though that corridor was, the boy who had lain unawares in that bed had got lost in it, as we all do, must, ever shall; that boy was as dead as any other of his blood in that violated cedar grove, and the man at whom we looked, we looked at across the irrevocable chasm, with pity perhaps, but not with mercy. So it took the sense of Stevens' words about as long to penetrate to us as it did to Anse; he had to repeat himself, "Now I say that you are wrong, Anse."

"What?" Anse said. Then he moved. He did not get up, yet somehow he seemed to lunge suddenly, violently. "You're a liar. You—"

"You're wrong, Anse. You didn't kill your father. The man who killed your father was the man who could plan and conceive to kill that old man who sat here behind this table every day, day after day, until an old negro would come in and wake him and tell him it was time to go home—a man who never did man, woman, or child aught but good as he believed that he and God saw it. It wasn't you that killed your father. You demanded of him what you believed was yours, and when he refused to give it, you left, went away, never spoke to him again. You heard how he was mistreating the place but you held your peace, because the land was just 'that damned farm.' You held your peace until you heard how a crazy man was digging up the graves where your mother's flesh and blood and your own was buried. Then, and then only, you came to him, to remonstrate. But you were never a man to remonstrate, and he was never a man to listen to it. So you found him there, in the grove, with the shotgun. I don't even expect you paid much attention to the shotgun. I reckon you just took it away from him and whipped him with your bare hands and left him there beside the horse; maybe you thought that he was dead. Then somebody happened to pass there after you were gone and found him; maybe that some one had been there all the time, watching. Somebody that wanted him dead too; not in anger and outrage, but by calculation. For profit, by a will, maybe. So he came there and he found what you had left and he finished it: hooked your father's foot in that stirrup and tried to beat that horse into bolting to make it look well, forgetting in his haste what he should not have forgot. But it wasn't you. Because you went back home, and when you heard what had been found, you said nothing. Because you thought something at the time which you did not even say to yourself. And when you heard what was in the will you believed that you knew. And you were glad then. Because you had lived alone until youth and wanting things were gone out of you; you just wanted to be quiet as you wanted your mother's dust to be quiet. And besides, what could land and position among men be to a man without citizenship, with a blemished name?"

We listened quietly while Stevens' voice died in that little room in which no air ever stirred, no draft ever blew because of its position, its natural lee beneath the courthouse wall.

"It wasn't you that killed your father or Judge Dukinfield either, Anse. Because if that man who killed your father had remembered in time that Judge Dukinfield once owned that horse, Judge Dukinfield would be alive to-day."

We breathed quietly, sitting about the table behind which Judge Dukinfield had been sitting when he looked up into the pistol. The table had not been disturbed. Upon it still lay the papers, the pens, the inkwell, the small, curiously chased brass box which his daughter had fetched him from Europe twelve years ago—for what purpose neither she nor the Judge knew, since it would have been suitable only for bath salts or tobacco, neither of which the Judge used—and which he had kept for a paper weight, that, too, superfluous where no draft ever blew. But he kept it there on the table, and all of us knew it, had watched him toy with it while he talked, opening the spring lid and watching it snap viciously shut at the slightest touch.

When I look back on it now, I can see that the rest of it should not have taken as long as it did. It seems to me now that we must have known all the time; I still seem to feel that kind of disgust without mercy which after all does the office of pity, as when you watch a soft worm impaled on a pin, when you feel that retching revulsion—would even use your naked palm in place of nothing at all, thinking, "Go on. Mash it. Smear it. Get it over with." But that was not Stevens' plan. Because he had a plan, and we realized afterward that, since he could not convict the man, the man himself would have to. And it was unfair, the way he did it; later we told him so. ("Ah," he said. "But isn't justice always unfair? Isn't it always composed of injustice and luck and platitude in unequal parts?")

But anyway we could not see yet what he was getting at as he began to speak again in that tone—easy, anecdotal, his hand resting now on the brass box. But men are moved so much by preconceptions. It is not realities, circumstances, that astonish us; it is the concussion of what we should have known, if we had only not been so busy believing what we discover later we had taken for the truth for no other reason than that we happened to be believing it at the moment. He was talking about smoking again, about how a man never really enjoys tobacco until he begins to believe that it is harmful to him, and how non-smokers miss one of the greatest pleasures in life for a man of sensibility: the knowledge that he is succumbing to a vice which can injure himself alone.

"Do you smoke, Anse?" he said.

"No," Anse said.

"You don't either, do you, Virge?"

"No," Virginius said. "None of us ever did—father or Anse or me. We heired it, I reckon."

"A family trait," Stevens said. "Is it in your mother's family too? Is it in your branch, Granby?"

The cousin looked at Stevens for less than a moment. Without moving he appeared to writhe slowly within his neat, shoddy suit. "No, sir. I never used it."

"Maybe because you are a preacher," Stevens said. The cousin didn't answer. He looked at Stevens again with his mild, still, hopelessly abashed face. "I've always smoked," Stevens said. "Ever since I finally recovered from being sick at it at the age of fourteen. That's a long time, long enough to have become finicky about tobacco. But most smokers are, despite the psychologists and the standardized tobacco. Or maybe it's just cigarettes that are standardized. Or maybe they are just standardized to laymen, non-smokers. Because I have noticed how non-smokers are apt to go off half cocked about tobacco, the same as the rest of us go off half cocked about what we do not ourselves use, are not familiar with, since man is led by his pre- (or mis-) conceptions. Because you take a man who sells tobacco even though he does not use it himself, who watches customer after customer tear open the pack and light the cigarette just across the counter from him. You ask him if all tobacco smells alike, if he cannot distinguish one kind from another by the smell. Or maybe it's the shape and color of the package it comes in; because even the psychologists have not yet told us just where seeing stops and smelling begins, or hearing stops and seeing begins. Any lawyer can tell you that."

Again the Foreman checked him. We had listened quietly enough, but I think we all felt that to keep the murderer confused was one thing, but that we, the jury, were another. "You should have done all this investigating before you called us together," the Foreman said. "Even if this be evidence, what good will it do without the body of the murderer be apprehended? Conjecture is all well enough—"

"All right," Stevens said. "Let me conjecture a little more, and if I don't seem to progress any, you tell me so, and I'll stop my way and do yours. And I expect that at first you are going to call this taking a right smart of liberty even with conjecture. But we found Judge Dukinfield dead, shot between the eyes, in this chair behind this table. That's not conjecture. And Uncle Job was sitting all day long in that chair in the passage, where any one who entered this room (unless he came down the private stair from the courtroom and climbed through the window) would have to pass within three feet of him. And no man that we know of has passed Uncle Job in that chair in seventeen years. That's not conjecture."

"Then what is your conjecture?"

But Stevens was talking about tobacco again, about smoking. "I stopped in West's drug store last week for some tobacco, and he told me about a man who was particular about his smoking also. While he was getting my tobacco from the case, he reached out a box of cigarettes and handed it to me. It was dusty, faded, like he had had it a long time, and he told me how a drummer had left two of them with him years ago. 'Ever smoke them?' he said. 'No,' I said. 'They must be city cigarettes.' Then he told me how he had sold the other package just that day. He said he was behind the counter, with the newspaper spread on it, sort of half reading the paper and half keeping the store while the clerk was gone to dinner. And he said he never heard or saw the man at all until he looked up and the man was just across the counter, so close that it made him jump. A smallish man in city clothes, West said, wanting a kind of cigarette that West had never heard of. 'I haven't got that kind,' West said. 'I don't carry them.' 'Why don't you carry them?' the man said. 'I have no sale for them,' West said. And he told about the man in his city clothes, with a face like a shaved wax doll, and eyes with a still way of looking and a voice with a still way of talking. Then West said he saw the man's eyes and he looked at his nostrils, and then he knew what was wrong. Because the man was full of dope right then. 'I don't have any calls for them,' West said. 'What am I trying to do now?' the man said. 'Trying to sell you fly-paper?' Then the man bought the other package of cigarettes and went out. And West said that he was mad and he was sweating too, like he wanted to vomit, he said. He said to me, 'If I had some devilment I was scared to do myself, you know what I'd do? I'd give that fellow about ten dollars and I'd tell him where the devilment was and tell him not to never speak to me again. When he went out, I felt just exactly like that. Like I was going to be sick.' "

Stevens looked about at us; he paused for a moment. We watched him. "He came here from somewhere in a car, a big roadster, that city man did. That city man that ran out of his own kind of tobacco." He paused again, and then he turned his head slowly and he looked at Virginius Holland. It seemed like a full minute that we watched them looking steadily at each other. "And a nigger told me that that big car was parked in Virginius Holland's barn the night before Judge Dukinfield was killed." And for another time we watched the two of them looking steadily at each other, with no change of expression on either face. Stevens spoke in a tone quiet, speculative, almost musing. "Some one tried to keep him from coming out here in that car, that big car that any one who saw it once would remember and recognize. Maybe that some one wanted to forbid him to come in it, threaten him. Only the man that Doctor West sold those cigarettes to wouldn't have stood for very much threatening."

"Meaning me, by 'some one,' " Virginius said. He did not move or turn away his steady stare from Stevens' face. But Anselm moved. He turned his head and he looked at his brother, once. It was quite quiet, yet when the cousin spoke we could not hear or understand him at once; he had spoken but one time since we entered the room and Stevens locked the door. His voice was faint; again and without moving he appeared to writhe faintly beneath his clothes. He spoke with that abashed faintness, that excruciating desire for effacement with which we were all familiar.

"That fellow you're speaking of, he come to see me," Dodge said. "Stopped to see me. He stopped at the house about dark that night and said he was hunting to buy up little-built horses to use for this—this game—"

"Polo?" Stevens said. The cousin had not looked at any one while he spoke; it was as though he were speaking to his slowly moving hands upon his lap.

"Yes, sir. Virginius was there. We talked about horses. Then the next morning he took his car and went on. I never had anything that suited him. I don't know where he come from nor where he went."

"Or who else he came to see," Stevens said. "Or what else he came to do. You can't say that."

Dodge didn't answer. It was not necessary, and again he had fled behind the shape of his effacement like a small and weak wild creature into a hole.

"That's my conjecture," Stevens said.

And then we should have known. It was there to be seen, bald as a naked hand. We should have felt it—the some one in that room who felt what Stevens had called that horror, that outrage, that furious desire to turn time back for a second, to unsay, to undo. But maybe the some one had not felt it yet, had not yet felt the blow, the impact, as for a second or two a man may be unaware that he has been shot. Because now it was Virge that spoke, abruptly, harshly, "How are you going to prove that?"

"Prove what, Virge?" Stevens said. Again they looked at each other, quiet, hard, like two boxers. Not swordsmen, but boxers; or at least with pistols. "Who it was who hired that gorilla, that thug, down here from Memphis? I don't have to prove that. He told that. On the way back to Memphis he ran down a child at Battenburg (he was still full of dope; likely he had taken another shot of it when he finished his job here), and they caught him and locked him up and when the dope began to wear off he told where he had been, whom he had been to see, sitting in the cell in the jail there, jerking and snarling, after they had taken the pistol with the silencer on it away from him."

"Ah," Virginius said. "That's nice. So all you've got to do is to prove that he was in this room that day. And how will you do that? Give that old nigger another dollar and let him remember again?"

But Stevens did not appear to be listening. He stood at the end of the table, between the two groups, and while he talked now he held the brass box in his hand, turning it, looking at it, talking in that easy, musing tone. "You all know the peculiar attribute which this room has. How no draft ever blows in it. How when there has been smoking here on a Saturday, say, the smoke will still be here on Monday morning when Uncle Job opens the door, lying against the baseboard there like a dog asleep, kind of. You've all seen that."

We were sitting a little forward now, like Anse, watching Stevens.

"Yes," the Foreman said. "We've seen that."

"Yes," Stevens said, still as though he were not listening, turning the closed box this way and that in his hand. "You asked me for my conjecture. Here it is. But it will take a conjecturing man to do it—a man who could walk up to a merchant standing behind his counter, reading a newspaper with one eye and the other eye on the door for customers, before the merchant knew he was there. A city man, who insisted on city cigarettes. So this man left that store and crossed to the courthouse and entered and went on upstairs, as any one might have done. Perhaps a dozen men saw him; perhaps twice that many did not look at him at all, since there are two places where a man does not look at faces: in the sanctuary of civil law, and in public lavatories. So he entered the courtroom and came down the private stair and into the passage, and saw Uncle Job asleep in his chair. So maybe he followed the passage and climbed through the window behind Judge Dukinfield's back. Or maybe he walked right past Uncle Job, coming up from behind, you see. And to pass within eight feet of a man asleep in a chair would not be very hard for a man who could walk up to a merchant leaning on the counter of his own store. Perhaps he even lighted the cigarette from the pack that West had sold him before even Judge Dukinfield knew that he was in the room. Or perhaps the Judge was asleep in his chair, as he sometimes was. So perhaps the man stood there and finished the cigarette and watched the smoke pour slowly across the table and bank up against the wall, thinking about the easy money, the easy hicks, before he even drew the pistol. And it made less noise than the striking of the match which lighted the cigarette, since he had guarded so against noise that he forgot about silence. And then he went back as he came, and the dozen men and the two dozen saw him and did not see him, and at five that afternoon Uncle Job came in to wake the Judge and tell him it was time to go home. Isn't that right, Uncle Job?"

The old negro looked up. "I looked after him, like I promised Mistis," he said. "And I worried with him, like I promised Mistis I would. And I come in here and I thought at first he was asleep, like he sometimes—"

"Wait," Stevens said. "You came in and you saw him in the chair, as always, and you noticed the smoke against the wall behind the table as you crossed the floor. Wasn't that what you told me?"

Sitting in his mended chair, the old negro began to cry. He looked like an old monkey, weakly crying black tears, brushing at his face with the back of a gnarled hand that shook with age, with something. "I come in here many's the time in the morning, to clean up. It would be laying there, that smoke, and him that never smoked a lick in his life coming in and sniffing with that high nose of hisn and saying, 'Well, Job, we sholy smoked out that corpus juris coon last night.' "

"No." Stevens said. "Tell about how the smoke was there behind that table that afternoon when you came to wake him to go home, when there hadn't anybody passed you all that day except Mr. Virge Holland yonder. And Mr. Virge don't smoke, and the Judge didn't smoke. But that smoke was there. Tell what you told me."

"It was there. And I thought that he was asleep like always, and I went to wake him up—"

"And this little box was sitting on the edge of the table where he had been handling it while he talked to Mr. Virge, and when you reached your hand to wake him—"

"Yes, sir. It jumped off the table and I thought that he was asleep—"

"The box jumped off the table. And it made a noise and you

wondered why that didn't wake the Judge, and you looked down at where the box was lying on the floor in the smoke, with the lid open, and you thought that it was broken. And so you reached your hand down to see, because the Judge liked it because Miss Emma had brought it back to him from across the water, even if he didn't need it for a paper weight in this office. So you closed the lid and set it on the table again. And then you found that the Judge was more than asleep."

He ceased. We breathed quietly, hearing ourselves breathe. Stevens seemed to watch his hand as it turned the box slowly this way and that. He had turned a little from the table in talking with the old negro, so that now he faced the bench rather than the jury, the table. "Uncle Job calls this a gold box. Which is as good a name as any. Better than most. Because all metal is about the same; it just happens that some folks want one kind more than another. But it all has certain general attributes, likenesses. One of them is, that whatever is shut up in a metal box will stay in it unchanged for a longer time than in a wooden or paper box. You can shut up smoke, for instance, in a metal box with a tight lid like this one, and even a week later it will still be there. And not only that, a chemist or a smoker or tobacco seller like Doctor West can tell what made the smoke, what kind of tobacco, particularly if it happens to be a strange brand, a kind not sold in Jefferson, and of which he just happened to have two packs and remembered who he sold one of them to."

We did not move. We just sat there and heard the man's urgent stumbling feet on the floor, then we saw him strike the box from Stevens' hand. But we were not particularly watching him, even then. Like him, we watched the box bounce into two pieces as the lid snapped off, and emit a fading vapor which dissolved sluggishly away. As one we leaned across the table and looked down upon the sandy and hopeless mediocrity of Granby Dodge's head as he knelt on the floor and flapped at the fading smoke with his hands.

"But I still don't . . ." Virginius said. We were outside now, in the courthouse yard, the five of us, blinking a little at one another as though we had just come out of a cave.

"You've got a will, haven't you?" Stevens said. Then Virginius stopped perfectly still, looking at Stevens.

"Oh," he said at last.

"One of those natural mutual deed-of-trust wills that any two business partners might execute," Stevens said. "You and Granby each the other's beneficiary and executor, for mutual protection of mutual holdings. That's natural. Likely Granby was the one who suggested it first, by telling you how he had made you his heir. So you'd better tear it up, yours, your copy. Make Anse your heir, if you have to have a will."

"He won't need to wait for that," Virginius said. "Half of that land is his."

"You just treat it right, as he knows you will," Stevens said. "Anse don't need any land."

"Yes," Virginius said. He looked away. "But I wish . . ."

"You just treat it right. He knows you'll do that."

"Yes," Virginius said. He looked at Stevens again. "Well, I reckon I . . . we both owe you . . ."

"More than you think," Stevens said. He spoke quite soberly. "Or to that horse. A week after your father died, Granby bought enough rat poison to kill three elephants, West told me. But after he remembered what he had forgotten about that horse, he was afraid to kill his rats before that will was settled. Because he is a man both shrewd and ignorant at the same time: a dangerous combination. Ignorant enough to believe that the law is something like dynamite: the slave of whoever puts his hand to it first, and even then a dangerous slave; and just shrewd enough to believe that people avail themselves of it, resort to it, only for personal ends. I found that out when he sent a negro to see me one day last summer, to find out if the way in which a man died could affect the probation of his will. And I knew who had sent the negro to me, and I knew that whatever information the negro took back to the man who sent him, that man had already made up his mind to disbelieve it, since I was a servant of the slave, the dynamite. So if that had been a normal horse, or Granby had remembered in time, you would be underground now. Granby might not be any better off than he is, but you would be dead."

"Oh," Virginius said, quietly, soberly. "I reckon I'm obliged."

"Yes," Stevens said. "You've incurred a right smart of obligation. You owe Granby something." Virginius looked at him.

"You owe him for those taxes he has been paying every year now for fifteen years."

"Oh," Virginius said. "Yes. I thought that father . . . Every November, about, Granby would borrow money from me, not much, and not ever the same amount. To buy stock with, he said. He paid some of it back. But he still owes me . . . no. I owe him now." He was quite grave, quite sober. "When a man starts doing wrong, it's not what he does; it's what he leaves."

"But it's what he does that people will have to hurt him for, the outsiders. Because the folks that'll be hurt by what he leaves won't hurt him. So it's a good thing for the rest of us that what he does takes him out of their hands. I have taken him out of your hands now, Virge, blood or no blood. Do you understand?"

"I understand," Virginius said. "I wouldn't anyway . . ." Then suddenly he looked at Stevens. "Gavin," he said.

"What?" Stevens said.

Virginius watched him. "You talked a right smart in yonder about chemistry and such, about that smoke. I reckon I believed some of it and I reckon I didn't believe some of it. And I reckon if I told you which I believed and didn't believe, you'd laugh at me." His face was quite sober. Stevens' face was quite grave too. Yet there was something in Stevens' eyes, his glance; something quick and eager; not ridiculing, either. "That was a week ago. If you had opened that box to see if that smoke was still in there, it would have got out. And if there hadn't been any smoke in that box, Granby wouldn't have given himself away. And that was a week ago. How did you know there was going to be any smoke in that box?"

"I didn't," Stevens said. He said it quickly, brightly, cheerfully, almost happily, almost beaming. "I didn't. I waited as long as I could before I put the smoke in there. Just before you all came into the room, I filled that box full of pipe smoke and shut it up. But I didn't know. I was a lot scareder than Granby Dodge. But it was all right. That smoke stayed in that box almost an hour."

NAPOLEON'S HAT UNDER GLASS [1]

By MANUEL KOMROFF

(From *Story*)

IN the gorgeous palace of Fontainebleau, just outside of Paris, on an embroidered silk cushion in a glass case, rests Napoleon's hat. This is the very hat he wore when, returning from Elba, he saluted his gathering army . . . the army that he led into the field of Waterloo. But all this was many years ago, over a hundred years ago, guides say when they conduct the large parties of visitors through the palace.

And before this glass case with its showpiece of history now stood a newly-married peasant couple from the country. She was a rosy-cheeked farmer's daughter and he was the son of a farmer in southern France. This was their honeymoon.

They stood before the glass case. She fingered her colored ribbons and he stared at the black felt hat in the case. Their red faces and big red hands were reflected in the glass. Their bodies seemed to sway just as they had swayed that very week when the village priest stood before them and recited the marriage vows.

"He was the greatest man in the world," she said.

"Yes, he was a great man. He was Emperor of almost the whole world."

"May his soul rest in peace."

"It must be a hard job to be an Emperor. I don't think I should like it. Too many papers and documents to read, and everything is . . . like in the fall of the year when we have to close ourselves in the house and the leaves become crisp and brittle. It don't seem natural to be an Emperor, does it?"

"Sure not, Emil. It must be very hard. But I think you could do anything you wanted to do. Nobody dreamed you would have the chicken house finished this summer, especially

134

with all the trouble we had with the old wine barrels that leaked and the bugs on the vegetables. But an Emperor don't have to read many papers. They tell him what it says and all he must do is to sign his name. And you can do that, can't you, Emil?"

"Sure."

"But it would be harder for me, Emil. This would be a nice place to live. But the servants would be watching you all day long. I would hate to have strange people watching me; but if you were the Emperor I would just have to do it and say nothing."

"Do what, Marie?"

"Oh, just do everything. Watch the kitchen to see that the rascals did not steal and do the things that ladies do, like making up the beds and sewing up new dresses and taking care of the house."

"It must be a hard job to be an Emperor. I don't think I should like it."

"If you wanted to be, I am sure you could be anything you like. You are so strong—and I love you so much."

At length they moved away from the glass case containing Napoleon's hat, and walked out into the gardens. Here they ate their lunch and looked into each other's eyes.

After a long silence she looked up and said: "You know, Emil, we should go back to the Palace before it closes and see the hat again."

"Poor Napoleon," Emil said.

"Yes. It is so sad. He was once Emperor of the whole world, almost, and now he is dead."

They walked back to have another look at the hat. And in the morning, under the pretext that it was on the way to the station, they went again and had a last gaze at Napoleon's hat under glass.

On the train she sighed: "It was a wonderful honeymoon, wasn't it, Emil?"

"Sure."

Then she whispered in his ear. "I love you, Emil."

He sat up straight and held her red hand. "I—thought maybe you loved Napoleon."

"Oh, yes, but that is different, Emil."

"How different?"

"Well, he is dead and I feel so sorry for him—it is so sad. He was such a great man and it is such a hard job to be an Emperor. You said yourself it was—you know you did."

"Yes, I said so, Marie, but I was thinking of myself and not Napoleon. It was easy for him because he always . . . well, he was all the time doing something big . . . he was a general. It is easy for a general to do all kinds of things."

"He was very brave and that is why . . ."

"That's why you love him."

"I love you too, Emil. I want you to be a great man and have people save your hat and . . . but not to be the Emperor."

Emil was jealous of Napoleon. He kept looking out of the train window watching the green fields and the long rows of tall poplars.

In the evening they were back on the farm. The fragrance of the green shrubbery and the loose damp earth filled their nostrils. In places the grass had grown during their absence. Here was a chance for a second harvest and they lost no time in removing their holiday clothes and getting back into their large comfortable wooden shoes. The shoes that have stamped down the fields of France for centuries. There was only an hour or two before sundown.

At night as they lay in bed breathing heavily, she whispered: "Oh, Emil, it is so good to be home again."

He pressed her hand.

"It must be hard to live in a palace," she added.

Again he pressed her hand.

"And so sad."

"You are thinking of the dead Emperor's hat!" He let go her hand.

"No, Emil, I was thinking, only foolishness. I love you, Emil." She put her arms about him and he kissed her eyes and fleshy cheeks and her moist red mouth—moist with the dew of the earth.

And Napoleon never came between them again. Only once did he again appear before them. This happened about a year later when Emil became the proud father of a baby boy.

"He is a prize baby," said the father.

And she tickled the child under the chin and added: "We will put him on exhibition . . . under glass."

Then they went through all the names of the ancient kings and Emperors that they could recall, but to their rural ears, each sounded foreign and sad.

The grapes were ripe and there was much work to be done around the place, but at odd moments they deliberated and often thought of Napoleon's hat in the show case. But in the end they named their little son John.

SPRING STORY [1]

By MERIDEL LESUEUR

(From *Scribner's Magazine*)

SHE opened her eyes and knew it was Easter morning. The white-lawn curtains blew out and in the half-open window as if signalling to some one outside. The air blew in upon her, cold, but with a strange fertile promise in it. She had been lying a long time, listening to the wind and the morning sounds outside. Her mother had called up the stairs many times. She was calling again.

"Eunice, aren't you going to get up at all? You must go with the boys to nine o'clock mass."

Eunice did not answer, but lay still, listening to the wind, pretending sleep. That freshening air seemed to blow right through the house. Her youngest brother had been shouting and running in and out all the morning, leaving the doors open. It was funny how suddenly, from the very sound of the voices, one knew that it was no longer winter. As she lay half dreaming she heard the laughter and the shouts of children on the street outside and behind the house. The voices seemed bright and shaken out. A milk-cart went by and the jingling of the horses' hoofs and the sound of the wheels had a new sound too, a loose, gay sound. In winter everything seemed muffled, sounds were frozen, but now outside they began to flow again, awaken and rouse and blow in her window with the strong sweet wind.

She sprang out of bed, the gusts of wind on her body, ran to the dresser and turned it about, moving the mirror downward at an angle. Now she could see herself lying in bed with her thin gold hair on the pillow, and her frail face smiling. She lay looking at herself, half entranced, while her mother called at the foot of the stairs, the voice sounding nearer than it did from the kitchen but still far away to the dreaming girl. "Eunice, I'm not going to keep those cakes warm another minute. It's eight o'clock!" The mother's voice, though near, sounded from another world. But in a few moments the girl got up, watching herself move in the mirror, as if in this way doubling her pleasure in her manner of being. She wandered about the room, touching her things that lay about; she leaned close to the mirror and lifted the fine hair from her forehead, gazing for a long time at her face. Sitting on the bed she began to slowly pull her stockings on, stopping to look at her feet, then to see her own face again, far away and lovely, in the slanting mirror.

Lying, walking, sitting in this room, she felt herself ripening and coloring. It was as if she felt upon herself, as upon the world outside, the blowing of a nourishing wind from some unseen space. She hung on a strange tree and day by day felt herself ripening and rounding in her flesh. This morning the wind blowing in the window seemed freighted, not only with the promise of the physical spring of the world, but with other promises for herself, blowing in upon her the dream of her future, the scent of unripe meanings which would one day mature.

Looking at her hands and feet they seemed to be shining with the vision of the things to be touched and the ways to be trod. "I will not close the window," she said to herself without voice, her lips moving, although she could not have told if she had spoken or not. "No, I will not close the window. Something will come in, something is sure to come in if I have the courage to leave it open. I am sure not to miss life then."

The cold air blew in silently. The white curtains waved, blowing out and then in, sudden gusts blowing with the wind upon her. Straight out the window she could see the great elm rising from the back yard. The top limbs looked as if they had begun to break open. They looked as if an excitement were upon the branches; a faint aura of reddish brown seemed to surround the tree. You really could not see the buds at all, but could only sense this excitement and the red irritation of the spiked branches. She could only see the top antlers rearing against the pale-blue sky. At that instant the sun came out in a faint shower of golden light that seemed to shatter down in a crystal rain upon the still-frozen earth. She ran to the window and put her bare arms in the light. They looked white with the little reddish hairs alight in the sun. Perhaps she too was going to burst into leaf and bloom. She laughed to think so and leaned out the window, the wind striking her, the curtains blowing about her in a confusion.

From below in the alley came up the sharp gay banter of young boys, excited like sparrows with the air and light. She could see them scrambling over the old fences, digging the last of the black snow up from the corners to throw at each other.

Then her uncle came up out of the cellar as if from the earth itself. He had a shovel and a rake.

"You've forgotten your coat," she shouted down at him, feeling she had to shout against the strong wind and the shattering light. "You've forgotten your coat," she sang out, feeling happy to cry out into the air like that. Startled, he looked up into the tree as if a blackbird had shouted at him. Eunice laughed, shaking her loose hair. "Here I am in the window, Uncle Joe."

He turned his face upward to her, so he looked like a gnome, half his size. "What if I have? What if I have?" he mumbled, half smiling. She saw that he was pleased with her.

"What are you going to do? Working on Sunday?" she shouted down, laughing.

"I'm going to uncover these canna bulbs so they'll get a sniff of this air and some warmth in them." He went with his shovel and rake to the corner of the house and began raking where the canna-bed had been the summer before. The girl, looking down on him, had, for an instant, a sharp picture of the dark leaves of the cannas standing there, amidst them the rising fold of scarlet, leaping in a twist of flame. The last year she had felt them as a rich, a troubling thing, as she had run past them in the dusk. Then the flames had withered and the rich stuff of the leaves had dried. Now, after a certain time, there they would be again, standing still and secret at the corner of the house for her to pass, a rich dark presence from another world. This year they would mark for her a different time. This she knew. No longer would she run past them in young play. These red flames would burn in a different time for her, stand up, marking a time that would be stranger and disquieting.

The uncle raking back and forth was a sharp figure in the morning and held for her some enchantment of meaning. For he was uncovering a plant that would grow up in a new time for her.

She watched him raking back and forth, his stooped back, his whole figure swinging to the rhythm of the raking. His body seemed to have grown to a curve, with a pull to its lines that had come from the many seeds he had uncovered in his time, the hoeing and the raking. This uncle had just come from a farm in Iowa the past year after Aunt Emma had died and his heart had got so bad the family thought it unsafe to leave him alone, so isolated. Now they passed him around from house to house among the uncles and aunts, and he did odd jobs like this. Eunice looked at him thinking his life was over; behind him and before him was only death. Still he came out to give the first life to the cannas.

He kept raking back and forth as she leaned out of the window watching. He had on a blue shirt and a small black cap. His figure was unlike the figures of the other men of her family. It was short and stocky, despite its age, with a vigor unknown to her before, with black hair on his square wrists and on his neck where he opened his shirt a bit. He had a strong odor of tobacco about him, almost overpowering, which she associated somehow with his strength, with his long past on the farm with horses and wheat and with the silent Aunt Emma, who was like some powerful wild grass herself. He moved in a way unknown to her. Not like her father and her uncles who lived in the city. He moved as if the meaning of his life were in his body and not in anything else, as if the pleasure too were there. So it was a satisfaction to her to be near him or to watch him working as she was watching him now as she leaned out of the upper window.

He raked back and forth, stooped and picked up the débris of winter, which was black and slimy, lifted it and put it in an old tub he had standing beside him. He uncovered the earth, which then looked as delicate as skin when the bandage has been removed, and there were the white blades of grass and the naked sprouts of the canna bulbs.

He turned his face toward her with pleasure. "Here they are. You can't fool them even under this rubbish. You can bet your boots they know when it's spring."

"How do they?" she called. He looked up at her again and his blue eyes looked blind. He did not answer her question. She felt awkward, as she often did around him when she had been foolish. He stooped again and picked up more of the slimy débris, dropping it into the tub. Above him the black elm was budding.

The wind blew off his black cap, exposing his close-cropped round head. He ran after the cap and put it tightly on his head, and came back to the canna-bed, leaning again over the dark earth, his short, strong body bent over it. The young girl leaned over too, looking down at the black earth he was uncovering. Still the wind blew fresh with something in the odor of it. The stocky man below went back and forth with the decay of winter, bending, lifting the dead stuff, raking again, uncovering the mist of green rising out of the earth.

"What time is it, uncle?" Eunice finally asked. He straightened and took a large gold watch out of the small pocket of his trousers. "It's quarter after eight. You've missed them pancakes with honey your mother give us for breakfast. I ate a lot of them."

"Say!" Jim, the brother next to her in age, came out of the kitchen door. He had just put on his shirt and was buttoning it. His face shone, newly washed. "You better hurry, Eunice. I been up since seven." He was pale in the bright light. "Jim," the mother called, "come out of that cold. And right after your bath, too." Jim went inside, banging the kitchen door.

Eunice turned back to her room, now dark to her dazzled eyes. She slammed the window down. The room seemed close and stifling, and she hurried, glad to be gone from it.

The way to the cathedral where the children were going led through a park whose winding paths went among the tall, upstanding trees. "Like black candles, they look," Eunice said to herself, walking between her brothers. Through the black maze of trees one could see the people hurrying, men and women with their children, groups of boys loitering, feeding the many squirrels that frisked greedily from the branches in spring hunger. Snow lay in the crotches of the trees yet and lay too at the bases. In places they had to step over little rivulets that ran over the walks. Men were taking up the board runway that had run from the warming-house down to the lake for skaters. Soon the ducks and swans would be upon the water. Pigeons came strutting down the walk with them, singing in their arched throats. From high among the budding branches came the sharp conversation of sparrows. Her brothers as they passed the croquet grounds were talking of spring sports, baseball, tennis. Eunice walked amidst her own thoughts and heard them as she now heard all the talk of her family, as something that went on at a distance.

This year she wouldn't play ball or run in the park at dusk with the gang like a wild Indian. This year she would put on a good dress after supper and walk delicately along the paths, with the boys in awe and amazement at the sudden beauty of her ways. She felt a new mode of life, a new way of being. "Jim, I don't see why you wear that crazy hat." His sallow face under the upturned collegiate hat annoyed her. "Well, you know what you can do," he said, for he felt the hat exactly right, going well with his own immediate idea of himself. The answer seemed so rude she thought she would cry, but she began looking at Johnny, who went beside them erratically, kicking an old tobacco-can. He would not stop it and only grinned at her.

They rose over a hillock and saw the towers of the church with pointed caps like two witches. Up a flight of stairs, from every street, the people were hurrying into the black spaces of the three dark doors. The bell was ringing from the bell-towers that rose amidst the sunlight. The fresh strong wind kept the trees blowing in a wild movement and seemed to have something to do with the gaiety and excitement of the many people hurrying to church. The three children walked faster, fearful lest they be late and have to attract attention. They half ran up the steps, slowed down at the doors, and entered with the hurrying people, hastily crossing themselves at the inner doors with the holy water from the font. They paused before the darkness of the interior, which came upon them softly after the wind and the light outdoors. Far down at the altar two little boys, moving in strict unison, were lighting the candles for the mass. The three children walked together down the central aisle, feeling they were being watched, and after a hasty bob by way of a genuflection, they slid one by one into a wooden pew and onto their knees.

Amidst her prayers, which she knew by heart and said without thinking, Eunice looked at the altars decorated with lilies and ferns. There was a smell of burning wax and of the incense from the last mass which still floated above them in the vaulting ribs and buttresses. The priest came, his black garments rocking about him. He was a slim old man, with a face looking as if it had been carved out of old wood like the statues of Saint Joseph and Gabriel on the side altars. He began the mass in a low humming voice. The little boys came, with the incense, the gong, moving in awkward youngness, their slim necks protruding from the white yokes, their big young feet swinging beneath their black robes. It gave Eunice a stab of pain watching them. They made her feel so much a girl.

The meaning of the mass she made up mysteriously herself. It made her sit in the trance of her own destiny, feeling through the ritual some hint of meaning that was never wholly graspable. The organ sounds came from behind them and fell and rose through the spaces; the choir of young boys sang in a high pitch. Their voices were strangely moving to the young girl. Hearing them, she had again a sharp knowingness that she would be a woman; something in the single, plaintive young male voices made her feel in her every fibre her own femininity. She could imagine their open mouths, their blank young faces, their earnest necks stretched upward, while out of their young throats came this high, plaintive singing, so effortless, so pure.

In the midst of her own dreaming she saw the thin white body ahead, hanging from the cross. Behind the flickering red candles in the dim recess stood that woman, His mother, amidst her draperies, that benign head drooping, looking down. Seeing the figure, she knew herself to be a woman too. Tears came to her eyes. The wooden altar in the apse of the dim church, the quaint figures looking outward with their pigmied human pathos, with so gentle a human grace, seen through her tears, filled her with a strange, a tumultuous compassion. There seemed to be sorrow in the world; the saints on the altars stood like any human men gentle from sorrow; the woman standing above the body of the prone man dead in anguish; the ways of the cross with the small tortured figures; and the priest proceeding about the mass, his tall, thin body, a line of tenuous sorrow, with a gentle droop lifting with effort upon itself the gray, lovely head.

The bells were ringing. Incense rose with the rising gray pillars, and above all, as if from a tree-top, fell that high-song of the boy choir, the single sustained pure note coming from the delicately upstanding throats of young boys. The many male voices all sounding together so sharp and clear made the girl feel confused and heavy. Looking at the back of the seat in front of her, she felt again that heavy knowledge of being a woman. The nearest she could get to the pain of such knowing was the vision of her mother, frail and sad and somehow defeated. To be a man was to be single and pure and unbroken. To be a woman was to be broken by an obscure defeat and mysteriously mellowed.

The ritual of the mass went on far down before her, as if the participating figures were so minute she might hold them in the palm of her hand, or as if the whole movement were going on within her.

And in all these symbols she felt vaguely a meaning of herself and what she would become and of a knowledge dimly awaiting her. Some faint knowingness of herself moved in her as the mass was enacted before her with its revealing of an inner altar, with all its intricate and provocative gestures of revealment. She too might turn at any moment and with as single a gesture as the priest made opening the great book before him—revealing the sacrament, taking from its inner place the chalice—with so simple a movement she too might open a space in whose depths lay the seed of her being. In this tension of suspense she watched the giving of the sacrament.

To her surprise it was all soon over, the moment had passed. She saw her brothers sitting beside her. The congregation wavered from the hard form into which the mass had seemed to mould them; it now broke, and moved. The two boys marched in again to the altar and snuffed out the candles. People were hurrying down the aisles to their Sunday dinners. Jim and Johnny wanted to be gone. The girl felt unhappy, baffled, but she rose and went with the scattering crowd out into the wind.

Outside the light seemed pale and wan upon the chill air. They hurried along buttoning their collars. Johnny found his tobacco-can, which he had hidden under some snow, and began kicking it home.

When they saw their own red brick house, Eunice dreaded the Sunday meal. Their dog came running out of the yard to meet

them. Jim pushed the animal away and went on ahead alone.
Eunice stooped to pat the beast but his affection palled her. He
wagged all over, his red tongue hanging out in an agony of gratitude for her attention. She could not stand it, having him all
over her like that. "Go 'way," she said. "Go 'way, Spud."
Johnny went around the corner of the house still kicking his tobacco-can, and the dog followed, turning his little doggish eyes
back upon her in reproof and sadness.

Going into the front door, she felt almost a fear that some one
would stop her before she got to her room. There was her father
calling out from the front room, where she knew he would be
sitting without any collar on, reading the Sunday papers, "Hello,
want the funny paper?" he called. She stopped tragically on the
stairs. "Ye gods," she murmured, closing her eyes dramatically,
"the funny paper!" Out loud she shouted crossly, "No, I don't,"
and ran up the stairs making a clatter.

In her room she flung herself on the unmade bed and lay like
an animal in ambush listening to the sounds downstairs. Johnny
was now batting the can around the back yard. She could hear
him. There was the incessant rattle of the many Sunday papers,
and the voice of her father sometimes reading the scandal or the
news out loud so her mother going from the kitchen to the dining-
room might hear snatches of it at least. As she feared, she heard
her mother ask where she was; then the tired, slow tread ascend-
ing the stairs. She flung herself against the wall, her back to the
door she knew her mother would open in a moment.

When she heard the familiar woman behind her she could see
with her eyes closed the face and figure of this woman, and she
was glad she had come into the room. If she might turn and ask
the older woman some question. But she did not know what the
question would be, and she had a feeling her mother would not
be able to answer it even if she found herself able to ask. "She
must have looked like me when she was young," Eunice often
thought. "What has happened?" Lying on the bed, the bewildered mother standing in the room behind her, the girl saw
every feature of the woman—her delicate body worn thin, her
slender neck, her face, once whittled to its delicacy by many
hopes, now gone into a tension of bewilderment and fatigue.
Something was marked there clearly. This marking signalled a

warning to the young girl, signalled some blight that had fallen on a dream her mother once had had. The imminence of a like blight haunted her.

The smell of pork roast came up the stairs through the door the mother had left open behind her. "Eunice, are you ill? What is it? Aren't you coming down to dinner? You haven't felt well all morning, have you?" she was asking, hovering over her in her delicate bewilderment.

"I'm all right. Please go away." She felt her mother pause, leaning over. "Oh, mother," she said to herself, wishing the mother of her own accord would say something to her. She felt the thin hand on her head: "You don't seem to have a fever." Eunice flung herself to a sitting position: "Of course I haven't. I suppose I've got to go down to dinner." She felt hunger with the strong warm odor of the pork coming up the stairs. Fixing her untidy hair at the mirror, she saw her mother reflected there too as she stood in the small space of the room, the worn hands under her apron, her flushed, worried face peering at her daughter in the little mirror into which they both were looking.

But nothing was said. Eunice followed her down the stairs, watching the familiar body, with its slight, dejected droop, go ahead.

"Well," said her father at the dinner table as he put a slice of roast on each plate, and they all knew by the tone of his voice that one of his jokes was coming. "So you don't read the funny paper any more, Eunice? She must be growing up, mother." He related—grinning palely, for he knew really how much he was hurting her—how he had been willing to share the funnies with her and she had shouted out to him, "like a fine lady," that she did not want them. Eunice looked down at her plate, feeling her cheeks flush.

Her mother changed the subject, speaking to Johnny: "Your cheeks are red as a beet, child; you must have been playing hard." Eunice saw the round face opposite her, his full apple cheeks chapped and reddened, his hair shaggy just as the wind had blown it. Uncle Joe, sitting alongside, looked at the boy affectionately, as if there was something between them.

"Let's go to the park, Johnny, and the keeper will take us over to the island and show us the duck eggs he is hatching," he said to the boy shyly, conscious of the others. "That'll be fun," the boy said, hacking his meat. Before she thought, Eunice was asking: "Can I go too, Uncle Joe?" "You stay home, Eunice," Johnny said, for he no longer liked her as well as he did. She had changed. "All right," the girl said quickly, ashamed and afraid lest her father tease her again, "I've got a date anyway."

But she had no "date." After the dishes were done she prepared to leave the house. She passed the door into the living-room and saw her father sitting by the window smoking. Her mother was sitting in her rocker looking almost as if she did not live there at all, but was a stranger who had come on a very long journey and was tired.

"Good-by, mother," Eunice paused in the door, "I'm going for a little walk." She hated to see her mother sitting there all afternoon like a stranger in the house. The mother looked up with her quick, startled eyes at the sound of her daughter's voice.

"All right, dear," she said, lowering the book she held. "Are you going with the bunch?"

"No, I don't know where they are. I just thought I'd go alone," Eunice said, feeling again that queer desire to cry.

"Oh," her mother said, raising her book.

Eunice still stood in the doorway looking into the littered room where sat her father and mother. Conscious of her there, the mother laid her book down on the floor and got up. Eunice started toward the outside door, saying hopelessly: "Well, good-by." And the woman followed her with that baffled air of indecision she so often had about her. At the door the two stood close together for a moment. "My, it's a fine day," the mother said, not looking at the day at all but smelling the fragrance of the close presence of her daughter.

"Yes, it is," Eunice said, not attending to the day, her eyes gone blind to the outside light as she stood so near her mother.

The girl turned suddenly and put her arms around the older woman, who stood awkwardly in the young embrace, not knowing what to think. Eunice let her go and ran down the walk to the street.

"You better wear your heavier coat, Eunice. There's a right chill wind blowing."

"No," called the girl, turning as she half ran and seeing the slight woman in the door of the shabby house, so that, walking along, she began to cry.

On the street she was afraid she might meet some one, so she stopped crying. The park was still deserted. She felt romantic and melancholy walking along under the tall, vaulting trees, but she met no one, so she soon lost interest in the feeling. She thought she would go to Fourth Street, where there were shops, and where the gang often "hung out." She would buy a chocolate bar, she thought, making sure she had a nickel in her pocket.

Coming onto the street she began to walk in an agony of self-consciousness, wondering whom she would meet. She saw ahead of her, at the corner of the cigar-store, a group of boys. She saw them become conscious of her as she was still in the next block. They turned, still talking and laughing, but with half an eye upon her approaching. She didn't know how she should carry herself, how she should walk approaching them. She felt herself superior and yet vulnerable. It was a confusing way to feel. As she came near, the boys stopped talking and stood watching her cross the street. She felt in an agony lest she slip on the melting snow, or perhaps her skirt was hanging in some way below her coat. Some of the boys in the group she knew at school.

"Hello, Red," she said in a mincing voice and they all took off their hats. At last she got by and into the drugstore. Inside she bought her candy.

One of the boys followed her. He leaned against the soda-fountain and talked to the clerk, wise-cracking for her to hear. She went over and began looking at a magazine. She felt the boy looking at her and she wished she had not come, yet she felt too that she was glad to be there.

She had not enough money to buy a magazine, so she was afraid to stand there looking at it too long. She feared that if she went toward the door the boy might open it for her. But she could stay no longer, so opening her candy bar she went to the door, feeling the boys turn to watch her walking. The boy did not offer to open the door. She went out and passed the window, seeing the two boys laughing inside, their grinning faces so young and so disordered.

Should she speak again to Red? She had decided against it when she found herself looking straight into his eyes and saying

again in that queer high voice that disgusted her, "Hello, Red,"
and seeing all the boys raise their hats at once, so comically. She
felt then like running as fast as she could. She felt almost as if
she were running swiftly, and was afraid she was, but she knew
she was walking quite slowly really, peeling the tinsel from the
chocolate.

After she had turned the corner out of sight of the group, she
felt depressed and would have liked to go back again. She went
on toward the park feeling lonely, wishing some of them might
follow her, imagining what might be said to a young man.

She sat down on a bench, watching uneasily the streets which
led into the park, thinking perhaps one of them would come.
Strolling couples came around the curve of the lake, stopped and
took each other's pictures, taking off their winter coats boldly.
She thought them common, holding each other's hands, kissing
so secretly behind the bare lilac-bush where she could see them
quite plainly.

Uneasy was her afternoon. She thought she would go back
for another candy bar but had not the nerve.

The young boys frolicked around the lake like monkeys, seeming quite mad in the spring wind, climbing trees, digging in the
mud, shouting at each other, fighting, screaming, calling half
around the lake, running to the cold water to get their feet wet,
shoes and all. Last year she had climbed that elm slanting out
over the lake. She remembered the thrill of sitting there between
the sky and water, her lean young self, like these boys, shouting
and singing.

The cold was getting into her limbs. The sun hung low behind
the trees, a pale, shaggy, round ball. The heat was all gone and
only the wind blew. She wondered where she could go, sitting
miserably on the cold bench while the dusk gathered in the dark
trees and the last couples and the last children went away. Far
around the lake, on their way home, she could hear two young
boys calling to each other.

Above her in the dusk arched the darkening trees. Occasionally a man passed along the walk behind her and she went tense
listening to his steps. Once a dark figure stopped uncertainly
and she heard him say something to her. She sat rigid, looking
blindly out over the lake until he had gone on. She became afraid

after that and got up and from habit went toward her home.

She saw the lights in the windows of her house. Some one turned the light off in the front room, so she knew they must all be in the dining-room. They would have cold-pork sandwiches.

Instead of turning into the house, she went on past it. She imagined that she did not live there. She went straight on in the uncertain dusk ahead.

Turning the corner out of sight of the house she trembled in excitement. It was as if she had disappeared from her familiar world. She might go on, making the right turnings, and come to the house where she would live, and to companions she did not yet know.

But she walked around the block and came upon the old house again. The light was still on in the dining-room. She crept around the house. Standing on tiptoe she looked in at the window where they were eating.

The light seemed to lie like a glare in the room and the family seemed horrible in it. Her mother sat at one end, her father at the other. Facing her sat Jim, his pale face looking ill in the light. She could see the back of Johnny's head and the broad back of Uncle Joe. Their lips moved as if they were speaking but she could not hear. The storm-windows had not yet been taken off.

She looked a long time. Tired of standing strained upward, she slumped down and seemed to fall out of the light into an abyss of darkness.

Creeping around the dark corner of the house, she smelled the newly upturned soil of the canna-bed. The morning when her uncle had uncovered them to the sun seemed a long time in the past. She felt herself again leaning out the upper window watching him, having that moment of brightness and wind.

Down on her hands and knees by the canna-bed she could see the white curved sprouts like scimitars just thrust from the earth. She put her finger on one of them and felt them hard and cold but with a moisture and this strong urgency, this upward thrust of power. They thrust upward, hard and single in the darkness, awaiting their day of flowering.

She parted the hard, naked stubs of the limbs of the lilac-tree and crawled behind it close to the house, sinking down on the ground. The body of the house was warm and she could hear going on inside the vague noises and movements of the people within, her father, her mother, her brothers. She listened and listened.

A stillness came up out of the blackness around her. People passed in front of the house along the walk. She could hear the quick steps of invisible children, the firm tread of many young men in the darkness.

She felt her eyes unbearably wide open and she listened and listened. The wind blew about her in the darkness as from another world.

After what seemed a long time the back door opened and her mother came out and stood on the steps. Reaching out she could have touched the woman's skirt.

"Eunice," her mother called softly, peering beneath her hand into the deep shadow that lay under the elm. The woman stood there a moment listening too. Then she went back into the house.

AN ARRIVAL AT CARTHAGE [1]

By SCAMMON LOCKWOOD

(From *The Frontier*)

ACROSS the Iowa prairie a train consisting of two freight cars, a combination baggage and passenger car and an ancient locomotive is laboring through ever-rising snow drifts. The early winter twilight is fast falling. It is January, 1882, and it is more bitter cold than any January since.

In the combination baggage and passenger car there are seven people, all huddled near the stove which is just to the right of the door leading to the baggage compartment. One of these is the ubiquitous drummer, on the road for a wholesale grocery concern in Des Moines. Another is a railroad laborer traveling on a pass from nowhere to nowhere. The other five passengers are all members of one family, three small children, a father and a mother. There is soon to be a fourth child and therefore they are all on their way to their mother's former home that she may be free from domestic toil during the travail that is before her and also that they may have food and shelter, for the husband is not one of the world's successes. Perhaps he has not yet found just the thing he can best do. He is an intelligent-looking man and his broad high forehead over keen dark eyes carries those slight elevations usually called "bumps" which phrenology tells us are indicative of unusual perception. He has been employed as a shoe clerk in a small town seventy miles back. But he lost that position partly because business was bad and partly because he had been more interested in loitering about the depot, trying to learn telegraphy, than in persuading people to buy shoes. So he has sold his few household possessions and, with his entire family, has taken this train to seek the refuge of an established and stable home until the baby should be born and he, the husband, find another job.

As he looked through a peep hole, scraped in the frost on the car window, he could see that the engine had ploughed through the drifts in a shallow cut or trough and come out upon a stretch of track which was higher than the surrounding country and therefore swept comparatively clear of snow by the strong zero wind.

Then the train stopped and the conductor got out and went forward to consult with the engineer. This conductor had not the appearance of the officials who watch over our limited trains to-day. He wore an old blue overcoat on which there was only one brass button remaining. Around his throat was a heavy knitted muffler with the ends tucked into the breast of the overcoat. On his head was an old blue conductor's cap to which, however, had been added a knitted protection for the ears and the lower part of the man's head. The bottoms of his trousers were thrust into heavy hob-nailed boots that had been generously anointed with neat's-foot oil. Although he was dressed for the weather it was with a gasp of relief that he climbed up into the cab of the locomotive.

"I thought fer a minute we wasn't goin' to make it," said the engineer.

The conductor shook his head vigorously and positively. "Tell you what, Gus," he said, "I don't believe we better try to git past the next town. They's you an' me an' Jack here"; he indicated the fireman, a subdued and inarticulate being, who had turned to hear their discussion; "an' they's seven passengers back there in the coach, an' they's Fred my brakeman an' that makes eleven, don't it?"

The engineer, who was warmly dressed like the conductor, but also much more plentifully upholstered by nature, nodded as one might nod who had accepted the utter finality of two and two making four.

"Well," continued the conductor, who had a walrus moustache over buck teeth and a stomach as concave as the new moon, and at all times the manner of a revivalist, "we ain't supposed to resk the lives of eleven human beings to git this train through to Des Moines. An' if we git snowed up out on this here prairie we'd all freeze to death or starve to death before any help could git to us."

"What'll we do?" said the engineer.

"Tell you," said the conductor, "Carthage is just ahead: we'd better lay over there, if we kin make it."

"Ain't nothin' there," objected the engineer.

"They's a deepo, ain't they?" The revivalist manner was more pronounced. "An' a stove an' firewood an' a bin o' coal an' a general store."

This inventory of the resources of Carthage seemed to impress the convex engineer, for he merely replied as he turned and looked out ahead, "Better be pullin' our freight then or we'll never get thet far; colder'n hell here."

"I'll stick here in the cab," said the conductor, "can't be more'n a few hundred rods."

Slowly the engineer opened the throttle, the cars clanked along behind the engine and then the entire train came to a stop with the locomotive drive wheels spinning around upon the icy rails. The engineer looked ahead. "Have to back her up and buck it," he said, reversing his eccentrics. They backed up about two hundred feet and then again proceeded forward at the greatest speed the engineer dared. He well knew that his only hope of getting through the rapidly rising drifts was by having plenty of momentum.

"Keepa feedin' her, Jack," he said to the fireman.

"How far you figure we gone since that last stop?" said the engineer after another minute or so had elapsed.

The fireman leaned on his shovel and considered. "Oh, mebbe ten mile."

"Carthage ought to be loomin' up along about here, but I can't make out nothin'. Hell!" And he quickly closed his throttle and applied the brakes. "Semaphore set against us, but no light on it; sompin' wrong."

The train came to a sudden, grinding stop. Air brakes were a novelty in those days and only found on locomotives and the newer passenger coaches.

The revivalist conductor was thrown violently forward. "Say," he said, as he regained his feet, "I bet you near made that lady back there have her kid."

The engineer peered anxiously out on both sides of the cab. "Better hustle ahead, Jack, an' see what's the matter with Amos," he said to the fireman. "He had the semaphore set dead against us and no light. Didn't see it till I was right on it."

"Just kinda feel your way slow," the conductor replied. "I wouldn't ask no man to walk that to-night. It's only a couple hundred feet, but that snow's like frozen sand shootin' into you."

"Well, if you're willing to take the responsibility of runnin' by a signal set against you," said the engineer with the caution of his trade.

"Hell, yes," said the conductor. "Anyhow ain't you run by it anyhow? An' a signal ain't no signal in the dark without a light, is it?" he added argumentatively.

The engineer without replying slowly opened the throttle and the train crept along until it drew up beside the station.

This structure of a pattern familiar fifty years ago was set back from the rails about twenty feet. It was perhaps thirty feet long by fifteen wide and the lower floor was divided into three sections; in the middle was the usual small office, projecting far enough out from the main building to enable the station agent while seated at his telegraph key to look along the track in both directions. Above this office was a gable end projecting from the sharply sloping roof, the ridge of which was parallel with the rails. Just below the windows in the small front gable was a long wide plank on which was the word "Carthage" in bold but faded capitals.

This new Carthage is merely a straggling prairie village of perhaps twenty houses and a rickety frame depot badly in need of paint. On one end of the wide plank which proclaims its historic name to the traveling public is the further information: "Des Moines 127 m." and on the other end "Denver 726 m."

On either side of the office are doors whereon large letters, also much faded, gave evidence of the conventional prudery by the words "Gents" and "Ladies." In the ladies' waiting room a certain male gallantry was subtly expressed by the absence of any ticket window; it was the part of men to buy the tickets and the agent's aperture looked forth upon the room assigned so definitely to "Gents" and was definitely marked, "Tickets and Information," the paint, like that on the doors, much faded but still legible. But in view of the chivalrous omission of a ticket window in the ladies' waiting room, the fact that the only stove in the

place was in the men's room must have been an accident. There
it was, however, and in cold weather women patrons of the road
had to choose between the danger of freezing an ear or a finger
or that infinitely greater danger of close contact and association
with the sterner and stronger and indubitably coarser sex.

This stove was like all stoves. A warm stove is the host to
which all visitors first turn their eyes and their steps. But cold
and lifeless as was this station stove it is forbidding, cheerless, and
spreads about it a sense of even greater desolation than if there
were no stove at all.

It was instantly obvious to the revivalist and concave conductor, to the convex engineer and to the subdued fireman, that
there was no fire in the stove. But they had been partly prepared
for this state of things by the absence of any light either in or
about the station.

So, as they entered, they knew at once before so much as striking a match that there was no fire in the stove. They knew it by
that dead and damp and motionless chill, so different from the
cold of out of doors, which always pervades an unheated room in
winter.

Fastened to the wall alongside the little ticket window was a
kerosene lamp and behind it a tin reflector which in its bright
youth had given back to the world ray for ray of the light that
it received. But now it was rusty and fly specked and old, and
even with the best will it could return but a small part of the
feeble radiance that the lamp offered it.

So, when the conductor had put a match to the wick, a sulphur
match whose fumes made his nostrils pucker up and his eyes
water, the gents' waiting room was still gloomy and cold.

"Amos'll git hell fer this," said the revivalist conductor, looking
around and wagging his head. "Mebbe fired."

"Do you have to report him?" ventured the engineer.

The conductor assumed an oratorical attitude, his left hand on
his hip and his right waving about. "Bounden duty," he replied,
"an' besides they's most likely too many know about it. Now if
it was only you an' me an' Jack here," he graciously included the
subdued fireman, "but there's the passengers; they might talk or
some one up at the village. Some way a serious thing like a station agent bein' off duty when a train's due is goin' to leak out an'

then what would happen to me an' you an'—" He stopped suddenly and looked about. "Where'n hell did Jack go to?" The subdued fireman had vanished.

The conductor, as usual, had been so absorbed in his brief oration that he had not noticed the fireman go into the station agent's office through the door alongside the ticket window.

But his question was answered almost immediately by the fireman himself who called out, "Hey! Commere! Quick!"

They followed his voice into the agent's office and saw him with a lighted match standing over the body of a man on a small bed just behind the door.

They knew instinctively that the man must be dead.

As the match held by the fireman burned out the conductor lit another and looked around.

On the table near the telegraph key was the station lantern. The conductor lit it and then came and joined the others standing beside the bed.

"Poor old Amos Dorley!" sighed the conductor, dropping an icy hand. "He'll never tap another telegraph key, least not in this world, an' we don't know, mebbe they ain't none in the next. Frozen stiff! Must a' died sudden a' sumpin'. Now how do you suppose—"

But again he was interrupted. This time by the traveling salesman from Des Moines, who burst in among them exclaiming, "Say, that lady's agoin' to have her kid right away an'—" He paused, seeing the dead man. "What's happened?"

"Old Amos frozen to death," said the engineer.

"Station agent," mumbled the fireman.

"Must a died a' sumpin'," repeated the conductor.

"Say, we'll have to get him out o' sight," said the drummer. "That lady'll have to come in here."

"That's so," replied the conductor. "No way to git her up to the village to-night. Take ahold, boys. Amos kin sleep upstairs to-night. Just as comfortable."

At the rear of the office, just behind the cot, were stairs leading to the floor above. Up there the four of them carried the dead man. They were not aware of the significance in what they were doing—the dead making way for the living and the yet unborn.

Above there were three rooms cluttered with a few pieces of

broken furniture, some lumber and empty oil cans and a pile of old freight receipt books and still older magazines. They found a torn tarpaulin and reverently covered the dead man and then went back down the stairs.

"Have to fix her up in the gents' waiting room," said the fireman. "Ain't no other stove." He said this as if a sound reason were needed for such a breach of decorum. If a woman had to have a baby in a public depot the least she could do was to have it in the ladies' waiting room.

"Now see here, Jack," the conductor answered, "I been through this five times an' I know what's got to be done. An' we got to have a fire in that stove and then heat some water. Got to have plenty of hot water. Have to melt the snow." He turned to the engineer. "Better call Fred and get him to huntin' every can and kettle he can find and fill 'em with snow. And you, Jack, bein' a fireman, get that stove red hot in jig time." He turned to the engineer. "Come on and help me carry that bed into the waitin' room. And say, Jack," he called to the fireman who was starting out the back door to find firewood and coal; "you'll have to keep a fire in that there coach. Them kids can't be in here with their mother while this party's goin' on, an' the rest of the station's too cold."

The conductor, having issued these orders in his usual revivalist manner, went out to the day coach to see how matters were progressing there. The woman was stretched across two seats which had been hastily arranged into a sort of a couch with the cushions from several other seats piled in between them. Her husband was bathing her face with a wet handkerchief and doing his best to reassure her.

"It's just a little sort of starting pain, Alice," he said. "It's not time yet. You'll be all right in a few minutes."

"No," she said quite positively. "I'm not mistaken." And then seeing the conductor, she said, "We must have miscalculated; have you a family?" She spoke in tones rather more refined than he was accustomed to and he realized at once that she was not the ordinary farm or village woman, whatever her present circumstances might be.

"That's all right, lady," he said cheerfully. "I have five myself and I got an idee what you've got ahead of you. We'll make you as comfortable as if you was in your own home." And then he showed his experience by a practical question. "How often the pains comin'?"

"Pretty close together now," the mother replied. "Can't we get up to the town?" she asked. "Some one would take me in for a few days."

"No gettin' up to town for you to-night," answered the conductor. "Mebbe not fer anybody, but somebody'll get up there in the mornin' and fetch the doctor if they is one. But if they ain't, why this sort of thing's happened before without a doctor and everything all right, too."

"I'll try to make it up to town," said the husband.

"Not on your life," replied the conductor, "your wife needs you. One of us will try to go, pretty quick." Then, turning to the woman, "Can you walk in to the deepo?"

The woman started to rise but sank back. "I—I guess not," she panted.

"Well, just wait a minute now and we'll get you in all comfortable," he said, and hurried out of the car and back to the station.

His orders were being carried out with willingness and speed. The fireman had given his snow-covered wood generous assistance with some kerosene from the station's supply and the stove was roaring. Cans of fast melting snow promised quick quantities of hot water and the bed of which the dead man had been so abruptly dispossessed had been brought in from the office.

"Say, Jack," said the conductor briskly, "grab a couple of them blankets and come along with me. We got to carry that lady in. She's a game one all right, but too far gone to walk. Then you and me can take a little tramp up to the village. It ain't more'n a mile but better two of us go in case one or the other don't make it. Worst blizzard I ever seen in all my days."

Jack took the blankets as directed and followed the conductor back into the coach. The woman was having a brief period of relief from her pain and thought she could manage to walk, but they refused to let her even so much as make the attempt. "Only bring it on again worse," said the conductor.

"Come," he said, "one of them seat cushions makes a good stretcher. Kinda short but then it's a short trip. Ha! Ha!

Hey, you," he called to the laborer who had sat stolid and silent and for all they knew uncomprehending at the other end of the car. "Come and help us carry this lady into the deepo. She's sick."

So they wrapped her in the blankets and then the four men, the husband, the conductor, the fireman and the laborer, carried her out of the car and into the rude room that had been so rudely and so hurriedly prepared for her. The three little children watched her departure with wide eyes. They were cold and hungry and frightened.

"It's all right, Effie," said the husband as they went out, addressing the elder child, a girl of about eight. "I'll be right back. Take care of John and Carrie."

After they had laid the mother upon the bed the conductor called the fireman into the little office and said, "Wrap yourself up good, Jack; you and me is goin' out for a little evening stroll to the village."

Trainmen on such runs in those days were always well equipped for extreme weather. They had heavy oiled boots and huge knitted scarfs and mittens and heavy ulsters. But what they needed most of all they did not have. They needed snowshoes. The drifts were so deep that it was impossible to wade through them. The railroad ran through a hollow and the village was on higher ground about a mile away. Much of the road was a shallow cut with banks on each side forming a long trough into which the snow had been drifting all afternoon. If the men could only have seen they would have found bare prairie along the sides of the road, but that much they could not see. The night was that dense black which a city man almost never knows. There may have been lights in the village a mile away but the fine driving snow obscured them. The men could only distinguish the course of the road by the few trees on either side looming up in a blackness even denser than the blackness of the night.

The men started out hand in hand, for they realized full well the danger of getting separated by even a few feet in that impenetrable night and with the screaming of the wind to drown out the loudest call. But they had gone hardly a hundred yards when the fireman pulled the conductor over to him and shouted in his ear, "No use, Hank, no man could get through half a mile of this alive. Better turn back."

"Guess you're right, Jack; we'd have three froze up men 'stead of one."

They turned and floundered back to the station and, when they arrived, they fully realized how impossible it would have been to get to the village.

The conductor led the way into the day coach where the laborer and the traveling salesman and the brakeman and engineer were waiting. "How is she?" the conductor asked.

"No change yet," said the engineer.

"Can't get to town?" asked the salesman.

"No, couldn't go a hundred rods," said the fireman.

"Now, boys," said the conductor, still in his revivalist manner which somehow seemed to match the gravity of the occasion, "we got death here amongst us and we got a new life a-comin' into the world an' we got no one to look to but ourselves; no chance fer any help no more'n if we was on a desert island. Now that lady's husband and I'll have to see her through. We both had experience an' that's all a doctor has in a case like this and jest somethin' about his position to make 'em feel easier. But we've got to be the doctor. Now there's some food of Amos' in there, canned stuff, flour, rolled oats, coffee an' tea and such stuff, so we don't starve. Anybody got any whiskey?" Of course the traveling salesman had a bottle of it in his bag. He got it out and gave it to the conductor.

"Now, Jack," the conductor continued, "give us a good pile of wood and a lot of coal to see us through the night and then some of you fellers give those kids somethin' to eat and get them to go to sleep and keep this car warm an' I'll see you in the mornin'."

As he entered the station he heard the click of the telegraph receiver. In the office he found the husband at the key. He turned as the conductor entered. "Been repeating the same call for the last ten minutes. I didn't know what this station's call was but thought I'd cut in and see if they was calling us."

"Hell!" said the conductor. "Do you know how to telegraph?"

The husband nodded.

"Why didn't you say so—still what's the use; there won't be no train through here for a week. What do they say?"

"Want to know what's the matter. I told them the agent was dead and your train here."

The conductor nodded and then jerked his head in the direction of the room where the woman was lying. "How she gettin' along?"

"She's easier for a time," he replied.

The conductor held up the bottle of whiskey. "This'll help her if she needs it."

The telegraph interrupted them.

After a pause the husband turned and said, "They want to know if I can take the job of agent until they can get a man through."

"Ain't you got a job?" said the conductor.

"No," said the husband, and explained his situation.

"Well," said the conductor, "forty-five dollars a month and upstairs to live in rent free and your coal and a place to raise vegetables and mebbe keep a cow and now and then a hell of a bawling out from the division supe, and no future working for this two streaks of rust and right o' way. That's what it is. Not so bad, not so bad for a handy fellow. Got any furniture?"

"I'll make some," said the man. "Pretty handy with tools. Guess I'll tell them that I want the job permanent." He turned to the key.

After a long interchange of dots and dashes he again faced the conductor. "They say it's all right if I suit the general agent of the division when he can get through."

The conductor held out his hand. "Well, Mr. Agent, here's congratulations and hopin' you get to be president of the road and take me off this rotten run."

The man rose to his feet his eyes shining. "I must tell Alice," he said. "She knows I always wanted to be a telegraph operator."

He went into the other room.

"Alice!" he said excitedly. "How do you feel now?"

"What is it?" she said. "What has happened?"

"I've got a job," he exclaimed. "Station agent here. We'll have upstairs to live in rent free, free coal, place to raise vegetables, keep a cow, forty-five dollars a month sure money all the time, too, Alice."

She smiled faintly. "I'm glad, Ed," she said. "But where is

the agent they had?"

"Oh, he's gone."

She nodded and then suddenly clutched at the bed clothes. "It's starting again," she whispered as beads of perspiration appeared on her forehead.

The next morning at about seven o'clock the conductor burst into the coach exclaiming, "Well, it's a girl, mighty nice little girl, an' everything's all right."

The men gathered around him.

"How's the mother?" said the engineer.

"She's all right; there's women have had it harder and again there's others had it easier, but she's all right and the gamest human creature I ever see."

"Anything more we can do?" asked the drummer.

"Somebody's got to get to town. Stark in there, that's his name, Edward Stark, mother's name's Alice—Alice Stark; well, Stark is sittin' there by the bed tryin' to make a pair of snowshoes out of the wicker backs of a couple of old busted rocking chairs he found upstairs. And damned if I don't think they'll work. That man is plumb handy. But anyhow we got to get to town. Most like they'll try to get down here." He looked out the window as he spoke. It was a dazzling January morning, clear, cold, dry, and the reflected sunlight from the snow making all blink and turn away.

"Fine morning," he continued. "Yes, we got to get milk for those kids. By the way, I haven't told them they got a little sister."

He approached the children; only the eldest was awake.

"Well, how is this little girl?" he asked.

"How is mother?" the child replied.

"Your mother is first rate and, what's better yet, you've got a new little sister."

The child looked up at him and calmly replied, "Then her name is Molly."

"Molly?" said the conductor. "How do you figger that out?"

"Because mother and father said so. There is a Molly Stark in the history book and we belong to her family and so mother and father said the next girl would be named Molly Stark."

"Well, now," said the conductor, "what do you think of that?"

MIST ON THE MEADOW [1]

By WILLIAM MARCH

(From *The Midland*)

WHEN Brother Hightower came at last from the twilight of the pine grove he saw before him a meadowland, filled with flowers—saffron and pink, bell-shaped and shaped like stars—lying damp and cool in the late afternoon and flowing richly to meet a line of cypresses that fringed the lagoon and marked where the marsh began. It had been dark among the trees, but the meadowland swam in a light fluid and amber, that blurred the outline of the cabin before him and softened the harshness of the clay plastered against its sides. The cabin was built of hewn logs that had weathered brown, and was set squarely in the midst of the meadow. At its back, a sagged chimney of sticks and red mud threw smoke into the air in a thin, curving stream.

Brother Hightower reined up his pony and removed his feet from the stirrups. "That must be the Gentry place," he thought. Before him stretched the meadow and the marsh, but to his left the land rose to irregular bluffs of red clay which hung like a shelf above the eastern edge of the lagoon.

He stretched his bony legs and turned to survey the cabin more carefully. Then he settled again to the saddle and began to think of himself and his mission. He thought of the sinfulness of the world, of the viciousness of men and of the souls he had somehow saved in his itinerant preaching years, and his heart flooded with a feeling of humility and power. He raised his arms to heaven and his eyes rolled upward. . . . "Lord! . . . Lord!" he moaned. "Make me worthy to serve in Thy vineyard! . . ." His face became distorted and he twisted with pain.

As he prayed, there came from across the meadow the voice of a man calling his pigs, and the answering sound of swine welcoming and disputing their supper. Hightower had dropped his reins, and the pony, with lowered mouth, wandered at will and cropped the grass eagerly. Presently the preacher removed his clerical hat and wiped the moisture from his forehead and his hands. Then he took up the reins again and guided his pony toward the cabin.

As he drew nearer, the squeals of the swine came louder to his ears, and he could distinguish easily the words the man was using: . . . "Hey, there—Emma! . . . Git outen that trough! Whoever learnt you manners? What would folks say, now, if they seen you actin' thataway?" Brother Hightower frowned at the joyousness in the man's voice. He halted his pony and dismounted stiffly. Before him was a sty, in which milled a dozen fat pigs, and a man who was feeding them slops and mash from a tin bucket. The man was dressed in a brown shirt and faded overalls, grotesquely patched with colored scraps which had also faded. His sparse red beard curled upward at the ends, and his head was entirely bald. He wore no shoes. His voice was affectionate, and he laughed continuously at the antics of his pigs.

"Git away, Emma, I tell you—give old Charley a chance. He ain't had a mouthful!" With his bare foot he shoved her away from the trough with a tolerant, loving gesture. . . . "I declare: That Emma's the *hongriest* sow ever I seen!" Again he laughed happily.

Brother Hightower cleared his throat sharply and said: "Good evening, and God be with you all." His voice was deep, with a rich, trembling intensity.

"Good evenin', preacher," the man said mildly.

"Is this the Gentry place?"

"Yes, preacher: I'm Jim Gentry."

"I allowed you was Jim Gentry. I'm the Reverend Hightower, the humblest of God's servants, and I'm on my way to hold a revival for the folks on Pigeon River."

Gentry walked to the edge of the pen and held out his hand. "I'm glad to make your acquaintance, preacher. I've heerd folks a-talking 'bout you. I've heerd it said Christ Jesus stood before you one time, honorin' and raisin' you up above all men."

Hightower bowed his head. "You have heard truly, brother. It was Him that gave me the wrath to make sinners quail and forsake their lusts. It was Him that gave me the power to heal the sick and a hand to cast out devils." Jim shifted his weight nervously and drew back, and with his bare, horny feet he stroked the backs of his swine.

Suddenly he turned and faced the cabin. "Exa!" he called loudly.

A woman appeared in the door. She was a tall woman, taller than her husband and almost of a height with Hightower himself. Between her decaying teeth was a sweet-gum brush which she chewed with a thoughtful, automatic insistence. Her eyes were pale under their bleached brows and blue veins stood out in her wrists. When she saw the stranger she drew back suspiciously, but her husband's voice reassured her.

"This here's the Reverend Hightower on his way to preach a revival at Pigeon River."

The name had a magic effect on Exa. She came down the steps quickly and approached the two men. "You don't come none too soon. The folks at Pigeon River are ungodly, I've heerd it said." She gazed at Hightower fiercely with her pale eyes, and Hightower stared back, his own eyes dark and dilated with emotion. "Ungodly and sinful, Sister Gentry," he whispered. . . . "Singing songs and dancing and lusting after flesh. . . ."

Exa spoke to her husband: "This is a holy man, Jim." But Gentry laughed foolishly and turned to finish feeding his pigs. Exa spoke again to the preacher: "We'll be proud to have you stay with us a spell. We hain't got much, but what we have is yours withouten even askin'."

"You are kind thoughted, Sister Gentry, but I aim to pass on my way at daybreak. There's work in the Vineyard of the Lord and the reapers are few." Exa nodded her head in complete understanding. "Come into the house, preacher; supper'll be ready right soon. Jim'll take care of your pony." Hightower turned then and followed her into the house.

The cabin consisted of two rooms and a lean-to. There were no lamps, but a blaze of pine knots lighted the room and cast great shadows against the walls. Hightower removed his hat and his black, tight-fitting coat, and Exa brought him water from the stove and poured it into a basin. When he had finished his wash and had combed out his damp, black hair, supper was being placed on the table. He seated himself at once and commenced a blessing, but almost immediately he was interrupted by sudden laughter and the sound of chains being shaken. He uncovered his eyes and gazed at the burlap curtains which screened the entrance to the lean-to, but he did not pause in his prayer. As he watched, there came to his ears a sound like the popping of a cork and a hiss such as some fabulous snake might make. Exa half turned in her chair, but her eyes remained downcast and devout. Again there came the rattling of a chain, angry and more insistent, and presently the hissing changed into an irritable and impotent chatter. Brother Hightower brought to an end his blessing and raised his head. He looked enquiringly at Jim.

"That's *Tolly*," said Jim proudly; "that's my boy, Tolly!"

Exa was on her feet instantly. "Oh, my po' baby—did its ma go and forget it? Did its ma clean forget little Tolly's supper? . . . Now that's a shame: that's what I call a mean shame!" . . . As she talked, she piled victuals on a tin plate, and presently she brushed the curtains aside and went to her son. The querulous chattering ceased at once. There was now the sound of lips being smacked and food swallowed sensuously. Occasionally Exa's voice was heard whispering some endearing phrase: "Eat it all, honey—greens is *good* for Mamma's baby . . ."

Gentry dragged one foot across the floor slowly. Then he looked down at his plate, as if to hide the pride in his eyes: "Tolly's the beatenest boy you ever seen," he said. "There ain't nobody like him in the county.—They just lost the pattern after they finished makin' old Tolly!" Then he leaned back in his chair and chuckled at some old recollection.

Brother Hightower frowned and shook his head. "But chains, Brother Gentry . . ." he began; "to put one of God's creatures in chains . . ." His voice thinned out into silence.

"Oh, pshaw!" said Gentry; "that don't mean nothing; Exa don't mean no harm by chainin' him up, but she can't be a-watchin' him every minute, after she done put clean clothes onto him, and iffen she didn't chain him up, Tolly'd just liable as not go get in the pen and wallow with the hogs."

Hightower looked up in surprise. "Will he do a thing like that?" he asked in an uncertain voice. Then an expression of distaste came over his face. . . . "Wallowing with hogs!" he repeated; "wallow in filth with hogs!"

"Sholy," said Jim; "sholy. Now what all's wrong with that?" Then he began to speak earnestly. "They're good clean hogs: them hogs is the best in this county; they're registered stock; I guess them hogs is better blooded by a whole passel than you or me, preacher. . . . It's their nature to wallow, and Tolly's nature to wallow, and I always say to Exa, if they don't mind Tolly in their pen, then Tolly ain't got no call to mind them."

Hightower shoved his plate away with a sudden gesture of disgust. He rose from his seat and walked to the fire, kicking at a log that protruded from the hearth and giving life suddenly to the shadows that seemed painted against the wall. But Jim continued talking in his soft, contented voice.

"He looks right cute there in the pen with them pigs, and him so covered with mud that nobody could say for sure what was hog and what was Tolly. . . . That boy Tolly—" he continued, "he sure is one case, now!—He sure is the very beatenest one! . . . But he's a real good boy and nobody can say different. He never meddled nobody's business and he never caused sorrow in his life. Sometimes of a morning he picks flowers in the medder or watches a humming bird all day, but then sometimes he goes to sleep against a cypress knee in the cool of the lagoon." Then Jim began to laugh louder and slap his leg. . . . "That boy Tolly!" he repeated proudly, "he sure is one case!"

The curtains parted and Exa came again into the room and seated herself at the table. Hightower made a deep, sympathetic noise in his throat. "I'm sorry for you, Sister Gentry, in your trouble." Exa bowed her head and looked down at her hands. There was a long silence and then Jim glanced at his wife timidly, turning at length to the preacher for support. "There was a young fellow through here last fall, come to teach school at Live-oak. He said we ought to send Tolly to the 'sylum. Said he might get cured iffen we done that."

Exa's eyes narrowed and her bleached brows became dangerous, as if the subject were a sore one. She rose from the table and walked backward slowly. "Nobody can take Tolly and lock him in a dungeon for a lunatic!" she said. She stretched her arms across the opening to the lean-to, and stared fiercely at the two men, as if her husband's words had somehow put in motion forces which would take the boy away. Brother Hightower walked toward her, his voice sweet with sympathy. "There, now, Sister Gentry! . . . Nobody's going to take the boy away. Brother Jim spoke without thinking. He's an earthy man and he knows not the yearning of the spirit nor the ways of God; but no man could be heartless enough to put God's own handiwork in an evil place of atheists and infidels where prayers are never heard and where His sacred word is flouted and scorned." He placed his arms protectingly around Exa's shoulders and guided her back to the table. "Sister Gentry, God has placed a heavy cross on you and yours, but rejoice and be exceedingly glad! For he punishes them that he cherishes, and you are his very dearly loved. . . . Rejoice, sister, and kiss the hand that chastens you! . . . Rejoice and be glad!"

Exa looked up pleadingly. "Preacher, what ails Tolly?"

Hightower walked across the room rapidly, his black hair tossing excitedly to his stride. Then he turned and faced the woman. His eyes were dilated and his hands were trembling. "Your son is possessed of a devil!" he whispered. There was a note of exultation in his voice. . . . "Your son is possessed of a very terrible devil!" he repeated.

"Aw, shucks, preacher," said Jim mildly.

When the meal was finished at length and Exa had cleared the table, a sweet mist was rising off the lagoon and a moon rode high above the trees. The pine grove lay quiet and dark to the north and the meadowland was an enchanted and a lovely place. The men had walked onto the porch and sat smoking their pipes. Hightower was talking of his conversion and Exa, washing her dishes, could hear his deep voice plainly.

". . . It happened nigh to dark, when I was ploughing in the field. There come a sound of wings about my ears and I seen the air was filled with angels. They roosted in the trees and sat white on the rails of the fence, singing a hymn of praise. I fell to my knees, knowing well the sinful life I had led. . . . 'Lord! Lord!' I said. . . . 'Wash me with blood, and make me as white as wool.' . . . I buried my face in the dirt and waited for death to take me, but something lifted me up, and Christ Jesus stood before me. I put my hands over my eyes, being unable to bear the sight of His glory, and swayed my head from side to side, moaning. . . . 'Spread My glory to all men, and preach My gospel to every nation!' he said. . . . 'Halleluiah!—Halleluiah!' sang the angels in voices as sweet and as high as a trumpet note.

" 'How can I preach for you?' I cried out; 'I, an unlettered man who cannot read Thy holy word!' . . . 'Doubt not, for thou canst really do these things!' he said in a voice of thunder. . . . 'No, Lord,' I answered, 'I never had no schooling and not one word can I read . . .'

"Christ Jesus raised his loving arm and I seen that he had a whip of scorpions. He brought it down across my shoulders time and time again. . . . 'It is written that My house shall be a house of prayer, and ye doubt that I am the Son of God come to save the world from sin!' . . . And me crouching between the rows of young corn, baring my breast to the whip and saying: 'Do with me what you will, gentle Lord. Beat me! Make me the lowliest of Thy slaves and I shall love Thee dearly! . . . Rend me limb from limb, if that be Thy sweet wish!' . . . And when they found me my mouth was cut and bleeding and my teeth was broke and there were great bruises on my back and chest to show where the whip had been. . . ."

For a moment there was silence, oppressive and brooding, and then Hightower began speaking again: "That night when I returned, word passed amongst the neighbor folk and they come to look at me, and to marvel, and I told them what they longed to hear. When a great crowd had collected, we walked down the road until we come to the settlement, and there, in the presence of them all, I called for a Bible and read aloud the Gospel according to St. Mark. And when the people who had known me all their lives seen that I could really read, they fell upon their knees, fearing, and I baptised them in the river and received them into the church of God. Then when it was dawn we walked down the road again, singing hymns of praise and waving green branches."

Exa put down her dishclout and stood silent in the room. The fire was dying into embers but the moonlight streamed brightly through the open window and the door. Her husband's voice, soft and apologetic, came to her ears. "I can't read none, neither . . ."

"Praise God for that, Brother Gentry! When God wants to give a man the gift of tongues or the gift of print he will signify His wish, as He done with me. And every book except God's

sacred Word should be burnt in flames. . . ." There was another long silence, so long that Exa feared the preacher would not
speak again, but presently he continued.

"That morning as I walked the road with my disciples praising
God and waving branches, I worked a miracle. A nigger come
running down from his cabin by the creek, toting a little black
girl whose legs were twisted and withered away. I put my hand
on the child, who had never walked a step, and commanded that
she rise up. And right away she rose up from the road and ran
skipping and laughing through the fields. And when my disciples
seen that they fell on their knees and kissed my dusty feet, but
I said: 'Verily, verily, praise not me, but render thanks to my
Father in Heaven, for I am not as mighty as He.' "

There was a silence between the two men. Jim Gentry pulled
upon his pipe with a faint hissing sound, but Brother Hightower
stared across the meadowland, his eyes dreaming and drawn upward. . . . "For I am not as mighty as He," he repeated sadly.

Exa's voice sounded suddenly from the doorway. "Can you
cast the devil out of Tolly, preacher?" Her nostrils were quivering with excitement and her white eyebrows were drawn together.
Hightower drew on his pipe deeply while Exa waited with
clenched fists for his answer. "I have cast out devils," he said
warily; "I have cast out many devils, Sister Gentry."

Jim Gentry got up from the steps and stood with his toes
pressed into the soft loam of a flower bed. "Now, Exa—you all
let Tolly alone, can't you?"

But Exa continued to stare at the preacher. "Can you cast the
devil out of Tolly?" Her fists were pressed against her breasts
and she was breathing heavily.

Brother Hightower stretched out his hands and bowed his head.
"I can if it be the will of God, Sister Exa."

"Now you all let Tolly alone, I tell you. He's not a-botherin'
nobody . . ."

But Exa and Brother Hightower paid no attention to Gentry.
They were staring at each other again with parted lips and furious, exalted eyes; and presently Exa went into the house and
unchained her son.

Tolly was undersized and sallow and no thought held his features together or gave his face significance. His forehead bulged

above his eyes and his jaw lay relaxed and toneless beneath his parted lips. He walked to the edge of the porch and held out his arms. "Fire! Fire!" he said eagerly.

"No, honey, that ain't fire—that's just the *moon!*"

"Tolly's got as much sense as you or me," said Jim; "Tolly's got as much sense as anybody, iffen he wanted to use it." Hightower shook his head vigorously. "It's the devils in him that call out for the fire!" he said.

Jim looked helplessly from the exalted face of his wife to the more exalted face of the preacher. A feeling of resentment came over him, but it passed almost immediately. He could never defy any one as powerful as Brother Hightower and he knew it. "Po' little Tolly!" he said sadly; "po' little Tolly!"

Exa seated herself and Tolly sat beside her, resting his meaningless face against her shoulder. Hightower regarded them carefully. "How old is the boy?" he asked. "He's going on twenty, preacher, but small for his age, as you see." Exa smoothed back her son's coarse, hemp-like hair and stroked his cheek with her hand.

Suddenly Hightower spoke directly to the boy. "Tolly, look at me, son!" But Tolly paid no attention. "Tolly! Listen to Brother Hightower; he's going to make you well again." Exa had risen to her feet, lifting the boy in her strong arms. Hightower had also risen, and presently he came over to the boy and placed his hands upon his forehead. Tolly hissed and spat and his face wrinkled with terror. "Tolly, ain't you 'shamed!" said Exa reproachfully.

"Don't blame the boy, sister: it's the devils in him that done that." He caught Tolly by the arms and held him firmly, and Tolly became very excited. He struggled and spat and tried to free himself. He began to chatter excitedly and later to make low, pleading noises; but Hightower held him tightly. "This is going to be an uncommon hard devil to rout, Sister Gentry," he said; "it might be best to chain the boy up while I pray."

"What makes you all keep a-pesterin' Tolly so?" asked Jim querulously; "he ain't done nothin' to you."

Exa gave her husband a single glance of scorn. Then she picked up the loose ends of the chain that circled her son's waist and snapped them through two bent spikes driven into the logs of the cabin. Tolly looked from one face to the other quickly. He drew close to the wall and clung there in terror, but Hightower pursued him relentlessly. He lifted the boy's face and gazed at him with deep, yearning eyes.

"Devil, come forth!" he whispered. Tolly began to laugh foolishly and to shuffle his feet, but he could not draw his eyes away from the preacher's eyes. Hightower swayed his head back and forth with a slow, steady motion and Tolly's head swayed with him. . . . "Come forth, devil, from this soul! . . ."

For a moment there was silence. Then a crane called shrilly from over the marsh and the swine, dreaming in their wallow, grunted twice and turned nervously.

Presently Hightower fell to his knees and began to pray in a deep, rich voice. He lay on the floor praying, his eyes distended and his hands splayed widely. Finally he rose to his full height and placed his palms against Tolly's cheeks. Tolly did not resist him now. He lay passive against the logs of the cabin, glancing from his mother to the preacher in terror. Hightower lifted his eyes to heaven. The muscles of his face twitched, his jaw was set and he talked cloudily through locked teeth. . . . "Grant me this miracle, Lord!" he whispered. "This miracle you done once with your own sweet hands!" . . . Then he forced back the boy's head until their eyes almost met and cried in a loud voice: "Come forth, devils, and depart from this boy!" Tolly began to tremble more violently. He rattled his chains and beat his head against the wall.

At that moment the pigs awoke and made a low, worried sound. They rose heavily and huddled together against the farthest wall of the sty, grunting in uncertain protest. Then they broke their grouping and trotted apprehensively around the pen, coming together, at last, in the center of the sty, to stand there, waiting, making a vague grunting noise.

Jim touched the preacher on his arm in mild protest. "Why don't you all go inside and shet the door?" he asked. "My pigs is getting upset with all this racket a-goin' on. . . . Them's blooded, high-strung pigs, preacher, and they can't stand this to-do."

But Brother Hightower did not even hear him. His voice was becoming stronger and more exultant. Again he lifted Tolly's

head, and again he gazed deeply into his shrinking eyes. . . .
"Come forth, devils!" he demanded. "Come forth and enter yon
filthy swine!" A strange echoing sound came from Tolly's throat.
He clutched the side of the cabin for support, clung for a moment,
and fell sharply to the floor.

Instantly the pigs began to squeal in terror, lunging furiously
against the sides of the pen. At the sound of their distress, Jim
Gentry sprang from the porch and ran to the pen and stood trying to quiet his pigs with soft, loving words, but they paid no
heed to him at all: they continued to squeal and hurl themselves
against the sides of the sty until at last its walls gave way against
their weight. Then the released swine ran across the meadow to
the east, in the direction of the bluffs, milling and whirling in
broken, furious circles and tearing each other with their teeth;
and when they reached the bluffs they continued to whirl, and a
moment later their bodies were silhouetted against the moon as
they pitched over the edge and into the water below.

Brother Hightower stood in silence, his body rigid, his eyes
flaming. Then he turned and faced Exa, praying rapidly, and
Tolly rolling on the floor. "I have performed the miracle of the
swine," he whispered, as if awed by his own power. "Bear ye
witness," he said; "bear ye witness to my holiness!"

At the preacher's words, Tolly crept eagerly to him, kissing his
hands and embracing his long legs. His face, which had once
been meaningless and content, was now meaningless and frightened. . . . "Save me!" he screamed over and over. . . . "Save
me from eternal torment!" Then his face began to twitch and
his body jerked spasmodically as Jim Gentry unsnapped the
chains that held him to the wall, and carried him into the house.
. . . "Po' little Tolly," he said; "po' little boy! . . . If ere a
man can show me where you're bettered withouten your devils, I'll
give that man a pretty." Then he looked sadly across the
meadow and closed the door to the cabin.

For the wind was changing and the mist that had hung above
the marsh began to thrust furtive arms between the trunks of the
trees and to spread over the surface of the lagoon. From the
lagoon the mist moved across the meadow with a slow, impercep-
tible motion, obliterating bushes and outhouses and familiar land-
marks. Soon the pine grove and the bluffs would be lost under

a covering overwhelming and impalpable; soon the horizon would be wiped away and the land blotted up completely, and nothing in all the world would remain except Tolly rattling his chains and Brother Hightower, with raised, enigmatic arms, praying hoarsely before the cabin.

HEEL, TOE, AND A 1, 2, 3, 4 [1]

By GEORGE MILBURN

(From *The American Mercury*)

ONE night Joe had been staring at the white paper in his typewriter so long that he thought he would go snow-blind. Finally he let his tilted chair down and began writing.

The types did a tap dance on the platen and words marched across the page: *"Wife:* Henry, have you got everything shut up for the night?"

Joe double spaced and wrote "Hubby;" but, before he could finish the line with the good one he had thought up for *Hubby* to say back to *Wife,* he heard a scratching on the iron grille of the basement window. He turned around in his chair and saw two hands gripping the bars and a twisted monkey-face squeezed between them.

"What do you want?" he asked.

"Say, buddy, how do you get down to the Lake from here?" the monkey-face said without moving its lips.

Joe got up and went over to the open window to see how any one could talk without moving his lips. He said, "You follow this street right on, and it'll take you to the Lake. It's only three blocks on over."

"What street is this, buddy?"

"This is Superior street—East Superior street," Joe said.

The stranger took his hands away from the window bars and sat down on the basement steps so that his head was level with the sidewalk and the window. Joe could see now that when he talked his lips did move a little. They jerked down on one side like those of a man rolling a cigar in the corner of his mouth.

He didn't make any move to go. Instead, he began explaining, apologetically. "Well, I know Chi' pretty good, but I ain't never been down to the Lake. I thought I would go down to the Lake to-night. Reckon is there any benches a man could sleep on down there at the beach?"

"Sure, you can find plenty of benches if you'll walk on up the shore a ways, up about Oak street."

Joe turned around and went back over to his typewriter again. But the bum kept on sitting there, hunched up on the basement steps. It annoyed Joe to have him sitting there looking in, and he was about to tell him to move on, when the bum said, "What're you doing, buddy? You writing a story book?"

"No, I'm writing two-line jokes," Joe said. "I make my living writing two-line jokes." Joe was proud of making his living by writing jokes.

The bum commenced talking again without paying any attention to what Joe had said. "Listen, buddy, you let me come in there, and I'll tell you some good stories you can write."

"What kind of stories?"

"Oh, all kinds of stories. Any kind of story you want to hear."

Joe got up and walked out into the hall and turned back the snap-lock on the basement door. The bum had moved quickly, because he was there at the bottom of the steps waiting when Joe opened the door. When he stepped inside he put his foot down on some plaster that had fallen and it made a loud gritting noise on the concrete floor.

"Sh-h-h!" Joe said. "Don't make so much noise. The land-lady lives right back there, and if she caught me letting you in she'd throw me and you both out in the street."

The visitor, stepping high, walked on past quickly and stood in Joe's room under the electric light, blinking. When Joe saw him in the light he knew that there wasn't any danger. The bum was a kid about sixteen years old. He looked tough, but not hard to handle. His back was twisted and he held his elbows out from his sides as if he had boils in both his armpits. His marmoset's face was broad and pleasant, but one of his eyelids drooped half-way shut. His other eye was as black and lively as a beetle.

II

"Start in," said Joe, sitting down in his chair.

"Well, what kind of a story would you want to hear?" the little bum asked, seating himself nervously on the edge of the cot.

"Just use your own judgment," Joe said. "You were the one that suggested this."

"Well, I can tell you about when I was handling greyhounds for the races out in Tia Juana and one day Roman Queen broke her leg and they give her to me to shoot. So I took her and set her leg and fixed it up and cured her. That dog sure did love me and I sure did love that dog. So one day Mr. Rambo, that was my boss, seen that Queenie was up and getting around again without much of a limp, and nothing would do him but he should run her. Well, she wasn't much account for running, the bone in her leg wasn't good and knit yet, but Mr. Rambo took Queen and shot her full of dope, and that day she run and win the race and Old Man Rambo win six grand. I sure did love that dog. But that last race tore her leg loose again and the dope and all was too much for her and I had to shoot her after all. How is that for a story? Is that the kind you like?"

"That's all right," Joe said. "Go slower and talk so I can understand what you're saying."

"Well, I've been all around. All over this country, Canada, and Mexico. I've been to Havana and Bonus Airs. I've just got out of a turpentine camp down in Florida. When the boom bust down there me and another kid was riding out in a Studie that was hot—that we had stole. We was almost to the line when the law caught us, and the judge shipped us off to this turpentine camp. They used to whup us regular, whether we'd done anything or not. But that turpentine gets into your hide and it gets so they can't hurt you so much when they cut you up with a cat-tail whip. I've got a back like a washboard. Here, let me show you something."

The little bum unbuttoned his coat and slipped his arms out of it gingerly. He bent his naked back over under the light bulb. The close, narrow welts on his back made it look like a piece of tan corduroy.

"Just feel that," the kid said. "Go on, just feel it."

Joe ran his finger tips along the leather-colored welts.

"That's what them cat-tail whips they use on you in a turpentine camp does to you," the boy said proudly.

"Well, me and this other kid was in there, and this kid was a wop kid from Chi'. He said that if ever he could get back to Chi' ever'thing would be jake for him and me both, because he could get me a job driving a beer truck for fifty bucks a week. He was a good kid all right. I sure did like him. So after a while he gets out and comes back to Chi' and before long he sends the money to get me out and sends me an address to come to here in Chi'. I didn't lose no time.

"I was riding the blinds out of Atlanta when a railroad dick come climbing down over the tender. She was hitting around seventy. I steps around on that little ledge out of sight, and when this yard dick sticks his beezer around trying to see where I had went, I lets him have it, and he goes over, squealing like a stuck pig.

"I got into Chi' this afternoon late, and I went around to this tobacco store on North Clark street, this address this buddy of mine had give me. When I got there they told me that this dago buddy of mine had been put on the spot day before yesterday and they had a big funeral for him yesterday. I sure liked that kid. Kid by the name of Liberatore. Old Vic Liberatore.

"Well, here I am now. That's the breaks. The next time you see me I might be wearing a silk shirt and smoking a two-bit cigar. That's the breaks. That's what they call the lawr of averages. I've had it to work out for me before. I've had the bucks before this, plenty, and I spent 'em, too. Say, buddy, you ain't got another Lucky there, have you?"

Joe pulled a package of cigarettes out of his shirt pocket and handed them over to the little bum. The kid took one, lighted it, and sent a blue veil eddying up around the electric light. He stood there, naked to the waist. Joe was looking at the bum's arms. From wrist to elbow they were splotched with livid scars. Some of the places were unhealed and they were open wounds.

"How did you burn your arms like that?" Joe asked.

"Them blisters? Buddy, if I told you how I got them, I'd have to tell you about Heavy Henderson. I don't know if I can tell you about Heavy, exactly. I ain't right in my head yet about Heavy. You see how I walk? Sort of on my heels? Some thinks I'm punch-drunk, but I ain't punch-drunk. I never have talked to anybody about this before, but I'll try and tell you about it.

III

"I wasn't more'n ten years old when I first started on the road. My old folks used to live in a little town in Missouri. I guess they still do if they ain't dead. That's been six or seven years ago. My old man always said that if ever I run off, I could just keep on a-running, because he never would send after me. So I run off.

"Well, I hadn't been out long before I met up with Heavy Henderson. It was in the jungles near Boise, Idaho. I had been having a pretty tough time of it, and I sure was needing somebody who was big enough to stand up for me.

"Heavy was a big, fine-looking man, and he was looking to get a good punk to do his moochin' for him. So when I come along Heavy and me joined up. Heavy was a good guy at heart; they don't make them no better than Heavy was. He'd 'a' done anything in the world for me, but I have to admit that Heavy did have a mean temper. Part of it was my fault, though. I was always kind of headstrong, and that made it hard for him to keep me in line. So Heavy used to have to put the bug on me pretty often. That's what made them burns."

Joe said, "Oh, I see!"

"You know what the bug is, don't you?"

"Well, it seems to me like I do, but I'm not quite sure," Joe said. "What is it?"

"The bug is what they call blister beetle, a sort of a little bug. The juice of it on you blisters to beat hell. Heavy nearly always used some kind of acid on me, but he called it the bug just the same. Ever' time I got so I wouldn't do like he said, or when I helt out something on him, Heavy would catch me and take and blister my arms. That worked two ways. For one thing, it hurt me a whole lot more than a whupping, and for another thing, the next day when I went into town to batter back-doors, why I could show the woman that opened the door the sores on my arms and tell her I had got scalded in an accident and that I was trying to get back to my folks. That always worked, and sometimes it paid off in money, too.

"I used to try to fight Heavy off, but that didn't do no good. That was one strong man. He had a big heart, and I bet that'd he 'a' gone through Hell for me, but, like I say, he did have a quick temper. When he got mad, he'd just burn the hell out of my arms. I guess I needed it sometimes. But Heavy sort of overdone it. Some of them sores ain't never healed up yet, and that turpentine I been working in is a quick healer.

"But I never could find it in my heart to anything else but respect Heavy. I sure did like him. He was as good a jocker as any kid could want. Wasn't scared of nobody, and I seen him mash a bird's face in for just grabbing me by the neck. I sure did like Heavy, but I never did know how much I liked him until after it was too late.

"The way it was, one night Heavy tanked up on white mule out in a place in Dakota. Man, talk about your raw liquor, that stuff was *raw*. I seen one guy take a snort of it, and an hour later he was having a hem'rage. But stuff like that didn't bother Heavy. He was a *man*. He had a set of cast-iron guts. We was waiting for a train, and Heavy was feeling good.

"I remember just as well. It was moonlight, and we was laying around a watertank waiting for the flyer. The drip from the tank made a funny sound where it splashed in the white chat down below. The moon made ever'thing look kind of like silver, except in the shadows. Old Heavy was propped up again' one of them watertank posts singing just as loud as he could sing. He was singing a song he knew about a bum that was one hell of a liar, and one day while he was setting there telling these lies a fly crawls up him and tickles him to death. It's a kind of a dirty song in places.

"Pretty soon we could hear a train working steam away off down the track. I don't know if you know how it is out there on the prairies, but the first thing you see is this long white light come shaking down the rails. It don't make no noise at all, just white and still. It sure is pretty. It puts me in the mind of one of them stories my old woman used to read out of the Bible. Then after awhile you begin to hear the drivers, away off acrost the plains. Pretty soon, when it gets nearer, it seems like the dark is just alive and beating with that sound.

"Well, this here was a manifest coming, a hot-shot freight. Heavy and me was passenger stiffs and we never did ride nothing slower than a fruit express. It was two hours yet before the flyer

was due, but Heavy took it into his head that he was going to
ride this rattler. Nothing would do him but we had to ride that
manifest freight out. He got stubborn spells like that when he
had been drinking.

"I thought he was too lousy drunk to even get on, and I tried
to talk him out of it. But he slapped my jaws, and nothing else
would do him, so we walked on down the track a ways, and when
she stopped for water, I got Heavy on.

"After we was on, Heavy took a notion that he would ride the
bumpers. You know how the bumpers is on a box car: there's a
block where the coupling pin is fastened on, and it sticks out far
enough for you to sit on it. Heavy was riding down there between two cars, sitting on the bumpers with his feet propped up
over the coupling pins.

"I was riding the tops right above him, where I could keep my
eye on him, like I aimed to do. I guess I must of drowsed off,
though. I never will get through blaming myself for what happened anyway. Pretty soon something woke me up. It was old
Heavy screaming. I climbed down to where he was. He had
went to sleep and let his foot slip down between the coupling
pins. The cars had jostled and the coupling pins had jammed
together and it had smashed Heavy's heel off. I felt of it, and it
was all bloody and mushy there in his shoe.

"God, I was scared! I knew that I had to get that train
stopped. Old Heavy was just like a daddy to me. I was so
scared that I didn't want to think about what had happened.

"I climbed back up on top, and I begin to run over the tops
toward the engine. It was funny, but you know something
popped into my head about that time, and I can't get shut of it
yet.

IV

"How I happened to run off from home: the Spring I run off
they was learning us kids at school a dance for some kind of a
doings they was having. I mean they *tried* to make me learn it
along with the others, but I never did like any sissy business like
that, and I wouldn't learn it. So they whupped me. My old man
always said that if ever I got a whupping at school I'd get one
twicet as hard when I got home. And when my old man set out

to whup me, he would just about half kill me. So I just didn't
go home that night. I left out of there. Well, of all the crazy
things, this tune they tried to learn me to dance to back in the
fourth grade at school popped into my head, and it kept running
in my head all the time I was high-tailing it down toward the
engine acrost them box cars.

" 'Heel, toe, and a one-two-three-four,' it went. 'Heel, toe, and
a one-two-three-four!' I got so I could make it come out even,
and when I got to the 'four' I would be at the end of a car and
I would have to jump acrost to the next one and begin all over
again, 'Heel, toe, and a one-two-three-four!'

"That seemed to me like the longest rattler ever I rode, and I
thought I never was going to reach that engine cab. Finally I
did, and I crawled up over the coal and jumped down into the
cab, screaming and bawling and carrying on. They couldn't make
out what I was saying, but they stopped the train. The head-end
shack got off and run down the track with me, and finally we
found the car where Heavy was, cussing and groaning. Ever'
time old Heavy groaned, it was just like some one had slit me
with a shiv. We got him off of there, and they carried him back
to the caboose. I plugged along behind the con and the shack
that was carrying him, and ever' time I took a step one of them
words—heel, toe, and a one-two-three-four—would snap into my
head. It just kept running through my head.

"And when the train started up again, it seemed like the wheels
was clicking, 'Heel, toe, and a one-two-three-four!'

"They put us off at a little town about fifteen miles up the line
so as I could get Heavy to a doc. I don't know how I ever did
get that croaker out of bed that night, because I must have been
crazy in my mind. Anyhow, the one I got must of been a horse
doc, because he just looked at Heavy's smashed heel once and
says, 'Um-mmm. Iron rust in it. I'll have to cut it off.' He fixed
up a little frame over Heavy's face, and he showed me how to
drop the ether. I let the drops fall, and as they dropped this
'Heel, toe, and a one-two-three-four' jerked through my head in
time to the drops.

"After a while the croaker started sawing. I could see the bone
show white through the raw meat. Zup! that saw would go
acrost, and I would think, 'Heel!' and Zup! it would come back,

and I would think, 'Toe!'; and then it would go zup-zup-zup-zup, and I would count, one-two-three-four.

"Pretty soon I passed out myself. I was awful sick that night, but I went to sleep there in the croaker's office on a couch he had there, and when I woke up the next day the doc told me that Heavy was dead. They claimed he died of lock-jaw. I don't know. I didn't cry or anything. All I done was lay there with that crazy dance tune running through my head.

"The buried Heavy that same day. They had him a coffin made out of a goods-box and they loaded that in an old wagon and hauled him out to the graveyard. I walked along behind the wagon. I remember how the dust let my feet go down in it easy like I was walking on clouds. And the wagon wheels was warped and they clocked back and forth, making a kind of a hollow sound in a regular beat, and that 'Heel, toe, and a one-two-three-four' kept time to that beat the wheel hubs made.

"I sure did hate to see old Heavy go. Nothing never has meant anything to me since then. I didn't take on or nothing, but I don't have no memory of what happened at the grave or how I ever got away from there. I get that way ever' onct in a while now. I'll be walking along and that 'Heel, toe, and a one-two-three-four' will start up in my head and I take to walking in time to it. Some thinks I'm punch-drunk, walking like that, but I ain't punch-drunk.

"And sometimes I have dreams at night. I drempt that I was running along the tops of a long string of box cars that seems like it hasn't got no end, and the cars is swinging and swaying and I'm screaming and screaming, but the engine whistle up ahead is blowing so loud I can't hear what I'm screaming. Only I know what I'm screaming. It's that 'Heel, toe, and a one-two-three-four!' "

V

The little bum stopped talking and peered at Joe with one bright black eye. "You think I'm as full of nuts as a peach-orchard boar, don't you? Crazy as hell, ain't I?"

He stood up. "Well, I guess I'll try and see if I can't get on down to the Lake," he said briskly.

Joe said, "No, you don't need to do that. You can sleep here to-night if you want to. I've got me a shower bath fixed up back there. You go in and take a good bath, and you can sleep here."

The little bum said, "No, I'll find me a bench down on the beach somewheres. You don't want me sleeping here. I'm crazy in the head."

Joe stood watching him get into his coat. The kid slipped his arms tenderly into the sleeves. When he had reached the door, Joe called, "Well, so long, then!"

"So long, buddy. Did I give you any ideas you could use for stories?"

"Sure, you gave me some swell ideas," Joe said. "I can get a whole batch of stories out of what you told me. Much obliged!"

"Well, so long then, buddy. You're O.K."

The basement door slammed. Joe heard a footstep on the bottom step. There was a pause. One on the second. Another pause. Then, in quick succession, four that brought his departing visitor to the sidewalk level.

Joe walked over to the typewriter and ripped out the sheet that had his half-finished married-life joke on it. He crumpled the paper and threw the wad on the floor. Then he sat down, fed in a fresh sheet, and tapped the space bar nervously.

He started writing rapidly, *"Kind Old Lady:* My poor man, what brought you to this miserable state?"

Joe double-spaced and wrote "Hobo." He paused to phrase a snappy comeback for *Hobo.* Off down the silent, lamp-lit street he could hear the footclicks growing faint.

THE KIMONO [1]

By IRA V. MORRIS

(From *Story*)

THE fact is I felt so pleased that Saturday afternoon I almost decided to take a taxi home from the station. It's not exactly an everyday event, is it, to receive a notice to go up to the boss's office, and when you push open the door, fully expecting to be blown up for some bit of inefficiency on your part, have him swing towards you in his swivel chair, smiling from mouth to ear, and exclaim, "Well, Mr. Van Dusen, I have some good news for you. We've decided to switch Mr. Sands to another department. Do you think you could step into his shoes? It means a substantial raise in salary, to begin at once."

Well, what could I say? I stammered out something about being honored and trying to do my best, and the boss grinned again and said, "That's all right, Mr. Van Dusen. We've always considered you a dependable sort of fellow." It does you good to hear a thing like that, I can tell you. After having had the old harness on for thirteen years, you feel at last that some one appreciates your work.

As I walked down Main Street and up Union Avenue it seemed to me that almost every one must realize something big had happened. Even the dogs seemed to bark in a new way that afternoon and the clang of the street cars had a kind of joyful note. When I got a hundred yards from the house I couldn't wait any longer, and broke into a run which I accelerated till I was fairly leaping along by the time I reached the front gate. I kicked it open, tore down the garden path and then up the front steps three at a time; I hadn't acted so crazy since I was a boy at school. The door was open, but I think I would have jumped right through if it hadn't been.

My wife was drying the baby after his evening bath when I

crashed into the room, and she was so surprised she almost
dropped him on the floor; but when she gave a look at my face
she also for some reason or other began to laugh with pleasure
(how young and pretty she looks when she laughs), and put the
baby back in its crib. In two words I told her what had happened—then, taking hold of her by the waist, whirled her about
the room till we were both of us completely out of breath, while
little Peter lay watching with his tiny face wrinkled into laughter
and his red legs kicking in the air. Suddenly my wife stopped in
the middle of a turn, and still laughing and trying to control her
laughter said, "Oh, Van, I'd almost forgotten. There's a telegram for you in the living room. It was addressed to you, so I
didn't open it."

For a minute a funny feeling of fear, or rather annoyance, shot
right through me. Could any bad news come at such a moment?
But going downstairs to get the wire my confidence came back.
I felt a strength inside me I had never known before. I even
felt that I could twist the wording of that telegram!

I tore open the yellow slip and read:

"Dear Harry welcome home your long lost brother who is going
to pay you back those five hundred simoleons he owes you am
motoring out in my car to spend the night with you Bill."

Well, it never rains but it pours. Back up the stairs I flew,
almost turning my ankle on the landing, and scared Peggy half
to death this time when I burst on her in the bedroom.

"Darling—Bill's back home! He's driving out to-night."

"No, honest? You're not joking?"

My wife jumped up and grabbed the wire from my hand.

"What a telegram!" Her face was wreathed in smiles. "Just
typical of Bill, isn't it?"

"He doesn't spare the pennies, does he?"

"He certainly doesn't. 'Motoring out in my car,' he says. Can
you imagine Bill owning a car?"

"Well, I can't imagine him owning anything, though I certainly
can imagine him borrowing some one else's," I replied.

"Now what do you mean by that remark?"

Peggy always did have a habit of defending my brother, even
when he was obviously in the wrong, as he usually was.

"Oh, nothing at all," I calmed her down. "I was only going to say that if I do get back those five hundred smacks I lent him, then I suppose miracles are possible after all."

"I always told you you'd get them back."

"Well, I'll believe it when they clink in my pocket."

Still, I'll admit that I felt pretty good when, leaving Peggy to put the kid to bed, I went to make up the living room sofa for Bill to sleep on and telephoned the butcher to send around a couple of extra chops for supper. I really had about said good-bye to those five hundred dollars, as well as to any prospects of ever getting a raise at the office, and now it all seemed to be coming out right at the same time, and without any effort on my part either. I never would have dared to ask again for that raise, just as I long ago gave up writing Bill about the money, and here were things falling my way in the end simply from sitting pretty and saying nothing. Funny life it was, wasn't it? But not a bad one—oh, not by any means! And in my delight I shouted to my neighbour, who was watering his garden with a broken hose patched up with court-plaster and sealing wax, "Say, Mr. Harrison, would you like to borrow my new hose?" and immediately regretted my generosity.

Bill drove up in time for dinner in a swell little blue runabout, and I went to meet him at the front gate.

"Where's Peggy?" was the first question ne asked, and when he caught sight of her in the entrance he ran up to kiss her, though he'd only shaken me by the hand. He was the same Bill as ever, spontaneous and careless and somehow a likeable cuss—good-looking with that slick, black hair of his which he brushed back from the forehead.

What he had been doing, we of course wanted to know and, tickled to death as usual when he could talk about himself, he sat down on the verandah swing without even taking off his hat and coat and was soon in the midst of the wooliest tale of luck and adventure I've ever heard. He had been twice around the world since he saw us last, shipped as able-bodied seaman aboard a tramp and spent six months in the Orient representing some oil firm or other, though God only knows what Bill had to do with oil. Still, it seemed to have been profitable, and the proof was when he pulled out a big wad of notes from his wallet and skimming off the six top ones, handed me so many hundred dollar bills, as he casually announced,

"The extra hundred is meant for interest."

What a chap Bill was anyway! He had the grand manner all right, I'll say that for him.

It wasn't till we had actually sat down to supper that I had a chance to break the big news about my raise in salary, for every time I tried to bring the conversation around Bill launched off on some new spell-binding yarn and Peggy would make signs to me not to interrupt. Finally, however, I managed to keep his attention long enough to blurt it out, and my brother did his best to look interested (I guess it was hard work for an egotist like Bill), and he murmured, "That's fine, old man. Congratulations."

And now this happening, which half an hour before had seemed so important that I almost took a cab back from the station, appeared insignificant to such a degree that it was almost impudent to mention it. That's the way Bill always made you feel—as if you hardly counted at all, might just as well tie a rock round your neck and jump into the lake.

When we got through supper we all sat down in the living room (Peggy said she'd wash the dishes in the morning), and Bill took out a lot of photographs of his travels and showed them to us. Here he was in a pull-over sweater and trousers that were too long for him standing arm-in-arm with two tough-looking guys before some sort of café; you could see the tables on the sidewalk. Bill said this was Buenos Aires. Then there was another showing him in a gorgeous green kimono standing beside a Japanese temple; he told us that they wore kimonos over there in broad daylight, like regular street garments, and that he had brought this one back with him and used it like a dressing gown. In fact there were pictures from all over the world, and in each of them, of course, Bill figured as the central personage; Bill sitting on a camel in front of the sphinx, Bill and a girl in front of Notre Dame in Paris, France, Bill and two other janes somewhere in Italy. I got fairly fed up with hearing his voice going on and on —this is me somewhere or other, this is me and some pal somewhere else, here's me and a girl friend in still another place. There was no mistaking him, even without his keeping on advertising his presence.

"You seem to be attracted to the skirts, Bill." I kidded him along, kind of out of spite, but he didn't seem to mind, felt rather complimented even.

"Sure—you've got to find something to do on a long evening, don't you? We haven't all got pretty wives sitting at home waiting for us like you married men."

When we had got through the whole bunch and had had everything explained to us, I thought I'd get out our album and show him what we'd been doing in the meanwhile, but Peggy, who usually took such a pride in our pictures, said,

"Why do you want to bother Bill with those?"

"Sure, Peggy," said Bill. "I'd love to see them—honest."

"They're mostly of the kid, you know," I explained apologetically. "But perhaps you'll be interested in some of the snaps we took at Norwood, Mass., last summer. We visited Peggy's aunt during the summer holidays."

"Sure, I'd love to see them."

But we had not gotten halfway through when Bill interrupted,

"Say—what do you folks say to stepping out a bit? There's the car, brimful of gas and just panting to be off. How about joggling into town and stepping out for some celebrations? Prodigal's return, you know, and all that stuff."

I might have guessed that Bill would suggest something of the kind! He never could stay at home one night and be quiet. And now that the suggestion was made I knew at once from the pleased look on Peggy's face that we were in for it. I suppose I could hardly blame her, seeing that we hadn't spent an evening in town for at least two months and that we certainly did have something to celebrate to-night, other than the prodigal's return, I mean. Only I thought that some one might have mentioned this last argument.

It was a cold hour's drive into town, leastwise for me sitting alone in the dickey seat and when we finally arrived, I gladly chimed in with Bill's suggestion to get a bottle of something or other before going on to a place to dance. We waited for him a few minutes in the car, which he had stopped before an innocent-looking Italian restaurant, till he reappeared with something sticking out of his overcoat pocket and a successful look in his eyes.

"Well, that's O.K.," he said. "Now where do we go from

here?"

"You're the judge," I told him. "Peggy and I aren't much up on the night game, you know."

"How about the Black and White then? There's a good Negro show there at midnight."

"Sounds all right to me," said I.

Well, it might have sounded all right, but it certainly didn't look it. It was a dark cellar of a place, you had to stagger down half a flight to get into it, and it was filled to overflowing with Negroes with diamond stick pins, half-naked chorus girls, and a smattering of other black and white riff-raff in various stages of intoxication. I thought we had come to the wrong place but Bill assured us it was quite all right. As a matter of fact he seemed to be known here, for the waiter called him by his name and showed us to what he said was a good table near the orchestra, though why it was better than any of the others I failed to see.

"Now, how about a little drink," suggested Bill, and he poured out three glasses half full of whiskey and sprinkled a little ginger ale on top. It tasted like vitriol but Bill swallowed his in three gulps and Peggy winced but managed to get away with a couple of swallows. The saxophone suddenly whined in my ear and the Negro orchestra burst into commotion.

"That's a good girl," said Bill with a laugh. "Now come and have a dance with your brother-in-law."

I watched them sidle through the raft of tables which separated us from the cleared space, and then she put her arm on Bill's shoulder and they were swallowed up in all the other couples dancing or pushing each other across the floor. They made a handsome pair, I thought, as I caught sight of them again at the other end of the room: they were dancing close together, as was every one else, and she was looking up into his face and laughing.

And for no reason in particular I suddenly remembered something that my mother had said years before when I told her that I intended marrying Peggy and she was trying to talk me out of it: that she would make a better wife for a wild, erratic sort of fellow like Bill than for a good, steady man who wanted to get on in the world. Well, that had all proved nonsense, I reflected. Here we had been married five years, going on six, and despite our occasional quarrels we certainly got on far better than most married people, while any tendency to flightiness that Peggy might have had seemed to have disappeared when little Peter came. What if she still did like a good time now and then? Surely no one could see any harm in that.

I sat sipping my whiskey and thinking in a pleased sort of way about the last few years and things in general. The stuff did not taste so bad after the first swallows and when I had poured myself a second glass and finished it I felt just about all right. Everything seemed to me to be pretty well planned and agreeable, more agreeable than I had ever known it before, or rather I felt that it had always been like this, but that I had never appreciated it till now. If one only worked hard and had confidence in oneself it seemed one got what one deserved in the end, even though things did look pretty hopeless more than half the time; it was all a sort of give and take, but when one finally got there it was worth the struggle. I was pleased with the present and with the past, while it seemed to me that the future was rosier still, that I would be given an even better position at the office and then I could save some money and buy some stock. Tapping on the table with my knife in time to the melody that filled the air, lulled by the dim lights and the whiskey and the swaying figures, I certainly felt on the crest of the wave—

"I'll say we had a wonderful dance," Bill's voice broke in on my reverie.

Peggy and he had wound their way back through all the tables and were sitting down before I was even aware that the tune had ended. I jumped up and helped her into her chair.

"I was thinking that you two made a fine couple together," I said. "You seem to be just cut out for one another."

"Really?" said Peggy, giving a poke at her hair as she smiled up at Bill.

"Oh, yes. Aren't you glad that you've got such a nice sister-in-law, Bill?"

"Of course," said Bill. "Don't you know that's why I came back from the Orient?"

We all laughed. Bill poured us out another round of drinks as the orchestra crashed into tune and I looked at Peggy, and nodded meaningly towards the floor. It was my first attempt at dancing in about three years, and considering the amount of whiskey I had gotten away with, I do not think it went so badly at all, even if we did almost fall down once and had to grab on to a table for support. I insisted that some one had tried to trip us up, adding wittily that perhaps it was because husbands and wives weren't allowed to dance together in a place like this.

"You're drunk, Van," said Peggy and she laughed. Pretty she looked to-night with her big black eyes all shiny and bright. I guessed that was the liquor, and the lines of her slim youthful figure showing beneath that blue silk dress, my favourite dress ever since we bought it together four years ago. She seemed in her element somehow in a place like this, though I guess she'd only been to such joints a few times in her life.

At three o'clock the Black and White closed. We were all of us pretty tight by then, but Bill said it was too early to go home and of course I agreed with him. After all, wasn't to-morrow Sunday and wasn't this party supposed to be a celebration—though what we were celebrating seemed a little mixed in my mind?

When I got up from the table my head reeled, so that I seemed to be walking on the ceiling, and the tables swam around and banged into each other and then into me, and all at once we were on the street, where a cold wind was slapping me in the face. I remember my hat flying off and rolling down the sidewalk and my chasing after it till I was almost run over by a taxicab, probably would have been if Bill hadn't yanked me aside.

Then I was back in the dickey seat, and we were tearing through the streets again while I held my hat with both my hands to prevent a repetition of its flight; we pulled up with a jolt and a crunching of brakes at the Italian restaurant where we had bought the whiskey.

"Get out," said Bill. "We're there."

I was sitting at a table opposite my brother and two brown glasses were in front of us again. My brain was muddled and I felt extremely drunk, yet in the back of my mind I knew that there was something very important that I had to say—I had been wanting to say it all the evening—but now I could not quite remember what it was. Perhaps if I had another drink I would remember. I drank the whiskey, and my brain was suddenly quite clear and I remembered.

"Bill," I said, leaning across the table. "There's something I want to tell you. Get married. Quit bumming around like you've been doing and try to settle down. It's the only way to be happy. Find yourself some nice girl—like Peggy here—some one you can love. Get a job. I tell you you've never known what happiness is—"

My head fell forward on the table. I could not finish the sentence, for my brain had begun to go around the room in enormous circles, round and round and round. From very far away I heard a voice—was it Bill's?—and then another gruff voice with an Italian accent. I remember noting the foreign accent and wondering who the man could be. Some one was taking me under the arms, trying to raise me up. I mumbled a few words and attempted to break away from him but only succeeded in falling back on the chair—or was it the floor? My feet would not do what I wanted. Then I was walking again or some one was pushing or carrying me; up something I stumbled, higher and higher up, and suddenly I was confronted with a door and then a bed. I fell down on it and closed my eyes—and my brain kept going round and round and round—

When I woke up in the room above the Italian restaurant it was broad daylight. I was lying on a bed with all my clothes on, and my head ached, and there was a bad taste in my mouth. Slowly the previous evening came back to me, and I remembered that I had been drunk for the first time in my life.

"Well, that *was* a celebration," I thought.

I tried to get up, but my head swam so that I was forced to lie down on the bed again; but in a few moments my head was clearer and I managed to stand up, and presently even staggered down the stairs.

A man in shirtsleeves with a mop was cleaning out the room where we had sat the night before. At my entrance he looked up and grinned in a friendly, understanding sort of way.

"Your head ache, what?"

I nodded to him.

"Want some water?"

He went to the tap and filled a pitcher which he handed to me, together with a note from Bill saying that he had put me to bed, as this seemed the only thing to do, and was going to take

Peggy back home in the car. I drank two glasses of water, gave the man a tip and left the restaurant.

I will never forget the train ride home that Sunday morning, with my head almost splitting open at every bump and feeling that I was going to be sick at any moment, yet not being able to when I tried. To make matters worse, the carriage was unheated, leastwise it felt as if it were, and my teeth kept chattering in my head from the cold. It was a terrible trip. How I cursed Bill then for ever luring me on that crazy party!

Peggy was tidying up the living room when I came in, and little Peter who'd been left in charge of our neighbours, the Harrisons, over night, lay in his carriage ready to be wheeled out for his morning walk. He smiled, raising his stubby arms towards me, as he saw me in the door; I'll swear the little beggar had already begun to recognize me. It certainly did seem good to be back home again after such a night; it made one realize how lucky one was to have a warm home and a wife and kid to come back to. The headache and the unpleasant train ride were at once forgotten, and I felt again a tingling of pleasure at the thought of my secure, well-ordered life, so seldom interrupted by violent adventures like last night's.

Bill had already left, my wife informed me. He was catching a train for the West Coast the same day, as he had told us, and he did not have the time to await my return.

"Poor fellow!" I exclaimed sympathetically. "He'd be much happier with a home and a family! What a life to keep dashing from one place to another without even time to rest for a few days in between. I'd go crazy in about a month."

"Yes, Van," said Peggy. "I guess you would."

I laughed and kissed Peggy on the cheek. Then I went upstairs to undress, for having slept in my clothes I felt sticky all over and thought it would be pretty nice to step into a good hot bath and soak out a little of that whiskey. I was still cold too and my fingers were so stiff that I could hardly undo the buttons. Pulling at my collar, my stud fell out on the floor and rolled under one of the twin beds; I made a futile stab for it before it disappeared. But I wasn't going to let that get away so easily! No, indeed—bitter experience having long since taught me the inconveniences of missing collar buttons.

Falling down on my knees, I began carefully rummaging around on the floor, and presently my hand touched, not the collar button, but something soft which I thought must be a sheet or pillow slip fallen through the crack between the beds. When I pulled it out, however, I discovered to my surprise that it was a sort of coat or jacket made of green cloth with yellow figures embroidered in the material. For some time I stood staring at it without realizing what it was; I seemed to have seen it before, and fairly recently, yet I could not quite succeed in placing it.

Then all at once it came to me: it was the kimono Bill was wearing in that picture where he stood beside the Japanese temple; the kimono which he used as a dressing gown. In a flash I realized what the thing was and what it meant lying under Peggy's bed and everything that must have happened in the room that night. And still staring at that bit of cloth with its beautiful design of interweaving dragons, the thought struck me that I had been absurdly happy the day before.

It seems that a guy just shouldn't be too happy in this world.

SHEPHERD OF THE LORD [1]

By PETER NEAGOE

(From *Story*)

THE Lord has many sheep.—Through the mouth of his chosen ones he commanded them to go and multiply like the sands of the seas. They are multiplying.—

Popa Anghel Boyer is shepherd of the Lord. A strong man Popa Anghel. The peasants rise when he passes and the women kiss his large hand; the left hand pats the young woman's cheek as she bends her forehead on his right hand. The old he blesses, laying a heavy blessing hand on their bent heads. Popa Anghel's boots are shiny and squeak proudly, as the shepherd stamps along the street.—When there is a wind his long moustaches are flowing streamers, black and shiny. But his spade-shaped beard, large and thick, flattens like an armor plate against his heavy chest. His long locks fall in curls over a neck, round and strong as a tree-trunk. The wide muscle-padded shoulders carry easily Popa Anghel's head.

Popa Anghel handles his four oxen with easy grace. The grace of power. Shouting to the heavy, long-horned animals keeps his voice alive. He sings in church and the saints on the windows tremble. He booms his sermons upon his congregation, and his words like waves against the breasts of the faithful. The candle flames stretch and shrink, waver and blink, when Popa Anghel booms his sermons in the house of the Lord.—

Popa Anghel's wife (priestess Andronica, the peasants call her) is wide-hipped, tall, full-chested. Generous breasts tremble maternally on her full chest when Andronica laughs. Her face and eyes laugh together and the breasts rock in unison.—Her skin is smooth as velvet, and her hands white and plump, her voice molten honey.—A sweetly fragrant burden in Popa Anghel's powerful arms.—"You crush my bones, you holy bear," she pants as Popa Anghel holds her, his face against her white throat.—

The house is large, the beds are fields of linen and virgin wool. Sweet mint and incense permeate the air of their nest. Popa Anghel and Andronica's nest.—

Popa Anghel has cattle, large-flanked, sleek and strong. Cows, oxen, horses, a bull and a stallion. For in animals the shepherd of the Lord favors the male; in his own species he loves the female.—

Popa Anghel has two daughters, Elizabeth and Maria.—Priests' wives and daughters are splendid females.—The Transylvanian peasant has good eyes.—"She could marry a priest," he says of a beautiful girl.—Elizabeth was seventeen then and Maria fourteen. Elizabeth was not a big girl—but she was plump—feeding on hallowed bread, honey and milk—and her skin was rosy and smooth. Her voice was full and her laughter rippled. The smell of ripe fruit, and her skirt was always snow-white.—The colorful aprons she wore had choice designs. The sleeves of her shirt were very full and puffed out from the shoulders to the wrists, where they gathered in embroidered bands, to emerge again in ruffled cuffs. But the wrist-bands were loose and when Elizabeth lifted her arms, the sleeves fell back to her very shoulders, wreaths of whiteness from which emerged the pink arms. But Maria was my friend. She was fourteen and I fifteen. Here my story starts.—

Popa Anghel's stone barns were veritable labyrinths. The fragrance of hay and straw sipped into the stone. Even the dust in Popa Anghel's barn was scented. Elizabeth, Maria, myself and two or three village boys played at hide-and-seek there during two of any summer vacations. I hid in the hay, dug myself into the straw and flattened out in some cozy corner. To be found by Maria was the greatest pleasure of my heart. By the time she came upon me Maria was exhausted, had to rest. She would sit down close to me; I would touch her cool arm in the darkness of our hiding place. At such times we talked in whispers, close to each other, and Maria's breath was sweeter than the fragrance of ripe straw.—She often bent so close to my face that the ringlets of her black hair touched my face.—

It was the time when I began to feel that girls are very splendid creatures, Maria their queen. The mere sight of Maria, walking across the yard, her apron flaring, released such flow of life in me that I could have jumped over the house or lifted one of the oxen on my back. When we walked side by side, our hands coming together, our fingers timidly embracing, there was a splendor on every object. My eyes were keen as an eagle's. The merest sounds were music. The immense mystery of life gushed from and through everything.—

We loved the brook in which we waded.—Maria's feet gleaming pink on the shimmering pebbles of its bed—and the water gurgled in its rush. We smiled upon the flowers in the fields and threw ourselves upon the warm ground inhaling the cool scent of the grass we crushed with our bodies.—We loved the sparrows who stole kernels from the sheaves stored in the barn. We loved them as we loved the stars and even God, who, we knew, was up in the sky, seeing everything that happened on the earth.—

But we knew, Maria and I, that we were the very core of everything, and God looked upon us from above, with grace and love. He was our father.—

Maria referred to her own father as Popa Anghel, because the villagers called him so. Maria feared Popa Anghel more than she feared God, because this powerful man lorded over his family with great zest. He was so fond of practical jokes that in church he swung the incense-chalice, filled with glowing embers, dangerously near to the mayor's nose. But everybody knew the mayor to be a miser and a tyrant, despite the great piety he showed on Sundays.—

In his gold-embroidered priestly garb, Popa Anghel looked very big.—He smacked the bundle of sweet mint, soaked in holy water, on the heads of his parishioners with great relish. He kept a serious face but his spade-shaped black beard seemed to laugh as it spread over the shimmering surplice.—Often his large moustache pushed out from under his nose as if mocking at some one, just when Popa Anghel raised his hand, with two fingers closed, the other three symbolizing the holy trinity.

I noticed that when young women kissed Popa Anghel's hand he would press it against their lips, before they could bow their forehead upon it as the custom is. When he prayed over some young widow whose husband had been taken by the Lord, his hand would caress the woman's cheeks as he adjusted his peplum over her head. But he uttered his prayer in clear words, in a soothing sing-song, so the woman was comforted and left the shelter of the holy peplum refreshed, but with flushed cheeks.—

But Popa Anghel did not like the mayor, nor could he bear the mayor's son, a tall square-shouldered young man of twenty, who followed Elizabeth everywhere. This young man, Jacob, was dark and sombre of looks, but he smiled so ingratiatingly that mothers of marriageable girls sighed and shook their heads when he did so. But Jacob had no eyes for other girls; only for Elizabeth.—Now I have learned some things—since those days—so I know that Elizabeth was a great beauty.

Elizabeth was then about seventeen; not tall but of such grace that even old men turned to look upon her when she passed them in the street. And she had a way of changing the expression of her violet-blue eyes from coldest haughtiness to a melting warmth which nobody could resist.—That is why Jacob could not live a day without seeing her.—For this reason, he became great friends with me. Passing Popa Anghel's, he would drop in to call on me with every kind of pretext. One time to show me a thrush he caught that very morning, another time to give me a new sheath for my belt knife, but more often to ask me into the fields to help him at some work—which I always loved to do.

I was flattered by Jacob's friendship, because he was stronger than the other peasants and the best wrestler in the village, not to mention his dancing.—Every girl in the village loved to dance the reel with him. In the first slow steps of this old dance, the man barely touches the waist of the two girls—his dancing partners—while, moving slowly to the right and to the left, he improvises in rhyme. A satire on some one or some commonly known event, but more often the man chants out in verse his heart's yearning.—Decided skill is needed to do this, for lacking that, the poor man will only betray his feelings to the amusement of the assembly. Jacob had remarkable skill in this kind of improvising.—He sang his praises to his adored one, comparing her to the moon—queen of the stars; to the sun, whose light and warmth is our life, placing himself, the adorer, in a sad or happy relation to the symbol of his worship, according to the condition of his heart at the time.—

Everybody listened to Jacob's rhyming, and mothers of lovely girls attributed his affection to their own daughters. Each one secretly, of course.—And many of the girls blushed and blinked to hide a tear.—But I knew to whom Jacob was singing,—I did not even have to look at Elizabeth to know it.—And Elizabeth never betrayed her feelings to anybody but myself, and to me only by her occasional glances at me. Her big violet-blue eyes remained otherwise screened by their long black lashes.—

My admiration for Jacob was especially strong because he could handle a long whip with uncanny skill.—He could crack the whip so it sounded like a pistol shot, and by lashing it back and forth, without once striking the ground, he produced with it a succession of reports like that of exploding firecrackers. But what mostly amazed one was the manner in which he would strike down a fruit from the tree. He swung the whip around, then with a quick jerk of the hand would lash the stem of the fruit and bring it to the ground.

In a whip duel he always disarmed his opponent.—With frowning eyes he watched for the favoring moment, to lash the whip-handle of his adversary and jerk it out of his hand.—The aim of a whip duel is no other than such disarming of the opponent.

Jacob was very generous towards me. He gave me his finest whip, thick as my wrist at the handle, tapering so gently towards the leash that it became twelve feet in length.—Jacob had pleated this whip himself, in four strands of white hemp, strong and shining as silk. The handle was hickory, smooth as polished ivory on the upper end but rough, for a better hold, at the lower.—

Under Jacob's rigorous tutoring, I succeeded after four weeks in managing the splendid weapon as well as Jacob. So well in fact did I handle the whip, that one day I strangled a crow with it.—The poor bird stood perched on a lump of sod in a newly ploughed field, its beak in the air and the head tilted to one side. —I aimed at the bird's neck.—The deadly leash coiled round it, with a snap—and the bird fell over with open beak.—

It may have been mere chance, but Jacob praised me for the accuracy of my aim and I felt prouder than Cæsar.

Jacob could sing well, in a clear tenor. My voice had broken already and was settling in a deep baritone. Jacob taught me many folk-songs. On evenings we walked up and down the village main street, singing in duet.

On a warm night in August, Jacob gathered six or seven young peasants and we went in front of Popa Anghel's house.—It was dark but the air was full of the fragrance of the fields.—We sat down under the locust tree and began singing. Softly, sadly, an endless tune. Occasionally a breeze would stir the foliage, rendering more sad, even, the melancholy monotone of our song.—

I became sadder and sadder under the influence of the night and the never-ending song. At length I burst out crying.—Jacob, near whom I was seated, put his arm around my shoulders.—My crying became a real lament, for with tears in my voice, I kept my place with the singers. Suddenly, Jacob's voice broke also. Then the other fellows' voices caught, and the chorus sounded like a group of mourners.—

How long we kept up our wailing, no one could tell, but a rude shock, a terrific donkey-braying, came suddenly, cutting into our lamentation. This unholy braying poured down upon us from one of the windows in the priest's house. We stopped instantly. We could see nothing, but all guessed that it must be Popa Anghel himself—who indeed it was.—For, after his ghastly braying, the priest thundered out in his booming voice:

"Pheu, Satan, may the holy cross kill you! Go back, devil, unto the flaming bowels of hell. Don't disturb the peace of one anointed unto the Lord."—

We crawled off softly on all fours. Once in the street, we took natural positions again and ran away on tiptoe.

Maria told me in the morning that both she and Elizabeth had heard us and cried until their pillows were soaked with tears. Only later she told me that when they heard the braying of their father they got cramps from laughing.—

Being at Popa Anghel's, I saw everything that came to pass there.—But the peasants say: "It is easier to watch a flock of rabbits than a woman in love." This is gospel truth. I never noticed anything about Elizabeth until one day, going into the barn, I saw something. But what I saw shall never pass my lips. I am honor-bound never to tell a soul. Elizabeth made me swear and then kissed me and pressed me to her heart.—For the kiss alone and for her embrace I would keep the secret eternally, not to mention Elizabeth's violet-blue eyes, as they implored me.

In the spring, soon after Easter, Popa Anghel married his

daughter Elizabeth to the school-teacher. A very handsome young man, with curly black hair, so genuinely patriotic that even now he wears the Roumanian garb on Sundays.—

When I arrived in the summer, Elizabeth was marvelously beautiful. She was not as rosy of color as before but a heavenly light shone in her eyes.—She was loved, and the peasants said, "Her husband carries her about on his palms."—The school teacher was an ardent lover indeed, for Elizabeth seemed to have forgotten Jacob, who was in the army. When he came for two weeks' leave in August, Jacob only spoke of books. He never mentioned his love.—Before we parted he said: "When I come back from service, I will go into the mountains to herd our sheep. Don't you see, Peter, the village is so small?—It is sad, so small it is."—

I soon forgot my sorrow for Jacob, because to me the village was a gay song; for Maria was there.—

We were big enough—Maria and I—to take our amusements otherwise than as children, but we did not. We ran about in bare feet, climbed trees, played in the barn and wandered in the woods. —What we both enjoyed most was swinging in the barn.—The swing was made of two heavy ropes, attached to the very peak of the barn roof.—Usually I sat on the board of the swing while Maria, standing facing me, drove it by bending from the knees and straightening up with a push.—We often touched the edge of the roof on both sides. When we swung so fast Maria's skirt flared catching my head in its folds, and she laughed so much at this that she had to ease her swinging.—I was never sorry for that, because then I could tickle her knee, and the smooth spot right in the back of it.—All she could do was to wriggle with strident shouts of laughter. When we heard the tramping of Popa Anghel in the yard, we quickly slid off the swing and disappeared in the hay.—

But this last summer of my stay at Popa Anghel's, the skies of my happiness began to cloud; Maria grew too fast.—She had passed fifteen, and was one inch taller than myself.—This was terrible enough in itself, but Maria made it worse. She adopted a protective air towards me—like a big sister managing a frail brother. I had to resort to cunning and the privileges of my sex to offset Maria's patronizing. And often did it at the expense of my feelings.—

One of the things I did—when the horse was needed in the fields—was to mount the horse bareback and ride proudly through the gate opened for me by Maria. In the street I set the horse trotting, then goaded him to a clumsy gallop, knowing that Maria was watching and envying me. She could ride the horse as well as I could (she insisted that she did it better, but I never believed her), but the horse was round as a barrel and too much of Maria's bare legs showed from under her skirts for Andronica's approval. Once she had tears in her eyes when she pointed to my trousers saying: "It is easy for you, in those ugly things."—She threw a twig at my head as I trotted out of the yard, haha-ing her.—Another time she swished a handful of nettles between the horse's legs and I had to flatten out on him and hold on to his mane. Maria shrieked with joy.—Arrived in the fields I worked with the peasants. At noon Maria and two women came with baskets of food. On such occasions Maria never failed to ask me, even coax me, to go back with her and take my luncheon with the family. Of course I refused, spending a miserable day thinking of her.

But I wanted to show Maria my independence; to show her how easily I did without her company. In truth, however, neither the flushed faces of the working girls nor the movements of their bodies (clad only in a full linen shirt with a belt and two aprons) consoled me. In fact their laughing and singing increased my longing for Maria.—

At first this stratagem of mine worked very well. Maria told me that the day was much too long for her without me. But Maria was much more clever than I thought. Soon she came to consider my behavior as a childish caprice and told me to my face that I was not as smart as I imagined. I had to look for other means to promote my superiority.—An opportunity came.—Being wealthy, Popa Anghel had a bull and a stallion.—They were used for breeding the cows and mares of the villagers.—Popa Anghel called the stallion Nestor.—No one but himself was allowed to exercise Nestor. Daily, Popa Anghel would lead the splendid animal into the yard.—A heavy pleated halter on the stallion's head and a long rope attached to it were the only means of con-

trol used by the priest. Nestor had flaming eyes, a long tail and
a wealth of mane. As soon as he came into the yard he let out a
terrific neighing, arched his neck, whipped his tail and began
prancing.—The priest gave him rope, turning on his trunk-like
legs, in the center of a circle formed by the galloping stallion.
Nestor's body was steel-gray. It shone like polished metal. His
black tail and mane flared with his movements. His hoofs, slender, high, trimmed and carefully filed, were like ivory. He had a
way of picking up his feet as if the ground under them were red
hot. His thin ankles were springs of steel. Popa Anghel, in his
thick, gurgling voice, would talk adoringly to Nestor. "There,
beauty, there, my brave one, limber up your limbs. Now, now!
Not so rough, my hero; there are no devils here.—You can beat
the very devil, my boy, so you can, my beauty."

The spade-shaped beard bobbed up and down on the priest's
chest as he spoke.—

Popa Anghel loved fecundity. Nestor and the bull were to him
symbols of male power and fructifying force. He would caress
the bull's flanks, press his face against the shining hide and inhale
deeply its odor. The bull would roll his eyes with animal wonderment and stretch his enormous neck. Lifting his massive head, he
released, from the depths of his huge body, trombone-like sounds.
—The priest laughed, answering: "Yes, my boy, sure—just as
you say," and slapped the bull's belly.—

There was a small yard in back of the barns. Wall-enclosed.—
Nestor and the bull performed their fructifying duties there.
Popa Anghel assisted with ritual officiousness, talking admiringly,
encouragingly, to Nestor or the bull, as the occasion required, one
or the other.—But, as soon as a peasant came, with cow or mare,
the priest boomed out his order, that all female folk retire into
the house. "Maria—there, girl—get in! What are you gaping
at, your mouth open as the barn door? Run in to your mother."
Maria had to run into the house at once.—But she looked at me
enviously and angrily, because I could stay in the yard until the
animal was led through the barn gates into the—sanctum—there
I was not allowed to enter.—

But, reconnoitering in the barn loft, I had found a square ven-
tilator, way up near the roof. It was large enough for me to
squeeze through, so that, without being seen from the yard below,

I could watch the ceremony.—So one day when I saw the mayor come with his mare, I sneaked into the barn. Nobody had seen me. I heard Popa Anghel talking to the mayor. Then he told him to lead the mare— "In there, you know," he shouted, adding, "She's a fine one, your mare."

I clambered to my post of vantage. Soon I heard Nestor's tramping on the barn floor. I looked down. The mayor was holding the mare by the bridle.

"Tie her to that post, man! Get away. Want your bones crushed," shouted the priest.—Hurriedly the mayor wound the rope around the post, slipped it through an iron ring and knotted it. Then he ran along the wall into the barn.—

Seeing the mare, Nestor let out a piercing neigh and reared on his hind legs.—He pushed his tail out straight, then he whipped it so it hissed.—The mare flattened her ears, neighing and dancing.—Popa Anghel gave rope to the stallion, dodging him: "Not too rough, my hero; gently, my boy! Now, you devil, don't murder her," he shouted. Nestor was biting the mare's neck, rearing up and away, when neighingly she snapped back at him.—Then he pawed the ground, snorting furiously. I heard a noise under his belly as of a club beating on a kettle-drum. Bam, bam, bam, it went, Nestor pawing and snorting. The priest's spade-shaped beard danced on his chest, a thick laugh rumbling out of him.

"Back there," he shouted to the mayor, who sidled nearer to the scene.—

Nestor reared up. His front legs gripped the mare's flanks. The mare danced and neighed—ears flattened—snapping at the stallion's head, as he was mouthing her mane with outstretched lips.—Suddenly, resting his whole weigh against the mare's body, the stallion set to pummeling her with his front legs.—I feared that the savage animal would kill the poor mare, who was being sacrificed to his ferocious passion.—

"His little love-play," grunted the priest over his shoulder to the mayor. Now the "love-play" stopped. For one instant both animals were still; then I saw Nestor's huge body well up, like a menacing swell, from rump to neck.—

"Aha—my hero," grumbled Popa Anghel.—

Leaving my peep-hole, I slid from the straw into the hay, fifteen feet below, where I sank up to my shoulders.—I stood there awaiting my breath, before trying to crawl out, when I heard something stirring in the hay—quite close to me. I listened. Some one was crawling towards me. Then I heard Maria's voice whispering: "I saw you."—

"Very well, if you did," I answered as softly.

"Where have you been?" she added, very close to me.

"Up there."

"Up where?"

"There on top of the straw." I pointed.

"Just so? What were you doing there?" Maria insisted.

"I? What should I do? Climbed on the straw!"

"To see what?"

"To see? What should I see there? It is dark, on top there."

"There is a shaft of light; I saw it from . . ." She pointed back.

"Yes! Well, there is a bit of light coming in," I admitted.

"One can look down there." She pointed toward the back of the barn.

"Maybe."

"Did you look?" Maria put her mouth close to my ear. This irritated me. She was too insistent and had a manner of questioning which I could not dodge.

"Yes, I did, if you want to know," I answered brusquely.

"You did—? Well—if father knew that!"

She certainly was exasperating.—I felt my face blushing; my eyes smarted with tears of anger. Whenever we discussed anything Maria had the upper hand of me. Her manner befogged my brain, so that I had to wait too long for the proper answer; she profited by my silence, to cram my head with a lot of words, confusing me still more.

But this time a light had come to me. With cruel relish I snapped at her: "And why weren't you in the house? Didn't Popa Anghel order you in?"

"No—he did not." She pulled herself up coldly.—I was not abashed. "Did he send you in here?" I asked with mock sweetness.

"Oh"—she moaned. "You are just a bad, vicious little urchin!" And stretching out on the hay, she cried softly.

I could see her shoulders shake. Something sagged, in the very core of me. I felt limp. With great effort I crawled out. Putting my face close to Maria's head, I began repeating: "What have I done? What have I done?" She covered her ears, her shoulders shaking the more, with stifled sobbing.—

I repeated these four words so often, that at length they seemed very stupid to me, in the presence of Maria's grief. I fell silent. —I put my hand on her head. Her hair was soft, alive. Her head seemed to beat against my finger-tips, like a heart. That made me terribly sad and compassionate with Maria. Leaning my face softly against her head, I began to cry also. We cried together, like that, for a long time.

At length, a feeling of lightness, a strange happiness invaded me, like the return of health in convalescence.—With each passing moment my well-being increased.—And, not only had my sense of smell become keen and refined, but my entire body was now as sensitive to touch as my finger-tips.—

I felt the fragrant air on my face as if it were something alive; my very clothes seemed like living skin, growing from my body.— I felt strong. Very strong. I felt as if a living force, a force of growth, were pushing outward, through the wall of my body. Carried away by this power, swung on a wave of warm light, I turned Maria to me—with a quick and agile move, and looked into her astonished eyes. Then, embracing her with all my strength, I bent to her ear, saying: "Maria—I love you."

For one short instant Maria looked at me earnestly; then her eyes smiled, her lips and her face smiled. She put up her arms,— her sleeves fell back to her armpits, and she smoothed my hair. Her fingers streamed delight into me. Suddenly she encircled my neck and pressed me to herself.—

We kissed on the lips, on the eyes, and swore eternal love to each other.—

It is known that our greatest weakness lies in the effort to eternalize an emotional state. Only Nirvana can be eternal because it is nothingness.—An emotion has an apex. There is to it an ascent and a descent. But this is wisdom, and how could Maria or myself know this, for all we had then was the great urge of life.—

I hope, for Maria's sake, that, like her father, she remained on life's side—unwise.—

The following summer my uncle took me into the mountains. He made me bathe in warm whey "to equip you for life," he said. We fed on corn mush and sweet cream—skimmed from sheep's milk cooling in wooden trays, and on that delicacy of the Carpathian shepherd—frozen mutton-stew. The odor of that dish, mixed with the fragrance of rosin and pine-gum, can resurrect the dead.—

The whey-bath, the morning baths in spring water, the rolling on the dewy slope until my body tingled, and my uncle's rations, gave me such vigor and strength that I wrestled with the shepherds the whole day. In the evening I wished for a bear to come along so we could have a real, rough tussle.—And I thought of Maria, wishing she were there.—Lying on the carpet of pine-needles, inhaling the heavenly air of the old forest, my thoughts were ever with Maria.—That feeling, first experienced in the barn, the feeling of an inner force pushing on the walls of my body, never left me. At times it became painful—for it had no other outlet than shouting, wrestling or running.—Because I was aware that this force surged purposefully—towards Maria, my love.— Only her presence near me could justify it and, perchance, relieve me from its pain.

I waited endless days, in torturing desire.—

Then—Maria came. Elizabeth with her husband, Jacob and Maria. What a day that was.—

The presence of a woman in the solitude of the mountains is more welcome than the first day of spring after a hard winter.— But who can describe the feeling if the woman happens to be the loved one?—

Maria and Elizabeth were the first to appear on the edge of the horizon. The shepherds saw them. With a shout they threw their caps in the air, and began jumping and pushing each other. They baaed, mooed and neighed—seized with a frantic animal joy.

I stood petrified, scanning the distance. They called to me: "See there—brave one! Female folks! Mother mine—female folks. Young, too . . . Young, sure! Sure as daylight!"— They sang.

"You can see the way they ride. Happy horses! Mother mine— Young, plump heifers."—

Even my uncle changed suddenly, when he saw them. His eyes sparkled, his black beard took on a bright sheen. A vibrant ring came into his voice.—He moved about quickly, ordering Dan to slaughter a young ram. Before the visitors reached us, the fire roared under the big kettle—started by him. He even peeled the onions, a peck of them, as fast as four womanly hands. He threw the onions in the kettle to simmer and yield up their flavor before the meat was put in.—An hour after, we were all seated on blankets, our mouths watering for the fragrant stew.—

My uncle lorded it over the shepherds, stroking his beard, his eyes on Elizabeth, who sat pensively, watching the distance, where naked mountain peaks glowed in the setting sun. When we ate, he sat near Elizabeth. With a wooden fork he pointed to the choicest morsels for her to pick.—

Aha, good uncle, I must tell this, for you even touched her hand several times. At her faintest smile, you laughed uproariously. But I was pouting with a fierce joy, watching you jealously, because I did not sit near Maria, as I wished.—

When the moon came up, the sheep were safe in the enclosure. The four shepherds played on their fifes. We danced, sang with them, Maria's piercing voice dominating the others like a cry.— I never left Maria, but Jacob remained always near her also.—

When the hour came for us to go to bed, Maria walked leisurely towards the spring—alone. I followed her unseen, by her or any one else. In front of the little pool into which the water trickled from a wooden pipe stuck in the rock, Maria stopped, stretching like a sleepy cat. I could hear her inhale the air. Then she cupped her hands under the streamlet and drank. With her wetted palms she patted her cheeks. That moment I came up to her.

The moonlight formed a halo around Maria—the water trickled shimmeringly into the basin. A light wind hummed in the fir trees beyond and played with Maria's hair. I felt lighter than the wind. I felt tall, my chest expanded, and I inhaled the scented air in long, deep breaths. A soothing warmth suffused my body, prickled my face.

Quietly, but with all the feeling I could put into my voice, I said to her: "Maria! Dearest, Maria!"

She looked at me steadily, without a smile; without the least move of her lively features. She stood and looked at me, the wind playing with her hair.

"Won't you say a word, Maria?" I asked softly.

Maria moved her arms as if they were wings. Then she said: "The air here is—you know—it makes me feel as if I were bathing in very clear water."

"Oh, yes! It is—just exactly—like the purest water. Maria, you know it is one year since we have been together."

"I know," she said, with a sudden animation, "and you have not grown at all. I have been looking at you."

"I? Oh, yes, Maria, I have grown a lot."

"It can't be noticed. Not a bit." There was laughter in her voice.

"But—I can throw you—Maria," I said courageously. She laughed out loud, slapping her thighs.

"I surely can. Want to try?"—

"I'll duck your head in that pool. I'll give you a second baptism," she laughed.

"All right, then do." I rushed upon her and the grappling started.—

Her legs were like stone pillars. Her arms like cables, around me. I could not budge her feet. Her body bent slightly under my efforts, now one way, now the other, but her spread legs stood planted on the ground. Grinding my teeth, I dug my fists into the middle of her spine. Maria's trunk expanded with a deep breath, her muscles stiffened. Her feet shifted for a better grip on the ground. In a flash I flew up in the air, her arms coiled around my waist. She held me above the ground, pressing my ribs with her arms. Then, with all her force she threw me, as if to plant me in the earth. I struck it with both feet at once, but my knees did not bend: anticipating her move, I spread my legs and stiffened them with all the force in me.—Arching my back I feigned pulling her towards me.—As she resisted I quickly pushed her backwards. We fell heavily, but before I could realize it, Maria was on top of me, clutching my shoulders and pressing them to the ground; I could hardly breathe.

She held me like that for a time, then bending to me, so close that her breath struck in my face, she asked pantingly:

"Well, great hero—who won?"

"Didn't I throw you?" I groaned.

"You pushed me all right, but—who is on top? Whose shoulders are pinned to the ground?"

"Who struck ground first?" I asked, trying to laugh.

"What of it? I did! But you—can you move?" With that she put all her weight on her outstretched arms.—My shoulders ached under the pressure.

"Yes," I teased, "but look where the pool is. You said you'd duck my head."

Maria turned slightly to look at the spring, unwittingly releasing her hold.

With a swiftness that surprised me even, I turned on my right shoulder and throwing my left arm around her waist, I threw Maria off—to one side. Instantly she grabbed my hair and swung my head backwards. My neck pained from the sudden jerk. I almost cried out in impotent rage.

"God Almighty—give me strength—" I hissed under my breath. But the coolness of the grass under my cheek felt good. The smell of the ground was sweet. The moonlight on Maria's face and shoulders, wonderful to look at. Her forearm rested on my face as she held my hair. She looked at me with smiling eyes. She breathed with parted lips—her strong teeth showing. I made no move for I realized suddenly that it all was wonderful. It was supremely delicious to be lying there, Maria and myself, side by side, on the fragrant grass, in the moonlight, listening to the breathing of the sheep and of the pine-forest.

Maria's warm arm rested on my cheek like a caress.—Even the feeling of her fingers clutching my hair was good. Occasionally a wave of pine-drenched air rolled over us and I heard the metallic rustle of some thistles close to my head. At the spring the water prattled endlessly. The tiny noise as infinite as the sky above.

Maria did not move—thank God—only her eyelids blinked now and then. Silently we looked at each other, then our eyes would turn and dive for an instant into the depth of the sky.—

After a time, as if awakened from a reverie, Maria released my hair and pulled her arm away, but remained as she had been. I was sorry to lose the touch of her arm on my face. I moved my head closer to Maria's, smiling happily. She answered me with her smile, then in a whisper she asked:

"Have I hurt you—Peter?"

"Oh, no, Maria, not at all, not the least, least bit."

"Truly not?"

"I swear—Maria."

"Then I am glad." She reached and stroked my hair. I took her hand, laid it on the ground and rested my face on it. After a while her arm got tired so she moved closer to me, leaving her hand under my face.—

For a long time we remained unmoving—looking only at each other. Then—the moon still shining on us, the water still tittering, a common impulse gathered us in each other's arms.—

When we returned to the cabin the moon was high.—All was silent inside, but Jacob sat leaning against the outside wall of the cabin. The white light of the moon fell on him, spilling from his ruffled hair over his bronzed face and chest—like a shimmering veil of water. Seeing us, Jacob stopped humming, but did not move. He pointed beside him, for us to sit down. Maria sat down close to him; I took my place near her. We sat silently, looking into the distance, an abyss of powdery light.—

The forest—close by—hummed softly and breathed upon us its scent.

"This is the queen of all my nights," Jacob said at length. Leaning forward he turned to me saying: "Do you remember— Peter—that song, 'Sleepy birds to their nests are flying'?"

I nodded.

"Let us sing it then, all three of us," he said, touching Maria's hand. We sang. First very softly, then louder, then quietly again, almost whisperingly, repeating many times the words of that melancholy genius—Eminescu.—Our song ended, softer than the breath of the forest.—

The lamenting song was the swan song of my love, for when we had fallen silent, Jacob turned to Maria, asking:

"Have you told him?"

"No," answered Maria.

"You have not? Why?"

Maria did not answer. Folding her hands in her lap, she leaned back against the wall and closed her eyes.—Jacob bent to look in her face.—

"Tell him now, then," he said.

Maria opened her eyes. Evenly, without a tremor in her voice, without a change on her face, looking straight in front of her, Maria said:

"Peter—I am going to be Jacob's wife; our fathers have agreed." I jumped up. Looked at them, sitting there, the moonlight full upon them. Then—in a gay but shrill voice—I cried:

"Surely! Of course! Yes, of course! My very best wishes to you—both. My greatest good wishes to you!" And I ran into the cabin.—

In the darkness I heard the breathing of Elizabeth and her husband. Cautiously I went to my bed in the chimney corner. Lying in the blanket, I began suddenly to wonder, how it happened that I did not see before the light which, coming from the windows, made two, clear, rectangular spots on the floor.—

For a long time I tormented my mind with the question: How is it I did not see those pools of light when I entered the cabin?—

LOAD [1]

By DUDLEY SCHNABEL

(From *The Midland*)

A NDERSON pushed his eye shade up and took the call. It was mama, talking in a guarded voice.

"The police wass just here for Benny," she whispered.

A wave of dread went down the father's big frame then, and his face, white and rugged like the hills of his native Iceland, was taut. Mama smothered a sob.

"Eee-ya? What now?"

He was night load dispatcher for the Public Service Company, and on the property they called him Cold Man Anderson. Stolid and rawboned he was, yet he seemed to belong in this bleak, immaculate room. Leaning now toward the telephone, his light brows came down to a hard line above his eyes, and he cupped a jutting chin into the mouthpiece. But some emotion tugged at his mouth, and twisted it.

All about were the instruments of the man and the job, which was command of the ebb and flow of a half million horsepower of electrical energy in the city below him. Under his large, freckled forearm lay a pile of disturbance reports and an evening paper. A small map glistened efficiently beneath a glass plate on the table top, and there were pads of cool blue report blanks. A worn leather pocket Bible showed beyond the litter. Prim and clean, the big white diagram board of the brown-paneled dispatching office half encircled him on the west wall, looking like a monstrous floor plan exactly drawn. A tradition of clean-cut rectitude, of hard inflexible purpose, stood forth from every feature, every aspect of the room.

"What now, mama?"

"The police wouldn't say nothing. Oh, God, Anderson! That's what I say, what now?"

1 Copyright, 1931, by John T. Frederick.
Copyright, 1932, by Dudley Schnabel.

216

"Hass he been home since last night, then?"

"No." A thick silence followed.

Cold Man's glance moved uneasily over the bank of meters above his left elbow, dropped to a load log sheet propped up across the table, wandered to the open newspaper page.

"There wass—a drugstore robbery this afternoon in Riverhill," he breathed into the mouthpiece. He would not tell her the rest of it now.

All that answered was a washing sound of breath at the other end, rhythmic, despairful. Mama was crying. He waited, shaking his head.

"Anderson, I told you many times—it would come to this. I told you—"

"Now, mama—"

"Ya, you always said that. 'Now, mama.' You shut up now. I told you many times, I said, 'Benny iss getting too big for me to handle, and he iss got bad company. You think you should make him stay in high school and go to Young Peoples,' like that. Ee-ya! He sneaked out on you. Oh, my boy, my boy! Now it iss the police, I tell you—"

"Wait a minute, mama. Hold the wire—"

The superintendent of power control, Mr. Blount, was calling his home over a direct wire.

"Watch the weather, Anderson," said Blount. It was the voice of the system, Blount's. Cold Man had to take note of every syllable. "Did you get your report?"

"Ya—yes, sir."

"Well, it's thundering up north here now. Have Cook Street test out his number six generator, in case you need it."

"Ee-ya." Blount was touchy to-night, snappish.

"Let me know if anything happens, and for God's sake don't let section three go out!"

"Ee-ya? What—" Section three ran out west, taking in Maychester, Cold Man's home district.

"Senator Evlinger is giving a speech in the Maychester auditorium to-night, taking a crack at the utilities, I guess. Public Relations sent down word from the vice-president's office to keep that circuit clear!"

Click. That was all.

"Hello, mama. Well—"

"What you been doing, making me wait when your boy—"

"It wass the boss, mama. I haf to."

"Well, please God my Benny gets away, anyway. I don't care, it ain't all his fault. You don't do nothing but work and eat and sleep. All he ever heard from you is load, load, load. What could I do? I hope they don't get him, whatever he's did, now!"

Cold Man shut his eyes tight, then opened them at a grinning dial and saw vaguely that the load on section ten was up some. Maybe mama was right about it. Even now, with his bad eighteen-year-old boy hunted by the police and mama crying about it at the other end of the telephone line, Cold Man would have to hang up and call the control station about section ten.

"Well, mama, I talked to him many, many times. Should I gif him a licking? He iss too big for that. I couldn't do nothing."

"Ya, you nefer could do nothing."

"Well, we better pray—" gentle as Cold Man's voice could be.

"Ah, pray!"

"—and let me know if something happens about it."

The bowl of soft light overhead beamed on his taffy-white hair and his taffy-yellow shirt. It made a half moon of shadow on the broad cheeks under the eyeshade, eclipsing the pain in his deep eyes. Through a double window those eyes might look down over the Loop, studded with myriad lights that were so much Cold Man Anderson's playthings he could wink them out with a word, and leave the city dark.

The company operator got Zymolski, engineer at the Cook Street plant.

"Eee-ya, number six," Anderson explained. "It iss going to be fireworks a little, I guess. And pick up fifteen t'oosand at a t'oosand a minute for section ten. I take it off St. Clements now." He did, a moment later.

They laughed around the big humming central stations, those control engineers, at Cold Man's "t'oosands." In fact, they laughed at him too, and called him Cold Man because he seemed coolly nerveless, a Scandinavian imperturbable, no matter what the trouble on the lines. The laughter was friendly, though, and they liked to tell new hands about the big Icelander on the night dispatching trick quoting Scripture when the power boss went after him, and how he could take the system through any armageddon of lightning that the elements might organize, Cold Man Anderson unassisted.

But mama, his thin dark Stavanger wife, sitting out in her Maychester house wagging jet earrings at the telephone, saw another Anderson. He was all that a man should be for a husband, but as a father, especially to Benny, she said, "Nei-da!"

Benny, straight and tall and dark-eyed like his Norse mother, had a subtle way about him that the father could not seem to sense. Benny had begun harmlessly enough a few years back with truancy, had gone on to pill pool and craps, blossomed into an affair about some stolen automobile tires, and so, as Cold Man had queried, what now? The evil breath of the big city was in Benny's moral lungs, mama knew. She had known it for quite a while, had cried to Anderson about it. But he could only go on saying, rumbling helplessly behind his neighborhood weekly, wiggling his great toes under the loose weave of his cotton sock out in the kitchen rocker, "Well, mama—"

Now he took the city phone again and asked for "Police 1000." It must have been the Maychester station that mama's callers had come from. Automatically he clicked off the substation locations in his mind, "Circuit three, Maychester, Elms Park, Riverhill—" Disturbed as he was, the complicated reflexes and gestures of his job ruled him with a hand of iron, and his fingers closed on a steel pencil to write across a report sheet, "8:03 P.M. 15,000 Cook St. up, 1M per minute. Ditto St. Clements Avenue down."

The police operator fiddled with the connection, and Cold Man, waiting, gazed far to the north from his eyrie over the twinkling streets and saw a pink sheet of quick flame behind a long gray thunderhead.

Beneath his quiet northern mien, shadows of hard dread and sorrow were mingling. Anderson loved his family as only a native of the model island can, loved mama in his stolid, deep-laid way, little Myrtle, Benny. For Benny was his son, and men of Anderson's kind like to have sons. He was rather proud of his three-quarter-size stucco cottage out there, his peonies and paint-brush and poppies, and the burdened winter apple tree in the back yard. It was all handy and pretty and snug, Cold Man's place, around the corner from the stores, close to the bright lights of Main Street, and to the railroad station. He was earnest about his election as usher in the Icelandic church, liked to pitch horseshoes of an afternoon with Pastor Culbertson, got along with his neighbors, his tradesmen, lodge fellows. Things like this trouble of Benny's were cruel, hurting dully down under the shell of ordinary system office demeanor.

"Maychester police, Sergeant Donohue."

"Eee-ya. This is Anders Anderson, I lif at 718 Adams Afenue. Iss it something the matter with my boy, sergeant?"

"What?"

Cold Man repeated it, gently.

"Jussaminute."

Circuit nine was wavering a bit. It was over north in the theater district, and curtains were going up on the big shows. Cold Man drew his newspaper over and read again the bitter story that ran down the first page.

"—were described by the fountain girl as youthful and well-dressed. One bandit wore a brown suit and had a purple handkerchief in his coat pocket, Miss Leland said. After the shooting, the two ran out the door and made their getaway in a blue sedan, found abandoned on Maychester Boulevard an hour later. It had been reported stolen this morning. Simpson, the victim of the bandit guns, is not expected to live."

Cold Man, pressing the receiver hard to his head, thought maybe that fellow with the purple handkerchief was Benny, all right. Benny had one of those things, and he had worn it that way too, like a dude. The last time Cold Man had mentioned it, Benny had said, "Says you?" or something nasty like that. Yet Benny had always been pretty kind to his mother, and she had stood up for him always, no matter what he had done.

It was funny, come to think about it, that these fellows had stopped running away when they got to Maychester. Just supposing now Benny had—that mama had—

Before Cold Man could get down to threshing out that sudden burning thought the connection rattled in his ear.

"You the father of Benny Anderson, 718 Adams Avenue?"

"Ya, I would like—"

"Well, we want him. Knew where he's at?" The voice was

throaty, overbearing.

"N-no, but if you will tell me something about it maybe I could think of something—"

"I'll tell you, mister. Your kid was in on a robbery and murder in a Riverhill drugstore this afternoon, see? He's out your way somewhere now. We went to your place—"

Murder! The man had died. Benny had shot him, maybe, and he had died. No, not Benny! Not Benny. What could you do now, put up a fight for him here?

"Ee-ya? Wait a minute. How you know it iss my boy in the murder?" That was what mama would do, fight for him. But if it was true!

"Ah, we know, Anderson. We got ways of knowing. I'm telling you, we went to your place, and your wife says he hadn't been home for a week. But we know him and his pal is around there, and we'll get him the minute he shows his mug, see?"

For a week, she had said! Cold Man wondered in a sudden confusing sweat why she would lie that way. He could not lie, even for Benny. Or could he?

"My boy iss a murderer then!"

It was a cry. Cold Man had known it from the moment mama called, it seemed. Something from that story in the paper had told him.

"Why, yeah—of course. You ain't surprised, are you? Hah. We ain't, Anderson!"

Benny, his own little boy that he used to hold on his lap in church, and teach how to talk quaint Icelandic, with its thorn-letter and umlauts and lilting phrases, at twilight on the porch. His boy creeping away in the darkness, afraid, from the law and the justice of the people. Mama biting her fingers, maybe, listening at the door, crying again. But Benny—

Mechanically Cold Man mustered St. Clements Avenue, Baker Street, on the load. Cook Street was the control, taking the swings back and forth over the city as the evening drifted on. Cook Street's sister stations were her energy bankers, waiting with simmering boilers to come through at Cold Man's beck, to cook up kilowatts and throw them out on the big trunk lines, to build up control capacity. Far out on the south side a steel rolling mill, clangorous and acres long, went into its night shift with a

bang, and the anemic finger on Anderson's circuit-five dial called
coldly on him for power. The big beacons out west in the Ever-
hard switch yards of the Great Southern railroad were sucking
the needle of section seven down. The Loop circuits with their
uncounted displays, their architectural outlines in light, their
bright-as-day streets, were ravening wolves bolting energy in
thousand-kilowatt chunks. But Cold Man Anderson sat in his
twelfth floor office and met these calls with an unwavering hand,
took on the load as it came with machine-like precision, knowing
beforehand it would come, how it would come, when, whence,
and wherefore. He was the kind of man a load dispatcher has
to be.

But the slim brown boy hiding out in Maychester—Cold Man
also was thinking about him, and saying little prayers under his
breath.

Now, to Baker Street, "Ya, all right. Drop ten t'oosand, reg'-
lar." To Addisonville likewise.

In the vibrating control room out at Baker Street, which was
a ganglion of two hundred thousand potential surging horses one
time, thirty thousand another, they heard Cold Man Anderson
and obeyed. A red-headed youth called student engineer relayed
the word to the turbine room, the boiler house, the night engineer. Grimy fingers came out from a denim pocket and closed
on a valve, set it back, shut down a row of mighty forced-draft
fans, slowed up the rumbling automatic stokers, eased up the
pumps. In the figured tile vastness of the turbine room, the
scream of live steam hitting the vanes of the turbo-generators, six
hundred pounds to the square inch, began to die away. The sec-
tionalized floor areas ceased their tortured quaking. Polished
hand rail and iron stair and sheer tile wall, the long gray robots
as big as mountain locomotives, jungles of valve wheels and pipes,
of control panels of black marine steel in Swiss watch precison
down in the dark of the turbine pits, all were as before, not changing a whit their aspect of spotless, bland complacency. Yet from
their habitation great giants of energy had lately fled, invisibly,
nimbly, all because Cold Man Anderson had spoken about
"t'oosands" over the phone.

"Nei, nei," muttered the load dispatcher, shaking his blonde
head over his steel pencil, heavily in tune with the nearing thun-

der to the north. "Not my boy! Not my boy!"

After it had been said, that prayer made Cold Man a little uncomfortable. It was as if he had petitioned, "Make it somebody else's."

He did not blame mama for the lie, though. He couldn't bring himself to it. And if by chance she had Benny now, down in the basement, or in a back closet somewhere while she set her thin bosom across the doorway in the face of the law!

"I don't care if he—" began Cold Man Anderson out loud, and looked, feeling chagrined, to reassure himself that he was alone in the room. The aspect of the place was a chill reminder that there men did not talk to themselves aloud about their private affairs.

Blount called again. The electric clock on the wall over the diagram showed 8:45 now, and Cold Man checked it against his watch as he lifted the receiver. A premonitory dark wind burst in the windows and pushed and rattled at his papers, and it smelled of rain.

"Did you get Cook Street fixed up?"

Blount's voice was far away in the receiver, but roundly authoritative.

"It's starting to rain up here now. Keep your reserve right on the spot, Anderson. I think she's going to be a peach."

"Ya. It iss okay now."

"And don't forget Senator What's-his-name! If you let the lights go out on him there's going to be hell to pay."

"Ee-ya." Click. Blount never said good-bye, merely hung up.

Now Baker Street was standing by on fifty thousand kilowatts, Addisonville on twenty-five, St. Clements on twenty, all base load. The frequency meter showed a smooth red line on the graph, not departing appreciably from the sixty-cycle axis. The system was waiting for the storm to break, waiting quietly, as a seasoned old boxer dozes in his corner before the gong.

One man against a storm, you might say. Cold Man Anderson sitting up there with his fingers on the pulse, his eyes on the sphygmomanometer of the city's power-and-light blood pressure. And thinking mostly about Benny, while a thunderhead came down from the north furious with lightning.

Ordinarily Cold Man did not have time to think about the job much.   There was the log, and the forecasts of the 24-hour load, before him.   According as the needles of the demand meters moved in front of his face he adjusted the give and play of energy out of the power pool in the city.   He could have looked on the system as a neurologist looks at his patient, so to say, seeing neither brick nor stone but only long tortuous miles of lead-covered copper cable snaking in, around and through the great body of structure and street and conduit, long threads of energy going out from his fingertips.   He might even have romanced over it, made a saga to establish it for the splendid thing it was.   Cold Man Anderson, though, did not look at it much that way.   He saw it as the source of a job that let him have his home and family and good name.   He was a part of it, a center of control, a machine more perfect than any in the mighty central stations, if not so strong.

Anderson did turn to watch the storm through the windows now.   Circuit two meantime had begun to act up as the lightning started snapping up there above the river.   He kept one eye on the dial, and so read the story of the tempest.   And all the time he thought about what he could do for Benny's sake.

"Hello, Cook Street.   Get number six on the line to stand by now, soon ess you can, ya."

That was Blount's idea, and anyway it was in the standing orders for a time like this.   The chief had figured it out and ordered it.   Figured it all out, down to a penny, to a split mill, where to start reserves boiling, how high to hold them, when to turn them loose.   At Cook Street, Addisonville, St. Clements, Baker, they all knew that.   Cold Man didn't have to take much of the burden of burning away a couple dozen tons of coal in the big drag-feed conveyors at Baker Street, say, or reckon the dollars that blew off in the boiler house safety valves when the load drop beat him to it.   The chief long ago had worried such things out, and Cold Man had the fruits thereof under his large fist.   All he had to do was to keep things moving by the book, by the clock, by the instruments and the swing of his own seasoned judgment in the lesser crises that came.   That made it easy, hard at the same time.   He had no excuses if he failed his orders.   But Cold Man Anderson did not fail.

When there was lightning, though, it was another matter.   The engineers had done their best with the budgets they had. The system was geared up and insulated and shielded and fortified from stem to gudgeon against lightning interruption, far as the money would go. They might have put in automatic re-closing equipment at the system's substations. There had been talk about it. In that case Cold Man's job would have been lightened greatly at such a time. But they hadn't, and his orders were plain. Always he was to try the circuit once, twice, thrice if necessary, and then go around by sections if the third try brought no answer from his board signals. Because, in a bad storm, there were sometimes simply too many volts. Then it became largely an affair of keeping things alive by the grace of God and that which made men call Anders Anderson "Cold Man."

The rain came in a gray curtain over the building tops. The load dispatcher was busy now. He could only work, and solace himself now and then softly with a part of the nineteenth psalm to the chief musician, the one he had chosen for his own and for Benny, if the boy some day should have straightened up and gone to work for the power company:

"His going forth is from the end of heaven, and his circuit unto the ends of it: and there is nothing hid from the heat thereof."

First, and for some time, it was circuit two. Then in a spectacular flash that tipped every misty minaret of the loop with false dawn, it was number nine, and nine covered the near north side, fed light to the ten thousand or so who sat in parquet or orchestra seats, gaped at a flickering, nasal screen.

Cold Man was after number nine like a lion. But the million-volt induced charge spilled over a transformer bank at Cook Street, and the lightning arresters could not quite digest it. Potentials reversed, the circuit collapsed like a gorged python, and in the long neat turbine room at Cook Street there was, in a manner of speaking, hell to pay. Yet before the operators could get down there, before the greasy firemen in the boiler house could hop to their valves, before the electricans could crawl over the sleek gray bellies of their stricken titans and sooth the strangling governors, Cold Man Anderson had it whipped. He got circuit nine going again through an interconnection with number one, northwest—it was right there on the big chart under his nose— and Baker Street had come to bat for Cook with twenty-five thousand KVA.

In the midst of action, and worry about Benny, Cold Man wondered for a moment if the crowds in the theaters would understand it was a bad storm, and not blame the system. It had been dark there, soft curtains of black velvet unfurling from the footlights and chandeliers, only five and three-quarters seconds. Then, Anderson knew, there had come a delicate pinkish brown, then a brighter yellow, and suddenly flaring light, as the arousing generators out Baker way joined struggling Cook Street to pick up the load. But most of ten thousand pairs of shoulders would heave, and as many voices whisper petulantly, "Well, it's about time—"

It *was* a peach, that storm. Blount had been a good prophet. He called once or twice, imperatively, about the trouble on section two. But not only Blount called. The office operator, in the midst of things sending an exasperated buzz against Cold Man's phone resonator, raked him over the coals.

"What's the matter up there?" she snapped. "Holy cow, they're ringing me three to the minute. 'No lights, what's the matter?' 'No lights, no lights.' Can't you fix it, dispatcher?"

"Ee-ya? Well, it iss a bad storm, operator. We do what we can."

"Uh-huh? Wait a minute—"

She was gone, then back again, while Anderson drove his pencil feverishly over his report sheets, trying to catch up with himself.

"—a guy just called from the Great Southern dispatcher's office and bawled me out. They've made a holler over at the opera house, too. They're mad because we got lightning, I guess. Can't you shoo this darn storm away, or something? I got magazines to read."

Just as Cold Man was trying to straighten out his thoughts about Benny again, a purple snake struck from the dark vapor wilderness overhead out south. This time it bit into the hard skeleton of a tower line structure, it appeared from the instruments. Circuit five showed low. But this was easy, and the rail mill scarcely paused in the gigantic shifting of its white-hot ingots and red-hot rails to wait for a tow-headed Icelander twenty miles away to cut it in again.

There was nobody in the mill who knew about Cold Man Anderson, or cared. Nobody in the show district's ten thousand either, in the hospitals, dance halls, night clubs, street cars, signal towers, offices, or homes. Except perhaps out at 718 Adams Avenue in Maychester. Mama, little Myrtle asleep in her small iron cot, Benny—

Little Benny, his boy. Benny had run for home, for mama, then. Killed a man, and run for home. Afraid! How it used to squeeze Anderson's heart in earlier years to see the little boy cry, afraid of some pitiable thing he had done or tried to do! That was the trouble now, all right.

The shifting fogs of rain that blurred the city lights below were thinning, and the thunder was a second or two delayed. Cold Man fumbled in the lunch box at his side and pulled out a dry sandwich, devoid of lettuce, opening his rough-hewn lips to eat.

There was a snapshot, dirty and cracked, in the load dispatcher's polished old billfold. He got it out and looked dimly at it. A picture of Benny at four, curly-haired, large-eyed, dressed in a little Norwegian peasant costume of mama's.

"Ah, he iss only a kid. I—maybe I ain't—been enough with him for a father."

If mama had him, if she only had him now, guilty or not! Would that be wrong? Somehow that would fix things better in Cold Man's mind. She would put her mother wings over him and talk to him, as she used to when Benny was a baby hurt at play.

It must be storming out in Maychester too, pelting rain down under a thrusting, irritable campaign of lightning, an admiral's salute of thunder. Nobody would be out, to speak of, except the police—and Benny. But the circuit was energized, number three was working. The system was doing its part for that senator fellow. And where the police were hunting for Benny, waiting for him as the policeman had said, where he was hiding, running for cover, skulking to get home or out of town, somewhere in his own neighborhood, they had light to see him by.

Cold Man Anderson rubbed a bit of dust from the surface of the old photograph, and put it carefully away. It trembled rather badly in his hands as he was slipping it into the wallet.

What if mama had him in the house, after all, now that the storm was going over? And what if circuit three should go out, somehow—

"Nei!"

Again Cold Man felt ashamed of his audible vehemence, and was glad he was alone. This idea that had clamored suddenly at him was obvious enough, yet such a thing had never occurred to him before in all his time on the job. For a few minutes, try as he might, he could not swallow his sandwich bites because of a dull ache in his throat; and not an untoward thing happened on the system.

No, it had never come to him like this before, Cold Man whispered to himself. It must be the devil at him, tempting him, like Pastor Culbertson had told about. If it should get dark in Maychester—dark in Maychester—

"Ah nei, nei!"

Even though he drowned the thought in his mind, he knew that an alibi would be easy. All you needed to say in the report was that it took you fifteen minutes, half an hour may be, to clear circuit three of a series of grounds brought on by an induced charge. Fifteen minutes outage out there could be written off in this storm.

Cook Street was calling to say the generator trouble was cleared, and it was ready to pick up again. Cold Man checked Baker Street, his knuckles showing white and hard, and smoothly number one circuit went free of its burden of keeping light for the fretful throngs gaping at shadows under the sign of the false face.

It struck Cold Man searchingly now that Maychester's police, on the hunt for Benny, needed the help of the system that night. They were asking for it without a word, and Cold Man was giving it to them, no matter the consequences. But in the dark of a stormy night before the rain had quite subsided, to steal a car, to hide its color, to find a paved boulevard for swift, silent flight —how could a handful of police squads prevent that if there were no light?

"Nei! No, no!" Cold Man fought with himself, put his face in his hands for a moment.

Cold Man Anderson was a fighter of lightning, and he knew it for a mercurial foe. A fellow never could count on it. The physicists said it was the friction of falling rain that built up the immeasurable potential in the storm cloud. Thence, they argued, as if that could help a man like Anderson any, came the lightning, an escape of pent ions across the resisting air gap to earth, the home of all lightnings. The passing storm so would gather its skirts, shake off its last rain drops to raise a fearful final pressure against the widening atmosphere behind it, and let go one devastating bolt for a parting shot. That is what it did in Maychester then, just as Cold Man finished the last crust of his dry beef sandwich. And the treacherous inductivity of the superpower lines feeding the Maychester substation did the rest. A tiny red light on the board sparked on, and a tiny blue one shut its eye, and the steady composure of the cold man cracked and fell apart. Circuit three was open—it was dark in Maychester.

Anderson sat for a moment motionless as a rock. Then a deep sigh shook him, tortured his big shoulders into life.

"—and for God's sake don't let section three go out!" came Blount's words into the staring room.

Like the irresistible drive of the big turbines he controlled, Cold Man Anderson began to move against the break on number three, closed in on it, with his teeth set hard into each other and sweat on his forehead. He put in a call for Zymolski.

The outside phone rang.

"Ya." His voice bawled and roared like the booming of gale-driven ice packs down out of the Arctic. And in his other hand he held the receiver that was waiting to carry Zymolski's answering voice to his ear.

"Anderson!" Mama's voice. In the murmur of failing thunder Cold Man could hardly catch her rapid words, so softly did they come. "It iss dark now—and he iss going. He will half to cross Main Street to get to the yards. Keep the lights off—you!"

Her voice was suddenly big and commanding.

"He's promised he'd get a boat and go back to grandma's to stay. To Reykjavik! He needs only half an hour of dark now—fifteen minutes, maybe! You hear?"

Anderson tried to interrupt, but she hurried on.

"The police iss out in cars, they don't watch the yards. Anderson, you got to—you *got* to gif him the chance—they're all around here, but I kep' him—"

"Well, mama—"

"They would put him in prison, and you can gif him a chance. What good are you up there, Anderson, if you can't—"

Prison? It was murder now, but mama didn't know that. They would put Benny in the electric chair.

"God help you, Anderson, if you turn those lights on now!" But section three was out. Three was out. Three— Mama's voice had broken now, terribly, as if she understood. "—your boy, I tell you—"

Imperturbable as time itself the meters were arrayed on their black board, coldly exact in the nice, trim swing of their delicate patrician needles. The white chart spread dispassionately out before Cold Man's staring eyes, a frigid reminder of organized duty, mechanical honor, inflexible scientific virtue. Number three was out, needing energy. There was a senator out there to whom Public Relations insisted on giving a break. Number three calling for orders from the load dispatcher—

Cold Man Anderson hung up on mama slowly, but with a face of iron, and eyes that stared like beads at nothing straight ahead. Zymolski, trained to wait, was on the other phone.

Forty-five seconds later Zymolski relayed his message back to Cold Man:

"All right, here they come now, Anderson. Shall I let number three have it?"

Once, long ago, Anderson had been afraid maybe he and mama would not have any kids, any boy—

"Ee-ya," he said, indistinctly. "Let 'em—haf it."

GENTLEMAN IN BLUE [1]

By LAURENCE STALLINGS

(From *The Saturday Evening Post*)

WHEN they found those old embroidery scissors under that stump to-day, I went a long way back in memory. To memories of blue. I remember how blue their uniforms were.

In those days the lane from the steps here to the clay road seemed about a mile long. It is no more than two hundred feet, but it bisected a universe for me. My mother had her flower garden in a little square which was fenced off with white pickets, and it was there, after my brothers went away, that I played.

I was playing store when the Yankees rode by the house down the Appomattox road and pulled in their horses at our gate. I can remember best how blue the cloth of their uniforms was, and how it glinted in the sun.

I had heard talk of Yankees before that, but they were the first we ever saw here. My father and brothers rode away in butternut gray, with nothing blue about them. Amos held me aloft to throw kisses to Jim when his time came to ride away to Virginia's battle line. Jim was, next to me, the youngest of mother's boys. He was well turned sixteen when he left. I seem to recollect his plaguing mother for some time to go, but I paid no attention to it. I was playing store mostly. I used to pretend I had a little store under that oak there. . . . No, that's a white oak. I forget the old one's down. My mother sometimes gave me things for my store. Empty tins and bits of harness catches, and an occasional spool for an extra clerk. My chief decoration was a broken conch shell with a picture of Vesuvius set in a little mirror in its bell. My Great-Uncle Randolph had brought it home with him after squandering his fortune abroad in the 40's.

They pulled in their horses, these men in blue. There must have been a dozen of them as they sat their horses and talked down at the gate by the clay road. I watched them a moment in wonder, but without fear. I did not at first understand that they were Yankees. They were men in blue—the most surprising blue. I watched them for a moment without fear. Then I understood that they were Yankees. Fear seized me, and I crept along the box bushes and ran around the house to the brick kitchen, calling for mother.

"Yankees!" I cried. "The Yankees have come to steal Spotsylvania Court House." My father had brought the pony home the year before, when he was on furlough. I don't recollect now what moved me, but the moment I saw the pony I said: "I'm going to call him Spotsylvania Court House." I did not know what it meant, or where it came from, but the name must have been in my mind, for that's what I called him. It seemed a very gallant name. "Yankees!" I yelled. "They've come to steal him!"

"Nonsense!" my mother said sharply. "Nonsense! No grown man wants to ride your pony."

In those days there were no stoves. Our cooking was done over an open fireplace, and I can remember the Negroes around the hearth that day. There must have been about twenty Negroes who lived around the house. Yard niggers. My mother often complained about so many being around, but we couldn't drive them off. They were from the carriage house, and from the loom house where mother supervised the spinning. There was a cobbler's shop and a smokehouse; but they're gone, too, all of them. They were of whitewashed logs and they made up a town square for us. The kitchen was in a turmoil when I said "Yankees."

Amos was our butler and coachman. He was putting fresh logs on the fire when I ran into the kitchen. He dropped the wood.

"You want yo' gun, Mis' Sarah?"

My mother was the calmest woman I ever saw. "Bring me my rifle, Amos," she said.

I held her skirt and started crying. It was a print of gray woolen with little, fine, red flowers and green leaves dotting it. I can remember the pattern.

"Stop crying, everybody," she said. "Stop it!"

Amos brought the gun. My mother took my hand and walked through the brick passage to the house, and went to the front door. Amos walked behind her. Amos had a hat with a cockade. He never wore it that I ever knew, unless for the Sundays when the bishop came to Amelia to preach and then home to dinner with us. Amos wore his hat with the cockade now.

I stopped crying just to see that cockade. It was a badge of distinction, a thing that rendered us immune from ordinary things such as Yankees. I know that his hat, which he put on miraculously, dried my tears before we reached the front door. Amos opened the door for mother to pass to the front porch. We all went outside—my mother in her print dress and kitchen cap, with her long light rifle which my father had given her on their silver anniversary, and I with my storekeeper's paper cap, and Amos with the hat. My mother could bark a squirrel with her rifle. Many a time I had seen her do it.

I doubt that more than a minute had passed since I ran to the kitchen. They were still down on the road; and just as I had said, they were Yankees. My mother's hand tightened over mine when she saw them. You can't imagine how far that road seemed to me, a little child, that day.

"Be mighty careful, Mis' Sarah," I heard Amos saying. Then he began mumbling to one of the slaves, who was whimpering inside the door. "Go lead de stallion away," he was saying sharply under his breath. "Go lead de stallion away down to de ice house, and git inside and stay wid him."

Our ice house was double-planked, with sawdust filling, and was three-quarters sunk in the earth anyway. It was soundproof. I knew Amos was placing big Logan where he wouldn't neigh and be heard.

I could hear Rupe's trembling answer, "Dey'd kill me. Dey'd kill me."

Amos was looking over my mother's shoulder at the men in blue down on the road. "Ise going to kill you as soon as dey leave, if dey don't," he said. "Go take de stallion down to de ice house."

There wasn't a Negro on our place who would have shut himself in the ice house with Logan. Except, of course, Amos. He and the stallion understood each other. Amos gave the stallion a pint of corn whisky every Sunday morning. I know my father allowed Amos a quart of whisky every week for his rheumatism, and the yard niggers said he gave half of it to Logan as regularly as he got it.

"It keeps him proud like me," Amos said. It was generally believed that Logan, when he heard the big meeting bell ringing over at Amelia every Sunday morning, would come to the bars and neigh until Amos brought him his whisky. I know that every Sunday morning he would tear up the turf of his pasture, throwing his heels and charging even the least bit of grass or a butterfly, galloping in short circles from the gate to his stall.

Our stallion's name was Logan, I said. My father had two. But Logan killed the other one fighting in the snow, when a field hand left the gate open the winter before. I remember how my mother said she hated to write my father that the little stallion was dead. "Your father has enough worry with that regiment of no-accounts," she had said.

Two of the Yankees were detaching themselves from the main group on the road. One of them dismounted at the main gate and opened it.

"Stop trembling," my mother said to me. "Keep cool, Amos." Amos narrowed his eyes and set the cockade hat at an angle. "Ise got de li'l' one-shot pistol," he said simply.

The Yankee who spurred forward through the gate is still in my vision. The picket fence has gone and the road is infinitely nearer, and one exaggerates childhood estimates; I am sure the Yankee's horse stood seventeen and a half hands at the shoulder. The Yankee simply lifted that big gray horse over the picket-fence gate, keeping to the gravel walk between the little, old-fashioned, button-chrysanthemum bushes.

I can never get the blue of his uniform jacket from my eyes. Not the yellow stripes or the brass buttons, nor the insignia at shoulder and cap are remembered vividly now. It is that powerful, flashing blue. It seemed immensely superior to the gray of my father and brothers. My father used to say "once in a blue moon" a lot when I was a child. Somehow, the blue of that smart jacket, under which the man's muscles moved and made it glint alive, seemed to have belonged to the man in the moon. That Yankee—the first I had ever seen—was a moon man. A blue— an intensely blue—moon man.

He pulled his horse in at the steps. These very steps. My

mother waited for him to speak. Amos did not move. Amos must have looked a fine figure to that Yankee. For Yankees think that some of the colored people are handsome. Amos must have been a very handsome man. He was very tall, with a peaked forehead and tightly wound hair that grew down almost to his eyebrows, and his head was as round as an acorn. His head was not unlike an acorn from a black-oak tree, for it was of dark, polished shell with a close-fitting top of black.

I heard Amos sigh as the Yankee lifted his own hard little cap in a sweep and by some trick of leg brought the horse low at his right shoulder, as he swept his cap along its withers to the ground. Both horse and man in the gravel path managed a bow that made my face tingle.

The Yankee was very grave as he eyed the rifle and the group of us. "We hate to disturb you, madam," he said, "but we'd like to trouble you for some fire to light our pipes." That was all he said.

"Amos," said my mother gently, "take a shovel of fire down to those gentlemen by the big gate." I could not take my eyes from this blue, though I heard Amos going back through the hall. "For I am sure," my mother was saying, "that they are gentlemen."

The Yankee smiled at this, his big, strong teeth flashing above his brown beard. "A lady is never uncertain in matters of this distinction," he said, smiling. "We thank you for the fire." He wheeled his horse sharply and gathered up the bridle for a run at the fence gate, holding the gray's head high and thrusting his feet home in the stirrups. I always rode Spotsylvania with box stirrups.

"Wait," my mother called sharply. "Are your men hungry?"

The Yankee turned his horse again, the blue of his back changing to the brass and blue of his front. "We could only eat, madam," he said, "if you have plenty to spare."

"Bread and butter," I said. "That's all we have now."

"What is better?" mother asked me.

"I don't know of anything," the Yankee said seriously.

"She never asked you," I said.

"Ask the gentleman to excuse you," mother told me. In our family, if some one said something rude to another, he was always excused to go to his room until evening prayers.

"Excuse me," I said. But I couldn't let go mother's hand to leave.

"There's no offense," said the man in blue. "I've a little boy in New Hampshire just like you. I'd want him to give your father a call-down under similar circumstances."

"I had thought better of New Hampshire," my mother said, leaning against a column. . . . That column there.

Amos came by the side gate with a shovelful of smoking coals, and carrying a big twist of our bright tobacco. He had put his hat away and was wearing the cook's white cap, one freshly starched. I knew that he did not believe the men at the gate were gentlemen, whatever my mother said. But there was something about the man on the gray that made me feel Amos would have worn the cockade to offer him fire. His jacket was of a blue more brilliant than the others.

"Amos doesn't want to be free," I said, hostile.

"No one does," the Yankee said, showing his teeth again.

"Nobody is," my mother said. She turned to the doorway, still holding my hand. "Will you ask your men to come around to the kitchen?" She opened the door. "And will you please come in, sir?" she said, leaving the door open.

Mother held my hand, walking the long hall, but she set her rifle in the corner by the clock. We went into the kitchen. The people there were silent. "How much hot bread is there?" she asked old Lizzie.

Lizzie made our bread because she knew where to hide the silver coins and how many fern leaves to put into the conjure bag when it failed to rise.

" 'Bout six pans," she said.

Mother looked them all over. "We're going to feed some soldiers," she said. "They are just like other soldiers."

"They have on very blue coats," I said.

"That's their only difference from our men," she said. "I don't want any weeping and wailing and carrying on when they ride up. Do you all hear me?"

They all heard, because they didn't say anything. When they "yes, sir," and "I sho will" and "I declare I truly did hear you," it means that they have been thinking of something else and have

LAURENCE STALLINGS 237

not heard. They haven't changed much since they were sold into slavery here, and I doubt that they ever will, whether this is good or bad for us or for them.

The Yankees did not ride around to the kitchen. They left their horses, with a picket, around by the gate, and they walked in their long boots slowly to the kitchen door. How blue their coats were when they came in! Not quite so blue as the first Yankee's on the gray, but terrifyingly so. I think the people in the kitchen felt as I did at first about their being men from the moon.

I sat on Amos' knee as they were fed, and marked with satisfaction how the hot butter, when they bit into the cut squares of the hot bread, dripped down onto the blue of their jackets. One of them put his hand on my head and called me "Bub," but I twisted away from it and they let me alone. The short one with big yellow slashes on his arms said that this house sat on a hill, so they could hold it just as they were against a hundred men. They ate the bread as fast as Lizzie cut it and buttered it, and they drank gourds of water from the big bucket. Suddenly I missed mother.

I began to cry. I ran into the hall and to the porch. The man at the picket line was eating bread, just as the rest were. I don't know how he got it. I went into the dining room. The Yankee was there at the table, eating bread with a knife and fork, and drinking buttermilk from one of the tumblers mother used when the bishop came to preach.

Mother sat at the other end of the table, but her bread was hardly touched. The dining room was always in half darkness, because mother said sunlight would fade the painted paper of the ceiling and peel the varnish on the wainscot. The Yankee's buttons were reflected on the table. He seemed to give off a blue light. I went to mother's side and stood by her.

"Here," she said, giving me small mouthfuls. "Mind the rug."

"They'll be coming home, then?" she said to the Yankee.

I could feel deep down that mother wanted to cry. It was the way she did when she wouldn't cry the time they brought the news that Great-Uncle Randolph had killed Mr. Harrison's eldest son; when they had a fight with shotguns over the ownership of one of great-uncle's yard niggers. Mother didn't cry until they left her, but I know that afterward she went upstairs and sank down by her bed and held on to one of the posts and cried.

There was something about what this Yankee was saying that made her want to cry. I could tell the way she put her arm about me when she fed me the bread.

"It will be over by to-morrow or next day," the Yankee was saying. "We're Sheridan's men. All of us are back of him, and he can't possibly get out."

"Back of father?" I asked, frightened.

"Back of General Lee," mother said. "Your father's all right."

"My father's the best one of General Lee's men," I said.

"He's a wonderful man then," the Yankee said. He had finished his bread. "We must go on," he said. "We might bring something down upon this house, remaining here." He got up from the table, and he bowed, and remained bowing until mother left the dining room holding my hand. "We are deeply grateful," he said.

As we came into the hall, Amos was standing there. I knew he had been watching. The Yankee spoke to him. "God knows I wish we were to be the last to trouble you."

"Just let mine come home to me," mother said. "It is all that I ask."

"We shall," the Yankee said. "It isn't that they'll come home. It's the thousands who will follow them that I regret."

Outside, the men were on the picket lines again, each holding his own horse. They swung into saddles when the big man came to the door with us, only one of them remaining on the ground to hold the big gray.

"May my little boy send yours a present from New Hampshire?" the Yankee asked. "Does he like maple sugar? Blocks of it?"

"We've never discovered a sugar he doesn't like," mother said.

The kitchen people were at the entrance to the brick hall. They were all peering around the door. "He's a damned Yankee," I said, "but he won't hurt you."

The big Yankee half shut his eyes then and sighed. As he straightened up and clicked his heels together sharply, I heard the people scamper back down the hall to the kitchen. He bent low and kissed mother's hand. He turned then and walked slowly down the steps and along the gravel walk of the garden, never looking back, his cap in his hand. Then he opened the little picket gate he had jumped when he first rode up, and he continued slowly, taking the gray's bridle and swinging himself into the saddle as though he was too tired to mount and ride again.

One of his soldiers, who rode up by him, had a small flag on a long staff which he carried with its butt in a saddle sling. The big Yankee took this pennon, which was red and yellow with a big "8" and a little "F" and rode over to our main gate, where he drove it with a hard thrust into the soft soil that is always there in the clay when the spring rains have swept the yard of the winter's dust. They fell in behind him, the others on their horses, and they rode away leaving the pennon on our gate. At the turn in the road where the cornfield is now—there used to be a grove of hickories there—all of them stood in the stirrups and their swords flashed in the sun as they waved back to us. Then they cantered around the trees and out of sight.

My mother stood looking after them a long time. She reached into her pocket then and brought out her small embroidery scissors with the filigree handles.

"Here," she said. "You can sell some scissors in your store to-day."

The scissors were forbidden property. I was never to touch them, for mother said the Lord only knew whenever she would get any more.

"But you'll need them," I said, "with your hoops and your embroidery."

"We are done embroidering," she said.

I didn't want to take them, but with mother ready to cry any minute, I had to. I resolved to hide them in the moss walls of my little store and give them back to her some day. I started into the flower garden. But there was a sound of many guns firing up the road.

When father used to let the Negroes all take muzzle-loaders out for the rabbit hunting around Christmastime guns would be popping that way, for every one shot quickly whenever the dogs jumped a cottontail. Father would never let me go if there was more than one gun, which Amos carried. At times when Amos carried me, he always looked to see where I was before he shot at a rabbit. But the firing up the road was heavier than we would hear on Christmas Eve.

I ran to my mother and held to her skirts, and she held me closely as we stood there, the popping coming nearer all the time. Amos came out again in his cockade and led mother back into the house and up the stairs. Then he ran to the front door and locked it and drew the curtains tight.

Upstairs we could hear the uproar from the kitchen. Mother ran out upon the sewing porch upstairs, for it overlooked the road. Presently the Yankees came in sight again. They were galloping, but each man would turn occasionally and rise in his stirrups and fire his short rifle—one not half as long as mother's—at something we could not see. I could see their blue coats sometimes over the trees and then between the branches as they streamed back down the road.

The last man to ride into view was the very blue one on the big gray. Mother caught me and sobbed when she saw him round the bend of the hickories that my father had to sell for timber later when he sent me off to the military academy. As they came back along the clay they bunched together at our gate and one of them tried to open it from horseback. His horse was fretting so that he had trouble seizing the catch. I knew anyway that he couldn't open it without dismounting. My brother Jim could do it, but that was because he practiced so hard. The latch was a bar that fell into a tongue catch, and there was a little iron trip which fell over it when it shot home.

The shots were coming nearer when the man on the gray rode into the men at the gate, waving his sword and beating them with the flat of it, trying to make them go farther down the road. He flashed his sword and got them off flying again, seizing the pennon out of the ground and thrusting it to the man with the yellow sleeves. They spurred up and started toward the bend going toward Amelia. There weren't so many of them as we had fed in the kitchen.

My mother gasped, and I could see over the trees more riders coming in great bunches, galloping hard. They were in gray, and their coat tails fluttered behind them in long ribbons, but their horses weren't so fast as the Yankee horses.

The big Yankee at our gate waited until they turned the bend and then began firing from a pistol. I think it shot four times before he threw it away. The gray riders were firing back at him now, galloping by the stable turnout. Father had said never to gallop a horse up to the stables, because that way gave the horse his will, which you should never give him if you wanted a good horse. But they weren't turning in at the stable.

"Run!" my mother screamed. "Run!"

I don't know if the big Yankee heard her. But he did just what he had done when he jumped our gate. He made a sweeping bow, horse and rider, and then turned and dashed off after his men.

There was a place up the road that father never could pack hard enough. No matter how many slaves worked on it, it was either mud or dust. It was a cloud of dust now from the stir the other Yankees made when they rode into it. The gray horse rode into it, the men in flying coat tails about a hundred yards back of him, from the stable gate to the bend there. The big Yankee fell from his horse just as the gray entered the dust.

I saw his blue jacket rolling as the other men galloped over him and into the dust after the others. Group and group of them came racing down our road and into the cloud of dust. I held to the banisters of the sewing porch, watching the clouds go past —clouds of yellow dust with figures, mostly hats and swords, rolling on the crest of them.

When it began to clear and they were all past, I discovered that Amos and mother had left me. They were down on the road, bending over the man in blue. The big gray stood there occasionally tripping over his bridle, waiting by them. Amos wanted to save his cockade from the dust, for he took it off and held it beneath his arm. Then he gave it to mother.

While she held the gray he picked up the Yankee and, folding him over the saddle, they came slowly up to the gate he had not let his men open. Mother carried the cockade and the little flat cap the Yankee had worn, and Amos led the gray. His jacket wasn't blue any more, for it was covered with dust, but just as they opened the gate I could see patches of it beneath his arms, shining as it had when he first put his gray over our picket fence and swept his cap along its withers in a bow from both man and horse. I went into mother's bedroom and cried on a post.

Amos took me over to Uncle Billy's to spend the afternoon, for he had sent word that the wood violets were out for the spring in the bowl of rocks we called the Wolf's Den. They say wolves used to live there. I stayed two days with Uncle Billy, and we spent many hours picking wood violets and shooting at a mark with his old gun. And I had a fine time playing store with two little black boys named Roy and Troy. When I came back home father and the boys were there. But they stayed in the back of the house all the time. It was so dusty on the porches, for the blue riders streamed by all day long.

When they found the embroidery scissors under that old stump to-day, it made me think of all this. I still remember how blue his jacket was when he lifted the gray over the picket fence and came down the gravel walk between those little button chrysanthemums.

THE FAMILY CHRONICLE [1]

By BERNHARD JOHANN TÜTING

(From *The Atlantic Monthly*)

THE war was over, the soldiers returned. They had left with music and songs—many had left; but now their number was small and their voices were low. The fragrance of the soil greeted them. The oaks loosened their leaves and spread a carpet of rust-brown brocade over the land. The war was over.

Then winter came and hung a garment of crisp white snow over firs and pine trees. The wind from the east blew rough and cold, rushed over the plains, and hardened to ice the water flooding the meadows.

Rudolf Schulte and his wife, Katharina Schulte, were alone in the room. It was in the late forenoon. The sun was far away in the southern sky and colored the frozen panes of the windows with a pale yellow light. The fire crackled on the hearth, but only in the upper corners of each pane had the ice flowers lost their leaves. Rudolf Schulte went to the desk, brought the family chronicle, and laid it on the table. His wife looked at him; he looked at her. As he turned the pages he recognized the different handwritings of the Schulten who had lived before his time here on the same farm. He knew the long family history by heart, but he liked to see it word for word, just as it had been written. He had blank sheets before him now. He gazed thoughtfully at the paper, turned the pen in his fingers, and put it back on the inkstand. He closed the heavy leather-bound volume and locked it in the desk again.

His wife shook her head. "Rudolf, have you written it down?"

"No, not yet. I do not know just what to write."

"Just write it down in a few simple words. A few simple words will do."

"Yes, a few simple words, I guess." He put on his long, heavy overcoat, and his high, sturdy build appeared still more powerful.

"Where are you going to-day?"

"I have to show him; you know how it is. He does not even know the boundaries. Nobody has ever shown him. He must know."

"Yes, he must know, but it is cold to-day. Death is blowing over the land."

"Yes, it is cold," and the tall, gray-haired man took his oak-wood cane and fur cap and left the room. He crossed the open yard, north of the house, and went into the stables. On both sides of the wide passage stood a long row of black-and-white cows, all thoroughbreds, valuable stock, the result of careful mating. He was still proud of the animals and proud of himself when he thought of his work here on Schulten farm; but a walk through the stables did not give him the great satisfaction it had given him in earlier years.

"Heinrich!" he called loudly. The answer came from the adjoining horse stable, and a young man of about twenty-five approached. "Heinrich, you take an axe and we shall go to the pines."

"To the pines," the young man repeated to himself while he walked to the tool room, "to the pines." He had been thinking of the approaching holiday, but now that it was so near . . . He should have told the old people. What could he say? How could he tell them without recalling the past to life, without causing them sorrow anew? But he had to tell them. He could not possibly wait until the last day.

"You must put on a heavy overcoat and your high boots. It is deadly cold. We cannot spare any more young men."

Heinrich went back into the horse stable. There he had his high boots and an overcoat. "We cannot spare any more young men," he mused. How could he possibly tell the old man? But he had to tell him, and it was, perhaps, somewhat silly to feel this way, to find it so difficult. Perhaps it was silly. Perhaps he saw a darker past than old Schulte himself.

II

Rudolf Schulte and young Heinrich Schulte walked over the fields. They were of equal height. Their broad, square shoulders and their determined strides gave them a strong family resemblance. They could easily be taken for father and son. They walked northward and made a new trail through the untrodden snow. Old Rudolf Schulte walked on the right side. With every second step the point of his cane left a narrow, funnel-shaped hole in the snow. In the distance before them the forest appeared like a white, heavy bank of clouds, supported by a dark wall of fir trunks. The old man lifted his cane and pointed to the right. "There, where the post stands out of the snow, is the line. The land on the other side belongs to our neighbor, Holtvogt. Our families have never had any difficulties. We have always helped each other, and I hope that will never change." He looked at Heinrich.

"No, that must never change," the young man said. Then came a long silence. Only the snow answered steadily to the men's steps—*knirk, knirk, knirk.* "Wonder whether he finds it difficult to tell me all about Schulten place," Heinrich thought.

"And do not forget," Rudolf Schulte again began, "the corner, about forty acres framed on two sides by alder bushes, must never be flooded. The soil is binding and inclined to be sour. Every fourth year it must be given a good portion of lime, otherwise bulrushes and moss will soon cover the surface and kill the good grasses. Lime warms and sweetens the soil."

Heinrich nodded. He had to know all this, he appreciated being told, and yet he did not like to listen to the words. It was as if the man were preparing for death, as if death would come and take him to-morrow. "Uncle, you are not so very old yet," he said, turning to Rudolf. He called him uncle, although they were not very near of kin.

"No, no, not so very old yet, but my days have been many, and the end comes in the sequence of the days." The men turned northeastward. The wind came straight into their faces. "It is cold, it is bitter cold," said the old man, and the wind drove tears out of his eyes. They ran down his cheeks and formed frozen crystals in his gray beard. He pulled the fox fur collar of his coat higher and drew his chin deeper into it. The wind whirled the snow in circles of white dust. The fence wires were singing in fine, metal-clear voices. Large swarms of gray-colored fog crows settled in the snow and called their sufferings into the cold day. From the woods came the bark of a hungry fox. The world was frozen. No mouse left its hole; the gopher slept his sleep of winter.

The men reached the forest. They stopped short and looked at one another. Here it was not so cold. The trees held off the wind. "The coldest day for years," old Schulte said.

"The winters in Russia were colder," replied Heinrich.

"Yes, and in the trenches it must have been insufferably cold." While he was still talking, Rudolf looked up at the high trees. "This patch here is not so old as it seems to be. I planted it out when I was in my best years, forty years ago. It has grown fast, but the wood is not hardened by age. It must stay for another forty before it is felled."

"Another forty," Heinrich said. "Then I shall be an old man."

"Almost—not quite. But, Heinrich, that is why the farm population here in the north sits so tightly in the saddle. One generation works for the next. No one expects that he himself will harvest the fruits of his labors. It is the unselfish work of a man that lasts and moulds the future. A lasting fruit needs time to grow."

Their way led into a dale. Not the slightest wind penetrated here. The sky was cloudless. The sun was far away, but without the wind it seemed warm. The trees were dripping. The moist snow shimmered brilliantly, and showed a slight touch of gold from the sun. The drops twinkled white, red, blue, green—their colors always determined by the background; and the background of the small dripping water pearls was composed of innumerable colors. When the snow slid off, branches snapped into their old positions. The young pine forest spread on both sides of the way. The trees were only man-high. The sun had freed the outer rows from the snow. All the small birds seemed to have gathered here. They were busy where the melted snow had exposed the soil. The warmth would last only a few hours; then the frost would come again, and no beetle, no fly, would dare to leave its hiding place.

The men looked at each tree. Heinrich's thoughts were far

away. "It is difficult," said the old man, "to find one, difficult to take one out where it will not hurt, but we have had one every year and we shall find one this year. This one, perhaps. No, it is difficult to take one out of the row without leaving a permanent gap. That one could be spared, but it is not symmetrical in growth. The branches are not the same length on both sides, and one side is too bushy, it seems."

"I should tell him, I am foolish not to tell him," Heinrich thought. "I am not a servant that I have to ask for a few days' vacation, but it is only considerate to tell him. I should have told him a week ago. Only a few more days and I shall leave."

Before he really had decided to speak, and before he had thought of just what to say, he began, "I am glad I do not have to spend the holidays this year where I spent them the last four years."

Rudolf Schulte looked at the young man. "Yes, I am, too," said he. "Thank God, it is over—but the end could have been a different one. The end was bad."

"Yes, the end was bad," Heinrich said, "but better a bad end than a worse continuation. The first time in four years that all of our family will be at home for the holidays—only one more week until then."

A sudden sadness struck the old man's soul. His face grew ash-gray. Ah, Heinrich was not his son! "All of you will be together then," he said.

"Yes, we shall all be home for the holidays."

"Of course, I expected you would go home for the holidays." They had come to the end of the pine grove. "Well, we have not found what we wanted."

"Aren't we going back this way? We have only looked at one side. Perhaps on the other side we can find one," said Heinrich.

"No, I guess not. I cannot find one this year, it seems. There are many, and yet there are none."

They walked homeward. It was easier to walk now with the wind behind. The buildings of Schulten farm came into sight. The roofs were covered with snow. The whole place seemed much larger now that the fields around were white. "All new buildings, Heinrich. They will last for generations to come, if they are taken care of—if the country is not ruled by those people who do not know, or do not want to know, the difference between 'mine' and 'thine.' Let us hope that time will never come."

Heinrich was silent. Of course that time would come. No farmer would remain owner of the soil; at least, he would not be allowed to call more than a few acres his own. They went into the stables. It was warm between the animals. Heinrich took a broom and swept the snow from his uncle's boots.

III

Rudolf Schulte went into the house to his wife. "It is warm here," said he.

"You have just been outside. It seems warmer to you than it is. The ice flowers are still blooming."

"Cold days—very cold outside."

"Where have you been?"

"We have been in the forests. I had to tell him many things he did not know."

"How could he know?"

"Of course he could not. He is going home for the holidays."

"He is going home!"

"Yes, they will all be home."

"I expected he would go. When will he leave?"

"I do not know."

"Did he not say?"

"He did not say."

"I suppose he will leave, then, a day before."

"Yes, a day before, I suppose."

"Perhaps he will leave sooner."

"Perhaps he will."

"How long will he stay away? Will he stay away over New Year's, too?"

"I do not know. He said they all would be home for the holidays."

"For the holidays. Then he will stay over New Year's. I expected he would. He has not been home on the holidays for the last four years. He really has to go. They expect him at home."

"Of course they expect him."

"I will bring you a pair of dry woolen socks."

"Never mind. I just want to take off my boots. My socks are dry."

"Here, these are better; change them near the fire. Do not go into the bedroom; the air is too cold."

"I have to go to the stables first to see whether the windows and doors are closed. The wind is deadly." He arose and went outside into the horse stable. "Heinrich, the clock struck one. It is time for lunch. You must come in. When are you going to leave, did you say?"

"A day, just a day before the holiday."

"And are you staying over New Year's Day?"

"No, I shall be back before New Year's Day. I shall, perhaps, stay away only two days."

"You must come in soon. It is time for lunch. And do not forget to close the doors when you leave the stable." Rudolf Schulte went into the house again, took off his boots, and changed his socks. "He is staying only two days," said he.

"Then he will be here on New Year's."

"Yes, on New Year's he will be here." The old man looked pleased. He lit his long pipe, sat down in his high-backed chair, and puffed the blue smoke toward the ceiling. "Yes," he said, "you see, Katharina, on New Year's he will be here."

IV

It was late on Christmas night. The moon was bright and growing. It poured its fullness over the fields and gave color to the flowers frozen in the windows. In the moonlight the buildings of Schulten farm stood out on the plain like an island in a Nordic legend. A row of strong oaks reached their bare arms into the ice-cold air, and their shadows wrote giant letters on the snow-covered roofs. If the first of the Schulten had planted these oaks they would be a thousand years old. The first-born son of each generation had taken over the soil, and had handed it down to the next in his line. The soil was holy ground.

Rudolf Schulte and his wife, Katharina, were alone in the room. She looked at him, he looked at her. This Christmas the war was over.

He opened the desk and laid the family chronicle on the table.

He read what his ancestor, Friedrich, had written during the Thirty Years' War. At that time Schulten farm had been one of the few places in this part of the country which had not been deserted, but Friedrich and his old mother, Elise Schulte, had been the only people on the place. His two sisters, Agnes and Gertrud, had been taken to Holland by the soldiers and had never been heard of again. No cattle had been left on the farm. Friedrich had saved one horse by burning out its eyes. The soldiers did not want blind horses. In 1628 all the buildings had been burned, and Friedrich—by this time he was left alone—had lived in the narrow high stone building which had been built centuries ago as a protection against robber knights.

Frau Schulte looked at her husband. "Rudolf, it is late."

"Yes, it is late." He turned a few leaves and read again. Gustav Schulte had seen the Seven Years' War. Hermann, Gustav's first-born, had fallen in 1759. One boy only was left, but he was sickly, and Gustav expressed his fear that the Schulten line might come to an end. That, however, did not come to pass. The boy developed into a strong man, improved the place, and left four sons. . . .

Rudolf Schulte went outside. The snow-covered buildings, the great white fields, were to him the death garment of his line. If only one of them . . . "It has come to the end with us Schulten." He went around the house and the barns and through the stables. If only one of them had come home. . . .

Frau Schulte had the photographs lying before her. Rudolf, Hermann, Heinrich, Ernst—four sons. . . . "O Lord, have we indeed deserved this? All four of them? Not one have you left to us, not one to Schulten." She looked at the framed documents on the wall. Each showed an angel consoling a dying soldier. Frau Schulte read once more:—

Rudolf Schulte, geboren 23. März, 1884, gefallen 4. August, 1914, bei Lüttich. Dulce et decorum est pro patria mori.

Rudolf would have been the next on Schulten farm.

Hermann Schulte, geboren 2. Februar, 1891, gefallen im Juli, 1915, in Russland. Dulce et decorum est . . .

Heinrich Schulte, geboren 29. März, 1895, gefallen 22. Juli, 1918, bei Chatteau Thierry . . . pro patria . . .
Ernst Schulte, geboren 6. Mai, 1899, gefallen 22. Juli, 1918, bei Chatteau Thierry . . . mori . . .

Ernst and Heinrich had only been children. Last Christmas the two boys had been on furlough and had trimmed the *Tannenbaum*. And this Christmas the war was over.

Frau Schulte could not hide the pictures. Her husband entered too soon. He opened the family chronicle again and turned the pages which he himself had written as the years had passed.

"Rudolf, have you written it down?"

"No, not yet."

"I guess you should."

"Yes, I guess I should."

"It is better to write it down. It would not be fair."

"You are right; it would not be fair to them. What do you think I should write?"

"Write it just in a few simple words. A few simple words will do."

"Yes, a few simple words. There is hardly any ink left, it seems."

"There is more. I will bring it."

"No, don't. I guess this will do. What do you think I should write?"

"Just write it down in a few simple words. Mention their names, perhaps, and their ages."

"Yes, their names and their ages, I guess. . . . Katharina, I don't believe this pen is any good. Is there another somewhere around?"

"Wait, I will see."

"Never mind, I suppose this will do."

V

"Have you finished, Rudolf?"

"Almost, not quite. I do not know just how to end." He wrote:—

Rudolf—Hermann—Heinrich—Ernst Schulte.

Fallen, World War, 1914-1918.

Our line has come to an end. I, Rudolf Schulte, the last of Schulten, leave this place to Heinrich Schulte, my cousin's son.

I curse whoever should dare to read this our history without the deepest of awe, and with the help of God do I curse whoever should dare to alienate our farm. So help me God.

RUDOLF SCHULTE
Anno Domini 1918, *December*

He put down his pen and closed the volume.

"Have you finished now, Rudolf?"

"Yes, I have written the end."

"It is late."

"Yes, it is late."

"The fire cannot do any harm?"

"No, it is almost out. . . . Well, Christmas is over, Katharina."

"Yes, it is over."

UNTITLED STORY [1]

By JOSÉ GARCIA VILLA

(From *Story* and *Clay*)

1

FATHER did not understand my love for Vi, so Father sent me to America to study away from her. I could not do anything and I left.

2

I was afraid of my father.

3

On the boat I was seasick and I could not eat. I thought of home and my girl and I had troubled dreams.

4

The blue waves in the young sunlight were like azure dancing flowers but they danced ceaselessly to the tune of the sun, to look at them made me dizzy. Then I would go to my cabin and lie down and sometimes I cried.

5

We were one month at sea. When I arrived in America I was lonely.

6

I window-shopped at Market Street in San Francisco and later when I was in Los Angeles I went to Hollywood but I remained lonely.

7

I saw President Hoover's home in Palo Alto but I did not care for President Hoover.

8

In California too I saw a crippled woman selling pencils on a sidewalk. It was night and she sat on the cold concrete like an

253

old hen but she had no brood. She looked at me with dumb faithful eyes.

9

The nigger in the Pullman hummed to himself. At night he prepared our berths and he was automatic like a machine. As I looked at him I knew I did not want to be a machine.

10

In the university where I went there were no boys yet. It was only August and school would not begin until September. The university was on a hill and there the winds blew strong. In my room at night I could hear the winds howling like helpless young puppies. The winds were little blind dogs crying for their mother.

11

Where was the mother of the winds? I lay in bed listening to the wind children crying for their mother but I would fall asleep before their mother had returned to them.

12

During the day the little blind puppies did not whimper much. It was only at night that they grew afraid of the dark and then they cried for their mother. Did their mother ever come to them? Maybe their mother had a lover and she loved this lover more than the little blind puppies.

13

I had nothing to do and I wrote home to my friends but my friends did not write to me.

14

One day a boy knocked at my room. He was young and he said he was alone and wanted to befriend me. He became dear to me.

15

The boy's name was David. He was poor and he wore slovenly clothes but his eyes were soft. He was like a young flower.

16

When David was sick I watched over him.

17

Afterwards David would not go anywhere without me.

18

Of nights David and I would walk through the streets and he would recite poetry to me.

"Sunset and evening star
And one clear call for me . . ."

This was the slowness of David, the slowness of the sunset, of the evening star.

19

One night David came to me and said he was returning home the next morning. He could not earn enough money on which to go to school.

20

I died in myself.

21

After David had gone I walked the streets feeling I had lost a great, great something. When I thought of him it hurt very much.

22

School opened in September. At my table in the dining hall we were eight. I liked Georgia, Aurora, Louise and Greg. There was another girl and her name was Reynalda but she was a little haughty.

23

The boys were Joe and Wiley. Joe came from David's town and when I asked him about David he said they had been like Jonathan and David in high school. Joe loved David and David, who was far away now, became a bond between Joe and me.

24

Sometimes Joe and I got sore at each other but when we thought of David we became friends again.

25

Joe wanted to become a preacher and Wiley would be a sports editor. I did not know what I wanted to be. First when I was a boy I wanted to be a movie actor but later I did not want to be a movie actor. I wanted to paint but Father objected to it because he said painters did not make much money.

26

Father was a moneymaker. When he had made it he did not want to spend it. When I needed money I went to my mother and she gave it to me because she was not a moneymaker.

27

Then I fell in love with Georgia. Georgia had golden hair and I became enamoured of it. In my country all the girls were black-haired. I asked Georgia to let me feel her hair and when I ran my fingers through it I became crazy about her.

28

Georgia and I went running around. Afterwards she wrote me love letters.

29

In one letter she called me My Lord, in another Beloved. But I called her just Georgia although sometimes I called her Georgie. When I called her Georgie I smiled because it was like a boy's name.

30

One day Georgia and I quarrelled and many nights thereafter I walked the streets muttering to myself. I did not know what I was saying. I called myself, You . . . but the sentence did not get finished. I would look at the sky and behold the stars and talk to myself.

31

One night I stopped talking to myself. I was no longer incoherent and the sentence on my lips that began with You . . . got finished.

32

The finished sentence was as beauteous as a dancer in the dawn. The sentence was finished at night but it was not like the night but like the dawn.

33

Later Georgia and I made up but everything was not as it used to be. The finished sentence was beauteous like a dancer in the dawn. After a time I did not care for Georgia nor she for me.

34

I went to school but I did not like going to school.

35

I said to myself I would be through with girls and love only the girl back home. I wondered if what had happened to me had happened or was happening to Vi. As I thought I got angry, not at myself but with Vi.

36

A girl should be constant.

37

I was angry with Vi, and in my fancy I saw many pictures of her with other boys. She was dancing and smiling and she had no thoughts of me.

38

Finally I dreamt Vi had got married and I woke up crying. Then I was no longer angry with Vi but with my father who had separated us. I wrote Father an angry letter blaming him. I said I would quit studying and did not care if he cut me off.

39

I was very angry. I became a poet. In fancy my anger became a gorgeous purple flower. I made love to it with my long fingers. Then when I had won it and it shone like a resplendent gem in my hands I offered it to my father.

40

My father could not understand the meaning of the gorgeous purple flower. When I gave it to him he threw it on the floor. Then I said, "My father is not a lover."

41

I picked the flower and it lived because my father refused it.

42

One morning at breakfast I told Wiley and Joe and the girls that I was quitting school and leaving for New York that afternoon. At first they would not believe me but I was quiet and pensive throughout the meal and finally they believed me. They wanted to know why I was leaving but I told them I did not know it myself.

43

At lunch they looked at me wistfully and I said: "This is our last meal together." I became very sad.

44

I shook their hands and Louise and Aurora asked me if I would write to them. When I left the table they followed me softly with their eyes until I turned at the door.

45

Joe and Wiley walked with me to my room at the dorm. They did not want to leave me and in my room I said they must go for I must pack my things. They wanted to help me but I said I was not packing many things. I made them go after we had shaken hands and promised to write each other. Joe and Wiley wanted to go to the station to see me off but I begged them not to. It would make me feel bad, I said.

46

And so I made Joe and Wiley go but when they had left my room I went to the window and looked at them long and I cried. I liked Joe and Wiley and Aurora and Louise—why was I leaving them?

47

Then I lay on the bed without moving. All the time I knew I was not truly leaving for New York yet I felt greatly hurt. In myself I was leaving and behind me I would leave Joe and Wiley and the girls. I would be lonely again as when I had first come to America.

48

I had said I was leaving for New York but it was not true. I was a liar because I had felt like telling a lie and I was angry with my father and in my mind I wanted to do something rash like leaving college and going about starving in a big city like New York.

49

In the big city New York, where I had never been, I was hungry and without money. I lived in the little dark room and it was dark and ugly for the rent was cheap. There was only one little window in the room and it was tight to open.

50

One night I opened the little window and a piece of paper blew in. It settled on the floor and then my mind began to work about it.—I am not alone. A lover is waiting for me outside. She has written me a letter calling me to her side . . . "I will go to you, sweetheart," I whispered tenderly.

51

Then a strong wind blew in and the paper moved.—It is a white flower trembling with love. It is God's white flower.—It made me think of my gorgeous purple flower which my father had refused and I wanted it to become God's white flower. Make my purple flower white, God, I prayed.

52

In New Mexico I had prayed before about my father, mother and sisters but in New York I prayed about a flower.

53

In New York it was colder than in New Mexico.

54

I wanted to buy a new suit and go to see a new UFA film but I had no money.

55

Because I wanted to have a new suit and to see a new German film and I had no money I walked around in the streets. I looked at the haberdashery windows and gazed at the new styles. There was a wine-coloured suit with roped shoulders and if I only had money I could have it. It cost sixty-five dollars.

56

In front of the big cinema it was very bright. In San Francisco I saw the Fox Theatre and I thought it was very big but this was much bigger. It was very lavish. Rich young ladies and thin gay gentlemen poured in. They laughed goldenly.

57

Then I got tired of waiting and I returned to my little dark room and the dark made me want a woman.

58

It was cold in the room and I thought if I had a woman I would not feel so cold. We would share each other's warmth.

59

Warming woman, warming woman, I sang. How beautiful the words. How beautiful the thought.

60

Then I turned on the light and in the lighted room I took a book and read. The story was about a liar. I thought of myself.

I had lied to Joe and Wiley and to Aurora and Louise and to every one at the table. It had occurred to me to lie and I did and now I was living up to my lie.

61

All these adventures in New York I have been telling you about happened in my room as I lay on the bed crying because I was a liar. But I was not afraid to cry.

62

Later I dressed and pretended I was going to the station where I was leaving. After a time when I got dressed I did not want to merely pretend and I left my room to go to the station.

63

On the way I met Aurora. She walked with me to the street-corner to bid me good-bye. She held my hands long and her hold was tight. Her hands were soft like flowers and thin like roots but they were strong lovers. Her hands made cruel love to my hands.

64

Write to me, her mouth said—but her hands, have we not touched the touch to last us for ever? The touch of music that knows no forgetting?

65

When I had already gotten into the bus and the bus started Aurora did not move. She stood at the corner, her eyes following me. She stood there long, immobile, and I waved my hand at her but only her eyes moved. Her hands that had been lovers were quiet now. Her whole body was become a quiet lover. As the bus moved away, in the far corner she was no longer a quiet lover but a song of serenity.

66

In the bus strange thoughts came to me: I have touched her hands. Why do I not love her the way I loved Georgia? Why have I not asked to touch her hair? Maybe if I touched her hair I would love her like I was maddened by Georgia . . . I should

have touched her hair. She would have liked it. We would have
become lovers.

67

As to Georgia I did not bid her good-bye and I did not care.—I
touched her hair. I ran my fingers through her hair. After I
finished the sentence that was beauteous as a dancer in the dawn
I did not care to touch her hair.—In the bus I could not understand why and it made me feel sad.

68

I got off at the station and waited for the 5.30 train. It came
and then it left. I watched it till I could not see it. I wondered
if I was in it.

69

Had I bidden myself good-bye?

70

Afterwards I walked through the town as if I had gone out of
myself. I looked for myself vainly. I was nowhere. I was now
only a shell, a house. The house of myself was empty.

71

My god had flown away and carried with him my gorgeous
purple flower. Will Father laugh now?

72

Where had my god fled? Where was he taking my purple
flower which my father had refused?

73

In the morning, on the campus, I met Aurora and she said I
fooled her. Later everybody said I fooled them. But to Aurora,
as I thought of her as she stood at the street corner, her hands
making love to my hands, and of her when she was a song of
serenity, I said: Your hands have told me an unforgettable story.
Your song of serenity has awakened me. Now let me feel your
hair . . .

74

My god was in her hair. My god was there with my purple
flower pressed gently to his breast. I opened his hands and he
yielded to me my flower. I pinned it to Aurora's hair. And as
the purple petals kissed the soft dark of her hair, my flower turned
silver, then white—became God's white flower. Then I was no
longer angry with my father.

THE QUARREL[1]

By LEO L. WARD

(From *Story*)

WITH a rusty tin full of coal oil in one hand and a clump of greasy rag in the other, he kicked at the screen door until it became dislodged from the jamb, and then edged his way out. The door slapped behind him and the released spring whirred for a moment or two as the old man shuffled away from the back porch, his face bent and frowning over the cup of coal oil that kept spilling upon his hand at almost every step.

He went over the lawn in a kind of hurrying half-run, passed through the dappled shade of the maple-tree, then across the narrow dirt drive and on toward a clump of burdock in a corner of the small farmyard. He set the cup on the ground, then began tugging and jerking at the handles of a plow that was half hidden among the weeds. He stood for a moment frowning at the plow and muttering to himself. Then he bent over painfully and began splashing the rusty share with the oil.

Little specks of brightness appeared here and there on the share as Nate Heming rubbed at it steadily. But the old man's brow was moist now, and a filmy, misty blur was gathering just before the gray lashes of his eyes, so that he could hardly see the brightness coming on the share. Suddenly dropping the stub of corn cob with which he had been rubbing at the rust, he lifted his body painfully and stood for a while shaking his head at the share and grumbling unintelligibly to himself. He rubbed the back of a greasy hand across his eyes and the little bright spots on the share suddenly began winking up at him.

"I . . . I can't scour the thing," he said. "I won't scour it."

Suddenly his head jerked backward angrily. A dense flock of blackbirds was passing over the barn. They swooped downward into the pasture with a great whirring of wings. Their raucous chattering ceased abruptly.

"Now look at that," the old man almost shouted, his shrunken face growing taut with lines of violent anger. "I'll tell you, I'm goin' to put an end to that."

He hurried away to the house, then in a little while returned, holding a single-barrelled shotgun crosswise before him. He stole around the corner of the barn, and a minute later the sound of a shot came from the pasture. A harsh din arose as the birds, lifting in a black cloud, went off northward over the fields in swift trailing flight. Then Nate Heming came back from the pasture, tramping heavily through the farmlot, the gun over his shoulder, his face flushed but relieved.

He was half way to the house when a woman burst out of the screen door on the rear porch and came toward him with long, rapid strides.

"Now what *are* you doin'? Don't try to fool me, Nate Heming. I heared you shootin' out there." The woman had planted her large body directly in front of Nate and her great jaws worked heavily while she talked.

Nate looked at the woman but said nothing.

"What you doin' with that gun, I said?"

"Been shootin' blackbirds. That's what I been doin', ef you want to know so bad."

"Give me that gun."

The woman snatched the gun out of Nate's hands, then pointed a brown arm toward the half-scoured plow over beside the fence.

"Now you git over that plow, Nate Heming. Just like I told you this morning. . . . You ought to been in that tater field an hour ago. Lord knows, you've had time to git a dozen plows scoured."

Nate put one hand in his pocket, turned casually and started toward the plow. The woman stood watching while he moved away, her face squinted into a fixed dry smile.

Half way to the plow the old man turned abruptly about, shook his fist violently at the woman and shouted, "I tell you, Sadie Heming, you ain't goin' to give me no dog's life this way. I . . . I'm not goin' to be worked to death. You just don't know what you're doin', you don't. You're just drivin' me right to my grave, that's what you're doin', Sadie Heming." The old man turned towards the plow again as he spoke of going to his grave, and his voice grew suddenly low and husky.

The big woman turned and went slowly toward the house, carrying the gun awkwardly at her side. But as she was crossing the dirt drive between the farm lot and the lawn she stopped and looked back. Nate was standing beside the plow, a corn cob in his hand, glaring at her. A grimace of disgust spread over Sadie Heming's face.

"Er you goin' to plow that tater field this afternoon or not?" she asked, lifting her voice to suit the distance.

Nate flung the corn cob into the burdock beside the fence. "No," he said abruptly. Then he spoke slowly and deliberately. "I guess I won't plow that tater field."

Mrs. Nate Heming went over to the maple tree and leaned the gun against it, then returned rapidly across the farm lot.

She stooped and picked up the can of coal oil and a corn cob, then rose and stood facing Nate, her mouth drawn tight over her teeth and her eyes flashing. "All right," she said in a low but unsteady voice. "You don't need to. *I*'m goin' to scour this plow, Nate Heming, and *I*'m goin' to plow that tater field. You don't need to."

Nate gulped audibly before he said, "Just you go ahead and try it. Just go right on an' try it, old woman." A thin smile pulled at the corners of his mouth and his whole body trembled slightly as he burst, first into a low, wheezy chuckle, then into a dry laugh. "I jess sees you a-plowin' that tater field. You'll learn, you'll learn what kinda work I have to do around here. . . . An' it won't be like fussin' inside a house all day neither."

Mrs. Sadie Heming jerked her head back and looked straight into Nate's flashing eyes as she said, "Yes, an' I'll tell you what *you'll* do. You go right up to the house and do the churnin'. *You* just *fuss* around the house onct and see how you like it. Yes, just march right on up there. The churn's ready, the cream's in it an' ever'thing. An' see you don't stop till the butter comes, neither. . . . An' then, Mister Heming, when the churnin's done you can start on them taters, cuttin' 'em up. They're right there on the porch, in the sack. And besides, you can milk the cow this evenin' too, when you git the taters done. . . . Yes, an ther's

suthin' else you kin do. You can git yer own supper this evenin'
. . . ef you expect to git any. Just like to see you gettin' yer
own meals onct. So, just go right on. Start to *fussin'* around in
the house, as you call it. The churn's all ready fer you."

Nate stood glaring petulantly at his wife, with a sickly grin
playing about the corners of his mouth. At last he turned without saying anything, and started for the house.

And scarcely a half-hour later Sadie Heming went out of the
farm lot, following an old gray team and a plow that scudded on
the ground before her, raising little puffs of dust about her long
swinging skirts.

It was not yet mid-afternoon when Nate burst open the screen
door on the back porch and went stumbling and limping in a
kind of headlong run across the farm lot toward the little dirt
lane that led past a small flaring corn crib and a low hog house
to the "tater" field. He could see a gray team moving slowly in
the field, and behind the team the tall figure of his wife bending
forward over the handles of the plow. He went straight toward
the team, lurching and jerking his body through the loose plowed
soil.

"You git in out a here," he cried, almost in a whine, as he
approached the plow. "I'm goin' to plow my tater field myself.
You . . . you git in out a here."

As the woman looked with some surprise at Nate a broad grin
spread slowly about her eyes and mouth. She tossed her head
upward and laughed, and the faded blue sunbonnet fell far back
on her thick grayish hair.

"Why, I thought you was goin' to do the churnin'," she said
and then laughed again.

"You do yer own churnin'," Nate shouted, "that's what you
do, an' leave me alone. I ain't goin' to do yer churnin' fer you.
I ain't goin' to do no slavin' fer you, Sadie Heming."

The woman slowly pulled the lines from over her head. "Awright, aww-right," she said almost good-humoredly, "just as you
say, Mister Heming. Go right ahead and plow it then, since I
see you don't like fussin' around the house so well." Her voice
rose, slightly shrill and thin with irony. Then she stepped over
onto the plowed ground and stood with one arm akimbo.

The old man's hands shook as he reached for the plow. He

was standing in the furrow now, violently jerking and slapping the horses with both lines. As the team moved away he grasped at the plow handles fiercely and stumbled on, staring intently at the curling loam beneath him. Once, as he went slowly up the field, he looked backward over his shoulder for an instant, then turned to fix his eyes again on the plow.

When he at last came to the turn of the land much of the anger had left his face. He breathed more freely and easily now. His hands no longer shook so violently. He looked back over the field. The woman was gone—he could see her in the lane, half-way to the house already. His eyes fell to the strip of plowed land beside him, and he examined it carefully. Wisps of grass and dried weed stalks showed here and there at the edges of the furrows. "Ughh . . . look a that. Fine job a plowin' *she* did. . . . Well, I knowed it. I knowed just what she'd do."

Sadie Heming could hardly see the "eyes" of the potatoes now, in the dusk that was creeping out of the little orchard and gathering slowly around the house. She examined each potato closely before cutting it into sections and dropping them in the pan at her feet. From time to time she looked toward the barn, then gazed uneasily down the lane toward the potato field. Her face was drawn and anxious, but no longer harsh.

At last she poured the potatoes into an empty gunny sack and went out from the porch with a large milk bucket swinging at her side. When she returned, not long afterward, from the direction of the barn, milk froth was spilling over the brim of the bucket onto her dress and her big loose shoes. She stopped for a moment with her hand resting on the little white knob on the screen, and looked again in the direction of the lane before going into the house.

She a lit small oil lamp and set it in its high bracket beside the kitchen window. She set the white oilcloth table with two big blue-rimmed plates, two large glass tumblers, a pitcher of milk, a plate of bread, the pink salt and pepper shakers, the little blue glass full of tooth picks. Then she put the meat and fried potatoes in the "warming oven."

She took her sunbonnet from the back of a chair and suddenly left the kitchen, and the screen door slammed sharply behind her as she walked swiftly toward the little lane leading to the field.

There was still light enough for her to see the horses moving in the field. She walked toward the team, striding heavily through the loose plowed ground, her skirts dragging in the black soil.

"Now, Nate, you better come in out a here," she said as she came up to the plow. "There's no use you stayin' out here all hours like this." The horses suddenly stopped at the sound of her voice, but the driver started to shout at them and to slap their rumps sharply with the lines. The team stood still, however, their heads drooped low over the furrow in front of them.

The woman raised her voice a little higher. "You know you ought to been in out a here an hour ago. Now come on. Onhitch them horses and come on in an' git some supper. You ought to be ashamed a this here stubbornness, Nate."

Nate Heming kept staring straight ahead at his team, paying no attention to the woman standing beside the plow. He continued to slap the horses and to shout more and more loudly. His shouting was becoming almost unintelligible, hardly more than a sustained howling and bawling.

At last one of the horses lifted its head and started to move, then the other moved forward also. The jerking and slapping and shouting continued.

Sadie Heming turned to the team and ran up along their side, calling to them to stop. "Whoa . . . whoaa . . . whoaaa . . ." She was almost screaming. The horses moved on, very slowly at first, but as the noise behind them increased they went faster, then faster and faster until the plow went forward so rapidly that the driver was forced into a half trot in the furrow behind it. The mingled screaming and shouting followed the team rod after rod up the field.

But at the corner of the land, where the team was swinging at the turn, the woman hurried forward and grasped a bridle rein. One of the horses, then the other, came to a full stop, and a few moments afterward they were both drooping their heads over the furrow as before. Gradually the shouting behind the plow lessened, and finally Nate Heming stood, mute with anger, staring at the woman.

"Now you just stop this craziness, Nate Heming," Sadie said when she had got back her breath from the running. "Just you come on in out a here, d'ya understand? Don't be stubborn like this, Nate." Her voice was suddenly not so high or harsh. "You'll make yourself sick at this kind a work."

The old man still gripped the handles of the plow. He was no longer glaring at the woman. He was looking straight ahead at the horses. He was crying.

The woman moved around to the doubletree and began to unhitch the tugs. Suddenly the old man pulled the lines from around his neck and violently flung them over the plow toward his wife. The buckle struck her cheek, stinging her sharply. Her hand went quickly to her face but she said nothing. She went on with the unhitching.

A few minutes later she was driving the team into the lane that led, now through a deep dusk, toward the house. Once as she went along she thought she could hear Nate's voice, lifted wild and angry behind her. She listened anxiously, but the jangling of the tug chains came clear and sharp in the damp dusk and she could not be sure what he said.

She put the horses in the barn, unharnessed them and fed them. As she came out of the door she saw Nate's figure standing at the corner of the barn. "Ever'thing's done now, Nate. You better come on up to supper." Her voice was quiet and gentle as she spoke. The dark figure at the corner of the barn did not answer.

Halfway to the house she heard a heavy thud behind her, then the jangle of chains. She knew he was rearranging the harness on its wooden pegs. She smiled faintly to herself as she walked on.

In the kitchen she took down the oil lamp from its bracket on the wall and set it on the table, then removed the meat and potatoes from the warming oven. She poured the greasy salt ham onto a white platter and the fried potatoes into a clay-colored bowl and set these on the table. Then she stood waiting over beside the window, her face tired and anxious but no longer taut or hard as it had been before.

She had waited for a long time beside the window when the spring on the screen door creaked and some one shuffled across the floor of the back porch. Then Nate appeared in the kitchen door. His face, grimaced against the light, looked very weary and very old. His squinted eyes flickered once or twice as he stared at his wife, and a slight petulant quivering ran along the gray line of his lips. He glanced once at the table, then his eyes lifted again to the woman's face. "Supper's ready, Nate," Sadie Heming said very quietly, pointing to the table.

"Awright," he said. His lower jaw was shaking violently as he spoke. "You better eat it yourself then. I don't want none a *your* supper." And he went, swaying, almost headlong through the low door that opened into the unlighted bedroom beyond the kitchen.

Sadie Heming ate very little, some bread and some milk and a few slices of fried potato. Then she cleared the table as noiselessly as possible, but little clinkings and clatterings arose whenever she set a dish away in the cupboard. At every slight noise of the dishes fresh lines would run out from the corner of her mouth, forming tiny pinkish webs under the wisps of grayish hair that had fallen down her cheeks.

When the dishes were done she went out to the porch and returned with a dish pan filled with potatoes which were covered with little white and purplish sprouts. She sat down beside the table and began cutting the potatoes with a small paring knife. Once in a while she would look toward the bedroom. She could see the corner of the great double bed, just visible in the dim light, that fell through the open door from the lamp on the table beside her. She heard sounds from the other room now and again . . . the quiet slap of a suspender falling against a trouser leg, the hard clap of a shoe upon the floor, the crackle of soil-caked overalls flung over a chair . . . then the creak of a bed slat . . . The cutting of the potatoes went on again, steadily, and there was no sound now except the lisp of the knife cutting through the soft flesh of the potatoes.

A loud heavy breathing came from the bedroom. It grew very loud and very slow, the labored breathing of a tired, exhausted body. The woman stopped the cutting, with half of a large potato held before her in her hand. She cut it in two pieces, then dropped these in the pan. She put the knife on the table beside her and let her hands fall in the hollow of her lap, then sat for a long while listening to the heavy breathing in the other room. At last she rose suddenly and impulsively from her chair and went quickly over to the door where she stood gazing into the darkened room. Her head was dropped slightly forward and she seemed to be looking down at the bed dimly showing in the light that fell over her stooping shoulder from the high lamp on the kitchen wall behind her. Once or twice her shoulders and her head shook convulsively but slightly, as though she was crying. After some time she turned slowly from the door and came back to the chair, where she sat down and with fumbling fingers took off her heavy shoes. She went very quietly back to the door again, but stopped there as before. For a long while she stood gazing into the half-dark of the farther room. Her shoulders no longer trembled. She seemed very quiet now. Finally her hand began playing idly with the fastening of her dress, and she moved as if to go through the door. Then she turned abruptly and came back toward the lamp in its high bracket against the kitchen wall. As she reached up for the lamp her broad, rough face showed wet and shiny against the light, and the line of her tight narrow lips was broken and softened in a faint smile. She blew the light out, and went through the sudden darkness of the kitchen toward the heavy breathing in the other room.

THE YEARBOOK OF THE AMERICAN
SHORT STORY
MAY 1, 1931, TO APRIL 30, 1932

ABBREVIATIONS

I PERIODICALS

A. L. ....American Literature.
A. Merc. ....American Mercury.
A. Sp. ....American Speech.
A. W. ....All's Well.
Adv. ....Adventure.
Am. ....American Magazine.
Ann. ....Annals of Our Lady of Lourdes.
Archive ....Archive.
Atl. ....Atlantic Monthly.
B. E. T. ....Boston Evening Transcript.
Blue Bk. ....Blue Book Magazine.
Book (N. Y.) ...Bookman. (New York.)
Books ....Books. (N. Y. Herald Tribune.)
C. D. N. ....Chicago Daily News Midweek.
C. For. ....Canadian Forum.
C. G. ....Country Gentleman.
C. H. ....Country Home.
C. H. J. ....Canadian Home Journal.
C. N. R. ....Canadian National Railways Magazine.
C. R. ....Cedar Rapids.
Cal. C. ....University of California Chronicle.
Can. ....Canadian Magazine.
Cath. W. ....Catholic World.
Chat. ....Chatelaine.
Chic. Trib. ......Chicago Tribune. (Syndicate Service.)
Clay ....Clay.
Col. ....Collier's Weekly.
Colop. ....Colophon.
Colum. ....Columbia.
Com. ....Commonweal.
Con. ....Contempo.
Cos. ....Cosmopolitan.
Crit. ....Criterion.
Dart ....Dart.
Del. ....Delineator.
Eng. J. ....English Journal. (College edition.)
Essex ....Essex Institute Historical Collections.
Ev. ....Everyman.
Fif. ....Fifth Floor Window.
For. ....Forum.
Free. ....New Freeman.
Frontier ....Frontier.
G. H. (N. Y.) ...Good Housekeeping. (New York.)

Gol. ....Golden Book Magazine.
H. H. ....Hound and Horn.
Hark. ....Harkness Hoot.
Harp. B. (N. Y.).Harper's Bazaar. (New York.)
Harp. M. ....Harper's Magazine.
Hol. ....Holland's Magazine.
House. ....Household Magazine.
Husk ....Husk.
J. o' L. ....John o' London's Weekly.
L. H. J. ....Ladies' Home Journal.
L. Merc. ....London Mercury.
Ly. ....Liberty.
M. L. N. ....Modern Language Notes.
MacL. ....MacLean's Magazine.
Man. ....Manuscripts of 1931.
Man. G. ....Manchester Guardian.
Men. J. ....Menorah Journal.
Mid. ....Midland.
N. A. Rev. ......North American Review.
N. C. ....New Copy.
N. E. Q. ....New England Quarterly.
N. M. Q. ....New Mexico Quarterly.
N. Mass. ....New Masses.
N. Rep. ....New Republic.
N. Y. ....New Yorker.
N. Y. Times .....New York Times Review of Books.
Nat. (N. Y.) ....Nation. (New York.)
Nativ. ....Nativity.
New R. ....New Review.
New S. ....New Statesman.
O. C. ....Open Court.
Op. ....Opinion.
Opp. ....Opportunity.
P. M. L. A. .....Publications of the Modern Language Association of
              America.
Pagy. ....Pagany.
Pict. R. ....Pictorial Review.
Pr. S. ....Prairie Schooner.
Pub. W. ....Publishers' Weekly.
(R.) ....Reprint.
Red Bk. ....Red Book Magazine.
Rom. R. ....Romanic Review.
S. E. P. ....Saturday Evening Post.
S. W. ....Southwest Review.
Sat. R. (N. Y.) ..Saturday Review of Literature. (New York.)
Scan. ....American-Scandinavian Review.
Sch. ....Scholastic.
Scr. ....Scribner's Magazine.
Scrip ....Scrip.
Sew. ....Sewanee Review.
Sh. St. ....Short Stories.
Sky ....Skyline.

ABBREVIATIONS

ABBREVIATIONS

277

St. Nich. ....St. Nicholas.
Stanf. ....1931 Yearbook of Stanford Writing.
Sto. ....Story.
Strat. ....Stratford Magazine.
S. V. ....Sovereign Visitor.
Sym. ....Symposium.
T. Q. ....This Quarter.
Tan. ....Tanager.
Tenn. ....Tennessee Historical Magazine.
Tor. ....Toronto Star Weekly.
Transit. ....Transition.
Un. ....Universe.
Un. C. ....Union College Bulletin.
V. F. ....Vanity Fair.
Va. ....Virginia Quarterly Review.
W. H. C. ....Woman's Home Companion.
W. T. ....Weird Tales.
W. W. ....Woman's World.
Westm. ....Westminster Magazine.
Yale ....Yale Review.
(161) ....Page 161.
(2:161) ....Volume 2, Page 161.

II. BOOKS

Adamic ....Adamic. Laughing in the Jungle.
Aldington D. ....Aldington. Stepping Heavenward. (English edition.)
Barber ....Barber. Cross-Country.
Barnard ....Barnard. One Generation Away.
Bates F. ....Bates. The Black Boxer. (English edition.)
Bates G. ....Bates. Sally Go Round the Moon. (English edition.)
Bates H. ....Bates. Threshing Day. (English edition.)
Becker C. ....Becker, *editor*. Golden Tales of New England.
Bennett D. ....Bennett. The Night Visitor.
Bennett E. ....Bennett. Venus Rising from the Sea. (English edition.)
Benson C. ....Benson. Christmas Formula. (English edition.)
Bishop ....Bishop. Many Thousands Gone.
Butts ....Butts. Several Occasions. (English edition.)
Byrne E. ....Byrne. Rivers of Damascus.
Canfield D. ......Canfield. Basque People.
Capek B. ....Capek. Tales from Two Pockets. (English edition.)
Caperton ....Caperton. Legends of Virginia.
Cobb M. ....Cobb. Down Yonder with Judge Priest.
Collier ....Collier. Green Thoughts. (English edition.)
Coppard K. ......Coppard. Nixey's Harlequin. (English edition.)
Corley B. ....Corley. The Haunted Jester.
Coyle ....Coyle. There Is a Door.
Cozzens ....Cozzens. S.S. San Pedro.
De la Mare F. ...De la Mare, *editor*. They Walk Again.

Powys G. ....Powys. When Thou Wast Naked. (English edition.)
Preedy ....Preedy. Bagatelle.
Pritchett ....Pritchett. The Spanish Virgin. (English edition.)
Pugh ....Pugh, *editor.* A Book of Short Stories.
Putnam ....Putnam and others, *editors.* The European Caravan. Part I.
Richardson ......Richardson. Barnegat Ways.
Roberts ....Roberts. Aly the Philosopher.
Romanov ....Romanov. Without Cherry Blossom.
Sayre ....Sayre. Rackety Rax.
Schnitzler F. .....Schnitzler. Flight into Darkness.
Shiffrin ....Shiffrin. The Other Cheek.
Sinclair D. ......Sinclair. The Intercessor.
Sitwell C. ....Sitwell. Far From My Home. (English edition.)
Slater ....Slater. The Secret Veld. (English edition.)
Spanish B. ......Wells, *translator.* Great Spanish Short Stories.
Stevens B. ....Stevens. Saginaw Paul Bunyan.
Strong D. ....Strong. The Red Ball. (English edition.)
Suckow C. ......Suckow. Children and Older People.
Summers ....Summers, *editor.* The Supernatural Omnibus.
Time ....Delafield, *editor.* The Time and Tide Album. (English edition.)
Tolstoy E. ......Fülöp-Miller, *editor.* New Light on Tolstoy.
Wakefield C. ....Wakefield. Imagine a Man in a Box.
Wells G. ....Wells, editor. The Best American Mystery Stories of the Year. Vol. 2.
Williams J. ......Williams. The Knife of the Times.
Williams-Ellis ...Williams-Ellis. Volcano. (English edition.)
Winslow D. ......Winslow. Blueberry Pie.
Zweig B. ....Zweig. Amok.

ADDRESSES OF MAGAZINES
PUBLISHING SHORT STORIES

I. American and Canadian Magazines

Adventure, Butterick Building, New York City.
Amazing Stories, 53 Park Place, New York City.
American Boy, 550 West Lafayette Boulevard, Detroit, Mich.
American Magazine, 250 Park Avenue, New York City.
American Mercury, 730 Fifth Avenue, New York City.
American-Scandinavian Review, 25 West 45th Street, New York City.
Atlantic Monthly, 8 Arlington Street, Boston, Mass.
Blue Book Magazine, 230 Park Avenue, New York City.
Canadian Forum, Aldine House, 224 Bloor Street W., Toronto, Ont., Canada.
Canadian Home Journal, Richmond and Sheppard Streets, Toronto, 2, Ont., Canada.
Canadian Magazine, 345 Adelaide Street W., Toronto, Ont., Canada.
Catholic World, 401 West 59th Street, New York City.
Chatelaine, 143 University Avenue, Toronto, 2, Ont., Canada.
Chicago Tribune, Fiction Department, 220 East 42nd Street, New York City.
Clay, Apt. 16-G, 302 West 12th Street, New York City.
College Life, 570 Seventh Avenue, New York City.
Collier's Weekly, 250 Park Avenue, New York City.
Columbia, New Haven, Conn.
Commonweal, Grand Central Terminal, New York City.
Contempo, Chapel Hill, N. C.
Cosmopolitan, 57th Street and Eighth Avenue, New York City.
Country Gentleman, Independence Square, Philadelphia, Pa.
Country Home, 250 Park Avenue, New York City.
Delineator, 161 Sixth Avenue, New York City.
Detective Story Magazine, 79-89 Seventh Avenue, New York City.
Elks Magazine, 50 East 42nd Street, New York City.
Fifth Floor Window, 230 East Houston Street, New York City.
Forum, 441 Lexington Avenue, New York City.
Front, Care of N. V. Servire, 15 Rietzangerlaan, The Hague, Holland.
Frontier, Care of Mr. H. G. Merriam, State University, Missoula, Mont.
Golden Book, 55 Fifth Avenue, New York City.
Good Housekeeping, 57th Street and Eighth Avenue, New York City.
Harper's Bazaar, 572 Madison Avenue, New York City.
Harper's Magazine, 49 East 33rd Street, New York City.
Holland's Magazine, Dallas, Texas.
Hound and Horn, 545 Fifth Avenue, New York City.
Household Magazine, Topeka, Kansas.
Ladies' Home Journal, Independence Square, Philadelphia, Pa.
Left, 218 West 3rd Street, Davenport, Iowa.

Liberty, 1926 Broadway, New York City.
McCall's Magazine, 230 Park Avenue, New York City.
MacLean's Magazine, 143 University Avenue, Toronto, Ont., Canada.
Menorah Journal, 63 Fifth Avenue, New York City.
Midland, 801 Monadnock Building, Chicago, Ill.
Munsey's Magazine, 280 Broadway, New York City.
New Masses, 63 West 15th Street, New York City.
New Mexico Quarterly, University of New Mexico, Albuquerque, N. M.
New Republic, 431 West 21st Street, New York City.
New Review, 42 bis, rue du Plessis-Piquet, Fontenay-aux-Roses, Seine, France.
New Yorker, 25 West 45th Street, New York City.
North American Review, 9 East 37th Street, New York City.
Opinion, 114 East 32nd Street, New York City.
Opportunity, 1133 Broadway, New York City.
Outdoor America, 222 North Bank Drive, Chicago, Ill.
Pagany, Care of Richard Johns, 9 Gramercy Park, New York City.
Pictorial Review, 222 West 39th Street, New York City.
Popular, 79 Seventh Avenue, New York City.
Prairie Schooner, Station "A," Lincoln, Neb.
Real Detective Tales, 1050 North La Salle Street, Chicago, Ill.
Red Book Magazine, 230 Park Avenue, New York City.
St. Nicholas, 155 East 44th Street, New York City.
Saturday Evening Post, Independence Square, Philadelphia, Pa.
Scribner's Magazine, 597 Fifth Avenue, New York City.
Short Stories, Doubleday, Doran & Company, Garden City, L. I., N. Y.
Southwest Review, Dallas, Texas.
Story, 126 Calle del 14 de Abril, Corp Mari, Palma, Mallorca, Spain.
Tanager, Box 66, Grinnell, Iowa.
This Quarter, 4 rue Delambre, Paris, France.
Toronto Star Weekly, Toronto, Ont., Canada.
Transition, Care of Eugene Jolas, 21 rue de Sévigné, Paris (III), France.
Trend, 978 St. Mark's Avenue, Brooklyn, N. Y.
Vanity Fair, Graybar Building, 420 Lexington Avenue, New York City.
Virginia Quarterly Review, 8 West Lawn, University, Va.
Weird Tales, 840 North Michigan Avenue, Chicago, Ill.
Western Home Monthly, Bannatyne and Dagmar, Winnipeg, Manitoba, Canada.
Westminster Magazine, Oglethorpe University, Georgia.
Woman's Home Companion, 250 Park Avenue, New York City.
Woman's World, 4223 West Lake Street, Chicago, Ill.
Yale Review, 125 High Street, New Haven, Conn.
Young's Magazine, 112 East 19th Street, New York City.

II. British, Irish, and Colonial Magazines

Adelphi, 58 Bloomsbury Street, London, W. C. 1.
All-Story Magazine, Fleetway House, Farringdon Street, London, E. C. 4.
Argosy, Tallis House, Tallis Street, London, E. C. 4.
Blackwood's Magazine, 45 George Street, Edinburgh, Scotland.

Blue Magazine, 13 Whitefriars Street, London, E. C. 4.
Blue Peter, 12 St. Mary Axe, London, E. C.
Britannia and Eve, Inveresk House, Strand, London, W. C. 2.
Bulletin, 214 George Street North, Sydney, N. S. W., Australia.
Bystander, 346 Strand, London, W. C. 2.
Cassell's Magazine, Tallis House, Tallis Street, London, E. C. 4.
Chambers' Journal, 38 Soho Square, London, W. C. 1.
Colour, 31 Craven Street, Strand, London, W. C 2.
Corner Magazine, Tallis House, Tallis Street, London, E. C. 4.
Cornhill Magazine, 50 Albemarle Street, London, W. 1.
Criterion, 24 Russell Square, London, W. C. 1.
Dublin Magazine, 2 Crow Street, Dublin, Irish Free State.
English Review, 6 Great New Street, London, E. C. 4.
Everyman, 13 Great Queen Street, Kingsway, London, W. C. 2.
Fortnightly Review, 13 Buckingham Street, London, W. C. 2.
G. K.'s Weekly, 2 Little Essex Street, Strand, London, W. C. 2.
Good Housekeeping, 153 Queen Victoria Street, London, E. C. 4.
Grand Magazine, 8-11 Southampton Street, Strand, London, W. C. 2.
Happy Magazine, 8 Southampton Street, Strand, London, W. C. 2.
Harper's Bazaar, 9 Stratton Street, Piccadilly, London, W. 1.
Home Magazine, 18 Henrietta Street, Covent Garden, London, W. C. 2.
Hutchinson's Magazine, 34-36 Paternoster Row, London, E. C. 4.
Illustrated London News, 346 Strand, London, W. C. 2.
Island, The Favil Press, 152 Church Street, London, W. 8.
John o' London's Weekly, 8 Southampton Street, Strand, London, W. C. 2.
Lady, 39-40 Bedford Street, Strand, London, W. C. 2.
Lady's World, Lennox House, Norfolk Street, Strand, London, W. C. 2.
Life and Letters, 10 Great Queen Street, Kingsway, London, W. C. 2.
London Magazine, Fleetway House, Farringdon Street, London, E. C. 4.
London Mercury, 229 Strand, London, W. C. 2.
Manchester Guardian, 3 Cross Street, Manchester.
Nash's-Pall Mall Magazine, 153 Queen Victoria Street, London, E. C. 4.
National Graphic, 346 Strand, London, W. C. 2.
New English Weekly, 38 Cursitor Street, London, E. C. 4.
New Magazine, Fleetway House, Farringdon Street, London, E. C. 4.
New Statesman and Nation, 10 Great Queen Street, Kingsway, London, W. C. 2.
Novel Magazine, 18 Henrietta Street, Covent Garden, London, W. C. 2.
Outspan, P. O. Box 245, Bloemfontein, Orange Free State, South Africa.
Outward Bound, Edinburgh House, 2 Eaton Gate, London, S. W. 1.
Pearson's Magazine, 18 Henrietta Street, Covent Garden, London, W. C. 2.
Premier, Fleetway House, Farringdon Street, London, E. C. 4.
Queen, Windsor House, Bream's Buildings, London, E. C. 4.
Quiver, Fleetway House, Farringdon Street, London, E. C. 4.
Red Magazine, Fleetway House, Farringdon Street, London, E. C. 4.
Romance, 3 Lancaster Place, Wellington Street, London, W. C. 2.
Royal Magazine, 18 Henrietta Street, Covent Garden, London, W. C. 2.
Saturday Review, 18-20 York Buildings, Adelphi, London, W. C. 2.
Scots Observer, 7 Royal Bank Place, Buchanan Street, Glasgow, C. 1, Scotland.

Sketch, 346 Strand, London, W. C. 2.
Soma, Care of K. S. Bhat, 61 Southwark Park Road, London, S. E. 16.
Spectator, 99 Gower Street, London, W. C. 2.
Sphere, 346 Strand, London, W. C. 2.
Story-Teller, Tallis House, Tallis Street, London, E. C. 4.
Strand Magazine, 8-11 Southampton Street, Strand, London, W. C. 2.
Sydney Mail, 38 Hunter Street, Sydney, N. S. W., Australia.
Tatler, 346 Strand, London, W. C. 2.
Time and Tide, 32 Bloomsbury Street, London, W. C. 1.
Truth, Carteret Street, Queen Anne's Gate, London, S. W. 1.
20-Story Magazine, 93 Long Acre, London, W. C. 2.
Universe, 1 Arundel Street, London, W. C. 2.
Violet Magazine, Fleetway House, Farringdon Street, London, E. C. 4.
Windsor Magazine, Warwick House, Salisbury Square, London, E. C. 4.
Woman, 34-36 Paternoster Row, London, E. C. 4.
Woman's Journal, Fleetway House, Farringdon Street, London, E. C. 4.
Yellow Magazine, Fleetway House, Farringdon Street, London, E. C. 4.

ROLL OF HONOR

MAY 1, 1931, TO APRIL 30, 1932

NOTE. *This list excludes reprints.*

I. AMERICAN AUTHORS

ADAMIC, LOUIS.
  Symbol.
ADAMS, BILL.
  Alien.
  Foreigner.
  Sailmaker's Yarn.
  Sea Wife.
AIKEN, CONRAD.
  Bow Down, Isaac!
ANDERSON, SHERWOOD.
  Mill Girls.
BEADLE, JOHN A.
  Trace of Man.
BENÉT, STEPHEN VINCENT.
  Death in the Country.
BESSIE, ALVAH C.
  Horizon.
BLACKMAN, M. C.
  Last Friend.
BOYLE, KAY.
  Christmas Eve.
  First Lover.
  His Idea of a Mother.
  Kroy Wen.
BRAGDON, CLIFFORD.
  Love's So Many Things.
BRAGIN, MOE.
  Cow.
  Flowers and Weeds.
  It Isn't Pie.
BRENNAN, LOUIS.
  Poisoner in Motley.
BURNETT, WANDA.
  Sand.
BURNETT, WHIT.
  Canal Third.
  Maker of Signs.
  Man Who Walked against the
    Sky.

Return of Queen Agnes.
  Sherrel.
CALDWELL, ERSKINE.
  After-Image.
  Corduroy Pants.
  Empty Room.
  Indian Summer.
  Rachel.
  Warm River.
  We are Looking at You, Agnes.
CALVERTON, V. F.
  There was a Man.
CAPERTON, HELENA LEFROY.
  Honest Wine Merchant.
CARLAW, D. V.
  Ohio in Her Bones.
CHAPMAN, WILLIAM.
  Christ in Sawyer Street.
CHERKASSKI, V. M.
  Boatman.
CHILDS, MARQUIS W.
  Renascence.
COATES, GRACE STONE.
  Dice.
  Easy Virtue.
CORNING, HOWARD MCKINLEY.
  Candle Glow.
COURNOS, JOHN.
  Story of the Stranger.
CRAWFORD, FRANCES ELIZABETH.
  What the Mayor Meant.
DE JONG, DAVID CORNEL.
  As the Lilies.
  Beneath a Still Sky.
  So Tall the Corn.
DIEFENTHALER, ANDRA.
  Hansel.
DRATLER, JAY J.
  Dark Victory.

284

EDMONDS, WALTER D.
  Big-Foot Sal.
  Blind Eve.
  Cruise of the Cashalot.
EXALL, HENRY.
  Music-Box.
FARRELL, JAMES T.
  Casual Incident.
  Nostalgia.
FAULKNER, WILLIAM.
  Centaur in Brass.
  Death-Drag.
  Doctor Martino.
  Fox Hunt.
  Hair.
  Hound.
  Lizards in Jamshyd's Courtyard.
  "Once aboard the Lugger."
  Smoke.
  Spotted Horses.
FISHER, A. E.
  Fine Woman.
FITZGERALD, F. SCOTT.
  Between Three and Four.
FOLEY, MARTHA.
  Revolution Can Wait.
FUCHS, DANIEL.
  Village by the Sea.
GODIN, ALEXANDER.
  On the Threshold.
GORDON, CAROLINE.
  Ice House.
  Mr. Powers.
GRANBERRY, EDWIN.
  Trip to Czardis.
HALPER, ALBERT.
  Farm Hand.
HARRIS, ROBERT J.
  Bell.
HARTLEY, ROLAND ENGLISH.
  Postscript to a Career.
HEMINGWAY, ERNEST.
  Sea Change.
HUTCHINSON, RUTH.
  Eyes.
JOHNSON, J. W.
  Off the Luke Road.
JOLAS, EUGENE.
  Dirge.
JONES, E. CLEMENT.
  Basket.

KNIGHT, CHATFIELD.
  Ship Goes By.
KOMROFF, MANUEL.
  Napoleon's Hat under Glass.
KREYMBORG, ALFRED.
  Always Too Late.
LATIMER, MARGERY.
  Guardian Angel.
LESUEUR, MERIDEL.
  Miracle.
  Spring Story.
LEWIS, JANET.
  Bokhara.
  Call.
  Pointe Chegoimegon.
LEWISOHN, LUDWIG.
  Romantic.
LOCKWOOD, SCAMMON.
  Arrival at Carthage.
MARCH, WILLIAM.
  George and Charlie.
  He Sits There All Day Long.
  Mist on the Meadow.
  Nine Prisoners.
  Sixteen and the Unknown Sol-
    dier.
  Snow Storm in the Alps.
METCALFE, MARY E.
  Gentlefolk.
MILBURN, GEORGE.
  Fight at Hendryx's.
  Heel, Toe, and a 1, 2, 3, 4.
  Love Song.
  No More Trumpets.
MORRIS, IRA V.
  Kimono.
  Old Age.
NEAGOE, PETER.
  Shepherd of the Lord.
  Village Saint.
NETHERCOT, ARTHUR H.
  Door.
OUTERSON, WILLIAM.
  Royal Yard.
PARKER, DOROTHY.
  Lady with a Lamp.
RANDALL, KENNETH C.
  Security.
ROOT, WAVERLEY LEWIS.
  Tinkling Brass.

SABSAY, NAHUM.
  Behind the Swamp There Was a
    Village.
SATTERTHWAITE, ALFRED.
  Mr. Rammer.
SCHNABEL, DUDLEY.
  Load.
SCOTT, EVELYN.
  Home.
SHUMWAY, ARTHUR.
  Easter Sunday.
SOKOLOFF, NATALIE B.
  Ivan.
STALLINGS, LAURENCE.
  Gentleman in Blue.
STEELE, WILBUR DANIEL.
  Man without a God.
STEVENS, JAMES.
  Rock-Candy Mountains.
  When Rivers Were Young and
    Wild.
TÜTING, BERNHARD JOHANN.
  Family Chronicle.
VAN TINE, PRUDENCE.
  Ghost Mountain.

VILLA, JOSÉ GARCIA.
  Daughter of Rizal.
  Footnote to Youth.
  Given Woman.
  Little Tales.
  Like My Box.
  Malakas.
  Resurrection.
  Son of Rizal.
  Untitled Story.
  Valse Triste.
  Walk at Midnight: A Farewell.
  White Interlude.
WARD, LEO L.
  Drought.
  Quarrel.
WHARTON, EDITH.
  Her Son.
WHARTON, ELIZABETH.
  Vermont Portrait.
WILLIAMS, WILLIAM CARLOS.
  Difficult Man.
WOLFE, THOMAS.
  Portrait of Bascom Hawke.

II. CANADIAN AUTHORS

CALLAGHAN, MORLEY.
  Absolution.
  Lady in a Green Dress.
  Lunch Counter.
  Red Hat.
  Silk Stockings.

  Younger Brother.
CREIGHTON, LUELLA BRUCE.
  Miss Kidd.
KENNEDY, RODERICK STUART.
  Brothers in Arms.

III. BRITISH AND IRISH AUTHORS

ADAMS, B. M. G.
  Souvenir de Venise.
BATES, H. E.
  Mower.
BENSON, STELLA.
  Destination.
  Search for Mr. Loo.
BRAND, NEVILLE.
  Returned.
BRANDT, ELIZABETH.
  Cricket.
CHARD, GIL.
  Unrecognized.
COLLIER, JOHN.
  Green Thoughts.
COPPARD, A. E.
  Smith of Pretty Peter.

DUNSANY, LORD.
  Curse of the Witch.
  Daughter of Rameses.
  How the Tinker came to Ska-
    vangur.
  Use of Man.
GOSSMAN, OLIVER.
  Film Fragment.
  Neighbours.
LYLE, MARIUS.
  Letter.
MAUGHAM, W. SOMERSET.
  Alien Corn.
MILES, HAMISH.
  Strange Episode in a West-End
    Hotel.

Noxon, G. F.
Bordeaux.
Porta di Roma.
O'Flaherty, Liam.
Proclamation.
Phillpotts, Eden.
Gypsy Blood.
Told to Parson.
Reid, Leslie.
Across the Heath.
Sackville-West, V.
Poet.
Strong, L. A. G.
Don Juan and the Wheelbarrow.

Walpole, Hugh.
Engaging Rascal.
Wells, H. G.
Queer Story of Brownlow's Newspaper.
Williamson, Henry.
Fair.
Wilson, Romer.
Loan.
On with the Dance.
Wyatt, Isabel.
Death Watch.

IV. TRANSLATIONS

Alekseyev, Gleb (*Russian*).
Return of a Red.
Asturias, Miguel Angel (*Guatemalan*).
Legend of the Tattooed Girl.
Bergman, Hjalmar (*Swedish*).
Actor's Day.
Bregendahl, Marie (*Danish*).
Hans Goul and His Kin.
Buchholtz, Johannes (*Danish*).
Devil Cheated out of a Soul.
Engström, Albert (*Swedish*).
Swedish Panoptikon.
Frank, Bruno (*German*).
Dressing Case.
Hazaz, H. (*Hebrew*).
Bridegroom of Blood.

Kafka, Franz (*Austrian*).
Three Stories.
Musil, Robert (*Austrian*).
Catastrophe.
Remarque, Erich Maria (*German*).
Annette's Love Story.
Josef's Wife.
Strange Fate of Johann Bartok.
Söderberg, Hjalmar (*Swedish*).
Blunder Sonata.
History Instructor.
Soïberg, Harry (*Danish*).
Asa's Mound.

BIOGRAPHICAL NOTICES

NOTE. *These notices refer only to American authors whose work appears in the Roll of Honor in this series for the first time. Biographical notices of other authors included in this year's Roll of Honor may be found, with one or two exceptions, in earlier volumes of the series.*

ARMFIELD, EUGENE. Born in North Carolina, 1904. Educated at the Universities of North Carolina and Harvard. Is working on a novel. Lives in New York City.

BEADLE, JOHN A. Is twenty-five years of age. Educated at Columbia College, Dubuque, Iowa, and at the University of Iowa. He is at present an assistant to a surveyor in the day-time and a jobbing saxophonist with several local dance orchestras at night. Lives at Dubuque, Iowa.

BLACKMAN, M. C. Born at Ida, Louisiana, September 29, 1902. Educated after a fashion at Louisiana State University and University of Missouri. Has been in newspaper work ever since. Is writing a novel. Lives in Detroit.

BRAGIN, MOE. Born in Russia, 1901. His parents brought him to America in 1905. In 1917, he hired out for the first time on a farm. He is now trying his hand at teaching. Lives in Brooklyn, New York.

BURNETT, WANDA. Born in Salt Lake City, Utah, June 28, 1907. "I have never worked on a newspaper—a natural field, it seems, from which all writers sprout,—and my University education suffered and lost importance in my desire to reach Europe, where I spent nine months of the year 1931. I did for several years, however, organize girls' orchestras—Mormon Musicians—which I led with much hope and no little disappointment, through the West. We played dances, theatres, and weddings, and even an occasional country funeral, for which we generally brought out our most serious waltzes and slow foxtrots and played with all the sadness we could possibly manage to tame from the wild strains of a popular jazz tune." Lives in Salt Lake City, Utah.

CAPERTON, HELENA LEFROY. Born in Richmond, Virginia, of Irish and Virginian parentage. Before she was a year old, she was taken to her father's home in County Down, Ireland, to live with her grandparents. She remembers nothing learnt in school. She has forgotten little absorbed in books and travel, so that it is difficult to say where she was educated, if at all. She married at eighteen. She has always written. Author of "Legends of Virginia," 1931. Lives in Richmond, Virginia.

CARLAW, DOROTHY VAIL. Born in Madison, Indiana. Thirty years old. Married. Her academic education was sketchy. She studied painting for several years in Indianapolis, New York, and Paris. She has only recently turned to writing. Is working on a novel. Lives in Paris.

CHAPMAN, WILLIAM. Born in New York City, 1905. He started to work part time on *The Brooklyn Eagle* when he was sixteen. Was married at twenty-one, worked for the Associated Press in Richmond, Virginia, for two years, and returned to New York where he started a small advertising business. He fishes, plays golf, despises Byrrh and Chianti, admires William Faulkner, and lives in New York City.

CHERKASSKI, VLADIMIR MOISEYEVICH. Born at Zaporozhie-on-the-Dnieper, Ukraine, Russia, February 2, 1906. Lived through the civil war and famine there. Visited the Caucasus. Lived in Moscow three months. Arrived in America, 1923. Graduated from New York University, 1930. Has been studying short story writing at the School of Journalism of New York University. Is writing a novel. Lives in Brooklyn, New York.

CORNING, HOWARD MCKINLEY. Born near Lincoln, Nebraska, October 23, 1896. Moved to Ohio and lived near Columbus as a child. Educated in the public schools of Linden Heights and Columbus. Has lived in Oregon since 1919. Author of two volumes of verse: "These People," 1926, and "The Mountain in the Sky," 1931. He is a florist when not writing. Lives in Portland, Oregon.

CRAWFORD, FRANCES ELIZABETH. Born in Pass Christian, Mississippi, December 3, 1900. She spent the early years of her life wandering from Mississippi to Georgia and from Alabama to Florida with her parents. She learned to read, according to a doting mother, at a miraculously early age. Having observed her own two children, "sons, nine and five years old," she very much doubts the truth of her mother's statements. She read voraciously as a child. At eleven, when she left Mississippi to live with a grandmother in Chicago, she had finished a set of Dickens and a set of Miss Mühlbach, and had pretty well exhausted the reserves of the family library. She wrote her first novel in two five-cent composition books when she was nine; it concerned the merits of plain little girls as over those with curls and blue eyes. From the time she reached Chicago, where she attended two private schools before being shipped off to a third in North Illinois, she worked diligently for the school papers. At the boarding school she attended for three years, she was an editor of the school quarterly. At college, where she lasted one semester, in South Wisconsin, she found no paper to edit, so she helped to organize a mimeograph one. Her nervous breakdown in the middle of the winter, followed by matrimony, put an end to all editing, for what now seems an unbelievably long time. She married in 1920, and has lived in Milwaukee since 1921. She has the two above-mentioned sons, a small house, a very nondescript car, and a lot of fun.

CREIGHTON, LUELLA BRUCE. Born in Stauffville, Ontario, August 25, 1901. Lived in Winnipeg from 1905 until the war. Taught country school in Ontario for two years. Graduated from the University of Toronto, 1926. Married. Lives in Toronto.

DIEFENTHALER, ANDRA, is married and has three children. Most of her time is devoted to making a home for her family and to gardening. The German-Americans whom she describes in her stories are her people. They all belong to the land. She lives in Chatham, New Jersey.

DRATLER, JAY. Born in New York City, September 14, 1910. Has lived in Connecticut, Florida and North Carolina, and has spent three years in Europe. Educated at the University of North Carolina. Was one of the founders of *Agora*. Was associate gunner for a smuggling crew for five months. Hopes eventually to rid himself of the associate hoodoo and blossom forth as a head man of something. Has written two unpublished novels and several plays. Two more rejection slips would give him enough to paper his room. Lives on Long Island, New York.

EXALL, HENRY. Born in Dallas, Texas, December, 1892. Cut classes for three years at the University of Texas, then took Law and eked out LL.B., 1916. Never practised. Cadet, First Officer's Training Camp, Leon Springs, Texas, 1917. In the Army for two years. Captain of Infantry. Then back to the soil—real estate and securities. Is still ahead on points, and expects the decision, even though a bank has its fang in his flank. Started writing stories at night in 1929 as an excuse for not going to the movies. Lives in Dallas, Texas.

FARRELL, JAMES T. Born in Chicago, February 27, 1904. Educated at Catholic Parochial and High Schools in Chicago, night-school, and the University of Chicago, but never received a degree. Did some bumming and has worked at various jobs in Chicago and New York. Author of "Young Lonigan," 1932. Lives in Paris.

FISHER, A. E. Born in Franklin, Massachusetts, 1902. Left as soon as possible. Educated at Harvard. Has been an instructor in English at Carnegie Institute of Technology since 1925, except for a year at the Sorbonne. Author of "To the Sun," "Marriage in Blue," and "Time and the Hour." Lives in Pittsburgh, Pennsylvania.

GRANBERRY, EDWIN. Born at Meridian, Mississippi. Educated at the University of Florida, Columbia University, and Harvard University, where he spent two years studying play-writing with George Pierce Baker. Served during the War with the United States Marines. Married. Author of "The Ancient Hunger," "Strangers and Lovers," and "The Erl King." Translator of "Amour Nuptial" by Jacques de Lacretelle.

HERBST, JOSEPHINE. Born in Sioux City, Iowa. Author of "Nothing Is Sacred" and "Money for Love."

HUTCHINSON, RUTH. Born in Granville, Illinois, March 5, 1908. Before she was three, she had lived in three States, and thereafter moved around at about the same rate. As accurately as she can remember, she has lived in almost all the known and most of the unknown places of Michigan, Wisconsin, Ohio, and Illinois, and during the hair-ribbon period was firmly convinced that Grand Rapids, where she lived a whole span of three years, was a mightier city than New York. Her parents were Canadian, her father a Congregational clergyman. He was a splendid personality, but his deacons were such a trial! For the last four years she has been living in Detroit and Chicago, studying part of the time at Northwestern University. Previously she had studied for two years at Lawrence College. Just now she is involved with a fraction of Chicago's four hundred thousand unemployed, doing case work for the Emergency Organization.

FUCHS, DANIEL. Born, 1909, in New York City. Educated in public schools and College of the City of New York. Teaches school. Lives in Brooklyn, N. Y.

GODIN, ALEXANDER (JOSEPH KATZ). Born in 1909 in Zhitomir, Volinskaya Gubernia, Ukraine. Parents poverty-stricken artisans working at home under feudal conditions. Father went overseas in 1913 to escape conscription. Sent money home till the war bottled up communications. Mother kept the family together through the war, two revolutions, civil war, three pogroms, and the famine. Came to New York in 1922. Self-taught. Married. Now working on a book which attempts to portray the agony of spirit of those who have come from abroad and their pitiful efforts to strike new roots. Lives in New York City.

JOHNSON, JOSEPHINE. Born in 1910. Has lived on a farm in Missouri for the past eleven years and hopes to live there always, unless it gets too terribly civilised and overfull. She has studied at Washington University and teaches magazine illustration. Lives in Webster Groves, Missouri.

KEMMERER, JOHN. Born in Iowa, 1901. Educated at Grinnell College, Harvard University, and Columbia University. Is a draftsman. Lives in New York City.

KREYMBORG, ALFRED, is the author of seven books of poetry, four books of plays, four books of prose and has edited several anthologies of poetry. He has been editor of *The Glebe, Others,* and *Broom.* He is co-editor of *The American Caravan.* Lives in Brooklyn, New York.

LOCKWOOD, SCAMMON. Born in New York City. He lived adolescently in Lincoln, Nebraska, and very dangerously in Chicago, Detroit, Toledo, and New York. He left Lake View High School, Chicago, during his second year, leaving behind nearly all the education in the place. Did newspaper work, mostly police reporting, in Chicago; worked as correspondent in various businesses, dictating seductive sales letters to reluctant buyers; then for too many years he was an advertising manager and writer of advertising copy. Married. Has travelled extensively. Divides his time between Greenwich, Connecticut, Fryeburg, Maine, and New York City. His only recreations are successful fishing for black bass, and passionate but futile conversations about religion, politics, literature, art, economics and the prohibition amendment.

METCALFE, MARY. Born at De Soto, Missouri, on a farm in the Ozarks. "We children always boasted that we were all born under the same roof. My family doesn't believe in moving around." Is a public school teacher, and likes her job. Lives with her father in St. Louis.

NEAGOE, PETER. Born in Transylvania forty-two years ago, of Roumanian parents. Although he comes of a line of intellectuals, his sympathies have always been with the peasants, among whom he passed his vacations in childhood, living the life of a rugged mountaineer of the Carpathian shepherds. He began a writing career at an early age, when, having written the love-letters for the servant girls in his home, he became the scribe to the neighbourhood servants. He studied philosophy at the University of Bucharest. At twenty-one, he went to America, where he became a naturalized citizen. Last year he spent four months in New Mexico, some of the time in an Indian pueblo. He talks five languages fluently, but says he thinks best in English. Author of "Ileana, The Possessed," and "Storm." Editor of "An Anthology of American Writers Abroad." Co-editor of *The New Review*. Lives in France.

NETHERCOT, ARTHUR HOBART. Born in Chicago, Illinois, April 20, 1895. Graduated from Northwestern University, 1915. Ph.D., University of Chicago, 1922. Was at Exeter College, Oxford, in 1919. Served in France and Germany as 2nd Lt. of Heavy Artillery, 1918-19. Now Associate Professor of English at Northwestern University. Married. Author of "Abraham Cowley: The Muse's Hannibal." Co-author of "The Writer's Handbook." Editor of "A Book of Long Stories." Associate Editor of *College Verse*. Lives in Evanston, Illinois.

PHILPOT, ADA S. Born in Chicago, where she still lives. Studied art and languages for four years in France, Germany, and Italy.

RANDALL, K. C. Born in Albany, New York, 1898. Spent his childhood and youth in Springfield, Mass. Worked in factories and for the railroad, and for a year on a farm before going to College. B.Sc. from Massachusetts Agricultural College. M.A. from Ohio State University. Is now Assistant Professor of English at Michigan State College. Lives in East Lansing, Michigan.

ROOT, WAVERLEY LEWIS. Born in Providence, Rhode Island, April 15, 1903. Educated at Tufts College, Massachusetts. Has lived in Europe since 1927 as correspondent for *The Chicago Tribune*. Is now news and literary editor to the Paris edition of *The Chicago Tribune*. Co-author of "The Truth about Wagner." Lives in Paris.

SABSAY, NAHUM. Born in Simferopol, Crimea, Russia, 1890. His father was a fairly well-to-do merchant. At the age of twenty he graduated from a seven-year commercial school, but his further studies were interrupted by the compulsory military service which, with a year off, he did for nearly seven years. He was in the war on the Belgian, Galician and Roumanian fronts. In 1917 he was commissioned ensign, took part in the Civil War at the end of that and at the beginning of the following year, and then escaped to America by way of Siberia.

Here, for over a year, he worked in shops and factories till he had saved a little money and learned enough English to resume his studies. He graduated from Harvard University in 1923. Until recently he was doing mining and geological work, but now gives all his time to writing. Lives in New York City.

SCHNABEL, DUDLEY. Born in Duluth, Minnesota, 1896. Educated at the University of North Dakota, 1918. Taught school in North Dakota for four years. Has been two years in newspaper work in Saint Paul, Minnesota, and in 1926 went into advertising. Married. Now engaged in railroad and utility advertising work. Lives in Indianapolis.

SHUMWAY, ARTHUR. Born in Janesville, Wisconsin, twenty-two years ago. Spent his boyhood in Florida and Illinois. Educated at Waukegan High School, and shortly gave up an attempt to attend the University of Florida as a working student in order to participate in the real estate boom as a soda clerk, automobile salesman, real estate salesman, and newspaper man. He has spent the past seven years as a newspaper man, except for a brief interval trying to act in a stock company, and has tried briefly during and since school days, labor, carrying mail, selling shoes, and tramping. Has worked for newspapers in Florida, Illinois, Michigan, and Indiana. Now employed as columnist. Married. Is writing a novel. Lives in Evanston, Illinois.

SLESINGER, TESS. Born in New York City, 1905. Educated at Swarthmore College and Columbia University. Has been engaged in newspaper work. Lives in Brooklyn, N. Y.

STALLINGS, LAURENCE. Born in Macon, Georgia, November 25, 1894. Educated at Wake Forest College and Georgetown University. Married. Was Captain of Marines in the War. Author of "Plumes," and the following plays in collaboration with Maxwell Anderson: "What Price Glory?", "The Buccaneer," "First Flight," and "Deep River." Lives in Yanceyville, North Carolina.

TÜTING, BERNHARD JOHANN. Born in Tütingen, Germany, 1899. He attended secondary school and university in Germany, served in the Army from 1916-1918, and came to America in 1924. Lives in Berkeley, California.

VAN TINE, PRUDENCE, will soon be thirty. Is writing a novel. Lives in New York.

VILLA, JOSÉ GARCIA. Born in Manila, Philippine Islands. His father is a physician, and wanted him to follow a medical career. He finished his pre-medical course, but could go no further. Has been writing short stories since 1925. Was expelled from the University of the Philippines in 1929 because it was claimed, he says, that his writing was immoral. He came to America in the summer of 1930, and graduated from the University of New Mexico. He is very unacademic because he believes academicism cramps the soul. As for the Philippines, he cannot stand the old-maidishness of its outlook on things. He is the founder and editor of *Clay*. Lives in New York City.

Wharton, Elizabeth. Born in Pittsfield, Massachusetts, July 16, 1897. Graduated from Bryn Mawr College in 1918. Since then has lived chiefly in France, Austria, and Germany. Lives in Berlin.

Wolfe, Thomas. Born in Asheville, North Carolina, October 3, 1900. Graduated from the University of North Carolina in 1920. Was a member of the Carolina Playmakers, and The 47 Work Shop. Pursued graduate work at Harvard University for three years. Was Instructor at New York University intermittently from 1924 to 1930. Author of "Look Homeward, Angel," 1929. Awarded a Guggenheim Fellowship in 1930. Lives in Brooklyn, New York.

THE BEST BOOKS OF SHORT STORIES
OF 1932

I. American Authors

1. Cozzens. S.S. San Pedro. Harcourt, Brace.
2. Faulkner. These 13. Cape and Smith.
3. Frank. City Block. Scribner.
4. McKay. Gingertown. Harper.
5. Neagoe. Storm. Paris: New Review Editions.
6. Stevens. Saginaw Paul Bunyan. Knopf.
7. Suckow. Children and Older People. Knopf.
8. Williams. Knife of the Times. Ithaca: Dragon Press.
9. Williams. Novelette and Other Prose. Brooklyn: To, Publishers.

II. British and Irish Authors

10. Aldington. Soft Answers. Doubleday, Doran.
11. Coppard. Nixey's Harlequin. Knopf.
12. Dunsany. Travel Tales of Mr. Joseph Jorkens. Putnam.
13. Hanley. Men in Darkness. Knopf.
14. Hughes. Omnibus. Harper.
15. Jacobs. Snug Harbour. Scribner.
16. James. Collected Ghost Stories. Longmans.
17. Kipling. Limits and Renewals. Doubleday, Doran.
18. Lawrence. Man Who Died. Knopf.
19. Maugham. First Person Singular. Doubleday, Doran.
20. O'Connor. Guests of the Nation. Macmillan.
21. O'Faoláin. Midsummer Night Madness. Viking Press.
22. Sinclair. Intercessor. Macmillan.

III. Translations

23. Pettoello, editor. Italian Short Stories. Dutton.
24. Pirandello. Horse in the Moon. Dutton.
25. Romanov. Without Cherry Blossom. Scribner.
26. Schnitzler. Flight into Darkness. Simon and Schuster.
27. Wells, editor. Great Spanish Short Stories. Houghton Mifflin.
28. Zweig. Amok. Viking Press.

VOLUMES OF SHORT STORIES
PUBLISHED IN THE UNITED STATES
AND CANADA

MAY 1, 1931, TO APRIL 30, 1932

NOTE. *An asterisk before a title indicates distinction.*

I. AMERICAN AND CANADIAN AUTHORS

ABBOTT, ELEANOR HALLOWELL. Minister who Wicked the Cat. Appleton.
ADAMIC, LOUIS. *Laughing in the Jungle. Harper.
APPLEGATE, FRANK. Native Tales of New Mexico. Lippincott.
AUSTIN, LILLIAN EDNA. Shudders. Meador.
BAILEY, TEMPLE. So This is Christmas! Penn.
BARBER, SOLON R. *Cross-Country. The Hague: Servire Press.
BARNARD, LESLIE GORDON. One Generation Away. Montreal: Dodd-Simpson.
BEACH, REX. Men of the Outer Islands. Farrar and Rinehart.
BECKER, MAY LAMBERTON, *editor.* *Golden Tales of New England. Dodd, Mead. Under Twenty. Harcourt, Brace.
BISHOP, JOHN PEALE. *Many Thousands Gone. Scribner.
BOTKIN, B. A., *editor.* *Folk-Say: A Regional Miscellany, 1931. Norman, Oklahoma: University of Oklahoma Press.
BRADBURY, SAMUEL LESLIE. Corn Tassel Tales of New England. Meadville, Pa.: The Author.
BRADFORD, ROARK. John Henry. Harper.
BRALLIAR, FLOYD BURTON. Zip, the Coon. Southern Publishers' Association.
BURGESS, ROBERT BRETTLE. "Bob" Tales. Meador.
BYRNE, DONN. Rivers of Damascus. Century.
CANFIELD, DOROTHY. *Basque People. Harcourt, Brace.
CAPERTON, HELENA LEFROY. *Legends of Virginia. Richmond: Garrett and Massie.
COBB, IRVIN S. *Down Yonder with Judge Priest. Long and Smith.
COHEN, OCTAVUS ROY. Cameos. Appleton.
CORLEY, DONALD. *Haunted Jester. McBride.
COZZENS, JAMES GOULD. *S.S. San Pedro. Harcourt, Brace.
CRANE, STEPHEN. *Maggie. Knopf.
CULLEN, JOHN PAUL. Hello, Wisconsin! Meador.
ELLSBERG, EDWARD. S-54. Dodd, Mead.
FAULKNER, WILLIAM. *Idyll in the Desert. Random House. *These 13. Cape and Smith.
FOLEY, MARY C., *and* GENTLES, RUTH G., *editors.* America in Story. Harper.
FRANK, WALDO. *City Block. Scribner.
GIBBS, GEORGE FORT. Old Philadelphia. 4 v. Appleton.

GILPATRIC, GUY. Half-Seas Over. Dodd, Mead.
GOODMAN, HENRY, *and* CARPENTER, BRUCE, *editors*. Stories of the City. Ronald Press.
GREER, HILTON R., *editor*. *Best Short Stories from the Southwest. Second Series. Dallas, Texas: Southwest Press.
GROVE, JOHN, *editor*. Omnibus of Romance. Dodd, Mead.
HAMMETT, DASHIELL, *editor*. Creeps by Night. Day.
HAWTHORNE, NATHANIEL. Mr. Higginbotham's Catastrophe. Boston: Berkeley Printers.
HEATH, JANET FIELD. Hygienic Pig. Chicago: Beckley-Cardy Co.
HECHT, BEN. Champion from Far Away. Covici-Friede.
HELD, JOHN, Jr. Flesh is Weak. Vanguard Press.
HELM, FLORENCE. Fatal Susan. Chelmsford Press.
HUME, CYRIL. *Myself and the Young Bowman. Doubleday, Doran.
JACQUART, ROLLAND. Prairie Lore. Sublette, Kansas: The Sublette Monitor.
JAMES, WILL. Sun Up. Scribner.
KEMMERER, JOHN. *Two Stories. Modern Editions Press.
KILBOURNE, FANNIE. Dot and Will at Home. Dodd, Mead.
LEWISOHN, LUDWIG. *Golden Vase. Harper. *Romantic. Paris: Titus.
LINCOLN, JOSEPH C. All Alongshore. Coward-McCann.
LONG, RAY, *editor*. Twenty Best Short Stories in Ray Long's Twenty Years as an Editor. Long and Smith.
MACGOWAN, KENNETH, *editor*. Sleuths. Harcourt, Brace.
McKAY, CLAUDE. *Gingertown. Harper.
MASON, ARTHUR. From the Horn of the Moon. Doubleday, Doran.
MILLER, ALICE DUER. Bishop's Nephew. Dodd, Mead.
NASON, LEONARD. Among the Trumpets. Houghton Mifflin.
NEAGOE, PETER. *Storm. Paris: New Review Editions.
NEW COPY, 1932. Columbia University Press.
O'BRIEN, EDWARD J., *editor*. Best Short Stories of 1931. Dodd, Mead.
OGDEN, MRS. GUSSIE D. Hits and Whims. O'Malley.
OWEN, FRANK. Della-Wu. Lantern Press.
PEATTIE, LOUISE REDFIELD. Pan's Parish. Century.
PERRY, M. EUGENIE. The Girl in the Silk Dress. Privately printed.
PUGH, CYNTHIA ANN, *editor*. Book of Short Stories. Macmillan.
RICHARDSON, A. P. Barnegat Ways. Century.
RUNYON, DAMON. Guys and Dolls. Stokes.
Saplings, 1931. Pittsburgh: Scholastic Publishing Company.
SAYRE, JOEL. *Rackety Rax. Knopf.
SECHRIST, ELIZABETH HOUGH, *editor*. Thirteen Ghostly Yarns. Swain.
SHIFFRIN, A. B. *Other Cheek. Newlands Press.
SPEER, ROBERT ELLIOTT. Owen Crimmins. Revell.
STEPHENSON, TERRY E. Shadows of Old Saddleback. Santa Ana, Cal.: Williams.
STEVENS, JAMES. *Saginaw Paul Bunyan. Knopf.
SUCKOW, RUTH. *Children and Older People. Knopf.
TERHUNE, ALBERT PAYSON. Way of a Dog. Harper.
WELLS, CAROLYN, *editor*. Best American Mystery Stories of the Year. Vol. 2. Day.
WHITCOMB, ROBERT. Time for Laughter. Brooklyn, N. Y.: The Author.
WHITE, STEWART EDWARD. Long Rifle. Doubleday, Doran.
WILEY, HUGH. Copper Mask. Knopf.

WILLIAMS, BLANCHE COLTON, editor. O. Henry Memorial Award. Prize Stories of 1931. Doubleday, Doran.
WILLIAMS, HARRY. Texas Trails. San Antonio: Naylor.
WILLIAMS, WILLIAM CARLOS. *Knife of the Times. Ithaca: Dragon Press. *Novelette and Other Prose. Brooklyn: To, Publishers.
WINSLOW, THYRA SAMTER. *Blueberry Pie. Knopf.
Wisconsin Writings, 1931. Mohawk Press.

II. BRITISH AND IRISH AUTHORS

ALDINGTON, RICHARD. *Soft Answers. Doubleday, Doran.
BAILEY, H. C. Mr. Fortune Speaking. Dutton.
BENNETT, ARNOLD. *Night Visitor. Doubleday, Doran.
COPPARD, A. E. *Nixey's Harlequin. Knopf.
COYLE, KATHLEEN. *There is a Door. Paris: Titus.
DE LA MARE, COLIN, editor. *They Walk Again. Dutton.
DINNIS, ENID. Out of the Everywhere. Herder.
DUNSANY, LORD. *Travel Tales of Mr. Joseph Jorkens. Putnam.
FLETCHER, J. S. Safe Number Sixty-Nine. International Pocket Library.
FOTHERGILL, JOHN, editor. *Mr. Fothergill's Plot. Oxford University Press.
FREEMAN, R. AUSTIN. Dr. Thorndyke Omnibus. Dodd, Mead.
GISSING, GEORGE. *Brownie. Columbia University Press.
HANLEY, JAMES. *Men in Darkness. Knopf.
HILL, CRAVEN. Survivor. Macmillan.
HUGHES, RICHARD. *Omnibus. Harper. *Spider's Palace. Harper.
JACOBS, W. W. Snug Harbour. Scribner.
JAMES, MONTAGUE RHODES. *Collected Ghost Stories. Longmans.
JESSE, F. TENNYSON. Solange Stories. Macmillan.
KAYE-SMITH, SHEILA. *Summer Holiday. Harper.
KIPLING, RUDYARD. Humorous Tales. Doubleday, Doran. *Limits and Renewals. Doubleday, Doran.
LAWRENCE, D. H. *Man Who Died. Knopf.
LYND, ROBERT, editor. Love Throughout the Ages. Coward-McCann.
MAUGHAM, W. SOMERSET. *First Person Singular. Doubleday, Doran.
MITCHELL, J. LESLIE. Cairo Dawns. Bobbs-Merrill.
O'BRIEN, EDWARD J., editor. Best British Short Stories of 1931. Dodd, Mead.
O'CONNOR, FRANK. *Guests of the Nation. Macmillan.
O'FAOLÁIN, SEÁN. *Midsummer Night Madness. Viking Press.
OPPENHEIM, E. PHILLIPS. Sinners, Beware. Little, Brown.
PREEDY, GEORGE. Bagatelle. Dodd, Mead.
ROBERTS, SWITHIN. Aly the Philosopher. Macmillan.
SAYERS, DOROTHY L., editor. Second Omnibus of Crime. Coward-McCann.
*Second Mercury Story Book. Longmans.
SINCLAIR, MAY. *Intercessor. Macmillan.
SUMMERS, MONTAGUE, editor. Supernatural Omnibus. Doubleday Doran.
TATHAM, H. F. W. Footprints in the Snow. Macmillan.
WAKEFIELD, H. R. Imagine a Man in a Box. Appleton.

III. TRANSLATIONS

BALZAC, HONORÉ DE (*French*). *Droll Stories. Modern Library.

BOCCACCIO, GIOVANNI (*Italian*). *Decameron. Modern Library.

CHEKHOV, ANTON (*Russian*). *Stories. Modern Library.

LEVINE, JOSEPH COOPER, editor (*Hebrew*). Echoes of the Jewish Soul. Bloch.

MAUPASSANT, GUY DE (*French*). *Adventures of Walter Schnafs. Translated by Lafcadio Hearn. Tokyo: Hokuseida Press.

PETTOELLO, DECIO, editor (*Italian*). *Italian Short Stories. Dutton.

PIRANDELLO, LUIGI (*Italian*). *Horse in the Moon. Dutton.

PUTNAM, SAMUEL, editor. *European Caravan. Vol. 1. Brewer, Warren, and Putnam.

ROMANOV, PANTELEIMON (*Russian*). *Without Cherry Blossom. Scribner.

SCHNITZLER, ARTHUR (*Austrian*). *Flight into Darkness. Simon and Schuster. *Viennese Novelettes. Simon and Schuster.

SIENKIEWICZ, HENRYK (*Polish*). *Tales. Dutton.

SPYRI, JOHANNA (*German Swiss*). *Renz and Margritli. Crowell.

TOLSTOI, COUNT LYOF N. (*Russian*). *Ivan, the Fool. Oxford University Press.

WELLS, WARRE B., *translator* (*Spanish*). *Great Spanish Short Stories. Houghton Mifflin.

ZWEIG, STEFAN (*Austrian*). *Amok. Viking Press.

ARTICLES ON THE SHORT STORY
IN AMERICAN PERIODICALS

MAY 1, 1931, TO APRIL 30, 1932

NOTE. *For articles in British and Irish periodicals, see "The Best British Short Stories of 1932."*

A

Adamic, Louis.
    By James W. Gilman. Op. Apr. 25, '32. (19.)
    By Benjamin Stolberg. Books. Mar. 27, '32. (5.)
    By Eda Lou Walton. Book. (N. Y.) Mar., '32. (74:688.)
Aldington, Richard.
    By Virgilia Peterson Ross. Books. Apr. 24, '32. (3.)
American Short Story.
    Anonymous. N. Y. Times. May 10, '31. (8.) May 17, '31. (7.)
    Jun. 14, '31. (7.) Nov. 22, '31. (7.) Dec. 13, '31. (19.)
    By Nancy Evans. Books. Dec. 6, '31. (18.)
    By Rachel Field. Sat. R. (N. Y.) Dec. 12, '31. (8:374.)
    By Percy Hutchison. N. Y. Times. Jan. 17, '32. (14.)
    By Burton Kline. Com. Sept. 30, '31. (14:520.)
    By Jerome Mellquist. Sat. R. (N. Y.) Jan. 23, '32. (8:473.)
    By Edward J. O'Brien. B. E. T. Oct. 10, '31.
    By Ben Ray Redman. Books. Feb. 7, '32. (13.)
    By Edith H. Walton. N. Y. Times. Nov. 22, '31. (9.)
    By Robert Whitcomb. Sat. R. (N. Y.) Jan. 2, '32. (8:435.)

B

Bailey, Temple.
    Anonymous. N. Y. Times. Dec. 20, '31. (19.)
Beach, Rex.
    Anonymous. N. Y. Times. Mar. 20, '32. (21.)
Beer, Thomas.
    By James W. Lane. Book. (N. Y.) Nov., '31. (74:241.)
Bennett, Arnold.
    Anonymous. N. Y. Times. Nov. 8, '31. (6.)
    By Florence Haxton Britten. Books. Nov. 8, '31. (2.) Jan. 24,
    '32. (7.)
    By George Dangerfield. Sat. R. (N. Y.) Jan. 16, '32. (8:460.)
    By Francis Hackett. Sat. R. (N. Y.) May 2, '31. (7:789.)
Bierce, Ambrose.
    Letters to Mrs. Allen Sickler. Cal. C. Jan., '32. (34:30.)
Bishop, John Peale.
    Anonymous. N. Y. Times. May 24, '31. (6.)

By Basil Davenport. Sat. R. (N. Y.) Jul. 18, '31. (7:975.)
By Virgilia Peterson Ross. Books. May 17, '31. (4.)
By William Troy. Book. (N. Y.) Aug., '31. (73:636.)
By Robert Penn Warren. N. Rep. Aug. 5, '31. (67:321.)
Blasco Ibáñez, Vicente.
  By Jenny Ballou. Books. Jul. 19, '31. (1.)
Bourget, Paul.
  By George N. Shuster. Book. (N. Y.) May, '31. (73:273.)
Bradford, Roark.
  By Hamilton Basso. N. Rep. Sept. 30, '31. (68:186.)
  By Jonathan Daniels. Sat. R. (N. Y.) Sept. 19, '31. (8:131.)
  By Percy Hutchison. N. Y. Times. Sept. 6, '31. (4.)
  By Guy B. Johnson. Nat. (N. Y.) Oct. 7, '31. (133:367.)
  By Constance Rourke. Books. Sept. 6, '31. (1.)
  By Robert Penn Warren. Va. Jan., '32. (8:153.)
British Short Story.
  Anonymous. N. Y. Times. Nov. 22, '31. (6.) Dec. 20, '31. (9.)
  By Dorothea Brande. Book. (N. Y.) Jan.-Feb., '32. (74:579.)
  By Elizabeth Brown. Books. Dec. 6, '31. (22.)
  By Gladys Graham. Sat. R. (N. Y.) Nov. 28, '31. (8:330.)
  By Edith H. Walton. N. Y. Times. Nov. 22, '31. (9.)
Byrne, Donn.
  Anonymous. N. Y. Times. Sept. 27, '31. (7.)

C

Cabell, James Branch.
  By Basil Davenport. Sat. R. (N. Y.) Feb. 13, '32. (8:521.)
Cable, G. W.
  By Margaret Bloom. Book. (N. Y.) Jun., '31. (73:401.)
Caldwell, Erskine.
  Anonymous. N. Y. Times. May 10, '31. (9.)
  By Malcolm Cowley. N. Rep. Jun. 17, '31. (67:131.)
  By Frederick Dupee. Book. (N. Y.) Nov., '31. (74:340.)
  By Norman Macleod. N. Mass. Jul., '31. (18.)
  By Gerald Sykes. Nat. (N. Y.) Oct. 21, '31. (133:436.)
  By T. K. Whipple. N. Rep. Jun. 17, '31. (67:130.)
Callaghan, Morley.
  By H. Steinhauer. C. For. Feb., '32. (12:177.)
Canfield, Dorothy.
  Anonymous. N. Y. Times. Oct. 11, '31. (4.)
  By Edwin Clark. Com. Dec. 2, '31. (15:138.)
  By Eleanor Mercein Kelly. Sat. R. (N. Y.) Oct. 24, '31. (8:228.)
  By Elizabeth Wyckoff. Book. (N. Y.) Sept., '31. (74:40.)
Cather, Willa.
  By Louis Kronenberger. Book. (N. Y.) Oct., '31. (74:134.)
Chinese Short Story.
  By Alice Tisdale Hobart. Sat. R. (N. Y.) May 9, '31. (7:812.)
  By Younghill Kang. N. Rep. Jul. 1, '31. (67:185.)
Cline, Leonard.
  By Dorothy Teall. Book. (N. Y.) Aug., '31. (73:624.)
Cobb, Irvin S.
  Anonymous. N. Y. Times. Apr. 3, '32. (7.)

Conrad, Joseph.
  By Irvin Anthony. Book. (N. Y.) Mar., '32. (74:648.)
  By Ford Madox Ford. Scr. Oct., '31. (90:379.)
  By R. L. Megroz. T. Q. Jul.-Sept., '31. (4:130.)
  By Henry L. Mencken. A. Merc. Jun., '31. (23:251.)
  By Christopher Morley. Atl. Apr., '32. (149:403.)
  By Charles Phillips. Com. May 20, '31. (14:82.)
  By Sir William Rothenstein. Atl. Feb., '32. (149:233.)
Coppard, A. E.
  Anonymous. N. Y. Times. Jan. 10, '32. (7.)
  By Margaret Cheney Dawson. Books. Jan. 17, '32. (2.)
Corley, Donald.
  Anonymous. N. Y. Times. Oct. 18, '31. (6.)
  By Margaret Cheney Dawson. Books. Sept. 27, '31. (7.)
Coyle, Kathleen.
  Anonymous. N. Y. Times. Dec. 27, '31. (9.)
Cozzens, James Gould.
  By Alan Burton Clarke. Book. (N. Y.) Jan.-Feb., '32. (74:583.)
  By William McFee. Sat. R. (N. Y.) Sept. 12, '31. (8:117.)
  By Jane Spence Southron. N. Y. Times. Sept. 6, '31. (7.)
  By Frederic Thompson. Com. Oct. 7, '31. (14:561.)
Crane, Stephen.
  By Ford Madox Ford. Scr. Oct., '31. (90:379.)
  By Ben Ray Redman. Books. Feb. 7, '32. (13.)
  By Vincent Starrett. Colop. Sept., '31.

D

De La Mare, Walter.
  By Sir William Rothenstein. Atl. Feb., '32. (149:233.)
Dingle, A. E.
  By A. E. Dingle. Am. Jan., '32. (19.)
Dostoevsky, Fyodor.
  Petersburg Reveries. Yale. Mar., '32. (21:645.)
  By Jennie Ballou. Books. Feb. 14, '32. (9.) Feb. 21, '32. (11.)
  By E. K. Brown. C. For. Jan., '32. (12:145.)
  By Babette Deutsch. Books. Nov. 1, '31. (5.)
  By Frederick Dupee. Sym. Jan., '32. (3:111.)
  By Joseph Wood Krutch. Nat. (N. Y.) Nov. 4, '31. (133:490.)
  By Alexander Nazaroff. N. Y. Times. Jun. 21, '31. (2.)
  By P. S. Porohovshikov. Yale. Mar., '32. (21:612.)
  By Gerald Sykes. N. Rep. Feb. 3, '32. (69:329.)
  By Avrahm Yarmolinsky. N. Y. Times. Nov. 1, '31. (4.)
Dreiser, Theodore.
  By Newton Arvin. N. Rep. Aug. 5, '31. (67:319.)
  By Florence Haxton Britten. Books. May 10, '31. (1.)
  By Henry Hazlitt. Nat. (N. Y.) Jun. 3, '31. (132:613.)
  By Robert Herrick. Sat. R. (N. Y.) Jun. 6, '31. (7:875.)
  By Peter Monro Jack. N. Y. Times. May 10, '31. (5.)
  By Lincoln Kirstein. H. H. Oct.-Dec., '31. (5:158.)
  By H. L. Mencken. A. Merc. Jul., '31. (23:382.)
  By Alan Reynolds Thompson. Book. (N. Y.) Jul., '31. (73:533.)
Dunsany, Lord.
  Anonymous. N. Y. Times. Sept. 20, '31. (22.)
  By Norah Meade. Books. Oct. 4, '31. (6.)

E

Ellsberg, Edward.
　　Anonymous. N. Y. Times. Mar. 20, '32. (7.)
English Short Story. *See* British Short Story.

F

Faulkner, William.
　　Anonymous. N. Y. Times. Sept. 27, '31. (7.)
　　By Sterling A. Brown. Opp. Nov., '31. (9:347.)
　　By Robert Cantwell. N. Rep. Oct. 21, '31. (68:271.)
　　By Edward Cushing. Sat. R. (N. Y.) Oct. 17, '31. (8:201.)
　　By Granville Hicks. Book. (N. Y.) Sept., '31. (74:17.) Books.
　　　　Sept. 27, '31. (8.)
　　By Marshall J. Smith. Book. (N. Y.) Dec., '31. (74:411.)
　　By Lionel Trilling. Nat. (N. Y.) Nov. 4, '31. (133:491.)
　　By Grenville Vernon. Com. Jan. 20, '32. (15:332.)
　　By Robert Penn Warren. Va. Jan., '32. (8:153.)
Flaubert, Gustave.
　　By Edmund Wilson. Books. Feb. 21, '32. (1.)
Frank, Waldo.
　　By Edwin Seaver. N. Rep. Apr. 13, '32. (70:248.)

G

Galsworthy, John.
　　By Joseph J. Reilly. Book. (N. Y.) Jan.-Feb., '32. (74:488.)
　　By Sir William Rothenstein. Atl. Feb., '32. (149:233.)
Garland, Hamlin.
　　By John Chamberlain. N. Y. Times. Sept. 27, '31. (2.)
　　By C. Henry Grattan. A. L. May, '31. (3:224.)
　　By Granville Hicks. Nat. (N. Y.) Oct. 21, '31. (133:435.)
　　By Amy Loveman. Sat. R. (N. Y.) Oct. 10, '31. (8:187.)
　　By George N. Shuster. Com. Nov. 4, '31. (15:22.)
　　By William Allen White. Books. Sept. 27, '31. (1.)
Garnett, David.
　　Anonymous. N. Y. Times. Jun. 14, '31. (6.)
　　By George Dangerfield. Book. (N. Y.) Sept., '31. (74:77.)
　　By Horace Gregory. Sym. Oct., '31. (2:551.)
　　By Fred T. Marsh. Nat. (N. Y.) Aug. 26, '31. (133:211.)
　　By Mary Ross. Books. Jun. 14, '31. (5.)
Gerhardi, William.
　　By Iris Barry. Books. Oct. 11, '31. (6.)
　　By Rose C. Feld. N. Y. Times. Nov. 22, '31. (27.)
　　By Henry Bamford Parkes. Nat. (N. Y.) Nov. 11, '31. (133:522.)
　　By Arthur Ruhl. Sat. R. (N. Y.) Oct. 31, '31. (8:244.)
Gibbs, George.
　　Anonymous. N. Y. Times. Nov. 15, '31. (20.)
　　By Emily Clark. Books. Dec. 13, '31. (20.)
　　By Elizabeth R. Pennell. Sat. R. (N. Y.) Oct. 17, '31. (8:206.)
Gissing, George.
　　By Morley Roberts. Va. Jul., '31. (7:409.)
　　By Robert Shafer. Book. (N. Y.) Mar., '32. (74:674.)
Gorky, Maxim.
　　By John Cournos. N. Y. Times. Nov. 29, '31. (4.)

By Joshua Kunitz. Nat. (N. Y.) Dec. 16, '31. (133:673.)
By P. S. Porohovshikov. Yale. Mar., '32. (21:612.)
By Johan J. Smertenko. Op. Feb. 1, '32. (16.)
By Mark Van Doren. Books. Nov. 22, '31. (3.)
Green, Paul.
By Julian R. Meade. Book. (N. Y.) Jan.-Feb., '32. (74:503.)

H

Hanley, James.
By Slater Brown. N. Rep. Mar. 2, '32. (70:79.)
By Margaret Cheney Dawson. Books. Jan. 24, '32. (3.)
By Percy Hutchison. N. Y. Times. Jan. 24, '32. (4.)
Hardy, Thomas.
By Samuel C. Chew. Books. Oct. 4, '31. (20.)
By Percy Hutchison. N. Y. Times. Oct. 18, '31. (18.)
Harris, Frank.
Anonymous. Nat. (N. Y.) Sept. 9, '31. (133:245.)
By Florence Haxton Britten. Books. Feb. 14, '32. (12.)
By Henry James Forman. N. Y. Times. Jan. 31, '32. (4.)
Harris, Joel Chandler.
By Herschel Brickell. Books. Nov. 29, '31. (1.)
By Sterling A. Brown. Opp. Apr., '32. (10:119.)
By W. L. Dance. A. L. Mar., '32. (4:82.)
By James W. Gilman. Op. Mar. 28, '32. (16.)
By Percy Hutchison. N. Y. Times. Nov. 29, '31. (2.)
By John Donald Wade. Va. Jan., '32. (8:124.)
Harte, Bret.
By Newton Arvin. Books. Dec. 20, '31. (1.)
By Henry Seidel Canby. Sat. R. (N. Y.) Jan. 30, '32. (8:485.)
By John Macy. N. Y. Times. Dec. 20, '31. (2.)
By Carey McWilliams. Nat. (N. Y.) Jan. 6, '32. (134:22.)
By Constance Rourke. N. Rep. Mar. 2, '32. (70:77.)
By John T. Winterich. Pub. W. Feb. 20, '32. (121:872.)
Hawthorne, Nathaniel.
Anonymous. Essex. Jan., '32. (68:65.)
By Elizabeth L. Chandler. N. E. Q. Apr., '31. (4:289.)
By Robert S. Forsythe. Sat. R. (N. Y.) Sept. 19, '31. (8:140.)
By Julian Hawthorne. Book. (N. Y.) Dec., '31. (74:401.)
By G. Hicks. Sew. Apr.-Jun., '31. (39:129.)
By A. A. Kern. A. Sp. Dec., '31. (46:1253.)
Hearn, Lafcadio.
By E. K. Brown. C. For. June, '31. (11:345.)
By Ray M. Lawless. A. L. May, '31. (3:228.)
By Joseph McSorley. Cath. W. Jul., '31. (133:502.)
Hecht, Ben.
Anonymous. N. Y. Times. Sept. 6, '31. (6.)
Anonymous. Sat. R. (N. Y.) Sept. 19, '31. (8:136.)
By Lisle Bell. Books. Sept. 20, '31. (6.)
By John Suesens. Pr. S. Fall, '31. (5:299.)
Held, John.
Anonymous. N. Y. Times. Dec. 13, '31. (7.)
Hemingway, Ernest.
By Arthur Dewing. N. A. Rev. Oct., '31. (232:364.)

By Merle Johnson. Pub. W. Feb. 20, '32. (121:870.)
By Leonard L. Mackall. Books. Jan. 31, '32. (19.)
Henry, O.
By John Chamberlain. N. Y. Times. Jun. 7, '31. (5.)
By George Libaire. N. Rep. Aug. 12, '31. (67:348.)
By Fred T. Marsh. Nat. (N. Y.) Jun. 17, '31. (132:660.)
By Thomas Orr. Ly. Jun. 13, '31. (16.)
By Hyder Edward Rollins. Sat. R. (N. Y.) Jun. 27, '31. (7:922.)
By George Seibel. Book. (N. Y.) Aug., '31. (73:593.)
By Carl Van Doren. Books. Jun. 7, '31. (3.)
Hergesheimer, Joseph.
By Geoffrey West. Va. Jan., '32. (8:95.)
Hudson, W. H.
By Sir William Rothenstein. Atl. Feb., '32. (149:233.)
Hughes, Richard.
Anonymous. Sat. R. (N. Y.) Jan. 30, '32. (8:490.)
By Ernestine Evans. Books. Mar. 13, '32. (8.)
By Anne Carroll Moore. Sat. R. (N. Y.) Apr. 16, '32. (8:673.)
By Eda Lou Walton. N. Y. Times. Dec. 6, '31. (11.)
By Frederic Thompson. Com. Jan. 6, '32. (15:278.)
Hurst, Fannie.
By Harry Salpeter. Book. (N. Y.) Aug., '31. (73:612.)

I

Irving, Washington.
By Harry Hayden Clark. Book. (N. Y.) Oct., '31. (74:210.)
By E. Goggio. Rom. R. Oct.-Dec., '31. (22:301.)
By E. H. Zeydel. P. M. L. A. Sept., '31. (46:946.)

J

Jacobs, W. W.
By Percy Hutchison. N. Y. Times. Sept. 27, '31. (5.)
James, Henry.
By Arthur Colton. Sat. R. (N. Y.) Aug. 1, '31. (8:21.)
By Ford Madox Ford. Scr. Oct., '31. (90:379.)
By Ernest E. Leisy. A. L. Jan., '32. (3:487.)
By Ludwig Lewisohn. T. Q. Dec., '31. (4:318.)
By Desmond MacCarthy. Sat. R. (N. Y.) Aug. 29, '31. (8:81.)
By Leonard L. Mackall. Books. Dec. 6, '31. (35.)
By James L. McLane. N. E. Q. Jul., '31. (4:577.)
By Robert Shafer. Book. (N. Y.) Mar., '32. (74:674.)
By William Troy. Book. (N. Y.) May, '31. (73:351.)
James, Will.
By Ross Santee. Books. Jun. 14, '31. (3.)
Joyce, James.
Anonymous. Transit. Mar., '32. (273.)
By Padraic Colum. N. Rep. May 13, '31. (66:346.)
By Stuart Gilbert. Transit. Mar., '32. (247.)
By Louis Gillet. Transit. Mar., '32. (263.)
By Eugene Jolas. Transit. Mar., '32. (250.)
By Thomas McGreevy. Transit. Mar., '32. (254.)

K

King, Grace.
　　Anonymous. Obituary notices in American newspapers. Jan. 15, '32.
Kipling, Rudyard.
　　By R. M. C. N. Y. Apr. 30, '32. (58.)
　　By Percy Hutchison. N. Y. Times. Apr. 24, '32. (3.)
　　By William McFee. Books. Apr. 24, '32. (1.)
　　By Christopher Morley. Sat. R. (N. Y.) Apr. 23, '32. (8:681.)

L

Lawrence, D. H.
　　Anonymous. N. Y. Times. May 10, '31. (8.)
　　By Iris Barry. Book. (N. Y.) Jul., '31. (73:547.)
　　By Ernest Sutherland Bates. Sat. R. (N. Y.) Feb. 13, '32. (8:521.)
　　By T. O. Beachcroft. Sym. Oct., '31. (2:540.)
　　By Ernest Boyd. Free. May 13, '31. (3:215.)
　　By Mary M. Colum. N. Rep. Jul. 15, '31. (67:238.)
　　By Basil Davenport. Sat. R. (N. Y.) May 16, '31. (7:828.)
　　　　Aug. 1, '31. (8:20.)
　　By H. J. Davis. C. For. Aug., '31. (11:426.)
　　By Frederick Dupee. Book. (N. Y.) Jul., '31. (73:526.)
　　By Horace Gregory. N. Rep. Jul. 15, '31. (67:239.)
　　By Percy Hutchison. N. Y. Times. Feb. 28, '32. (4.)
　　By Joseph Wood Krutch. Nat. (N. Y.) Mar. 23, '32. (134:345.)
　　By Henry Bamford Parkes. Nat. (N. Y.) Jun. 17, '31. (132:661.)
　　By Lorine Pruette. Books. May 24, '31. (6.) Feb. 14, '32. (3.)
　　　　Mar. 6, '32. (7.)
　　By Alan Reynolds Thompson. Book. (N. Y.) Jul., '31. (73:492.)
　　By Henry Tracy. Sat. R. (N. Y.) Jul. 11, '31. (7:960.)
　　By George Sylvester Viereck. Ly. Oct. 10, '31. (15.)
Lewisohn, Ludwig.
　　Anonymous. N. Y. Times. Aug. 23, '31. (6.) Oct. 11, '31. (7.)
Lincoln, Joseph C.
　　Anonymous. N. Y. Times. Aug. 2, '31. (6.)
　　By Arthur Warner. Books. Aug. 16, '31. (10.)
London, Jack.
　　By George Sylvester Viereck. Ly. Oct. 10, '31. (15.)
Longfellow, Henry Wadsworth.
　　By James Taft Hatfield. A. L. May, '31. (3:136.)

M

McFee, William.
　　By Leonard L. Mackall. Books. Feb. 7, '32. (19.)
McKay, Claude.
　　Anonymous. N. Y. Times. Apr. 3, '32. (7.)
　　By Rudolph Fisher. Books. Mar. 27, '32. (3.)
Mann, Thomas.
　　By Louis Kronenberger. N. Y. Times. Jul. 12, '31. (8.)
Manning, Frederic.
　　By Leo Kennedy. Book. (N. Y.) Aug., '31. (73:657.)
Mansfield, Katherine.
　　By Leonard L. Mackall. Books. Jan. 17, '32. (15.)

Marie-Victorin, Frère.
    By Felix Walter. C. For. Mar., '32. (12:223.)
Mason, Arthur.
    By Pauline Sutorius Aird. Sat. R. (N. Y.) Nov. 14, '31. (8:280.)
Maugham, W. Somerset.
    Anonymous. N. Y. Times. Sept. 20, '31. (6.)
    By Dorothea Brande. Book. (N. Y.) Nov., '31. (74:336.)
    By Florence Haxton Britten. Books. Sept. 27, '31. (2.)
    By Lee Wilson Dodd. Sat. R. (N. Y.) Oct. 17, '31. (8:206.)
    By Gerald Sykes. Nat. (N. Y.) Nov. 25, '31. (133:576.)
Maupassant, Guy de.
    New Letters. Va. Apr., '32. (8:204.)
    By Ernest Boyd. Va. Apr., '32. (8:204.)
Maurois, André.
    By Justin O'Brien. Book. (N. Y.) Jul., '31. (73:530.)
Melville, Herman.
    By Robert S. Forsythe. Sat. R. (N. Y.) Sept. 19, '31. (8:140.)
    By L. Howard. M. L. N. May, '31. (46:291.)
    By L. Morris. O. C. Sept., '31. (45:513.) Oct., '31. (45:621.)
    By O. W. Riegel. A. L. May, '31. (3:195.)
    By Russell Thomas. A. L. Jan., '32. (3:432.)
    By B. M. Wainger. Un. C. Jan., '32. (25:35.)
    By John T. Winterich. Sat. R. (N. Y.) Feb. 13, '32. (8:531.)
Miller, Alice Duer.
    Anonymous. N. Y. Times. Mar. 20, '32. (21.)
    By Garreta Busey. Books. Feb. 28, '32. (5.)
Mitchell, J. Leslie.
    Anonymous. N. Y. Times. Oct. 4, '31. (22.)

N

Neagoe, Peter.
    By Samuel Putnam. New R. Apr., '32. (68.)
Nervo, Amado.
    By John E. Englekirk, Jr. N. M. Q. Feb., '32. (2:53.)
Norris, Frank.
    By Florence Haxton Britten. Books. Aug. 23, '31. (13.)
    By John Chamberlain. N. Y. Times. May 3, '31. (2.)
    By C. Hartley Grattan. A. L. Nov., '31. (3:349.)
    By F. Walker. Cal. C. July, '31. (33:320.)

O

O'Connor, Frank.
    Anonymous. N. Y. Times. Sept. 20, '31. (22.)
    Anonymous. Sat. R. (N. Y.) Sept. 26, '31. (8:147.)
    By George Dangerfield. Book. (N. Y.) Jan.-Feb., '32. (74:584.)
    By Felix Walter. C. For. Feb., '32. (12:189.)
O'Faoláin, Seán.
    By John Chamberlain. N. Y. Times. Mar. 27, '32. (7.)
    By William Troy. Nat. (N. Y.) Apr. 27, '32. (134:495.)

P

Patterson, Pernet.
    By Theodore Morrison. Book. (N. Y.) Jun., '31. (73:416.)

Peattie, Louise Redfield.
    By Amy Loveman. Sat. R. (N. Y.) Aug. 22, '31. (8:68.)
    By Mary Ross. Books. Aug. 23, '31. (2.)
"Philibin, An."
    By Shaemas O'Sheel. Com. May 13, '31. (14:55.)
Pirandello, Luigi.
    By Margaret Cheney Dawson. Books. Jan. 24, '32. (3.)
    By Harold Strauss. N. Y. Times. Jan. 24, '32. (7.)
    By Charles A. Wagner. Op. Feb. 29, '32. (15.)
Poe, Edgar Allan.
    By Edward J. Breen. Com. Dec. 9, '31. (15:156.)
    By John E. Englekirk. N. M. Q. Aug., '31. (1:247.)
    By J. De Lancey Ferguson. A. L. Jan., '32. (3:465.)
    By Cortell Holsapple. A. L. Mar., '32. (4:62.)
    By James Southall Wilson. A. Merc. Oct., '31. (24:215.)
Preedy, George.
    By Louise Maunsell Field. N. Y. Times. Jun. 21, '31. (7.)

R

Richardson, A. P.
    Anonymous. N. Y. Times. Sept. 27, '31. (20.)
Romanov, Panteleimon.
    Anonymous. N. Y. Times. Mar. 6, '32. (7.)
    By Fred T. Marsh. Books. Feb. 14, '32. (7.)
Runyon, Damon.
    Anonymous. N. Y. Times. Sept. 6, '31. (15.)
    Anonymous. Sat. R. (N. Y.) Sept. 12, '31. (8:117.)
    By Murray Godwin. N. Rep. Oct. 14, '31. (68:240.)

S

Sayre, Joel.
    By Edward Angly. Books. Feb. 14, '32. (5.)
    Anonymous. N. Y. Times. Feb. 14, '32. (6.)
Schaffner, Jakob.
    By A. W. G. Randall. Sat. R. (N. Y.) Apr. 2, '32. (8:637.)
Schnitzler, Arthur.
    Anonymous. N. Y. Times. Nov. 15, '31. (7.)
    By George Dangerfield. Sat. R. (N. Y.) Jan. 23, '32. (8:473.)
    By Pierre Loving. Books. Nov. 8, '31. (3.)
    By Otto P. Schinnerer. Nat. (N. Y.) Nov. 11, '31. (133:517.)
    By Harry Slochower. N. Rep. Nov. 18, '31. (69:22.)
Scott, Evelyn.
    By Harry Salpeter. Book. (N. Y.) Nov., '31. (74:281.)
Shiffrin, A. B.
    Anonymous. N. Y. Times. Nov. 22, '31. (7.)
Short Story.
    By Ben Ray Redman. Books. May 17, '31. (12.)
    By Blanche Colton Williams. Clay. Winter, '31. (6.)
Sinclair, May.
    Anonymous. N. Y. Times. Feb. 21, '32. (7.)
    By Mary Ross. Books. Mar. 6, '32. (4.)

Spanish Short Story.
  By Betty Drury. N. Y. Times. Feb. 21, '32. (8.)
  By Angel Flores. Books. Apr. 3, '32. (11.)
Stevens, James.
  By Charles J. Finger. Books. Feb. 7, '32. (7.)
  By John T. Frederick. Mid. Mar.-Apr., '32. (19:55.)
Stevenson, Robert Louis.
  By Christopher Morley. Atl. Apr., '32. (149:403.)
  By Edwin Muir. Book. (N. Y.) Sept., '31. (74:55.)
  By Austin Strong. Sat. R. (N. Y.) Apr. 16, '32.
Strong, L. A. G.
  Anonymous. N. Y. Times. Aug. 16, '31. (9.)
  By George Dangerfield. Book. (N. Y.) Sept., '31. (74:77.)
  By Margaret Cheney Dawson. Books. Aug. 16, '31. (4.)
  By Dayton Kohler. Book. (N. Y.) Aug., '31. (73:570.)
  By Theodore Purdy, Jr. Sat. R. (N. Y.) Jun. 20, '31. (7:912.)
Suckow, Ruth.
  By Florence Haxton Britten. Books. Aug. 16, '31. (6.)
  By J. T. Frederick. Eng. J. Jan., '31. (20:1.)
  By Fred T. Marsh. N. Y. Times. Aug. 23, '31. (4.)
  By Catherine Royer. Book. (N. Y.) Oct., '31. (74:191.)
  By G. M. A. Grube. C. For. Jun., '31. (11:350.)

T

Tenenbaum, Joseph.
  Anonymous. N. Y. Times. Aug. 9, '31. (15.)
Tieck, Ludwig.
  By E. H. Zeydel. P. M. L. A. Sept., '31. (46:946.)
Tolstoy, Count Lyof N.
  Letter. N. E. Q. Oct., '31. (4:777.)
  Anonymous. Sat. R. (N. Y.) Nov. 14, '31. (8:298.)
  By John Cournos. Yale. Sept., '31. (21:210.)
  By Frederick Dupee. Book. (N. Y.) Aug., '31. (73:665.)
  By Alexander Kaun. Sat. R. (N. Y.) Jun. 27, '31. (7:925.)
  By Catherine Radziwill. Com. Aug. 19, '31. (14:386.)
  By Count Lyof N. Tolstoy. Westm. Sept., '31. (10.) Dec., '31.
    (36.)
  By Avrahm Yarmolinsky. Books. May 7, '31. (6.)
Turgenev, Ivan.
  By Catherine Radziwill. Com. Aug. 12, '31. (14:361.)
Twain, Mark.
  Anonymous. N. Y. Times. Oct. 4, '31. (2.)
  By Ernest Sutherland Bates. Books. Oct. 18, '31. (1.)
  By Percy H. Boynton. N. Rep. Jan. 27, '32. (69:302.)
  By L. Cooper. M. L. N. Feb., '32. (47:85.)
  By Bernard De Voto. Book. (N. Y.) Oct., '31. (74:172.) Sat. R.
    (N. Y.) Apr. 2, '32. (8:640.)
  By A. V. Goodpasture. Tenn. Jul., '31. (1:253.)
  By Granville Hicks. Nat. (N. Y.) Oct. 28, '31. (133:463.)
  By Fred W. Lorch. A. L. Nov., '31. (3:309.)
  By Constance Rourke. Sat. R. (N. Y.) Jan. 23, '32. (8:474.)

W

Wakefield, H. R.
  Anonymous. N. Y. Times. May 24, '31. (6.)
Walker, Charles R.
  By Catherine Royer. Sat. R. (N. Y.) May 2, '31. (7:800.)
Wallace, Edgar.
  Anonymous. Obituary notices in all American newspapers. Feb. 11,
    '32.
Wells, H. G.
  By Sir William Rothenstein. Atl. Feb., '32. (149:233.)
Wetjen, Albert R.
  By Frederick Dupee. Book. (N. Y.) Jul., '31. (73:526.)
  By Arthur Warner. Books. May 10, '31. (5.)
Wharton, Edith.
  By R. P. Blackmur. Free. May 6, '31. (3:190.)
White, Stewart Edward.
  By Charles J. Finger. Books. Mar. 27, '32. (4.)
Wiley, Hugh.
  Anonymous. N. Y. Times. Feb. 14, '32. (17.)
Winslow, Thyra Samter.
  Anonymous. N. Y. Times. Feb. 21, '32. (17.)
  By Stanley Walker. Books. Mar. 6, '32. (6.)
Woodington, Charles.
  By G. M. A. Grube. C. For. Aug., '31. (11:433.)

Y

Young, Stark.
  By Grace Leake. Hol. Dec., '31. (4.)

INDEX OF SHORT STORIES IN BOOKS

MAY 1, 1931, TO APRIL 30, 1932

I. AMERICAN AND CANADIAN AUTHORS

316   THE YEARBOOK

II. BRITISH AND IRISH AUTHORS

A

III. TRANSLATIONS

MAGAZINE AVERAGES

MAY 1, 1931, TO APRIL 30, 1932

The following table includes the averages of distinctive stories in thirty American periodicals. One, two, and three asterisks are employed to indicate relative distinction. "Three-asterisk stories" are considered worth reprinting in book form. The list excludes reprints.

PERIODICALS	No. OF STORIES PUBLISHED	No. OF DISTINCTIVE STORIES PUBLISHED			PERCENTAGE OF DISTINCTIVE STORIES PUBLISHED		
		*	**	***	*	**	***
American Mercury	19	14	10	6	69	53	32
Atlantic Monthly	25	16	9	4	64	36	16
Canadian Forum	11	11	4	1	100	36	9
Canadian Magazine	57	10	1	1	18	2	2
Catholic World	24	8	0	0	33	0	0
Clay	31	28	20	18	90	65	58
Collier's Weekly	233	27	3	3	12	1	1
Columbia	28	10	2	0	36	7	0
Cosmopolitan	125	30	6	3	24	5	2
Delineator	51	8	0	0	16	0	0
Forum	12	9	6	6	75	50	50
Frontier	22	17	9	4	77	41	18
Good Housekeeping (N. Y.).	60	13	3	0	22	5	0
Harper's Bazaar (N. Y.) ...	40	10	6	6	25	15	15
Harper's Magazine	38	30	20	13	79	53	34
Hound and Horn	10	10	8	5	100	80	50
Ladies' Home Journal	57	6	2	2	11	4	4
MacLean's Magazine	99	12	3	2	12	3	2
Midland	56	43	27	13	77	48	23
North American Review	20	15	7	2	75	35	10
Pagany	42	32	19	8	76	45	19
Pictorial Review	57	10	3	0	18	5	0
Prairie Schooner	19	18	10	3	90	50	15
Saturday Evening Post	283	41	6	3	15	2	1
Scribner's Magazine	44	42	28	16	95	64	36
Scrip	10	7	1	1	70	10	0
Story	41	41	37	27	100	90	66
This Quarter	24	22	16	11	92	67	46
Transition	12	9	7	3	75	58	25
Woman's Home Companion.	53	6	1	1	11	2	2

The following tables indicate the rank, by number and percentage, of distinctive short stories published, of seventeen periodicals coming within the scope of my examination which have published an average of 50 per cent or more of distinctive stories. The lists exclude reprints, but not translations.

By Percentage

1. Story 100%
2. Hound and Horn 100%
3. Canadian Forum 100%
4. Scribner's Magazine 95%
5. This Quarter 92%
6. Clay 90%
7. Prairie Schooner 90%
8. Harper's Magazine 79%
9. Midland 77%
10. Frontier 77%
11. Pagany 76%
12. Transition 75%
13. Forum 75%
14. North American Review 75%
15. Scrip 70%
16. American Mercury 69%
17. Atlantic Monthly 64%

By Number

1. Midland 43
2. Scribner's Magazine 42
3. Story 41
4. Pagany 32
5. Harper's Magazine 30
6. Clay 28
7. This Quarter 22
8. Prairie Schooner 18
9. Frontier 17
10. Atlantic Monthly 16
11. North American Review 15
12. American Mercury 14
13. Canadian Forum 11
14. Hound and Horn 10
15. Forum 9
16. Transition 9
17. Scrip 7

The following periodicals have published during the same period ten or more "two-asterisk stories." The list excludes reprints, but not translations.

1. Story 37
2. Scribner's Magazine 28
3. Midland 27
4. Clay 20
5. Harper's Magazine 20
6. Pagany 19
7. This Quarter 16
8. Prairie Schooner 10
9. American Mercury 10

The following periodicals have published during the same period five or more "three-asterisk stories." The list excludes reprints, but not translations.

1. Story 27
2. Clay 18
3. Scribner's Magazine 16
4. Midland 13
5. Harper's Magazine 13
6. This Quarter 11
7. Pagany 8
8. Forum 6
9. American Mercury 6
10. Harper's Bazaar (N. Y.) 6
11. Hound and Horn 5

Ties in the above lists have been decided by taking relative rank in other lists into account.

DISTINCTIVE SHORT STORIES
IN AMERICAN MAGAZINES

MAY 1, 1931, TO APRIL 30, 1932

NOTE. *Only distinctive stories are listed. The list includes a few American stories published only in British periodicals. One, two or three asterisks are prefixed to the titles of stories to indicate distinction. Three asterisks prefixed to a title indicate that the story is listed on the "Roll of Honor." The figures in parentheses after the title of a story refer to the volume and page number of the magazine. Where successive issues of a magazine are not paged consecutively, only the page number is given. While every effort has been made to indicate the nationality of authors correctly, I assume no personal responsibility for the accuracy of my classification in this or other lists.*

I. AMERICAN AUTHORS

A

ABDULLAH, ACHMED.
  *Beside the Still Waters. Del. Nov., '31. (20.)
  *From Whence Cometh My Help. G. H. (N. Y.) Dec., '31. (40.)
  *When War Gods Call. Cos. Feb.. '32. (30.)

ADAMIC, LOUIS.
  *Dog-Robber. Ly. Oct. 24, '31. (42.)
  ***Symbol. Pagy. Apr.-Jun., '32. (135.)

ADAMS, BILL.
  ***Alien. Adv. Nov. 15, '31. (18.)
  ***Foreigner. Atl. Apr., '32. (149:428.)
  ***Sailmaker's Yarn. Atl. Sept., '31. (148:353.)
  *Saving of the "Tavy." Sh. St. Mar. 25, '32. (115.)
  ***Sea Wife. Adv. Aug. 15, '31. (2.)
  **Carolina Wilderness. Scr. Jun., '31. (89:611.)

ADE, GEORGE.
  *Fable of the Two Mandolin Players. (R.) Gol. Oct., '31. (14:238.)

AIKEN, CONRAD.
  ***Bow Down, Isaac! Harp. M. Jul., '31. (163:175.)
  ***Mr. Arcularis. Crit. Apr., '32. (11:399.)

ALBEE, GEORGE.
  **Initiation. Sto. Mar.-Apr., '32. (61.)
  **Meeting. Pr. S. Spring, '31. (5:149.)
  **Sketch of an Old Woman. Pr. S. Winter, '32. (6:39.)

ALDRICH, THOMAS BAILEY.
  **Struggle for Life. (R.) Gol. Dec., '31. (14:407.)

ANDERSON, SHERWOOD.
  ***Mill Girls. Scr. Jan., '32. (91:8.)

ANDREWS, GEORGE LAWRENCE.
  *Justice in the Hills. House. Mar., '32. (1.)
  *Path of Vengeance. S. V. Jan., '32. (3.)

APPEL, BENJAMIN.
  *Rabbit. Mid. Nov.-Dec., '31. (18:180.)
  **Summer Witches. Pagy. Apr.-Jun., '32. (32.)
  *Turners Become Wealthy. Mid. Aug., '31. (18:105.)
  *White Mice and Perfume. N. A. Rev. Sept., '31. (232:246.)

APPLEGATE, FRANK.
  *New Mexico Legends. S. W. Jan., '32. (17:199.)

ARMFIELD, EUGENE.
  **No Retreat. Pagy. Oct.-Dec., '31. (85.)

CROSBY, JANE SNOWDEN.
*People Who Go to Museums. Mid. Mar.-Apr., '32. (19:37.)

D

"DAGVAR."
*Green Easter. L. H. J. Apr., '32. (14.)

D'AUTREMONT, JAMES.
*Prize Pony. Scrip. Mar., '32. (3:38.)

DAVIS, BRION.
**Purgatory Freight Train. Frontier. Mar., '32. (12:213.)

DAVIS, RICHARD HARDING.
*Romance in the Life of Hefty Burke. (R.) Gol. Oct., '31. (14:202.)

DE FORD, MIRIAM.
*Plagiarism. Frontier. Mar., '32. (12:247.)

DE JONG, DAVID CORNEL.
***As the Lilies. Clay. Autumn, '31. (1.)
***Beneath a Still Sky. H. H. Apr.-Jun., '32. (5:422.)
*From Thunder to Thunder. Pagy. Apr.-Jun., '32. (84.)
**Little Brown Dog. Clay. No. 3. (28.)
**Old Men. Mid. Sept., '31. (18:136.)
***So Tall the Corn. Scr. Apr., '32. (91:209.)
*Under the Bridge. Nativ. No. 2. (43.)

DELANO, EDITH BARNARD.
*Snow for Christmas. C. G. Dec., '31. (7.)

DERLETH, AUGUST W.
*Nella. Pagy. Jan.-Mar., '32. (3:134.)
**Old Ladies. Mid. Jan.-Feb., '32. (19:5.)

DIEFENTHALER, ANDRA.
***Hansel. N. C., '32. (162.)

DOBIE, CHARLES CALDWELL.
***Hands of the Enemy. (R.) Gol. Jun., '31. (64.)

DOUGLAS, MARJORY STONEMAN.
*Bees in the Mango Bloom. S. E. P. Dec. 12, '31. (12.)

DRAKE, FRANCIS VIVIAN.
*Big Flight. Atl. Jun., '31. (147:699.)
*Spring Morning. Atl. Jan., '32. (149:33.)

DRAPER, EDYTHE SQUIER.
*In Washington Tonight. House. Feb., '32. (6.)
**Parnells. Clay. No. 3. (16.)

DRATLER, JAY J.
***Dark Victory. Sto. Jun.-Jul., '31. (62.)

DUNCAN, THOMAS.
*Death of a Champion. Mid. May, '31. (18:21.)

DUNSING, DOROTHY.
*Thief. Pr. S. Winter, '32. (6:19.)

DWYER, JAMES FRANCIS.
*Woman with the Green Mole. Ly. Nov. 7, '31. (42.)

E

EDMONDS, WALTER D.
***Big-Foot Sal. Harp. M. Jul., '31. (163:137.)
***Blind Eve. C. G. Jul., '31. (7.)
***Cruise of the Cashalot. For. Jan., '32. (87:24.)

EMORY, WILLIAM CLOSSING.
**Etching in Frost. Mid. Jun., '31. (18:58.)

EUNSON, DALE.
*Sun-Dog. W. H. C. Nov., '31. (7.)

EWERT, EARL CRANSTON.
**Gun Park. Pr. S. Summer, '31. (5:224.)

EXALL, HENRY.
***Music-Box. S. W. Oct., '31. (17:39.)

F

FARR, DOROTHY.
*Dancing Abbess of the "Fir Cone." Sch. May 2, '31. (5.)

FARRELL, JAMES T.
***Casual Incident. Sto. Sept.-Oct., '31. (54.)
**Mary O'Reilley. Mid. May, '31. (18:3.)
***Nostalgia. C. D. N. Aug. 12, '31. (6.)
**Spring Evening. Sto. Mar.-Apr., '32. (43.)

FARSON, NEGLEY.
*His Own Affair. Adv. Aug. 15, '31. (65.)

FAULKNER, WILLIAM.
***Centaur in Brass. A. Merc. Feb., '32. (25:200.)
***Death-Drag. Scr. Jan., '32. (91:34.)
***Doctor Martino. Harp. M. Nov., '31. (163:733.)
***Fox Hunt. Harp. M. Sept., '31. (163:392.)
***Hair. A. Merc. May, '31. (23:53.)

***Heel, Toe, and a 1, 2, 3, 4. A. Merc. Apr., '32. (25 :473.)
***Love Song. S. W. Oct., '31. (17 :45.)
***No More Trumpets. A. Merc. Dec., '31. (24 :421.)
MINTZER, MURNEY.
*First Command. Col. Dec. 19, '31. (26.)
MITTLEMANN, BELA.
*In the Fullness of Time. Fif. Apr., '31.
MORAN, HELEN.
**Silver Fox. L. Merc. Apr., '32. (25 :535.)
MORRIS, IRA V.
***Kimono. Sto. Jun.-Jul., '31. (5.)
***Old Age. Sto. Sept.-Oct., 31. (71.)
MULLINS, HELENE.
*Pension. Com. Oct. 14, '31. (14 :572.)
MURPHY, ALISON.
*Island. Cath. W. Sept., '31. (133 :683.)

N

NASON, LEONARD H.
*Night in the Hay. S. E. P. May 30, '31. (14.)
*Storm on the Post Road. S. E. P. Mar. 12, '32. (10.)
NEAGOE, PETER.
***Shepherd of the Lord. Sto. Nov.-Dec., '31. (5.)
***Village Saint. Transit. Mar., '32. (75.)
NEEDHAM, ELIZABETH.
**Sigurdson. Frontier. Nov., '31. (12 :53.)
NETHERCOT, ARTHUR H.
***Old Ones. Mid. Jul., '31. (18 :72.)
NEWLAND, MARGARET ROWLEY.
*Fiddle. Husk. Oct., '31. (11 :1.)
NIELSEN, ELLEN.
**Niels' Father. Mid. Oct., '31. (18 :160.)

O

ODELL, R. IRVINGTON.
*Bit of Old London. Pr. S. Summer, '31. (5 :217.)
O'HARA, JOHN.
*Alone. Scr. Dec., '31. (90 :647.)
OLDHAM, DEMMA RAY.
*Liza Rides the Storm. Pict. R. Aug., '31. (10.)

*Teacher's Pet. Pict. R. Jan., '32. (10.)
OLSON, TED.
*Full Circle. Frontier. May, '31. (11 :319.)
OPPENHEIM, JAMES.
*Stanner. Transit. Mar., '32. (82.)
OUTERSON, WILLIAM.
**Black Death. Atl. Oct., '31. (148 :462.)
***Royal Yard. Atl. Jul., 31. (148 :84.)
*Sheath Knife. Ly. Dec. 19, '31. (44.)
**Ship's Bread. N. A. Rev. Nov., '31. (232 :455.)

P

PARKER, DOROTHY.
***Lady with a Lamp. Harp. B. (N. Y.) Apr., '32. (56.)
PARRY, RICHARD EDWARD.
*Lifeboat Number Five. W. H. C. Dec., '31. (13.)
PELLEY, WILLIAM DUDLEY.
*Fiddler in the Dusk. House. Feb., '32. (1.) Mar., '32. (6.)
PETERKIN, JULIA.
**Ashes. (R.) Gol. Jun., '31. (51.)
PETERSEN, ELIZABETH BENNECHE.
**Kiss for a Blue-eyed Sailor. G. H. (N. Y.) Jan., '32. (60.)
*Lost Spring. G. H. (N. Y.) May, '31. (38.)
**Witch's Gold. G. H. (N. Y.) Oct., '31. (58.)
PIERRE, WALTER S.
*Underground. Frontier. May, '31. (11 :332.)
POE, EDGAR ALLAN.
***Berenice. (R.) W. T. Apr., '32. (19 :567.)
POLLOCK, CHANNING.
*Poor Little Man. Col. Nov. 21, '31. (13.)
*To What Red Hell. Ly. Sept. 5, '31. (46.)
POST, MARY BRINKER.
**Pat Kelly's Wife. Pr. S. Fall, '31. (5 :291.)
*Precipice. For. Jun., '31. (85 :369.)
POST, MELVILLE DAVISSON.
***Twilight Adventure. (R.) Gol. Dec., '31. (14 :427.)
PRATT, THEODORE.
*Roman. N. Y. May 9, '31. (35.)

SNELL, MINA.
*Fifty Cents. Sky. Nov., '31. (26.)

SOKOLOFF, NATALIE B.
***Ivan. Adv. Jun. 15, '31. (49.)
*Jester of Moscow Kremlin. Adv. Feb. 1, '32. (64.)
*Prince and the Rebel. Adv. Dec. 15, '31. (102.)
**Prince's Messenger. Adv. Oct. 1, '31. (92.)
**Scourge of the Volga. Adv. Sept. 1, '31. (138.)
**Spray of Blue Feathers. Adv. Nov. 1, '31. (129.)

SOUTHARD, SHELBY EDWARD.
*Polish Soldier. Sch. May 2, '31. (9.)

SPALDING, MATTINGLY.
*Bothered. Scrip. Dec., '31. (3 :12.)
*Church. Ann. Apr., '32. (48 :295.)
*Gibby. Scrip. Jun., '31. (2 :129.)
*Running Off. L. H. J. Jun., '31. (12.)
*Victim. Ann. Feb., '32. (48 :237.)

SPRINGER, FLETA CAMPBELL.
**Ceremony in White. Harp. M. Sept., '31. (163 :456.)

STAIT, VIRGINIA.
*Don Juan. Westm. Dec., '31. (10.)
*Interdict. Archive. Nov., '31. (5.)

STALLINGS, LAURENCE.
***Gentleman in Blue. S. E. P. Feb. 20, '32. (8.)
*Return to the Woods. Col. Mar. 5, '32. (30.)
*Vale of Tears. Cos. May, '31. (26.)

STEELE, WILBUR DANIEL.
**Conscience. Pict. R. Jan., '32. (16.)
***Man without a God. L. H. J. Nov., '31. (3.) Dec., '31. (16.)

STEVENS, JAMES.
*Downfall of Elder Barton. A. Merc. Dec., '31. (24 :461.)
***Rock-Candy Mountains. A. Merc. Mar., '32. (25 :301.)
***When Rivers Were Young and Wild. W. H. C. Jul., '31. (26.)

STOCKTON, FRANK R.
***Widow's Cruise. (R.) Gol. Jun., '31. (56.)

STRUCKMAN, ROBERT T.
**Train. Frontier. May, '31. (11 :341.)

SUCKOW, RUTH.
*Three, Counting the Cat. G. H. (N. Y.) Sept., '31. (30.)

SULLIVAN, RICHARD.
**Robin. Mid. Mar.-Apr., '32. (19 :35.)

SWAIN, JOHN D.
**One Head Well Done. (R.) Gol. Jan., '32. (15 :40.)

T

TABER, GLADYS B.
**Rabbits. N. C., '32. (185.)

TARKINGTON, BOOTH.
*Instrument of Providence. Col. Apr. 9, '32. (7.)

TARLETON, FISWOODE.
*Heritage. Am. May, '31. (24.)
*Resurrection Gap. Adv. Jul. 1, '31. (125.)
*Signs and Wonders. G. H. (N. Y.) Apr., '32. (61.)

TERRELL, UPTON.
*Afternoon Off. Mid. Aug., '31. (18 :98.)

THIELEN, BENEDICT.
**Art. Scr. Jun., '31. (89 :662.)

THOMAS, DOROTHY.
**Grandma Hotel Adams. A. Merc. Dec., '31. (24 :490.)
*Jeeter Wedding. A. Merc. Sept., '31. (24 :72.)

THOMAS, JEAN.
**"Poure Hippo." Mid. Jan.-Feb., '32. (19 :24.)

THOMPSON, DONALD.
*Helping Hand. N. Y. Apr. 9, '32. (16.)

THOMPSON, ISABEL M.
**Ebony. Opp. Oct., '31. (9 :312.)

THOMPSON, JIM.
*Gentlemen of the Jungle. Pr. S. Fall, '31. (5 :285.)

THURBER, JAMES.
*Cholly. N. Y. Sept. 19, '31. (17.)

TICHENOR, GEORGE.
**In Passing. H. H. Jan.-Mar., '32. (5 :208.)

TITUS, HAROLD.
*Frame House. Mid. Oct., '31. (18 :150.)
*Moulting Time. T. Q. Mar., '32. (4 :532.)

TUCKERMAN, ARTHUR.
**Love's a Grown-Up God. Scr. Mar., '32. (91 :133.)

WINSLOW, THYRA SAMTER. (*Cont.*)
*"Wishes." Chic. Trib. Aug. 16, '31.
WOLFE, THOMAS.
***Portrait of Bascom Hawke. Scr. Apr. '32. (91:193.)
WORKING, PAUL.
*Hit the Pocketbook. N. A. Rev. Mar., '32. (233:209.)
WYNBUSH, OCTAVIA B.
**Noose. Opp. Dec., '31. (9:369.)

Y

YELLEN, SAMUEL.
**Death of a Girl. H. H. Oct.-Dec., '31. (5:24.)

Z

ZUGSMITH, LEANE.
*Appointment at Five. Scr. Sept., '31. (90:313.)
**Picture. A. Merc. Mar., '32. (25:318.)

II. CANADIAN AUTHORS

B

BARBEAU, MARIUS.
*Handsome Dancer. Tor. Apr. 16, '32.
*Witch Canoe. Tor. Feb. 20, '32.
BARNARD, LESLIE GORDON.
*Beyond the Rim. C. H. J. Apr., '31. (10.)
*Midnight Miracle. C. H. J. Dec., '31. (16.)
BEDER, EDWARD ARTHUR.
*Wattman. C. For. Dec., '31. (12:98.)
BETTS, MABEL W.
*Strength of the Coutures. Tor. Feb. 20, '32.
BIRD, WILL R.
*Love of Bride Crowdy. Chat. Apr., '32. (10.)
*Lucky One. Can. Jun., '31. (13.)
*One Night at Pin Tickle. Tor. Dec. 26, '31.
*Sunrise for Peter. MacL. Jun. 1, '31. (16.)
BOWMAN, LOUISE MOREY.
*Gray Man and Red Bird. Can. Mar., '32. (7.)
BROWN, ELSIE.
*Furnace. Tor. Aug. 8, '31.

C

CALLAGHAN, MORLEY.
***Absolution. N. Y. Dec. 5, '31. (20.)
***Lady in a Green Dress. Can. Feb., '32. (13.)
***Lunch Counter. N. Y. May 2, '31. (17.)
***Red Hat. N. Y. Oct. 31, '31. (18.)
***Silk Stockings. N. Y. Apr. 16, '32. (16.)
***Younger Brother. N. Y. May 23, '31. (16.)

COOKE, HELEN MARGARET.
*Mart House. Tor. Oct. 3, '31.
CORNELL, MARY.
**Uninvited. C. For. Aug., '31. (11:418.)
CREIGHTON, LUELLA BRUCE.
***Miss Kidd. C. For. Oct., '31. (12:17.)
CUNNINGHAM, LOUIS ARTHUR.
*Barratry. Tor. May 23, '31.
*Spaniard's Gold. MacL. Jan. 15, '32. (24.)
*Would Ye Be Loving a Sailor? Tor. Jan. 9, '32.

D

DENT, W. REDVERS.
*Judgment. MacL. Sept. 1, '31. (3.)

F

FARMER, BERTRAND J.
*Toll Bridge. Tor. May 16, '31.
FORSYTH, R. B.
*Late Harvest. Tor. May 30, '31.

G

GRANT, GEORGE H.
*Pilot. Tor. Jun. 13, '31.
GRAY, BERYL.
*Mary Sylvia—One Day. Can. Mar., '32. (3.)
*Stowaway. Chat. Mar., '32. (19.)

H

HARDY, REGINALD.
*Soil. Tor. Apr. 23, '32.

I

INNIS, MARY QUAYLE.
*Aunt Belle. C. For. Sept., '31. (11:455.)
*Holiday. C. For. Jan., '32. (12:140.)
*Party. C. For. Jun., '31. (11:334.)

III. BRITISH AND IRISH AUTHORS

ALMEDINGEN, EDITH M.
**Perspectives. Com. Feb. 17,
'32. (15:435.)
ARLEN, MICHAEL.
***Shameless Behavior of a Lord.
(R.) Gol. Oct., '31. (14:197.)
AUSTIN, F. BRITTEN.
*Eve—The Woman Rules. S. E.
P. Apr. 2, '32. (8.)
*Shattered Atom. Blue Bk.
Feb., '32. (19.)

B

BAPTIST, R. HERNEKIN.
**Civilization. Harp. M. Apr.,
'32. (164:525.)
**Red Riding Hood and the
Wolves. Harp. M. Mar., '32.
(164:457.)
BATES, H. E.
***Mower. T. Q. Sept., '31.
(4:37.)
BEACHCROFT, T. O.
**Joey's Law Case. T. Q. Sept.,
'31. (4:114.)
BECKE, LOUIS.
**Mrs. Liardet. (R.) Gol. Jan.,
'32. (15:95.)
BELL, J. J.
*Fugitive. Hol. Mar., '32. (8.)
BENNETT, ARNOLD.
*Honor. (R.) Gol. Dec., '31.
(14:391.)
BENSON, STELLA.
***Destination. Harp. M. Dec.,
'31. (164:23.)
***Search for Mr. Loo. Harp. M.
May, '31. (162:653.)
BLACKWOOD, ALGERNON.
*Fire Body. N. A. Rev. Sept.,
'31. (232:219.)
***Valley of the Beasts. (R.)
Gol. Apr., '32. (15:355.)
BOTTOME, PHYLLIS.
**Liqueur Glass. (R.) Gol. Apr.,
'32. (15:349.)
BRAND, NEVILLE.
***Returned. T. Q. Mar., '32.
(4:399.)
BRANDT, ELIZABETH.
***Cricket. Sto. Jan.-Feb., '32.
(34.)
BURKE, THOMAS.
*John Brown's Body. V. F.
May, '31. (37.)
BUTTS, MARY.
**Green. Pagy. Oct.-Dec., '31.
(1.)

C

CHARD, GIL.
***Unrecognized. Sto. Jan.-Feb.,
'32. (69.)
COLLIER, JOHN.
***Green Thoughts. Harp. M.
May, '31. (162:691.)
COLLINS, WILKIE.
**Blow Up with the Brig! (R.)
Gol. Jul., '31. (56.)
CONRAD, JOSEPH.
***Brute. (R.) Gol. Nov., '31.
(14:334.)
***Conde. (R.) Gol. May, '31.
(43.)
COPPARD, A. E.
***Smith of Pretty Peter. For.
Sept., '31. (86:173.)
CONSTANDUROS, MABEL, and HOGAN,
MICHAEL.
*Alfie's Manger Story. Pict. R.
Dec., '31. (7.)
COULDREY, OSWALD.
*Noisy Slinger. Atl. Jun., '31.
(147:720.)

D

DANE, CLEMENCE.
*Across the Years. C. H. J.
Feb., '32. (3.)
DICKENS, CHARLES.
**Thirteenth Juryman. (R.) Gol.
May, '31. (36.)
**U. M. I. H. M. C. B. & P. D.
Company. (R.) Gol. Apr.,
'32. (15:303.)
DINGLE, A. E.
*Devil in the Jade. MacL. Jun.
15, '31. (20.)
*Johnny Boker. MacL. Nov. 1,
'31. (11.)
*Pearls for Swine. Hol. Feb.,
'32. (11.)
DUNSANY, LORD.
***Curse of the Witch. Harp. B.
(N. Y.) Jan., '32. (82.)
***Daughter of Rameses. Harp. B.
(N. Y.) Sept., '31. (100.)
**Drink at a Running Stream.
V. F. May, '31. (48.)
***How the Tinker Came to Ska-
vangur. Harp. B. (N. Y.)
Jun., '31. (96.)
**Pearly Beach. V. F. Mar., '32.
(29.)
***Use of Man. Harp. B. (N. Y.)
Aug., '31. (84.)

E

ERTZ, SUSAN.
*Black and Scarlet. S. E. P.
Mar. 19, '32. (14.)

P

PAIN, BARRY.
*Lovers on an Island. (R.) Gol. Jul., '31. (62.)

PHILLPOTTS, EDEN.
***Gypsy Blood. Cos. Nov., '31. (48.)
***Told to Parson. MacL. Apr. 15, '32. (7.)

PRIESTLEY, J. B.
*Bad Companions. Cos. May, '31. (56.)

R

REID, LESLIE.
***Across the Heath. T. Q. Mar., '32. (4:501.)

S

SABATINI, RAFAEL.
*Night of Hate. (R.) Gol. Jan., '32. (15:1.)
*Pasquinade. (R.) Gol. Feb., '32. (15:101.)

SACKVILLE-WEST, V.
***Poet. N. A. Rev. Aug., '31. (232:141.)

"SAKI" (H. H. MUNRO).
**Background. (R.) Gol. Nov., '31. (14:313.)
***Interlopers. (R.) Gol. May, '31. (27.)

SMITH, LADY ELEANOR.
*Sweet Spanish Ladies. Del. Dec., '31. (8.)

STEVENSON, ROBERT LOUIS.
*Fable of the Sinking Ship. (R.) Gol. Mar., '32. (15:221.)
***Story of the Young Man with the Cream Tarts. (R.) Gol. Sept., '31. (14:138.)

STRONG, L. A. G.
***Don Juan and the Wheelbarrow. Yale. Mar., '32. (21:581.)

T

THACKERAY, WILLIAM MAKEPEACE.
***Devil's Wager. (R.) Gol. Feb., '32. (15:145.)

TOWNEND, W.
*Sport! Cos. Oct., '31. (28.)

W

WALPOLE, HUGH.
***Engaging Rascal. Harp. B. (N. Y.) Jan., '32. (54.)
*Silver Mask. Harp. B. (N. Y.) Mar., '32. (66.)
**Staircase. House. Oct., '31. (1.)
*Whistle. Yale. Dec., '31. (21:330.)

WELLS, H. G.
***Queer Story of Brownlow's Newspaper. L. H. J. Feb., '32. (8.)

WETJEN, ALBERT RICHARD.
*Family Affair. S. E. P. May 16, '31. (8.)
*Masters of the Craft. Col. Jan. 2, '32. (30.)
*Squall. Adv. Aug. 1, '31. (74.)

WILDE, OSCAR.
***Sphinx without a Secret. (R.) Gol. Aug., '31. (14:63.)

WILLIAMSON, HENRY.
***Fair. Com. Jul. 15, '31. (14:278.)

WILSON, ROMER.
***Loan. Sto. Sept.-Oct., '31. (64.)
***On With the Dance. T. Q. Dec., '31. (4:357.)

WYATT, ISABEL.
***Death Watch. T. Q. Mar., '32. (4:420.)

WYLIE, I. A. R.
*Outcasts. Pict. R. Feb., '32. (14.)
*Road Through. W. W. Apr., '32. (4.)

IV. TRANSLATIONS

A

ALEKSEYEV, GLEB. (Russian.)
***Return of a Red. Cos. Jun., '31. (38.) [malan.)

ASTURIAS, MIGUEL ANGEL. (Guate-
***Legend of the Tattooed Girl. Transit. Mar., '32. (8.)

AVERCHENKO, ARKADY. (Russian.)
**Elephant Hunter. (R.) Gol. Sept., '31. (14:117.)

B

BALZAC, HONORE DE. (French.)
***Red House. (R.) Gol. Feb., '32. (15:163.)

BARBUSSE, HENRI. (French.)
***Funeral March. (R.) Gol. Jun., '31. (31.)

BAUM, VICKI. (German.)
*In a Little Border Town. Cos. Jun., '31. (44.)

NERVO, AMADO. (*Cont.*)
*Resuscitator and the Resuscitated. N. M. Q. Feb., '32. (2:61.)

P

PUSHKIN, ALEXANDER. (*Russian.*)
***Amateur Peasant Girl. (*R.*) Gol. Jun., '31. (40.)

R

REMARQUE, ERICH MARIA. (*German.*)
***Annette's Love Story. Col. Nov. 28, '31. (10.)
***Josef's Wife. Col. Nov. 21, '31. (14.)
***Strange Fate of Johann Bartok. Col. Dec. 5, '31. (18.)

S

SALTYKOV, MIKHAIL. (*Russian.*)
**Nostalgic Ram. (*R.*) Gol. Oct., '31. (14:217.)
SODERBERG, HJALMAR. (*Swedish.*)
***Blunder Sonata. Scan. Sept., '31. (19:552.)
***History Instructor. Sto. Sept.-Oct., '31. (61.)
SOIBERG, HARRY. (*Danish.*)
***Asa's Mound. Scan. Aug., '31. (19:478.)

STRINDBERG, AUGUST. (*Swedish.*)
***Love and Bread. (*R.*) Gol. Nov., '31. (14:364.)

T

TOLSTOY, COUNT LYOF N. (*Russian.*)
***God Sees the Truth, but Waits. (*R.*) Gol. Jul., '31. (69.)
TURGENIEV, IVAN. (*Russian.*)
***Song of Love Triumphant. (*R.*) Gol. Jan., '32. (15:69.)

Y

YAKOVLEV, ALEXANDER. (*Russian.*)
*Chinese Vase. Cos. Jul., '31. (48.)

Z

ZOLA, EMILE. (*French.*)
***Maid of the Dauber. (*R.*) Gol. Sept., '31. (14:111.)
ZOSTCHENKO, MIKAIL. (*Russian.*)
*Bridegroom. Sto. Jan.-Feb., '32. (16.) N. Rep. Mar. 9, '32. (70:99.)
**Slight Mistake. Sto. Nov.-Dec., '31. (27.) Gol. Feb., '32. (15:157.)

THE END